OUR FRIENDSHIP IN RUINS

A NOVEL

AMY BUCHANAN

Our Friendship in Ruins

Copyright © 2026 by Amy Buchanan

Published by Amy Buchanan

Cover illustration and design by Gabriela Romero Lacruz

Copy editing by Sapphic Library Author Services

Proofreading by Sapphic Library Author Services and Tiffani Rasberry

For anyone fighting for their dreams.
Don't let the bad days win.

And to those who stood with me while I fought for mine.
I can't list you all, but I love you immensely.

1

QUINN

EARLY APRIL — FOUR WEEKS UNTIL SUMMER BREAK

ALL ROADS LEAD TO ROME. Except this one, which leads to hell and is paved with my friend's good intentions.

The brick building looms in front of me like a harbinger of doom, even though it's usually one of my favorite buildings on campus. It's where I do some of my best work and normally fills me with a sense of purpose and confidence. But today, the library is enemy territory.

"I can't believe you talked me into this," I mutter to my friend, who's taking her own steadying breaths by my side.

"I stand by the idea," Inez says, shaking out her arms. "You're our only hope."

I side-eye her. "Stop trying to take advantage of my lifelong Princess Leia obsession. Those powers should only be used for good, not evil."

Also, if I'm the only hope for the Billings staff, we're fucked, but she doesn't need to hear that. Again.

I love my job at Billings College. The students are enthusiastic, the campus is in the heart of Boston, and the other staff members have become my own little family over the past eight years.

But one part of it blows. An unspoken war on campus. A toxic, never-ending battle at the heart of every interaction.

On one side is the staff. The good, brilliant, and kind employees of Billings College who work tirelessly to help students grow and develop. We're the student activities folks, helping them find a community on campus. The housing people who, quite literally, give them a home away from home. And of course, the crème de la crème—the career counselors like me, who make sure students have an actual future after college.

On the other side is the faculty. The evil, condescending professors of Billings College. They're the worst of the worst. Business professors who give students opposite advice about resumes, despite our telling them what we're hearing from employers. Architecture professors who think they can design a better internship program than the person with a literal degree in it (read: me). English professors who look down their noses at my super fun romance novels because they're not *literature*.

It is a truth universally acknowledged that a Billings professor in possession of a tenured position must look down on the staff.

No, I'm *not* biased, or "projecting past hurt" from my parents, as my ex-therapist liked to say.

"I'm just saying, this could work," Inez says. "You can be really charming when you want to be."

I narrow my eyes at her. "I'm pretty sure there was an insult in there."

My friend, who is normally so sweet she'll give you a cavity, mimes locking her lips.

"You can do this," she says, giving my hand a squeeze. "*We* can do this. But if you really don't want to, we'll walk right now. Self-ishly, I want you in Rome with me this summer, but at the end of the day, I just want what's best for you. You're my priority."

There's a decade of support to back up this claim, even if I'm doubting her love for me now. Because this woman, who's adamant she wants what's best for me, is making me lay myself bare in front of the enemy in the hope we can come to a ceasefire.

At the beginning of this year, we started hearing whispers that the professors were making moves to change the landscape of Billings forever. Apparently, they're over our "interruptions and interference in classes." Yes, I can see how our coming into class to present on different opportunities could mess up their lesson plans, but we bring value, too.

Instead of actually talking to us, they've decided to be petty and write in the university bylaws that staff are not allowed to be involved in academics. A complete hard-line separation of church and state, even if the years of study and expertise we each bring to our areas could complement their classes. With the vote happening at the beginning of the next academic year, this is our last chance to stop it.

Because, much to the faculty's chagrin, they need me.

Those same bylaws they're planning on using to screw us have screwed them first. Dr. Lewis, who was supposed to teach an internship class in the Rome program this summer—the class that *I* designed, BTW—backed out at the last minute. Every other business professor already has summer plans lined up, and those pesky bylaws require any professor at Billings to have a master's degree and relevant experience on the subject.

You know who fits that bill? Me. The assistant director of internships, who they think should have "no involvement in the classroom."

I shake out my arms, bouncing up and down on my heels— ones I almost never wear but put on today like the extra inches will make them actually see me—and push through the front door. I blindly follow Inez down to the front of the presentation room, running through my arguments in my head on repeat. She goes straight to the computer to get us set up, while I look out at the stadium seating.

Billings has been around for almost two hundred years, and most of the buildings reflect that. Beautiful brick exteriors and heavy wood paneling inside. Warm classrooms and a cozy library with plenty of places to sneak away with a good book when life is driving you up a wall. But this is one of the more recently renovated rooms—white walls with white tile floors, light gray desks and dark gray seats. Cold, figuratively and literally. If this isn't a sign of things to come, I don't know what is.

I groan into the echoing space, planting my hands on my wide hips and letting the fabric of my pencil skirt ground me. "This is such a bad idea. The faculty won't cave. They guard the academics like they're the last Roman legion and we're the barbarian forces looking to bring about the downfall of Western civilization."

"Those barbarian forces successfully invaded, and so will we." She punctuates the last few words with a slap on the flimsy presentation podium that tips precariously with each hit.

I drop my head to the cold surface, but she grabs me by the shoulders and yanks me until I stand straight, hunching down so our faces are level.

"Okay," she says, shaking my shoulders like it'll stir up some optimism lurking deep down. "Give me the pitch."

I plaster on my fakest smile. "Dear Billings faculty. Thank you for lowering yourselves enough to meet. You honor us poor plebeians with your presence."

Inez meets my pleased expression with one of disappointment. "Take this seriously, Quinn. If this initiative passes…"

She trails off and starts worrying her lip between her teeth. I hear what she's not saying. What we've both said in anger plenty of times. That if Billings keeps getting worse, we'll leave. There are dozens of universities we could move to—thousands if we're willing to leave Boston—all with non-toxic work environments.

There are plenty of professors who are kind, welcoming, and collaborative. They just don't come to Billings.

But she wouldn't actually leave, just like I didn't mean it last week when I declared I was leaving after a biology professor mansplained how internships work. This is our home. Even the thought of her leaving—of me being left behind again while she moves on to something better—stirs a panic low in my stomach.

"Fine, I'll be serious," I say, rolling my head from side to side. "First, I'd like to thank the faculty senate for making time for us today. I'm excited by the prospect of taking on this internship course for the summer. As you know from my original presentation"—which they approved and then handed over to Dr. Lewis like I hadn't meant it for me to begin with—"I have extensive experience related to internship courses. Paired with my Italian fluency and familiarity with Rome, I feel confident in my ability to serve the students' needs.

"However, I'm worried about what I'll come back to at the end of the summer. In my opinion, the need for me to step in at the last minute demonstrates that your planned initiative will lead to nothing but issues for the students down the road. Since this situation clearly demonstrates what staff bring to campus, I wouldn't feel comfortable taking this role, only for a rule to be passed a few months later that would cut me and any other employee on campus off from potential ways to help students."

Not a full ultimatum, but the threat is clear. Drop the initiative, or cancel the class that the students have already planned their schedules around. Despite my issues with the professors, I can admit the Billings faculty cares deeply for their students. I just have to hope they love them more than they hate us.

The thought of this not going my way makes me sick to my stomach. My entire career has been spent prioritizing my students, and I know there are some in the class who need it to graduate. But this decision to split the campus in half—to prevent any sort of collaboration or growth—will hurt all the students at Billings, so I have to risk it.

But god, a summer in Rome sounds incredible. A chance to return to my favorite place in the world, home to all my best childhood memories. Three months of fresh tomatoes from the market you can eat like an apple, of perfectly churned gelato and chatting with baristas over the bar while sipping sublime espresso. And getting paid for it. How is that not the dream?

Before Inez can give me notes, the door at the top of the auditorium swings open, and we both tense. No one shows up to these meetings early. We thought we'd have time to run through everything and troubleshooting any technical issues, and we're only a minute in.

When Colton Miller's tall, lean figure slips in and closes the door, my whole body relaxes, like he's an even more effective form of Valium.

Okay, so not *every* professor is the enemy.

When my other best friend was offered a tenure-track position at Billings a year ago, I was torn. The idea of having him close again made my heart soar, but I was worried that the culture on campus would poison our friendship. But like with everything else in his life, Colton refuses to be cowed, rolling his eyes whenever I tell him to meet me off campus for coffee or fixing his signature scowl on his face when I try to push him behind a bush to hide from a professor walking toward us.

I'm not going to sacrifice nearly a decade and a half of friendship because they all have sticks up their asses.

It's been magical having him back with me this year. Then came the request for him to join the Rome program. Yes, not one, but *both* of my closest friends are going on this trip. I finally got Colton back after a decade of him traveling between Rome and Chicago, getting his PhD and becoming Roman history's new golden boy. I don't want to surrender him back to his one great love, at least not without me being there, too.

Colton's never been one to give out his smiles easily, so when he spots us at the front of the auditorium, all we get is a small quirk of his lips.

It's still bizarre having him on campus after he only existed within my six-inch phone screen for so long. My fingers tingle with the desire to reach out and touch him, to prove to myself he isn't a figment of my imagination.

"How are you two feeling?" he asks, all somber gravity.

Inez gusts out a breath. "Like I'm gonna be sick."

"It'll be okay," I say, reaching across the podium to squeeze her hand as the two of us seamlessly shift between consoler and consoled.

Inez has terrible anxiety over presentations, which, sadly for her, make up a decent third of the work she does at Billings. We spent half of grad school coming up with coping mechanisms. It works well when she's doing low-key pre-departure orientations with a handful of students, but standing up in front of a group that's rooting for you to fail is a whole other beast.

Colton jerks his head toward me. "And how are *you* feeling?"

"Like you aren't supposed to be here," I say, crossing my arms over my chest and shaking my head at him. "Did I dream that extensive conversation about how you should stay away so people don't think you're siding with the staff?"

He turns so he's leaning his side on the podium, facing me fully. My eyes skim over him without permission. The past decade has been kind to him. He's always been cute in a scraggly hair, metal-band-shirts-that-were-too-big sort of way. But this isn't the eighteen-year-old Colton Miller I met the first week of freshman year, all sarcasm and scowls to cover his fear of not fitting in at our expensive private college. This isn't even twenty-two-year-old Colton, nervous smiles and held-back tears when I dropped him off at the airport, both of us emotional over the fact that we wouldn't see each other for a full year. We had no idea that one year would turn into ten.

I watched the changes play out virtually. The way his shoulders continued to broaden. The new haircut that showed off his jaw, the lines of his face sharpening until you could cut yourself on them. The confidence that grew in his eyes as he proved himself again and again. But it was muted, like looking at a picture of St. Peter's Basilica so often that you assumed you'd be unaffected in person, only to find yourself bowled over by its grandeur. I'm sure the impact will wear off eventually—it has to, right?—but even a year later, seeing him in person hits me like a Mack truck.

My eyes can't stop clocking all those changes, across his chest and to his forearms, cruelly exposed by his rolled-up sleeves. I rip my gaze away.

Yes, he's grown up. Doesn't mean I need to notice it this much.

"I seem to recall a lecture from you," he says, his head tilting side to side, "but I don't know if I'd call it a conversation."

"They'll see you supporting me and then they'll hate you and you won't get tenure and all the hard work you've put in will be for nothing and I'll hate myself for the rest of my life. I don't want to hate myself, Colton. You've met me. I'm awesome."

Colton's been working toward a tenured position with his special brand of tunnel-vision determination since we were nineteen. Aligning with campus culture is taken into consideration during tenure review, especially at a small institution like Billings, and being the one and only professor to be friends with the staff is *definitely* going against campus culture here.

His mouth stays stubbornly straight, but the dimple in his left cheek pops the smallest bit, like he's trained his lips not to smile but can't wrangle his cheeks under control. "Seems dramatic."

"It's really not dramatic," Inez says with a sigh. "You've been here for a full academic year and you haven't noticed it?"

"I've noticed faculty and staff don't spend time together, but I don't think it's as bad as you two make it out to be."

"What about the way they talk over me in the Rome meetings?" she asks.

Colton winces. "Okay, yeah, I can recognize there's some... tension. But I still don't think being friends with a staff member will cause drama."

"We've been over this," I say. "Billings demands you pick sides! How do you think the Capulets and Montagues would've reacted if Romeo and Juliet were chatting in the middle of Verona's piazza?"

He lifts an eyebrow, one side of his mouth losing the battle against his smile. "Are we star-crossed lovers? Seems I missed a step."

"You know I mean two people on different sides of a feud. Stop trying to be clever when I'm freaking out!"

I push his shoulder with a laugh, and he grabs my hand, tugging me into his chest. I tense for half a second before letting my head find its home right over his heart, the steady beat settling my own. Even with my heels boosting me up to a solid five foot five, he dwarfs me as he let his large hand skim up and down my back.

I missed this over the last decade. We had our weekly calls and daily texts, my steady stream of consciousness and his sarcastic commentary of life in Italy. But I'm an affectionate person by nature, and I've always needed physical connection with the people I love. I missed feeling him, missed his reassuring hand running over my back and those hard forehead kisses when I came up with an idea that inspired him.

And if there's a distracting new awareness that runs through my limbs from those touches? I'll stubbornly ignore that.

"You shouldn't be here," I say into his chest, even though I'm beyond grateful that he is. He's always been there. The only one I've been able to count on.

His chuckle reverberates through my body. "I wasn't going to miss this."

I tilt my head to look at him, the minuscule curve of his lips showing he isn't taking this threat seriously at all. "I'm worried about you, Colt. Associating with me is a risk."

"Worth it," he says, that curve growing the smallest amount, and I pinch his side. He yelps and grabs my hands, anchoring them behind his back. "I'll stay quiet and in the back. If anyone asks, I'm here because I'm a professor in the program and wanted to see what they decide. Deal?"

"Deal." I bury my head back in his chest. "Thank you for being here."

"What was that?" he asks, all dry humor.

"I hate you."

Colton's phone buzzes in his pocket, and he lets go of my hands to fish it out, my own last name flashing across the screen. Both of us tense, and I pull back quickly. He silences the call, slipping the phone back into his pocket.

"Take the call, Colton," I say, turning away from him. My father won't appreciate being ignored. At least, he never used to. I may not know him anymore, but men like him don't change.

I've spoken to him a grand total of two times in the past decade, a perfunctory greeting at my brother's engagement party where we both clearly agreed not to ruin his day, and once that same weekend when I begged him to get us access to the campus dining hall as a favor for a friend who had no idea how much it cost me. He followed that favor up with a text that just said, *The door's open when you're done being stubborn.*

Of course, his version of "not stubborn" means doing exactly what he demands of me with no consideration for my own feelings.

"I'll call him back later. Tell him I was in a faculty meeting."

I nod and busy myself with the notecards I brought for the presentation.

Colton grips my chin, forcing me to look at him. "If this is too hard now that I'm back, I don't have to work with him."

I'd never ask him to throw away his career just because my relationship with my family imploded. My award-winning, internationally respected professor of a father may be an epic asshole, but he's also the most influential member in Colton's field and willing to mentor him despite his connection to me. And now that he's poured years of public support into Colton, he'd be extra vindictive if Colt cut ties.

I force a smile that Colt immediately sees through, but he lets me have it. "Hell no, let's make having to deal with his bullshit worth something. Call him back. There's time before we start."

He looks into my eyes, trying to suss out if I'm really okay. The truth is I'm not—I'll never be okay with how everything went down—but I'm not *not okay* enough to have him commit career suicide.

"Okay," he finally says. "I'll make sure to get him off the phone quickly so I'm back in time to heckle you with the other professors."

I swing my foot at his ass, and he scurries out of the way just in time. "I kind of love you," I call as he runs up the stairs.

He stops halfway up, turning to me with a broad smile, the one with the dimple that makes my heart feel like it's grown too big too quickly à la the Grinch. "Kind of? I'm moving in the wrong direction."

I laugh and turn back to my flashcards. Inez is immediately at my side.

"Can you two just kiss already?" she asks in a low voice, her eyes on Colton, who's undoubtedly dialing my father as we speak.

I nudge her with my shoulder. "You know we aren't like that."

We've heard some variation of this for fourteen years, though Inez's comments have kicked up considerably since he came back to Boston. No one can seem to accept that we are, and have always been, just friends. There may have been a blip of attraction now and then on my side, but nothing worth risking our friendship over.

He's been my person since the first week of college, when I word vomited my enthusiasm all over him and he responded by asking genuine questions instead of making fun of me. I spent all freshman year waiting for the moment I'd be too much for him, like I've been for everyone else, but it never came.

Inez purses her lips and side-eyes me, the embodiment of the *Sure, Jan* meme.

"Men and women can be friends, you know!" I say.

"I absolutely agree. But not you two."

I scoff. She can say what she wants, but our friendship is deeper than any romantic relationship I've ever seen. Romance fades, even when the relationship is built on a solid foundation of friendship. And when those relationships end, so does the friendship. Who in their right mind would risk it?

"Don't we have more important things to focus on than your matchmaking attempts?" I ask Inez, fluttering my notecards in front of my face like a fan.

"Ready for this?" she asks, tugging on one of her long, dark brown curls.

"Is *no* an acceptable answer?" I ask with a laugh.

She wraps her arms around my shoulders, laughing with me. "Not really."

The door opens again, and this time, a group of much less friendly faces walk through. No more time for second-guessing. It's showtime.

2

COLTON

I LET myself have one last look at Quinn before I slip out of the auditorium. Ten years apart, and her effect hasn't worn off a bit. I may as well still be an awkward eighteen-year-old, mesmerized by her dark expressive eyes and the way her mind jumps so quickly from topic to topic.

I thought these feelings would fade while I was abroad. A decade without seeing each other in person should have cured me of this, but it was like she was right next to me every day. A whiff of limoncello may as well have been Quinn behind me, her citrusy scent hanging in the air. Her laugh, loud and unabashed, echoed in my head when my new colleagues didn't even chuckle at my deadpan sarcasm. And on the days when the cursor blinked on the screen, my research nowhere near done and the pressure pushing down on me like a medieval torture device, she was the only one I wanted to talk to, no matter how many other women I tried to build something with.

I pull up my missed call log, hitting Richard Riley's contact and fighting back my anger at the way Quinn's eyes went carefully blank at his name. There's nothing careful or vacant about her. She's meant to be loud. Passionate, with thoughts flowing out of her like the constant stream of water from the fountains around Rome.

My phone rings out five times before Richard picks up, and I can practically see him sitting at his giant wooden desk, watching the lit-up screen and waiting until the last second to pick up as one of his weird power plays.

I hate the man. And I idolize him and then hate myself for idolizing him. He's a horrible father, and I'll never forgive the pain he's inflicted on the most important person in my life. But he's also brilliant, and he's dedicated a lot of time and energy to helping me build a name in the field. The darkest part of me—the part that's a terrible friend who doesn't deserve her—always sighs in relief when Quinn insists I keep working with him.

"Colton, how are you doing, son?"

I flinch every time he calls me that. When I was in college, I'd fantasize about Quinn realizing she had feelings for me, the two of us building a life together and me being welcomed into this impressive, overachieving family like an equal. Now, it makes my skin crawl, him claiming me as his own while dismissing the person who *is* his.

"Doing well, Richard. But I'm about to go into a faculty senate meeting, so I'll have to keep this short."

A clap sounds down the line, like he's slapped his hand on his knee. "I knew you'd dive straight into building a name on campus. Never forget how important service is for your tenure package, you hear me?"

"Yes, sir," I answer dutifully, although I've been through this conversation a dozen times between him and my other mentor, Dr. Cassia.

While Richard's support is somewhat performative—he wants to claim ownership of my successes—Dr. Cassia's been in my corner since freshman year, just like Quinn. The two of them took an angry, defensive kid who was sure he'd never fit in on a university campus and turned me into who I am today. They're the reason I had the confidence to go off the path I'd planned, the reason I believed supporting my mother and pursuing my passion weren't mutually exclusive.

"Now, about this summer," Richard says, "I'll be in Rome longer than expected. I wanted to get something on the calendar."

Even though he's settled in Florida and I was getting my PhD in Chicago, both of us have spent plenty of time in Rome over the last decade. Whenever our time overlaps, we get together, spending the whole time talking shop and very noticeably avoiding the elephant in the room. I haven't heard him speak Quinn's name once since she decided not to go into our field. It isn't like she was dead to him—parents of deceased children still talk about them. It's like she never existed to begin with.

"Sounds great," I say, knowing there's no point in avoiding the inevitable. "But I don't have my exact schedule yet, so I'll have to let you know. Send over the dates."

A lot of my summer plans are dependent on how Quinn's presentation goes, but I'm not going to bring that up with him.

He grumbles on the other line. "I'll never understand why you chose a liberal arts college over the research institutions that were interested in you. A university like mine would never leave the schedule to the last minute like this."

I thought long and hard about what direction I wanted to take my career, and going back to a small college like my undergraduate experience felt right. Eighteen-year-old Colton's decision to go to Chadoin University was based on nothing more than the fact that they gave me the most money. No one in my small town in West Virginia had gone to college, and my priority was getting the most practical degree possible so I could start making money for my family. It was pure luck—or destiny, if I want to get real Italian about it all—that I was randomly assigned to a Roman history elective, where a chaotic girl dropped into the seat next to me, talking a million miles a minute. By the end of the semester, I was equally in love with the girl and the subject.

Unlike when I was choosing my undergrad, I *did* have the luxury of choice this time around. Money's still a consideration—and likely will always be, if the bills piling up from my mom are any indication—but it isn't the *only* consideration anymore. Despite my first impression, I found myself at Chadoin, and I think I'll continue to grow at Billings.

Dr. Cassia understands that, even if Richard thinks I'm throwing my potential away. It's mind-blowing that I had multiple tenure-track offers when so many of my colleagues didn't have any. But when I saw an open position at Billings, I knew in my gut it's where I'm meant to be, and only half because Quinn's here, too.

But rather than explaining that—again—I mumble my agreement and wrap up the call. If this presentation works out and Quinn comes with us to Rome, we'll have to talk about her dad. She won't be able to avoid seeing or thinking about him like she normally does.

I slip back into the room right as Inez kicks off the presentation. Her light brown skin has gone ashen as she stumbles a bit over the words she rehearsed so perfectly in Quinn's apartment yesterday, but she gets it all out.

I looked over the materials sent to the senate and helped them practice their presentation, starting with the explanation for the last-minute change, followed by why Quinn's so qualified, before they hit them with the ultimatum that they refuse to call an ultimatum.

Their argument is sound. Still, they're fighting an uphill battle.

Billings's Faculty Senate is small. The large auditorium's only a quarter filled with about thirty faculty representatives, plus President Munchen and the deans of each college. These meetings are open to anyone, but no one except the senators show up, until me. I know Quinn worries about me, and I know there's some truth to what she's saying, but I'm not going to leave her without support.

The lines deepen on Quinn's face as Inez wraps up, and I can practically hear her running through her proposal as she takes in the tired, bored faces in front of her. One professor yawns loudly, making no attempt to cover it up. Quinn pretends not to notice as she starts on her portion of the presentation.

My college experience was dedicated to studying each side of Quinn. I loved them all—the wild enthusiasm when she was working through an idea out loud, the loopy, sleep deprivation-driven humor when she procrastinated on a paper, the soft, sleepy smiles when she woke up after crashing on my futon during a study session. But there's something particularly magical about this side of her. Strong, composed. Driven by passion. I can't imagine denying her anything.

"Since this situation clearly demonstrates what staff bring to campus, I wouldn't feel comfortable taking this role, only for a rule to pass a few months later that would cut me and any other employee on campus off from potential ways to help students," Quinn finishes, chin held high as she stares down the audience.

There's silence for three seconds, and then a dozen professors jump in all at once.

"Are you truly saying…"

"How dare…"

"The audacity…"

Quinn lifts her hands, and the professors shockingly fall silent again. "If we could have one question at a time, please, I think that would be more productive."

The red that creeps over some of their faces shows exactly how they feel about Quinn's command, but everyone in the room can recognize that screaming over each other accomplishes nothing.

Dr. Richardson from the marketing department is the first to speak up. "Students need this class, Ms. Riley. Are you really going to hold their futures hostage?"

Quinn flinches. The first question, and they went right for the jugular. "That's not my intention. I *want* to teach them. I've dedicated my career to helping students, and I believe this summer will change those students' lives. But tell me what would have happened to these students if your initiative had passed last year? I wouldn't be *allowed* to teach, or to consult on the KMG internship program you're all so passionate about, or any of the other ways I've served campus over the past eight years. I'm taking a gamble that bringing this conversation to you will lead to us all coming to the same conclusion."

"And what conclusion is that?" asks a professor I don't know.

"That our students deserve a campus that provides them the best support possible, and shackling our employees will prevent that from happening."

Dr. Richardson nods thoughtfully. He's always been one of the more open-minded professors on campus, even if he is a bit of a conceited prick. A few of the other professors murmur to the people beside them, and while I can't understand the words, it seems positive.

Then Dr. Yoder stands, pushing his wire-rimmed glasses up his nose as he clears his throat. I've had a few interactions with him—he sits on my tenure committee—and none of them have been particularly pleasant.

"Why," he starts, a sneer taking over his wrinkled face, "are we having this discussion to begin with? Let's find a professor from any department to step in for this class and be done with the drama."

Quinn's smile is viscous as she walks up the stairs and hands him a sheet of paper. "Sir, would you mind telling us what the highlighted portion of the Billings bylaws states?"

"In order to teach a course, one must have..."

His back is to me, but his posture goes ramrod straight as he processes the words on the page. They can't tap someone else. Quinn's their only choice, and the flash of satisfaction in Quinn's eyes tells me that fact is written on Dr. Yoder's face.

"This is just like the staff, trying to encroach on the academics," he says, changing tactics. "First with the never-ending requests to present during our class time, and now trying to dictate the decisions the faculty senate makes."

A throat clears lightly, and everyone turns their attention to our president. "Let's keep the discussion on the topic at hand," she says with quiet authority.

He scowls, but doesn't argue. Quinn somehow manages to keep her smile relaxed and professional when I know inside she's doing that awkward wiggle dance she does when she's ecstatic. I let out a smug smile on her behalf.

But before she can enjoy her victory, Dr. Guarino, one of the most respected members of our community and another professor on the Rome program, raises his hand. The other professors fall silent.

"Ms. Riley, I'd like to thank you for your presentation and the time you've given us. Please know that what I am going to say is not a criticism of you."

Quinn tenses.

"However, the decisions this senate makes are not done so lightly. I vote we deny this petition and tell the students to choose another class in the program. They have plenty of options."

Quinn can't stop herself. "With all due respect, Dr. Guarino, that's unfair to the students."

"Perhaps you should have thought about that before you laid out this ultimatum."

Quinn's face goes from its regular pale hue to crimson in seconds. She lets her eyes wander up to me, and I give a little shake of my head. Her lips pinch like she can hold in the words, but she's already too far gone.

I open my mouth to stop whatever shit show is coming, but she beats me to it. "You think I want to do this? You think I want to have to choose between the immediate needs of my students and the long-term health of this college? No, I didn't put myself in this position. I was put here by pompous professors who care more about proving a point than serving their community."

The room sucks in a collective breath. None of the professors would have spoken like that to Dr. Guarino, and they certainly won't tolerate that sort of disrespect from staff. Even Quinn's allies turn against her. Her eyes are desperate as she watches their demeanors change.

"This *pompous professor*," Dr. Guarino says, his light Italian accent deepening, "is feeling more confident by the second in our decision to distance the two sides of our campus."

The red fades from Quinn's face, the fight going out of her eyes and her shoulders hunching. My tiny warrior is disappearing before my eyes. I would have lived a very different life without that fire, and I can't see it go out.

Without thinking it through, I stand from my seat and walk down the steps of the auditorium. Every eye follows me, and my stomach churns from the attention.

Spontaneous decisions are not my thing. Every action I take—from the research I select to the way I've trained my accent out of my voice—is meticulously planned to make the most of my shot at tenure. There's a reason I have such a strong reputation on campus after only one academic year, and it's not from running to the front of a senate meeting without a fucking plan.

I don't know what I'm going to say when I get to the front of the room. All I know is I can't leave her up there alone. Quinn's wide brown eyes look up at me, her expression anguished, like I'm throwing myself on my sword for her. When I take a spot next to her, I turn my attention back to the senate.

I run a hand down the leg of my pants to anchor myself. "I know I'm not on the faculty senate, but I am a professor in this program. I'm also relatively new here, which has some disadvantages, but also gives me a fresh perspective. It seems... shortsighted... for us not to at least pause to consider what Ms. Riley is proposing."

The professors are silent for a beat, and then, as if they have synchronized internal timers, all start talking at once. Mostly arguing against me, and my blood turns cold. The way they look at me shifts the same way it had for Quinn when she insulted Dr. Guarino, suspicion lining their faces. Maybe I should've listened to Quinn's warnings.

"You may be onto something here, Dr. Miller." All eyes turn back to President Munchen in the front row. "Perhaps that's exactly what we need. A pause."

She taps a finger against her lips, something churning behind those intelligent hazel eyes as she stands and takes up the spot on Quinn's other side. "Our campus has been at a tipping point for a while. I was on board with the faculty's original plan, but I'll admit Ms. Riley has presented some compelling arguments.

"I propose we put a pin in the initiative. Let's have Ms. Riley teach the course as a test of the... unexpected value staff may bring to our academic programs. At the end of the summer, we can reconnect to discuss the success or failure, and what that means for our campus."

Quinn bounces on her toes. "How does the staff know this is in good faith? That it isn't just a way to get us to run the class while you all plan to pass the initiative anyway?"

President Munchen's smile isn't unkind, but has a pitying quality about it. "You don't. But I would ask"—she pauses to glance meaningfully around the room, stopping significantly on Dr. Guarino—"that everyone involved go into this experiment with an open mind. And as a sign of our commitment, we'll assign a faculty member in the program to act as a resource for you in case there are issues to troubleshoot. No one expects perfection, but we need to see the true value, even through the challenges. Is that acceptable?"

Quinn's throat bobs while she considers, and I can see the moment she realizes there's no other choice. It's not a win, but it *is* an opportunity.

When Quinn nods her head once, President Munchen claps her hands. "Fantastic. The only thing left to sort out is which professor you'll work with."

She makes eye contact with Dr. Guarino, whose jaw flexes from how tightly he's grinding it. He gives a subtle shake of his head. The impact of the rejection infuses itself into Quinn, and I see it transform her body. It's so reminiscent of her body language whenever her family comes up—quiet and closed off in a way that's unnatural for her.

I should keep my mouth shut. Should let President Munchen make the call. Then, even if she does pick me, it would be her choice. But the professors have made Quinn feel alone far too often, and I want her to know that I'm choosing to stand with her.

"I'll do it," I say, and any nerves I have are wiped away by the grateful look on Quinn's face.

"There you have it," President Munchen says brightly, patting Quinn on the shoulder before turning back to the auditorium. "I hope you all will give this new plan a chance. Let's put it to a vote."

I fight the urge to reach for Quinn's hand while the chair calls for the vote. My eyes fly back and forth, taking a quick tally of the hands raised in favor. The proposal passes. By the skin of its teeth, but still.

We're going to Rome.

3

QUINN

I LOOK around at the mayhem I've created in my bedroom. I have two days before my flight to Rome. Two days to figure out how to fit ten suitcases' worth of clothes into three bags. It isn't going well, but I'll figure it out.

For the first time in years, I let myself enjoy the memories of the city that defined so much of my life.

Sitting on the wall outside the Pantheon with gelato dripping down my chin while my father gesticulated wildly, explaining how the pillars had been looted like it mattered to his five-year-old daughter.

My first kiss at twelve with Tomasso, the son of one of my dad's contacts and my annual summer playmate, which ended with us in a fit of giggles over how wrong it felt to kiss someone who was practically a sibling.

My heart bursting as tears filled Colton's eyes the first time he saw the city when we were twenty-one and studying there together our junior year. Rome has always been the home of my heart, but it felt like *more* during those few months when I was there with Colton.

I haven't set foot in the city in over a decade. Once I graduated and blew up my relationship with my family, I wasn't particularly welcome on their annual trip. And with student loans up to my ears, I can't afford to take myself. The joy in my work and the freedom from my parents' control are worth what I left across the ocean, but now that it's within reach, my whole body sings in anticipation.

From down the hall, I hear my front door swing open and closed. A few seconds later, Colton leans into my room, his hands braced on either side of the doorframe, scowl in place. "How many times do I have to tell you to lock your damn door?"

"I locked it when I got home!"

He raises an eyebrow. "And it magically unlocked itself? I didn't know you had a sentient door."

I point at him. "If that's what you're into, have I got a novella for you. A man gets turned into a door, and he'll only turn back if the woman who lives in the apartment fu—"

"Stop trying to distract me with your batshit reading habits," he says, one side of his lips hitching up.

I sigh. "I'm sure one of my roommates left it open for their friends."

He shakes his head. "You've gotta get roommates who aren't in college."

"Find me people who can afford this place without mommy and daddy footing the bill, and I'll kick these babies out in a heartbeat. But a girl's gotta pay her loans."

Colt's face softens at the last word. It's the closest we ever come to discussing my family stuff. I don't like talking about it, both because it sucks ass and because afterward he always feels guilty about working with my dad, and then I feel guilty for making him feel guilty and we both just feel guilty and sad. Great way to spend the day! Rehashing how their love and support was contingent on me following a certain path never makes me feel better anyway.

They'd given me everything when I was young. There was always money in my bank account and a ticket home for the holidays, no matter how brief the visit. My parents and three older brothers dropped anything if I needed them. I grew up feeling loved and important, basking in the glow of their support. It was a blessing, until my entire support system was ripped away from me without warning, and I was left with no coping skills to deal with the loss.

I was crushed when they cut ties at Dad's request—or rather, Dad's demand. He isn't an easy man to go against. But I realized if their support was so easily taken away when I didn't do what they wanted, it wasn't support at all. It was control, and I have no interest in it.

There wasn't a peep from any of them until last year, when Bradley prostrated himself at my feet and said he couldn't get married without me there, winning me over with that same timid sweetness that made him unable to stand up to Dad back then. I agreed, with the understanding that I'd have as little contact with the rest of the family as possible.

Colt heaves a sigh. "I know you don't want to, but we need to talk about your dad."

"I don't have a dad," I say cheerfully, telling myself if I smile and joke about it enough, it'll stop hurting. "He made that decision for me."

"You know he's going to be there this summer."

"In a city of nearly three million people? How ever will I avoid him?" I ask dramatically, and Colton rolls his eyes.

"You aren't going to talk about this, are you?" He sighs and rubs his brow. "Sometimes I wish I'd never applied for that damn fellowship."

My gut twists at the mention of the Harrow fellowship. It was a defining moment of Colton's life when he won at the end of undergrad. The shock on his face when they called his name instead of mine is seared into my brain. I didn't want anything to take away from his victory, so I hid the shit show of everything surrounding the fellowship as long as I could, until he called from Rome one day asking why the hell my dad suddenly wouldn't say my name.

"Don't ever say that," I say. "I was happy for you then, and I'm happy for you now."

Colton's jaw tightens. "Your family sucks."

I release a contented sigh. "I know. That's why I stole yours."

"Borrowed mine," he says with a raised brow.

"Pretty sure your mom would say she's mine," I say with an evil little smile. "Haven't you always wanted a sister?"

He levels me with a stare. It's heavy and loaded and even though his eyes never leave mine, I feel it across every square inch of my skin. "You are *not* my sister, Chaos."

I love when he calls me that, the nickname that has belonged solely to him since I cornered him the first week of our freshman year, flying between topics like a monkey on cocaine jumping through trees. The split second of self-consciousness when he first said it was quickly washed away by the smile he tried to cover with his hand.

A group of river dancers start performing in my stomach as he walks over to lie across the small portion of the bed not covered in my clothes. He's too big for the space, his long legs stretched out and his head propped on one hand. My eyes follow the line of his body, heat creeping up my neck at the image of him reclined on my bed.

No, definitely not my brother.

"Do you want to talk about a plan for this summer?" he asks.

I scowl down at the dress in my hands. No, I don't need a plan. I have the experience to run this class well, and my talent will speak for itself, contrary to what the faculty members expect. They won't be able to deny the value the staff contributes when it's right in front of them. Even knowing Colton's intentions are good, the question digs under my ribs.

"No, thank you," I answer primly.

He lifts a brow at my civil tone, the awkward, formal one I use with professors but have never used with him. He holds my gaze, staring into my eyes like he can read my thoughts and is daring me to speak my mind.

It takes less than a minute for me to crack. "Look, I know everyone expects me to fail, but I was a TA my entire graduate career and am an expert in the field. I don't need a strategy to trick the faculty into thinking I bring something to the table."

Colton props himself up on his elbow. "That's not what I'm saying. No one is going into this hoping you'll fail."

"Dr. Guarino is," I say quietly, unable to meet his eye.

"I hate to tell you this, Quinn, but Dr. Guarino was perfectly civil until you called him pompous."

I groan and run my hands over my face, the lace of the dress scratching my skin. He's right—I never should have said that to Dr. Guarino—but Colton also can't understand. He hasn't dealt with years of being dismissed, of being talked over and ignored. Of presenting irrefutable proof of your success and impact, and still being treated like a flippant, unnecessary part of campus.

I've tried placating and sweet, strong and stern, self-deprecating and friendly, and none of it has made any difference. My voice is treated with a fraction of the respect and consideration of his, even when talking about my own field. I can recognize that in this instance, Dr. Guarino wasn't terrible, but he still threw away my idea for no other reason than it didn't align with campus culture, and that was triggering.

"I know I fucked up, okay," I say. "But I felt backed into a corner. I'll be better. And I really do feel good about this summer."

"Good," he says, his expression stern but his eyes soft. "What about the class? Want to talk about that?"

I fight down my knee-jerk defensiveness. "I've read every resource Billings offers on methodology and planning. I've reviewed the syllabi for internship classes across the country. I've even practiced my first day introduction in the mirror like a kid excited about their one line in the school Christmas play. I think I'm good to go."

I try to play off the self-consciousness as a joke, but I can't help the flood of fear. I have experience, but it's been eight years since I ran a classroom. My father's voice echoes in my head. *Of course you can't do this, Quinn. You're weak, throwing away everything because you can't handle a little rejection. Your class is going to be a mess, and the professors will see every misstep.*

Colton tucks his hands behind his head as he shakes it in mock disappointment.

"You'd think someone who spends their days convincing people to do internships would put more faith in the benefits of hands-on learning. I'm sure there's a thing or two I've picked up over the years that aren't in the pamphlets."

He always knows the perfect approach to pull me out of a spiral. No placating words or tearful heart-to-hearts. Just pure, logical facts. He has experience I don't, and he wants to help. The short burst of frustration fades from my veins.

I stop folding the clothes and sit down next to him with a huff. "Fine. What do I need to know?"

He shifts up on his elbow to look up at me, his expression so serious, my body tenses. "The most important thing? Know that everything is going to go to shit."

"Excuse me?" I ask.

"Every time."

A laugh bursts out of me.

"Laugh it up, but it's true," he continues. "No matter how many classes you teach, things will go wrong. So, plan for it. If you think a discussion in class will take twenty minutes, plan what will happen if it takes twice that time or half that time. Students will always screw it up for you."

"You make the work sound rewarding," I scoff.

He drops back onto the bed again, smiling up at me from his lounging position and my stomach starts up a gymnastics routine. "It's the best job in the world. And the worst."

"Your insight's been so helpful," I say, shaking my head at his proud little grin.

I push off the bed, and we settle into a comfortable silence. I start folding the clothes again, trying to judge if this stack will fit in my last suitcase. Colton eyes them skeptically, too.

"Did you know there's this cool invention in Rome?" he asks. "You put clothes into it, and it makes them clean."

I toss a piece of clothing at him. "Fuck off. It's a lot, but it's hard to find cute plus-size clothes. I don't want to need a certain type of outfit and not be able to find something that looks good. I'm covering all activities."

He lifts the article I threw at him, and I realize too late what it is. His fingers pinch the straps of a babydoll nightie as it spills down toward the bed. I can barely make out his face through the sheer lace cups and the blanket of embroidered material that would fall just far enough to give me some modesty, if there were any real coverage to the white fabric.

His lace-obscured eyebrows lift, a smirk playing on his lips. "Planning for *every* type of activity, are we?"

My eyes go wide. "I didn't mean to throw that at you."

I lunge for the fabric, but he's quicker, shuffling off the other side of the bed and holding it up again.

"Too late. Tell me, Chaos. Are you looking for an Italian fling?"

Now that he mentioned it, an Italian fling is exactly what I need. I've barely dated this past year. No one could seem to keep my attention past a date or two, and while I don't want a relationship, I could use some regular tension relief.

I laugh, scrambling after him. "You're such a dick. I'm probably not even going to take it."

He pushes back into the small space between my bed and the wall as I round the bed to reach him. He lifts the negligee in front of his face and raises his voice an octave. He affects an accent, more Scarlet O'Hara begging Rhett to stay than his old mountain man charm.

"Please, Quinn. I've always wanted to see the beauty of Italy. Don't leave me behind."

"I hate you so much."

"Not *so* much. Only a little."

I shake my head and go to yank it from his hands. He pulls back, making me stumble into his body. He places a hand on my hip to steady me, and I gasp, that hazy awareness I've felt over the past year suddenly bursting into high definition. My gaze runs down to where we both still clutch the cloth, before jumping up to his eyes again. His lips twitch, not a full smile, but his eyes dance at how clearly flustered I was.

Tingles shoot through my limbs, and I let him tow me another inch closer with the fabric. My heart thuds so loudly I'm sure he can hear it. His eyes never leave mine.

"Bring it, Quinn." His voice is smooth, like that first sip of limoncello that somehow both warms your body and sends a shiver through you.

I gulp, still unable to look away. "I don't know if I like how it looks."

He quirks an eyebrow. "Need another opinion? Maybe you should try it on."

I'm out of my depth here. He's messing with me. He is *definitely* messing with me.

Right?

A part of me wants to call his bluff. To strut out in nothing but this wisp of lace and see how well he holds up then. I won't do it, but I'll enjoy watching that smirk wiped from his face when he thinks I'm going to.

I lift my chin. "Good idea."

I'm not prepared for his reaction. He flies right past shock, too fast for me to even savor the victory, and straight to a pure hunger that shoots through me. His eyes slide down from my face, lighting me up every place he looks. I take an unsteady breath as he takes his bottom lip between his teeth.

His challenging gaze finds mine again. "Get to it, then."

The loud ringing of my phone breaks the tension, and I scamper away like I'm Superman and moving fast enough will turn back time on the last five minutes. He tosses the negligee onto the bed with the rest of my unfolded clothes.

What the fuck was that?

In the four years of our in-person friendship—of seeing each other practically every day—there was never anything romantic between us. No drunken kiss, no stress-relieving hookup. I recognized he was an attractive guy, even back then, but there was nothing substantial enough to act on. I hadn't been willing to risk our friendship, and I definitely won't now. I'd never survive losing him after everything else I've lost.

And Colton doesn't flirt. Like, ever. Not with the girls he dated in college, and definitely not with me. I don't like the reminder that he's changed. The physical differences I expected, had seen hints of on our video calls, but there was only so much you could see about the way someone carries themselves when they're stuck on a couch thousands of miles away from you. There have been years of small adjustments and growth that I didn't get to be a part of. It makes my stomach churn.

Or maybe that's something else. Like that damn smolder. Who the fuck taught him that? Everything in my body tightens.

Would it be hot? Probably.

Would it be a terrible decision? Without a doubt.

I need some space. This year's been so busy that Colton and I have barely had time together. Now that the semester's over, we've seen each other every day this week. I'm on a contact Colton high, like I stayed inside a newly painted room for too long and am feeling the effects of the fumes. I just need to open a window, and I'll feel back to normal in no time.

We'll be together in Rome for three months, but I can keep it together and avoid situations like this. Maybe take our hangouts out into the city instead of one of our apartments.

And. No. More. Lingerie.

"Hey, Inez," I say as I answer.

"Are you working out?"

"What?"

"You're breathing heavily."

I shoot a quick glance at Colton, thankful he can't hear her side of the conversation. "No, just packing. What's up?"

"I need to talk to you about housing for the summer. We've had a situation."

"Colton's here. Should I put you on speakerphone?"

"Yes please. It'll save me a call later." I pull the phone away from my ear.

I put it on speakerphone and sit down on the bed next to him. "You've got us both."

"Our regular apartments fell through. Their old pipes burst and flooded our floor. They can't get it all fixed up until July. We've used the same apartments for over a decade, but of course, they give out the year *I* manage the program," she says, with diabolical glee in her voice.

"You're enjoying this," I say in mock outrage.

"No, I'm not," she replies, too quickly.

"Yes, you are, you little psycho!"

She whines. "I can't help it! I love a problem to fix! It's the best part of the job."

There's nothing Inez loves more than moving things around behind the scenes to achieve the perfect solution. As the oldest cousin in her massive Puerto Rican family, she's grown up managing the people around her and putting out fires.

It's probably why she ended up in the study abroad office,

which is exciting and fun and rife with a million problems a day, ranging from canceled flights to natural disasters. She's never happier than when everyone else is panicking.

"I fully support the little chaos demon you are," I say. "So what do we do?"

"I found something else, but we have to change up the configuration. Dr. Keck is going to get her own place since she's bringing her whole family." I try not to think about my own family, how I was the kid lugged around on my dad's study abroad trips year after year. "That leaves six of us. I found two apartments in the same building with three rooms each, so we'll split. Colton, would you mind staying in our apartment?"

"Of course. I'd rather be with y'all, anyway," Colt says, and I savor the little twang he only lets out in private, the real Colton hiding under the professional Dr. Miller exterior.

"Amazing! I'll call them now and get it sorted out. Thank god. I thought we would end up on the streets for a minute there," she says before rushing off the phone to call the next person.

I glance around the room as the new details settle in my mind. My eyes land on the white bunch of lace on the top of my clothes and then shoot to Colton. He's looking back at me, but I can't make out his thoughts.

Well, there goes my plan for space, shot to shit.

I suck my teeth. "So… roomies."

He chuckles, surveying my luggage. "You better hope it's a penthouse if you plan to fit all of this."

"I'll stick stuff in your room."

"No."

I grab a handful of my clothes and turn back to him. "Two drawers," I say, and he tsks, shaking his head. "One drawer?"

He walks to the corner of my bed, one finger hooking the negligee. "I probably have space for this."

I shoot up and snatch it from his hand, tossing it back in my underwear drawer with a scowl. "Fine. I'll fit everything in my room."

He heads for the door. "It looks like packing is a long-term project. I'll pick up dinner while you keep working."

I tell myself not to watch him walk away. My brain commands my legs to stay locked, but they still walk to the doorway. I tell my eyes to mind their own business, but they somehow find his ass in those perfectly tailored slacks. I finally get control over my traitorous body and yank it back into my room like I'm fighting demonic possession.

Nope, nope, nope.

I'm going to take the next however long it takes to pick up food to reset. When that man steps back through my door, I'll be composed, friendly, and definitely *not* horny. And I'll be packed.

But before I can stop myself, I tiptoe across the room to the dresser. I glance around like I'll find hidden cameras to catch my guilty actions. I pause to listen for the door to make sure he isn't circling back for something.

And then I sneak that damn negligee into my suitcase.

4

COLTON

MAY — THIRTEEN WEEKS
TO WIN OVER THE FACULTY

I STEPPED foot on a plane for the first time a week before my twenty-first birthday.

It was fucking terrifying.

West Virginia and Boston are close enough that when I needed to visit, I was able to take a train or, in desperate times, a shitty bus that made me wish I wasn't going home at all. But planes were uncharted territory.

Without me asking, Quinn flew to Pittsburgh so we could fly out to Rome together. I spent the entire three-hour drive from home to the city a nervous wreck. But she was waiting there for me at the airport, two giant suitcases behind her and a backpack almost as big as her body strapped on. She talked for half of the almost ten-hour flight about the spots she wanted to show me— never making me feel bad for being too nervous to respond and letting me squeeze her hand every time my stomach dropped.

Like that first flight, I spend this one pushed up against Quinn, trying to focus on the movie in front of me instead of the way her leg presses against mine.

The memory of her flushed skin as we held that scrap of nothing between us plays on a constant loop, like it's transposed over the tiny screen on the back of the seat, a thousand times more vivid than the superhero movie I put on. I don't know what came over me in her apartment that day. It was like the angel on my shoulder passed out from the shock of the lingerie, leaving me defenseless against the devil pushing me to see how far we'd go, and now I'm left with a million what ifs.

What if Inez hadn't called?

What if Quinn had followed through?

What if I'd kissed her when her eyes flicked to my lips?

It's going to be a long summer sharing an apartment with her.

Once we gather Quinn's six thousand bags, we grab a cab to our new place. It's worth the extra cost—and fear, as the cabbie swerves between cars at an unholy speed—to see the city flying past us, flashes of concrete, marble, and steel making you feel like the taxi's a time machine providing glimpses into history. It doesn't matter how much time I spend here. Nothing can pull my attention from the world laid out before me. Not even Quinn.

When the cab drops us in front of an old building that definitely doesn't have an elevator, Quinn looks between our luggage piled on the sidewalk and the small wooden door to our building. Then she clears her throat and gestures to her bags. "Well, get to it, Colton."

I laugh. "Excuse me?"

She rolls her lips together in a failed attempt to hide her smile, especially since she's never been able to figure out how to keep it from reaching her eyes. "You're a strong guy. Should only take you three or four trips to get it all up there."

"And what will you be doing while I take care of this?"

"There's too much for one trip. Someone has to stay with the extra bags to keep them from being swiped by some guy on a Vespa."

I eye the bag closest to me. "I don't think that technique would work. This bag is bigger than a Vespa."

She laughs and tugs the luggage in question closer to the building with a little grunt. "Fine, then to protect them from some guy in a giant van."

"And why, exactly, am *I* the one who has to take up all the bags when *you're* the one who packed two years' worth of clothes?" I ask as I cross my arms over my chest. I'll carry the bags, but I'm going to get a *please* out of her first.

"Because you have all of that," she says, patting my biceps, and I don't think I imagine the pressure of her fingers tightening.

"What do you say, Quinn?" I ask sternly.

She flutters her lashes, over the top and dramatic, and it shouldn't be as cute as it is. "Please?"

"Good girl."

Her grip definitely tightens on my arm that time, her eyes widening.

She recovers less than a second later, punching my arm with a laugh. "I never should have given you that stack of romance novels. It's like I walked up to Thanos and handed him the Infinity Stones. The women of Rome are in danger."

I chuckle, shaking off my disappointment. Of course her mind goes there. She'd never consider me for herself.

Even on my most hopeful days back in college, I never expected more than friendship from Quinn, who is all light and joy and can have her pick of whomever she wants. Her friendship is enough. More than enough. It's everything. That moment in her apartment is messing with my head, making me see and hope for things I'd long given up on, and if I don't want to mess up the most important thing in my life, I need to get my head on straight.

I grab the first two bags, grunting as I hoist them up. "The fuck did you pack in these?"

She yells a singsong *thank you* at my back as I make my way up for the first time. When we complete the last trip up—first for Quinn and third for me—I need a cold beer and a flat surface. Quinn knocks on the door of our new place, and the door tears open a second later.

Inez, who has been dragging the luggage into the apartment as I brought it up, is bouncing on her toes, a beaming smile on her face. "Welcome home, you two!"

We follow her inside, and my eyes run over the the apartment. It couldn't be more stereotypical if it tried. Charming—if cold and uneven—terracotta bricks jostle our suitcases like we're still out on the Roman streets. Stucco walls, painted a warm yellow, feel like a hug in the bigger rooms and suffocating in the tiny kitchen off the foyer. The exposed wooden beams would do any modern farmhouse proud, but make it seem like we've stepped back in time when paired with the rest of the apartment.

It has a large living area, with a couple plush leather couches and a massive dining table. I wonder how anyone is supposed to host a dinner party to fill that table when the kitchen can barely fit three people. It's odd and old and perfect.

Inez points out the doors off the living room. "I took the one on this side. It's smaller than the other two. Those rooms each have a desk, and I figured you'd appreciate a place to grade papers away from the school."

"This is incredible. Thank you," I say.

She smiles and nods before pointing back to the two remaining doors. "Those two are up for grabs. They're basically the same, so it doesn't matter. The only difference is the corner one has a better view."

At the word view, Quinn's and my eyes clash together. We're two gladiators in the arena, sizing up the opponent, and that view's our ticket to freedom. I'd do a lot of things for this woman —giving up a room with a view isn't one of them.

Our fingers twitch towards our suitcases like this is the Old West. Each waiting for the other's move. Each afraid to pull their eyes away and give the slightest advantage to the opponent. I half expect a tumbleweed to roll between us.

I'm not sure who moves first, but suddenly we're both scrambling for our suitcases. Unfortunately for Quinn, she brought three times as much as me. As she reaches for one bag, I knock another one down between her and the room. My other hand closes around my suitcase as I shoot off toward the far door.

Her laughter rings out behind me. "Asshole."

I grin over my shoulder and see her scrambling over the suitcase, all luggage left behind in pursuit of the prize. But she can't catch up to my long legs.

I fling my suitcase into the room, slamming the door behind me and flipping the lock with a satisfying click. Quinn's body hits the door a second later. The doorknob turns, but there's no way she's getting in with that deadbolt.

"You're such a cheater!"

"It's not cheating. It's strategy. Ask Sun Tzu."

I toss my suitcase on the bed and yank open the drawers of the rickety dresser as she messes with the door again.

"Colton Ford Miller, don't you dare unpack that suitcase in my room."

"Not your room, Quinn Livia Riley."

I start blindly throwing clothes into the drawers. Half of this stuff will need to be hung up later, but that's not the point.

"You tricked me with that tricky suitcase..." She struggles to finish the sentence, too frustrated by my victory. "...trick!"

"It's cute when you get flustered and lose your words."

Her fist bangs against the door again. "Your mother would be so disappointed in you."

"My momma raised me to be a winner," I say, letting my accent slip back in full force.

I toss the empty suitcase under the bed. I allow one more laugh before I school my expression and walk to the door.

Quinn's leaning on the couch across from me with an adorable scowl.

"You're a dick."

I feign concern. "Did you want this room? I'm sorry. I wish I had known before I unpacked." She shoulders past me with narrowed eyes. "Welcome to my crib."

She glances over her shoulder with an infuriatingly sexy smirk. "You're dating yourself, Dr. Miller."

She saunters over to see the view I haven't taken the time to look at in my mad dash to claim the bedroom. With her back to me, my eyes run down her body.

I saw the physical changes through our video calls and the hundreds of pictures she sent me, but it had all been theoretical to a certain point. When I thought of her over the years, she was the last way I'd seen her in person, twenty-two with a giant smile on her face and tears sliding down her cheeks as she dropped me at the airport. My brain's still processing the changes in person.

She's even more beautiful now with her blond hair cut short. I'm temporarily mesmerized by the way it swings over her shoulders as her head follows the path of the Roman skyline. She has laugh lines around her eyes now, and I'm grateful that she's spent most of our time apart smiling even in the midst of her hurt. She's put on weight that makes her look like an ancient statue of Venus brought to life, all lush curves built for grabbing.

I look back up to find her watching me over her shoulder with a raised brow, and I clear my throat. "How's the view?"

"Spectacular, you asshole." With a final scowl at me, she turns back to the window.

I come up behind her to see for myself. She's right. The oranges, yellows, and reds of the buildings catch the sun. Clotheslines dotted with drying laundry hang between them, a sign that the neighborhood still holds on to its local population. Plenty of the buildings are showing age, their facade damaged and discolored, but that's part of the joy of Rome. Everything's old. Centuries old. Every crumbling building and hole-in-the-wall courtyard makes me wonder what it's seen over the course of its history, so significantly longer than my own. I'm a blip, a mayfly. It should terrify me, but I find the consistency and grandeur of this place more comforting than intimidating.

Our apartment is in Trastevere, a historically local neighborhood that is becoming more popular with students, artists, and tourists by the day. The dome of Saint Peter's Basilica shines in the distance, capping off the perfect image of Rome. I'll never get over the contradiction of these historical sights next to the crumbling facades and ruins that litter so many corners. The juxtaposition of a city collapsing under the weight of its own history next to the greatest—and most pristine—artistic and architectural feats.

I look down at the side of Quinn's face, her eyes misting as she gazes over the city. She's stunning, even more gorgeous than the view outside my bedroom window, and I'm struck by how lucky I am for the thousandth time.

"It's been a while since I thanked you," I say.

She rolls her eyes even as her lips curve up. "That again?"

"Yes, that again. You're the reason I have this life."

"You would have figured something out," she says, fiddling with her shirt like my gratitude makes her uncomfortable.

"I don't think I'd be living under a bridge now if you hadn't stepped in. But I wouldn't be here. I wouldn't have a career I love and a chance to travel the world doing it. Your belief in me changed everything, and I'll never stop saying it."

She teases her lip with her teeth as she squeezes past me, plopping down in the plush armchair set up in front of my new desk.

"I don't think I've ever said this out loud, but you changed everything for me, too."

I cross my arms and lean back against the windowsill. "Oh, yeah?"

"Yeah. You were my first student." I laugh and her smile grows. "Seriously! You had so much potential and were being left behind by an educational system that acted like you should know everything. It wasn't fair. I got more joy out of helping you than I got out of all my classes combined. It was the first time I questioned if the life laid out for me was the one I wanted."

"Dealing with my brooding bullshit was enjoyable?"

"Helping you figure out what you wanted to study and what you could do with it was enjoyable. Knowing I made a difference in your life was enjoyable. I'm not saying you don't make a difference, too, but it didn't feed my soul like it fed yours. You showed me that."

I walk over and pull her up for a hug. "Then I guess we're even."

She lays her head on my chest, right over my heart. "Even."

Quinn's affectionate by nature. I learned that quickly and thoroughly when I thought she was also interested in me freshman year, only to find out that she started seeing a girl who lived on her hall. But it doesn't matter that her hugging me or kissing my cheek or twining our arms together as we walk is platonic, my heart kicks up every time. She probably thinks I have a heart condition after all these years.

"Want to blow off unpacking and go grab some food?" she asks.

I lean back from the hug to look down at her. "Absolutely, I do. Let's reintroduce you to your city."

Quinn bounces on her toes, all joy and excitement like the first day I met her. And just like then, I let her drag me along, out of our apartment and into the city.

Fourteen years later, and I'd still follow this girl anywhere.

5

COLTON

FOURTEEN YEARS AGO

W‍HAT THE FUCK am I doing here?

I look at the students filing into the small auditorium. They drop into seats with their designer clothes and thousand dollar laptops, talking to each other without a care in the world.

I can't relate to these people any more than I could relate to the people back home who cared more about the Mountaineers' football team than what they could learn if they actually went to the team's college.

I'd been ready to leave Grand Creek behind me when I graduated high school. Everyone there fell into two categories. The first group acted like I thought I was better than them because I was going to college. And the second? They put me on a pedestal —which was worse. The smart kid who was getting out against all odds; they pinned me with their hopes and dreams but never took the time to know me. An ideal instead of a human being.

But I had the promise of escape and the hope that I'd find my people in college. A hope that's quickly vanishing as I listen to the guy behind me bitch about his parents because they wouldn't pay three hundred dollars a month for a parking spot.

I glance back at their bags and down at my backpack, the same one I've had since ninth grade. It's old and faded, but it doesn't have holes, so I see no reason to replace it. I'm not spending a cent of that scholarship money unless I have to.

I was lucky as hell to get a full ride to such a great school. I can recognize that, while also recognizing I don't belong here. My expectations need to shift. I'll hunker down in the library for the next four years, get the fuck out of Boston, and help set my mom up in a nicer place. A place that's her own, like she's always wanted.

"Oh my god, I'm so excited about this!" a random blond girl says as she throws herself into the seat next to me. I look around for whatever friend she's talking to, but there isn't anyone.

"Are you excited, too?" She's talking a mile a minute and doesn't give me time to answer. "I've been dying for this class. Dr. Cassia is, like, my personal hero. She's so smart. And did you know she's actually from Rome? She grew up around all this stuff we're gonna talk about. And a woman. So many of the big names in the field are men, but she kicks so much ass that they all worship her. And she's consulted on, like, all the big movies and TV shows about Rome. Everyone wants to hear what she thinks. It's, like, the coolest thing ever, right?"

I stare, dumbstruck by the information dump.

She teases her bottom lip with her teeth, and I realize that this whirlwind of a girl is mind-blowingly hot. Her long, blond hair falls over her shoulders, and even in her Chadoin sweatshirt and jeans, I can tell she has curves that could stop my heart. Those wide chocolate eyes are stunning, even though they dart around like she's looking for an escape route.

"Sorry, not cool?" she asks. "I get overexcited. Sometimes it's hard to stop the words."

"My advisor put me in the class."

God, could I sound more boring?

Her shoulders cave in. "Yeah, of course. That makes sense. Sorry again."

She faces the front of the auditorium, fiddling with her bag as she scans the room for a different seat. I'm struck by an irrational and overwhelming fear that if this girl walks away from me right now, the rest of my life will be wasted. She lifts her bag, and I panic.

"What movies?"

It comes out too fast and too loud, but at least she hasn't left yet. She blinks her wide eyes. A slow smile curves her lips, and I find my gaze locked on them. After a beat, she drops her bag back to the ground and turns toward me.

"All of them. I mean, obviously not like *Spartacus* since she's not ancient"—*What the hell is* Spartacus? But she hardly takes a breath, so I don't have time to ask—"but modern ones, you know? Do you like movies about ancient Rome? I think they're so much fun. My dad and I always watched them growing up, so maybe they hold a special place for me. But there are other things we do, just the two of us, and the Rome movies are still my favorite, so who knows? What do you do with your dad?"

It's my turn to blink at her. I don't know if I can keep up with this girl, but I've never wanted to do something more.

"God, I'm sorry. I'm doing it again, aren't I? My brothers tell me I'm a lot. I'm working on it. I can leave you alone. You probably didn't expect to get cornered by a chatterbox on the first day of class."

"No," I cut in, a bit too forcefully. This conversation may be hectic, but it's the first time since I arrived in Boston that I haven't been fixated on all the ways I don't fit in. I'm not ready to give that up, so I take a breath to steady myself. "No, I like hearing you talk."

She bites her lip to hide her smile, but she can't keep it from her eyes. They crinkle into perfect crescent moons.

I don't know exactly what it is. Her stream of consciousness that's weirdly relaxing? Her complete, unfiltered excitement to be at Chadoin? The embarrassment on her face when she thought she talked too much? But suddenly, I feel like I can breathe again. Like I'm not the only one adrift in this new and terrifying world. She's chaos incarnate, and I want to exist solely in the whirlwind of her enthusiasm.

"Great!" she says. "Because I'm in desperate need of some friends. I don't know anyone at Chadoin and I can already tell my roommate won't be my person. So, friends?"

I don't want to be friends. I want to drag this girl back to my dorm and kiss her until neither of us remember our names. My dick twitches and I try to think of anything I can to stop it. I don't want to scare her off. And I need friends, too.

"Sure. I'm Colt."

She reaches over to shake my hand, but before she can tell me her name, Dr. Cassia comes through the side door by the board. The mystery girl was right. She's cool. She does all the same syllabus bullshit as every other professor, but she also shows pictures of different sites and tells us stories about the things we'll learn about that semester. It's a frivolous class I'm forced to take to graduate, but it's the first lecture I've sat in that feels inspired.

When she lets us go for the day, my mystery girl twirls to face me.

"That was great, wasn't it?" She pulls her long blond hair up into a ponytail, and my eyes home in on her graceful neck, leading to the thick, tempting curves of her body. "This is gonna be the best semester ever. I literally came to Chadoin to learn from Dr. Cassia and I got her in the first semester. I'm going to learn so much from her. God, I'm hungry. I was late this morning because everyone in my dorm decided to shower at the same time."

Don't picture her in the shower, Colton.

"I didn't have time to go by the dining hall. I need to find a grocery store to get some breakfast food to keep in my room. Want to go grab lunch, Colt? Oh, shit. I never introduced myself." She laughs loudly, and I find myself grinning along.

"Don't worry about it, Chaos," I say, the nickname slipping from my tongue, and I run a hand over my smile at her indignant face.

She narrows her eyes at me, but a smile plays on her full lips. "It's Quinn. Quinn Riley."

"It's nice to meet you, Chaos."

She lets out a delighted laugh and nudges me with her shoulder, which only hits about halfway up my biceps. "I've never had a nickname before!" She slips her arm through mine, and my stomach jumps at the contact. "So, tell me. You got a state to go with all that twang?"

I fight back the groan climbing up my throat. I've been in Boston for a week and have already heard all the asshole comments about Southern accents. They think my voice means I'm not as smart as them, which is rich coming from *Boston*, of all places. Plus, my accent isn't even Southern. Not like they care to differentiate anything below the Mason-Dixon line.

I pry my arm out of Quinn's grasp. "West Virginia."

She grabs my hand and forces me to face her.

"Did I say something wrong?"

I shrug like it's no big deal when in reality, this has been eating me up. "People here hate on accents is all."

"Oh my gosh! I didn't mean to make you think that! I don't have one, but I'm from northern Florida, which is pretty much southern Georgia. We've got plenty of Southern accents there, so it's like a warm slice of home. Although yours is different. I couldn't have placed it, but I guess it's West Virginia."

I fight the twitch of my lips. "Yeah, people lump together the Southern and Appalachian accents, but they're not the same."

"Appalachian," she repeats, mimicking my local pronunciation, biting off the *latch* like she's savoring the syllables in her mouth. She smiles that crescent-moon smile again. "I love it. Forgiven?" She looks up at me with hopeful eyes.

"Nothing to forgive, Chaos."

She loops her arm back through mine and tows me toward the dining hall. When I look down at this hectic, exciting, overwhelming girl, I decide I'll let her tow me anywhere.

6

COLTON

MAY — THIRTEEN WEEKS
TO WIN OVER THE FACULTY

PLATES of fried food stretch over the surface of our table, except for one little bowl of pasta in the corner, hoarded by Inez like gold.

Quinn whines across the table from me. "I can't eat anymore."

I lean forward, grabbing a *supplì* from the platter and tearing it in half, the deep-fried exterior breaking open to reveal rice and cheesy goodness. The flavors explode on my tongue as I force it between my lips. Our eyes were bigger than our stomach, but we can't stop. Not when the little Jewish-Italian grandmother who runs the restaurant has already popped over twice to ask how we're doing. She won't take kindly to us leaving a ton of food on the table.

Quinn dragged us to the Jewish Quarter, one of the most authentic neighborhoods in the city. For hundreds of years, the Catholic Church forced the Jewish community into this handful of blocks, leaving them with few resources in an area that flooded several times a year when the Tiber rose, until they built a retaining wall in the twentieth century. Those centuries of pain gave way to a strong community, identity, and the best food in Rome.

The cuisine is a unique combination of Jewish and Italian foods. Artichokes and rice and fish that all burst with flavor. But it's almost exclusively fried, a technique started as a way to maintain lower quality ingredients that's now continued out of tradition. After eating crappy plane food, our bodies aren't equipped to handle it.

Quinn sends a pathetic little look to Inez. "Help us, Inez. Please."

Inez pulls her bowl of *amatriciana* closer to her chest. "If I eat that much fried food, I'll be bloated for a week."

Quinn drops her head back with a little whine. "We're so fucked, Colt."

A ringing from Quinn's purse interrupts our groaning, and she bites her lip when she turns the phone toward me to show my mother's name.

"Don't answer that," I yell, frantically trying to pull my phone out of my pocket. If I can call her back before Quinn answers, I'll have plausible deniability.

Quinn wiggles her eyebrows at me and swipes to answer the video call. "Momma Miller!"

"Hi, my sweet boo," Momma says.

"We made it to Rome," Quinn says, leaning close to Inez and holding up the phone. "Say hi to Inez."

"Hi, Gerry," Inez says cheerfully.

"Hi there, sugar. It's so good to see you! How are you feeling about the program?"

"Wait," I interrupt, "how do you know my mother?"

"Holiday check-ins," Inez says with a bright smile for my mother, jumping into her plan for the upcoming week.

Yet another thing I've missed over the last decade. The first year I was in Rome, Quinn was alone in Boston. She was newly friends with Inez, but not nearly close enough after only four months to spend Christmas with her huge Puerto Rican family. My fellowship didn't cover a flight home, and my mom was going to be all alone for the holidays, too. For Quinn's present, I reserved a rental car and sent her down to Grand Creek. They've spent every major holiday together since. Seeing the two of them joking on the screen—often at my expense—was the only thing that got me through those lonely holidays, and I've been beyond grateful to be back with them this year, and hopefully for every year after.

"Are you two with my deadbeat son?" she asks, and I don't need to be able to see the screen to know she has a teasing smile on her face.

Quinn raises an eyebrow at me. "Oh yes, such a deadbeat with his PhD and all those important professorship offers."

"Anyone can be a deadbeat if they don't answer their mother's calls when they promised to check in by a specific time."

"Sorry, Momma," I call out, and Quinn hands me the phone. The second it's in my possession, I say, "It's Quinn's fault."

Quinn gasps. "*Traditore!* What did I ever do to you?"

I raise an eyebrow. "Your idea to go get food distracted me."

Quinn moves around the table to the open seat next to me. "*I didn't know about the call. I'd never forget you, Gerry.*"

"I know, darlin'," she says, blowing Quinn a kiss through the phone.

It's both weird and wonderful seeing how much my mother has welcomed Quinn into her life. It's been the two of us as long as I can remember, the sperm donor who helped create me off doing whatever real deadbeats did when they left their wife with a newborn baby and no money.

My mother did everything for me. She took on extra jobs to pay for my expensive SAT prep courses. She drove me to Boston and Philadelphia and New York for college scholarship interviews instead of relaxing on her rare days off. She read dozens of dry books about the college application process so she could understand a world she never had a chance to explore.

I swore I'd be successful, that I'd be the first Miller to get out of Grand Creek and make enough to support us. I refused to be another man who made promises he didn't keep.

"Gerry, did you see the article I sent you about Christmas?" Quinn asks, snapping me out of my reverie.

"The one about doing a trip instead of exchanging gifts?"

"Yes! I figured now Colton's home, we could each present our ideas on Christmas Day and then vote. What do you think?"

"I love it," she says, then sends a chastising look in my direction. "I'm just relieved Colton's finally at a job that doesn't make him work over the holidays."

My chest tightens, and Quinn slides her hand under the table to squeeze mine. She knows the truth, that there wasn't enough money left over after paying for my mom's housing for me to fly back every year. When my mother assumed I couldn't get off work, I didn't correct her.

Momma continues. "There's nothing you two could give me that would be better than spending more time with my kids."

"Quinn's not my sister," I say without thinking. If she's supposed to be my sister, I need some serious therapy.

"Your only child doesn't like to share," Quinn mock whispers, and my mom laughs.

I shoot Quinn a stern look. "I'm taking *my* mother over there to talk."

"Spoilsport," she yells at my back.

I turn back, smiling widely, and Quinn's answering smile sends tingles to every corner of my body. "You can stay here and finish all this fried food for us."

Quinn's groan chases after me as I walk away from the restaurant and down the street. I lean against the first wall I find that isn't part of the stretch of restaurants.

"How're you doing, Momma?" I ask.

"Nothing to complain about. Ruthie's still driving me crazy at the factory, but apparently it's against HR policy to duct tape someone's mouth for talking too much." She shrugs innocently, and I laugh loud enough to earn stares from people sitting on the patio of the nearby restaurant.

She continues talking over my laughter. "I do have to call that horrible Bobby, I'm sure you remember him"—she always says that and I never remember them—"he's a pain in the ass, but he's the best person to help with the kitchen renovation I was telling you about."

I clear my throat. "And he can stay on budget?"

A couple years ago, I finally saved up enough to buy her a house. I sent her a dozen listings that were in the budget I'd come up with. Cute houses and condos. But then she called me, her eyes shining with tears as she showed me the listing for her dream house, a little bungalow within walking distance of downtown Grand Creek. She'd spent so much of her hard-earned money helping me achieve my dreams, and I wanted to give her one of her own, even if it meant stretching my finances beyond their limits.

She took my ability to buy that house as a sign that I was making a ton of money. Which... I'm not. My pay isn't bad, but I don't have disposable income, especially between my rent and Momma's mortgage.

But I've never been good at saying no to her. So when she wanted to paint her house a soft blue with white shutters, I footed the bill. And when she mentioned her decades-old couch wasn't very comfortable anymore, I sent her money to redecorate. And when she asked if she could renovate the kitchen so it was open to the living room—*It'll be perfect for my girls' nights*—I said yes without even thinking about it.

I mentally calculate what I'll need to move around to make this reno work. Adding any new expenses will stretch my budget to near breaking, but I can make it work for now, especially since

I'm subletting my apartment in Boston while I'm gone, and the university is covering my expenses here.

"It won't be too much, baby," she says, setting the phone down to fill up her cup of coffee and leaving me staring at the ceiling. She always busies her hands during uncomfortable conversations. "I won't go more than a little bit over budget."

Her laughter, teasing and sweet, rings through the phone, and it should make me feel better, but the lines of my budget spreadsheet feel like they've wrapped around my lungs, pulling tighter and tighter.

Quinn's been on my ass to talk to my mom about all of this, but she doesn't get it. She has no idea what it's like to owe everything to another person and to have a limited time to pay them back properly. I've seen how much my mom's changed over the years. The long days standing in the production line at her factory job are showing. It had been noticeable even over video calls, but when I saw her in person this past July, it knocked me for a loop. Every moment of those ten years apart are written in the lines of her face, in the strands of her hair that have gone completely gray. I don't know how much longer I'll have her, and she should get to experience all the things she wants—all the things she sacrificed for me—before I lose her.

I sigh. "Try to stay in budget, Momma."

She barks out a laugh, grabbing the phone so I can see her face again. "Always so serious! I need someone who'll get my vision. Bring Quinn back. I always did like that girl of yours better than you, anyway."

I groan. "You know she's not mine, Momma."

"Only because you're too damn stubborn to say something and make her yours. I got it when you were leaving, but why not speak up now?"

I rub my palm over my eyes. "She doesn't look at me like that."

I've spent a decade and a half watching for something from her, any hint that she might be interested in more. We've had a couple charged moments since I've come home, but she's always quick—very, very quick—to bring up how lucky we are to have our friendship. She may be attracted to me, but does she want something real with me? Absolutely not. She's never hidden any of her thoughts and feelings. If she wanted to be with me, she wouldn't have been able to hold her tongue.

I've seen her walk away from friendships with other people after they confessed their feelings for her. She sat on my bed at least a half dozen times, talking about the awkwardness, how she didn't know how to behave around them anymore. The thought of her walking away from me is crippling.

"Sounds like you're a scaredy-cat," she says.

We've hashed out this conversation dozens of times over the years. But she doesn't really care about this topic today. This was evasion, pure and simple.

"Mother—"

"Ooh, you know it's serious when you bring out *mother*."

"Please stop playing around."

"Okay, okay. I'll ease up," she says, lifting the hand not holding the phone before her eyes go soft. "I'm so proud of you, sweet boy. This big, beautiful life you've built for yourself. People who love you and the world to explore and a fancy job you get to do forever."

Despite all the time and effort she's put into understanding my life, she's never fully grasped what the "tenure track" portion of my job title means. I'm not even close to lifetime security yet. There are plenty of reasons someone on the tenure track may not get tenure, and losing tenure at Billings would put me back at square one. Or worse, in the adjunct faculty pool, where contracts are unreliable and pay is shittier than underpaid elementary school teachers. And if I lose my position, there's no way I'd be able to pay for a kitchen renovation. Shit, we'd probably have to sell Momma's house.

I drop my head forward. I can feel the weight pushing my body down on itself. I won't fail her. I can't.

There's a familiar pang—a combination of fear, frustration, guilt, and regret. I could have chosen something more stable. I knew, even back then, that it was my job to help my family. Yet I gave up my business degree for something that wasn't a guarantee. I'd been miserable with all of those numbers and metrics freshman year of college and I love my life now, but enjoying my work will mean nothing if I can't support my mother.

"Will you at least think about telling Quinn how you feel?" she asks, bringing me back into the moment and the perfect girl sitting thirty feet away.

"Of course," I answer. "I'll think about how I'm not gonna do it."

She barks out a laugh. "You're a pest."

Her smile's bright enough to shine across the Atlantic, and I feel a tug deep in my gut. "I had to get it from somewhere."

After we say our goodbyes, I turn back to our restaurant and spot Quinn with Inez, head thrown back like she's bowled over by her amusement. Her laughter—my favorite sound in the world—echoes off the concrete and cobblestones, settling into my bones and easing some of my anxiety. We aren't together, but she's by my side, easing some of the stress and fear, and that's enough.

7

QUINN

MAY — TWELVE WEEKS TO WIN OVER THE FACULTY

I'M GOING TO COLLAPSE. Any second, my tiredness is going to win the fight against the multiple espressos pulsing in my veins, and I'll drop to the ground like Sleeping Beauty. *Here's your precious princess.*

I spent the past week putting out fires with Inez, everything from talking down freaked-out parents to finding out that the school space we'd rented has also been rented to another university for part of the summer and we'll have to share. She's been on a problem-solving high all week, right up until yesterday, when she remembered the orientation she has to host today.

We sat up all night practicing, finally going to sleep a couple hours before the sun came up, and I don't do well on little sleep. I either turn into a hyperactive, sleep-deprived clown or an over-emotional demon, but I don't have time for a nap. So here I am, hyped up and pacing our living room.

When the bathroom door flies open, I try to stop my pacing in its tracks, but the combination of caffeine jitters and sleep-deprived sluggishness don't pair well together, and my feet end up tangled underneath me. My body continues forward, and I reach out to brace myself, only for my hand to come down on Colton's wet, hard chest. He grips my hip to steady me, but not before my body lines itself up perfectly with his.

My brain short-circuits. It's the only logical explanation for why I can't pull my eyes away from the contrast of my pale hand against his bronze skin, or why my fingers push more firmly into the muscle, testing the strength buried beneath. I can't be responsible for the deep breath I take, inhaling the woodsy scent mixed with something so undeniably him, laced with memories of laughter and tears and so much love.

Colton bends his knees slightly to catch my gaze, his brows pulling together in confusion even as his lips kick up. "Quinn?"

I push away from him faster than I've done anything in my life, taking a solid five steps back until my legs hit the coffee table.

"You okay?" he asks.

"Where are your clothes?" I ask manically, apparently combining both of my sleep-deprived identities into a hyperactive demon.

He glances into the bathroom and then back at me like I was speaking Aramaic. "I... just got out of the shower."

I sputter, trying to latch on to something logical. "I just think if we're all sharing this apartment, we should keep our clothes on."

He rolls his lips together, crossing his arms over his chest in a way that makes his biceps do ungodly things. "Does my nakedness bother you, Chaos?"

Yes, his wet, naked body bothers me, but he can't know that.

I scoff and wave a hand. "Not me. You're practically my brother. But Inez may be uncomfortable."

His posture straightens, lips drawing back into a hard line as his hand comes down to clutch the fabric of the towel slung low over his hips. He sends a look around the apartment, his eyes settling on the closed door where Inez is getting ready, her favorite reggaeton hype playlist floating out through the crack under her door.

"Sorry about that," he says as he rushes off to his room. "See you in a few minutes for coffee."

"What are you talking about?" I call at his back.

He pauses in his doorway, turning to face me and leaning back against the frame in a way that makes his stomach flex like one of the models on my romance novel covers.

"Coffee with the faculty?" he asks. When I shrug, he exhales a heavy breath. "You didn't get an invitation to coffee with the other professors this morning before orientation?"

My stomach bottoms out. No, I didn't get an invitation. I'm torn between embarrassment and righteous indignation. On one hand, of course they didn't invite me. They look down on me, and me taking on an academic role isn't going to magically fix their perspective. On the other hand, I *am* a professor in the program. I stepped in and saved their asses when they needed someone, and the least they could do is treat me with respect.

When I shake my head, Colton mutters a low curse. "Get dressed. We're going to get coffee."

I smile, though it probably looks more like a grimace. "That's okay. You go."

"No," he says furiously. "You're a professor in this program, too."

"Crashing a party I was intentionally not invited to isn't the way to make friends and influence people, Colt. And, before you inevitably offer, you aren't blowing them off. You need to network with them for tenure. I'm fine. Go, make a good impression, and I'll see you in a couple hours." He opens his mouth to argue, but I cut him off. "Please."

He watches me for a couple seconds and then nods, slipping into his room.

I knew they wouldn't welcome me with open arms, but knowing something and actually experiencing it is different.

I hate feeling unwelcome, of being a part of the "out" group. I've spent the past decade avoiding situations where I'd experience it, but this summer's hitting all the soft spots I've protected. It rubs somewhere deep inside me, the same bruise that made me create a finsta to see the family trips and holiday photos on my brothers' pages, despite the fact that I'm absolutely, totally, completely fine with my family stuff.

Inez slips out of her room, hair and makeup pristine. "Are you ready to go?"

"Shit," I say with a glance at the clock. "I'll get dressed."

As I throw on my clothes and rush out the door, I promise myself I won't let the professors get to me. I have a job to do, and I'm going to blow it out of the water, whether they want me to or not.

THE STUDENTS HAVE OFFICIALLY ARRIVED.

Inez is holding a giant green flag with *Billings College* printed across it over her head, and it isn't even close to the strangest thing in Piazza Navona.

As one of the most popular sites in Rome, the piazza is as crowded as always. Tour groups push against each other like they're in a mosh pit, trying to get to the front to hear their tour guide. Dozens of living statues stand on boxes scattered through the piazza, moving only to claim their tips. Caricature artists sit by their easels, lazily watching the tourists like ambush predators, waiting for one of them to wander close enough to pounce. Behind us, Angelo—a staple of the piazza—blows through his stadium horn before calling out "We are open," like everyone can't see the patrons already filling the outdoor tables of his restaurant.

The students are slowly gathering on the cobblestones between two of Bernini's greatest fountains, alternating between yawning and gawking at the world around them. Our school for the summer is retrofitted into an old apartment building, tucked back on a quiet street through a nondescript red wood door. No outward sign that it's anything more than someone's home. Since the students are coming from their various apartments and homestays, Inez decided to have everyone meet in the famous piazza before leading them to the school for orientation.

Inez walks through the mass of students, talking to some she knows from Boston. It's a pre-presentation technique we came up with to help Inez remember she has friendly faces in the audience when her presentation anxiety sets in. The other professors aren't talking with the students, so I keep myself removed, too. It's unsettling, both being a part of something and being outside of it. On campus, I know my role. I'm the advisor, friendly and approachable. But here? I don't have a place yet, and I don't like it.

The professors claimed one of the few stone benches the moment they arrived, four of them barely fitting across. They apologized profusely to Colton about there not being space for him. To me, they said... nothing. In fact, no one has acknowledged my presence in the fifteen minutes we've been waiting for the students to arrive. Colton was immediately pulled into a conversation about the *Aeneid* with one of the professors, and the others have blatantly ignored me. So I stand here, torn between my natural desire to speak and my certainty that they don't want me to.

Inez finally calls for everyone's attention, making it through her introduction flawlessly, and I clutch my hands together to keep from clapping for her.

Before leading them to the school to tackle all the fun stuff—like culture shock and behavioral expectations, woohoo!—Inez cedes the floor to Dr. Guarino to introduce the faculty.

Dr. Guarino has been at Billings longer than I've been alive. He's been teaching in this program almost as long, happy to come back to his hometown every summer. His students apparently love him as much as the professors who idolize him back in Boston, which I don't get. He seems like a grumpy motherfucker.

The professors all stand from the bench, and I hurry into place beside Colton. Dr. Guarino runs through the introductions, going straight down the line.

Dr. Larsen, the art history professor he gleefully teases about their ongoing debate on whether Michelangelo or Bernini was the more talented sculptor.

Dr. Keck, the architecture professor he praises for her research on how neoclassical architecture has influenced public buildings across the United States.

Dr. Aguilar, the literature professor he calls a pioneer in the study of epic poetry.

Dr. Miller—a reminder that Colton is one of them—who he says is the only person he'd believe knows more about this city than he does.

And then he reaches me.

"And last, we have Ms. Riley, who—"

"Professor Riley." Colton's voice booms around us even in the open piazza, cutting off Dr. Guarino and making everyone straighten at the command in his tone. "She's a professor on this trip and will be addressed as such."

Dr. Guarino lifts an eyebrow. Colton raises his chin in response, something stubborn and aggressive stretching taut between them. I feel a surge of gratitude that Colton not only recognized the dig, but spoke up against it publicly.

But as much as I appreciate the support, a conflict like this between two such stubborn men won't lead to anything productive, for me or for Colt.

So I laugh. "This is a great example of how changing roles affect the way people view you. I've been in one position for so long that it can be hard to take on something new. The students in my class will have to navigate it too, going from student to student *and* employee. We'll talk about that more next week."

Dr. Guarino nods and turns back to the students. "Yes, *Professor* Riley"—I can't imagine anyone misses the sarcasm laced in that honorific—"is teaching a class for the students in internships this summer."

And that's it. Every other professor received praise for their work over the years. But I'm just here. I went in expecting this, so why does it dig under my ribs?

Colton's jaw clenches as Dr. Guarino hands the orientation back over to Inez, who gives me a sympathetic smile before leading the students through the winding streets off the piazza to our school.

I fall into step beside Colton, whispering, "Don't pick fights with the other professors."

He whispers back. "They can't talk to you like that."

"It'll be a long summer if you fight with them every time they dismiss me," I mutter.

He chuckles and leans closer, so close I can feel the breath of his words ghost along my ear and neck. It's the only reason I shiver when he whispers, "You're worth fighting for, Quinn."

I block out the chattering around me as I breathe in the city—*my* city. Looking strictly at time spent here, it shouldn't feel this important. My summers here were nothing compared to the eighteen years I'd spent in Florida and the fourteen in Boston. And those summers weren't even perfect, magical times. Yes, I always loved Rome, but there was a lot of loneliness here, too. We weren't here for my fun or exploration. We were here for my father's work, and I was expected to find ways to occupy myself while he and my mother focused on their respective research.

But Rome speaks to me. It buzzes with an energy that matches my own. It's not frozen in time like so many historic locations around the world. It's bustling, the modern age weaving and converging around the past like a river splitting for a small island. The scent varies widely based on where you're standing, the rich aroma of baking cheese, lemons, and espresso hanging in the air, then randomly washed out by the stench of garbage or urine. This isn't the Disney World version of Italy. It shows you its truest self, inviting you to be a part of it rather than an observer. It's loud, busy, and often gross, but it's real.

Colton forces the hot and exhausted students to pause, pointing out that from the corner where we stand, they can see a modern skyscraper, an eighteenth-century church, a Renaissance palace, a medieval building, and the ruins where Julius Caesar was assassinated. And even though I've stood in this exact stop hundreds of times, I'm once again struck by the magnitude of this city's history. All the things it has seen and will see.

Once we finished up the orientation, Inez promised free gelato for anyone interested. About half of the students took her up on the offer, and she rushed ahead to pay before flooding the gelateria with fifty students, leaving Colton and I to lead them there.

"Why'd we have to walk this far for free gelato? We've passed at least a dozen other gelato places," one of the students complains, undoubtedly thinking about the bed that's calling to his jet-lagged body.

"Trust me," I say over my shoulder. "It's worth the walk."

"And we couldn't have taken the metro? It's hot," another moans.

Colton stops, and the whole Billings progression stops with him as he faces the students. "A lesson for you all. This isn't Boston with T stops on every corner. Rome's metro doesn't even come to Trastevere because every time they dig, they find something with more historical significance than our entire country.

You can take your chances with the buses if you want. Good luck."

A loud snort escapes me before I can stop it, and everyone turns to look at me. Colton narrows his eyes at me as I cup my hands over my nose and mouth.

"Sorry, guys," I say. "Dr. Miller has a complicated history with the Roman bus system."

The students' gazes ping-pong between us.

"Don't," he says in a low tone.

I bite my lip to trap in my laughter, and he holds my gaze, daring me to make the next move.

"Oh, come on! Someone has to tell us," says Markus, a student I worked with in Boston.

Colton turns to him with a sigh. "Professor Riley and I studied together in Rome. I had a not-so-great experience on the bus when I first arrived, and she won't let me live it down."

"There are bus strikes here," I cut in, trying to hide the laughter in my voice. "The drivers will pull the bus over to the side of the road and leave without a word. It happened while Dr. Miller was on one right after we arrived, and he thought they were trading out drivers, so he sat there for... a while."

"How long?" Markus asks in the midst of the students' laughter. Colton mumbles the answer, and Markus lifts an exaggerated hand to his ear. "What was that, Doc?"

He clears his throat. "Twenty minutes."

They holler in laughter again.

"I was twenty-one. We all do stupid things at twenty-one." He raises a significant eyebrow at the group.

"What else did you do?" a student I don't know yet calls out.

I open my mouth, but Colton cuts in before I can speak. "Are you sure you want to play 'who did more stupid stuff on their study abroad,' Professor Riley?"

The blood drains from my face, the smirk on his own telling me exactly where he'll go if I push him. That night we went out in Florence, when we all got wasted at a little tourist trap bar next to the Duomo and I ended up dancing on the bar. Pretty standard drunk college kid activities, until I slipped, falling off the back of the bar and bringing an entire shelf of liquor bottles down with me. Not my finest moment.

I laugh lightly, glancing around. "That's enough story time for today, children."

They groan at me, and I wave for them to continue down the street as Colton joins me at the back of the group.

"The bus? Really, Quinn?"

I watch him out of the corner of my eye. "Not gonna lie, watching you squirm was gratifying. Sorry for killing the cool guy vibe you're going for."

"I'm not going for a cool guy vibe," he says indignantly.

"Bullshit you aren't! You got that whole stoic, sexy Indiana Jones professor thing going on. I bet all the students attracted to men sit in the front row making starry eyes like in *Raiders of the Lost Ark*. Any student write *love you* on their eyelids yet?"

Colton's brow shoots up. "Sexy?"

Shit. What's wrong with me?

"Oh, shut up, I didn't mean *you*. I meant cool professors in general," I say with an epic eye roll.

He smiles his biggest smile with the dimple in his left cheek. "I didn't know Indiana Jones did it for you."

"Indiana Jones does it for everyone." I poke his dimple. "Now put that thing away."

"You called me a sexy Indiana Jones type, and you expect me not to smile?"

I subtly elbow him in the side and quicken my pace to catch up with the students. The problem is he *had* become a sexy Indiana Jones type, minus the whip. And double shit, now I'm thinking about him with a whip.

I have to get this attraction under control or risk losing my best friend. My family, really. Relationships have never been my strong suit. They all go down in flames faster than Rome under Nero's rule, and, like him, I end up standing on the roof, fiddling and dancing and emotionally removed from the destruction below me. I'm broken. And if past experience is any indication, transitioning back to friends after a relationship never goes smoothly.

Colt's my person. His family is my family. Our attraction would eventually collapse and take our friendship with it. A few orgasms aren't worth a decade and a half of friendship, even if the idea of him in a fedora and unbuttoned shirt is ridiculously appealing.

Five minutes later, we arrive at the gelateria. Inez greets us at the door, passing off tickets for the students to take up to the gelato counter.

"This is on every list of the top gelaterias in Rome," one student says as we enter. "We walked thirty minutes for a tourist trap?"

"There's a difference between famous and touristy," Inez answers, never looking up from the tiny papers in her hands. "And once you taste this gelato, you'll understand that difference. You're welcome."

I fight my way through the throng of people trying to hand off their tickets to the workers behind the counter. The mirrors behind them make the space feel open, even though the gelateria is crammed full. There's something soothing about the crush. I started every summer of my childhood with the same cone—a chocolate hazelnut blend based on a famous Italian treat—from the same place, and it's comforting to know this store looks and feels the same after all these years away.

Inez is still talking some students through the ordering process when Colton and I get our cones and start to make our way out of the building. We're nearly to the door when a deep, achingly familiar voice calls out, "Colton."

I spin toward the voice on instinct, both of us freezing when my eyes meet my father's. He's an imposing figure, well over six feet with thick hair that has gone mostly gray in the ten years we've barely spoken.

"Hi, Dad," I say, my voice coming out quieter than I planned, and I hate myself for it. He shouldn't have this much of an impact on me anymore.

He crosses his bulky arms over his chest. "Quinn. I heard you were here this summer."

It isn't friendly, but it isn't combative, either. I see a glimpse of who I'd thought he was when I was a little girl. Stern, but loving.

"It's a great program. I'm excited to be here," I say, letting myself smile at him for the first time in a decade.

"Yes, well, you could have been teaching for years if you hadn't thrown your career away on a whim."

And there it is.

"You should shadow Colton's class this summer," he continues.

"I have my own class to focus—"

"His is a real class," he says, and it feels like a fist to the stomach. A small part of me thought he'd hear I'm teaching and be impressed, but I should have known better. Just like I should have known better when I thought the professors would treat me as an equal.

When I don't argue, he continues. "There's still time for you to turn this around if you'd like to talk about your options."

He means my "options" to go back to school and get a PhD I don't want in a field I don't love, just because my father thinks I should.

When I'd told my parents I wanted to work in student development instead of pursuing my PhD in Roman history, their first instinct was to offer me counseling for my "obvious mental breakdown." When I didn't accept that, they cut me off financially, hoping I'd be too weak from a lifetime of coddling to figure it out myself. When I still didn't capitulate, they cut me off emotionally. They uninvited me from holidays and told my brothers not to make contact either. He told them it was their responsibility to help me realize I was *wasting my potential and the years and money they poured into my education*, and they listened. I don't think it was even because they agreed with him. They knew they had to pick a side, and I wasn't worth losing Dad's approval for.

It was radio silence for years, until I started getting texts and emails from my dad explaining how I could "get back on track" with my career. I ignored every one of them. He doesn't want a daughter, he wants a successor.

My brothers all went into academia, but different fields. I was the only one desperate enough for my dad's attention that I convinced myself I loved Roman history the same way he did. Then I watched Colton struggle freshman year with the business major he hated, and the things he said hit a bit too close to home. It took me another four years and a whole ass undergraduate degree to finally admit it. Every single fear I had leading up to that decision—that my parents would be disappointed in me, that I was only close to Dad because I was interesting to him—was proven true.

Colton's hand comes to my lower back, grounding in its support. "Richard, did you see my email?"

I appreciate him stepping in to distract from the lecture Dad would have jumped into.

Dad's full attention turns to Colton, the one who followed through and became the superstar he'd always pushed me to be. "The article will be great, son."

The *son* finally does me in. I excuse myself, though my dad barely looks in my direction, and head out of the building. I wave off the students I know and disappear down one of the small streets across from the gelateria, making it a few feet down before collapsing. The cold concrete of the wall cools my body as sobs wrack me. My gelato melts quickly in the Roman heat, dripping down until it covers my hand and starts sliding down my forearm.

This is why I told my brother I'd come home for his wedding, but won't have any other contact with my family. No matter what I do or how proud I am of my own accomplishments, it takes a handful of words for my father to tear me down. To remember that I wasn't worth sticking around for, even for the people who were biologically programmed to care about me.

A pair of loafers comes into view through the tears, and the cone's plucked from my hand. Colton's back in seconds, the gelato safely deposited in the trash, and I'm in his arms.

"Colt, you're going to get gelato all over you."

"I don't care," he says before pressing his lips to my forehead in a hard, reassuring kiss.

His arms tighten around my back, and I let myself fall into the safety of this man. This scent—cedar and old books—soothes the deepest part of my soul, the part that fears I'm just not lovable enough. I lost my family, but I still have him.

"I'm so sorry, Quinn," he whispers onto my hair.

I bury my head in his chest. "It's fine."

"No, it's not fine. He can't treat you that way. I'm going to tell him that when we get dinner next week."

"You are not," I say as I push him an arm's length away, and he jolts at the harshness of my tone. I sigh and try to breathe. He doesn't deserve to be the outlet for my anger. "I get that it's hard now that you have to actually see the way he treats me, but I don't want you to say anything. In fact, I'm begging you not to. I can handle his bullshit, and you need him. Plus, what are the chances we'll run into him again?"

Colton watches me carefully, that brilliant mind of his clearly whirling, and I know he can see it all. The anger and frustration, but even worse, the little girl inside of me that wishes she was enough to be worthy of her family's love. I know he wants to say something, but he must be able to tell that I'm barely holding it together, so he nods.

I lift my hand with a grimace as I study the melted gelato. "Ugh, such a mess."

I look up at him, begging with my eyes to play along, to bring a bit of levity to this shitty moment.

Finally, he sighs, his lip twitching up. "A public embarrassment, Chaos."

"They'll throw me in jail to clean up the streets."

He gestures to my gelato-covered arm. "At least you have something to eat."

"True," I say, eyeing the last bit of the gelato I was finally about to taste again.

I run my tongue up the line of my thumb and suck it into my mouth, closing my eyes and groaning as the hazelnut and chocolate explodes on my tongue.

"Fuck, that's delicious," I say.

I feel a breath gust against the side of my head, but when I glance at Colton, he's looking back down the street toward the gelateria.

I sigh. "I'm gonna head inside and clean off my hand."

"I'll get you another," he says, his voice tight.

I smile and tap his chest with my clean hand. "See, this is why you're my best friend. Always looking out for me. But I'm good. The students want to get home, so I'll come back later."

I flick my pointer finger with my tongue to get one last taste and moan.

"How is this so much better than everywhere else? I'm gonna spend the day pissed because I remember how good it is, but can't have more. One taste isn't enough." I say before turning away from Colton and stomping off toward the shop.

He stays behind me, but I think he mumbles, "Nowhere near enough."

8

QUINN

FOURTEEN YEARS AGO

"The smell of garbage," I say, opening my mouth to catch the M&M Colton throws to me.

I bought a bag for each of us so we could play the wonderful new game I invented called the Bitching Game. We throw one piece at each other for every shitty thing we list, until either the reasons run out or the candy does.

We spent the last twenty minutes listing everything we hated about Boston in minute detail. It's late October, and between the stress of midterms and the excitement of our newfound freedom wearing off, we're both feeling some serious homesickness.

"The crowds on Boylston," he replies, opening his own mouth. The M&M lands with a satisfying plunk.

"How early the sun sets," I continue.

"The way the Green line shrieks like a banshee."

"The severe lack of high-quality barbecue."

"The way people quack at you from those annoying duck boats."

I gasp and clutch my chest. Hating public transportation's one thing, but the duck boats are a goddamned institution.

"I love the duck boats!" I say. "They drive on land *and* in the water! It's like a real-life *Chitty Chitty Bang Bang*."

"I don't know what that is."

"Seriously? Old movie with Dick Van Dyke? Car that can drive, fly, and float?" He shrugs. "The point is, the duck boats are amazing."

He throws an M&M at my forehead. "We agreed, no negativity shaming."

I sigh, trying to fight back my smile. "Fine. Fuck the ducks."

He gives me a definitive nod, his own smile tugging at the corner of his lips. "Anything else we hate?"

"I don't think so," I say, stroking my chin. "Have we reached our limit?"

"Never thought I'd see the day."

"You know what that means." I smile widely, and he groans as I start shaking my arms. When he doesn't join, I lean across the twin mattress to force it. "We agreed! Once we got it all out, we would shake off the negativity and focus on what we loved!"

"I'm not shaking like a dog, Chaos." But I'm persistent, and he finally caves, swinging his arms a couple times. "Happy?"

"That, my friend, is what we'd call a half-assed attempt. But I'll take it." I settle back on my side of the mattress. "Now, positivity. I'll go first. I love that I can sit outside for more than five minutes without sweating, unlike at home."

Colton crosses his arms, but I've learned a few tricks over the past couple of months of our friendship. He may not speak up a lot, but he always caves if I hold my tongue for a few minutes.

He sighs and runs his hands through his long, messy hair, pulling it back, and I'm temporarily dazed by the sharp line of his jaw. God, this boy could kill if he pulled that hair back.

"The Public Garden is pretty." He says it like it's a personal offense, but at least he's talking.

"Oh, especially right now, with the leaves changing."

"The architecture's cool."

"The fact that everything here is old. It's like walking through history!"

He smiles a little at that, then ducks his head like his enjoyment embarrasses him. "The food from different places. You don't see much of anything in Grand Creek."

"The antiquing!"

"Okay, add that to my negativity list," he says with a raised brow.

It's my turn to toss M&M's at him. A handful bounce off his chest and roll off the bed.

"If I can't negativity shame you for hating adorable sightseeing vessels, then you can't shame me for loving old things."

He holds up his hands in surrender and smiles that broad, dimpled smile that he makes me fight for. I want a trophy room filled with pictures of him just like that, a plaque beside each one stating what I said to earn it.

I glance down at the pile of books between us. We're supposed to be studying, but neither of us have worked up the energy to start.

"Are we doing this?" I ask, gesturing to the offending pile.

"Guess we gotta."

The bane of my existence, my calculus book, sits on top of the pile, mocking me. Colton tosses it over before grabbing his finance book, both of us settling in.

The words and numbers blur on the page in front of me. I look over at Colton's scrunched up brow as he reads something in the book, seeing he's clearly as excited about studying as I am. I throw my book back down.

"We need to do something fun. Something to get our minds off the stress so that we can focus."

"I am focused, Chaos."

"Really? Look at me." I wait until his gaze meets mine, holding it for a few seconds. "Tell me the last thing you read."

He narrows his eyes. I take his silence as confirmation that he's retained about as much as I have.

"Come on." I smack my palms against my lap. "We're going to the Esplanade."

"Why in the world are we going to the Esplanade?"

"To go kayaking on the Charles River."

"Quinn, I gotta study. Plus, it's cold."

I flop back again. "Fine. You're no fun."

"I'm fun."

"Yeah? Then prove it."

I lean forward now, daring him to do something spontaneous. His gaze flicks down to my lips. The glint in his eye charges the air, like I'm sitting by the giant Tesla coils at the science museum, bolts of lightning dancing around me. I may not be struck, but it's all close enough that the hair raises on my arms and my stomach tightens. I gulp and shift, uncomfortable with the new sensation.

But a few thundering heartbeats later, he turns his attention back to his textbook. "Midterms, Chaos."

A gust of air rushes out of me. Relief. Right? He's cute, really cute, underneath that grunge-rocker exterior, but he's also my closest friend here. Random blips of attraction, of curiosity, aren't worth the risk of losing him. Who would force me to study, or chuckle instead of complain when I get us kicked out of the library for talking too much, or listen to me prattle on with actual interest instead of the dead-eyed stare I get from most people when I can't make the words stop?

I've always made friends easily. People are drawn to you when you're naturally talkative, the person who always breaks the uncomfortable silence. But there's a huge difference between making friends and establishing deep friendships. Usually, with time, I either settle into the role of the entertaining friend—our relationship more of a performance—or I have to learn how to temper myself. The enthusiasm that drew people to me quickly becomes *too much* for most.

Colton's different. He never rolls his eyes at my excitement. And in those—admittedly rare—moments when I need the calm and quiet, he sits with me in it. He never asks me what's wrong, like I'm a broken toy whose batteries need to be checked.

I shake off the strange moment between us. "Fine. We'll save the fun for after midterms. But I'd like it noted that this is against my will."

He chuckles and tosses another book into my lap. "Move on from calculus and you'll be happier. Why don't you work on the midterm essay for Cassia?"

Is it bad that researching my essay sounds barely less miserable than studying calculus?

I groan. "Essays are boring."

"You realize that's half of what you'll do when you're a professor, right?" he asks without looking up from his book.

I feel a pinch of anxiety at that. My plan has always been to become a Roman history professor like my dad. He'd started me in Italian lessons before I could remember, and Latin lessons weren't far behind. We watched Roman movies and read Roman books and discussed Roman stories. While I love those talks, these academic journals are tedious.

But I'll learn to love it.

"I'm just not in the mood for all that reading," I say. "Don't you think it's exhausting?"

Colton shrugs. "I like reading about it. It's way more interesting than the busy work I'm doing for my business classes. Plus, when I have my face buried in a book, people leave me alone. Usually."

"If that was your subtle way of telling me to leave you alone and let you study, you're gonna have to be more upfront. I don't really do subtle."

Colton laughs again. "I noticed, Chaos."

He turns back to his textbook without another word, and I watch him for a few more minutes. Forcing my friendship on him that first day of class was the best decision I've made since coming to Chadoin. It's surprising, how comfortable I feel with him so quickly. Maybe it's the way he lets me blabber on without judgment, or how I know those smiles are real because he doesn't give them out easily. Or maybe it's what he said on the first day of class.

I like hearing you talk.

"Colt?"

I have to roll my lips together to hold in my laugh at his classic long-suffering sigh. "What is it, Quinn?"

"I thought of the best part about Boston."

He straightens from his hunched position over the textbook and gestures for me to continue.

I give him my biggest smile. "Getting to meet you."

He tries to hide his answering smile, but there's no stopping it. A slight blush takes over his cheeks. "Get back to studying."

I groan and flip open my book. A couple of minutes later, when I'm fully immersed in an analysis of why yet another emperor was murdered by his own guard for the *good of Rome*, Colton clears his throat. I look up to find him watching me with a curious gaze.

"What's up?" I ask.

"Meeting you is the best part for me, too."

9

QUINN

JUNE — TEN WEEKS TO WIN OVER THE FACULTY

THIS IS MORE rewarding than I expected.

Three classes in, and I'm loving it. This isn't my first experience in front of students. Between undergrad and grad school, I've been a teaching assistant half a dozen times, but this is the first time I've run a classroom myself. I'm responsible for it all—the lesson plans and the classroom management and the learning outcomes—and it's a beautiful experience watching the ideas I jotted down in my little polka-dot notebook turn into active learning for my students.

I've never doubted my decision not to get my PhD. It wasn't the right field for me, and I'd have been miserable if I spent my life living for others. The one-on-one student interactions I get every day in Boston have always been my favorite, but I can't deny how exciting it is to be in front of a group, watching them learn from and with each other.

The students file out of the room, animatedly chatting about their internships as I call out a reminder that their journals are due by midnight. I'm buzzing as I gather my things.

Inez pops her head into my tiny classroom. "Oh my god, is that the brilliant professor, Quinn Riley?"

I laugh, tossing a crumpled up piece of paper her way. "Fuck off."

"I heard her students love her."

"Everyone loves me," I say, lifting an eyebrow in challenge.

Inez drops her voice low, affecting a Bostonian accent. "I heard she has a perfect score on Rate My Professors." Her voice lifts into a high, squeaky voice. "I heard all her students refuse to study with any other professor ever again because they were so inspired by her."

"Damn right they were inspired," I say, looping my bag over my shoulder. I step close, dropping my voice lower. "It's going so well, Inez! I think this might actually work."

"So you're ready to admit I was right?" she asks, the sweetest little smirk on her face.

"I'll admit," I say, dragging out the words, "that there was... some value in your plan."

"Stubborn little shit," she says, hip checking me as we head down the hallway.

We're about to turn the corner into the school's shared lounge when we hear voices.

"How is it going, Anthony?" Dr. Guarino says from around the corner.

"Great! Probably one of my favorite classes I've taken."

Heat radiates through my chest, spreading through my limbs like the Roman sun warming my body. I gesture toward the room, widening my eyes at Inez, who does a little happy wiggle. Dr. Guarino grumbles something I can't hear as Anthony exits the lounge, giving us a little wave as he heads out of the school. Inez is about to step into the room when I hear another person speak. I grab her wrist, tugging her back before she comes into view.

"You didn't expect her to do so well, did you?" someone else asks. It has to be one of the other professors, but they haven't spoken to me enough for me to pick them out.

"One student said one positive thing," Dr. Guarino says. "That doesn't mean the class is actually going well."

The woman tuts. "I doubt my first students would have spoken so positively about me. I know it's been a while for you, but think about how hard your first classes were."

"Was that an old man joke, Andrea?" Dr. Guarino asks. The easy camaraderie between them, one that I'm not welcome in, digs deep.

"If the geriatric slippers fit," she answers with a laugh. "The real question is if how well she does actually matters."

"I agree," another disembodied voice says, and I stifle a groan when I realize this is a group conversation between most, if not all, of the professors. "The staff are a systemic issue. One person doing well in the classroom doesn't change that."

Dr. Guarino grunts. "The faculty agreed to this little *experiment* to appease President Munchen. Once the summer is over, we won't have to worry about this again."

My vision swims. I knew this was a possibility, but to hear them say that they aren't taking this seriously, that the decision is already made and the hard work I'm putting in is pointless, feels like the ground has been ripped out from under me. In an instant, all of that joy and optimism I was carrying from the class turns to lead in my hands, dragging me to the ground.

I'm not enough. I'll *never* be enough.

Inez is gripping my arm, squeezing tight and whispering something in my ear, but the words don't register. When I finally look up, her face looks as devastated as I feel. I'm failing her and all the other staff members who are relying on me to fix things.

"Professor Riley?" I look up to see Colton, just through the front door of the school. His students filter in behind him, blessedly turning down the hallway toward the classroom.

Instead of following, Colton walks down the hallway to meet

us. I make a dramatic shushing motion with my hands, pointing towards the door to the common room.

"What's going on?" he asks, his eyes flicking between me and Inez.

I rub my hands back and forth over my face, hoping it'll help me focus on something other than the tears trying to escape. I open my mouth, but saying it out loud will push me over the edge.

He runs his hand up my arm. "Talk to me."

I want to talk to him, but I can't force the words past my lips. How can I admit how useless I feel, how utterly defeated, when I know he'll want to make it better? That the only way he can make it better is by putting himself in direct opposition with one of the most powerful professors on campus?

I shake my head, and push past him. Both he and Inez call after me, but I don't turn back as I rush down the steps and push through the heavy wooden door to the street.

I start walking toward the Piazza della Rotonda. Sitting in front of the Pantheon always helps center me, reminding me of how small my troubles are in the grand scope of history. But halfway there, I remember the way my best friends called after me. Inez usually gives me space when I'm upset, but Colton won't. If he plans to check on me, that's the first place he'll head, and I need space. So I change tack and cross the river to another spot I love. I climb the Janiculum Hill, letting the strain of my legs from the incline burn away all my thoughts of how terrible I am at my job.

I walk through the park at the top, quieter than most parts of Rome. This isn't one of the seven ancient hills, so fewer people go out of their way to come here. The people who *are* around me almost exclusively speak Italian. The overlapping conversations are impossible to make out, but I allow myself to sink into the cadence of speech, to enjoy the time I have here before I have to go back to Boston and face how I failed.

Gravel crunches under my feet as I wander the paths lined by busts of *Risorgimento* freedom fighters, men who fought and died for a unified Italy in the nineteenth century. Every five feet, there's a new bust, each face more judgmental than the last. They seem to say, *We united an entire country, and you can't even unite six people.*

I can't say how long I've been walking when I reach the monument to Anita Garibaldi, wife of the famed Italian revolutionary leader and a legendary figure in her own right. I sit at the lone bench in front of the massive structure, staring up at this wild, brave woman. Shame creeps under my skin. People like her exist, and yet I'm so easily cowed by a few closed-minded professors.

The phone in my hand feels heavier than usual as I look down at it, realizing I've pulled up my father's contact without consciously choosing to. It must be some long-buried instinct to seek his guidance, and for one solitary second, I let myself consider calling him the way I would have when I was younger. But his name, big and bold at the top of my screen, doesn't give words of encouragement. It spews negativity, a lecture about how I've wasted my time on my graduate program and how I'd have a place with the professors if I'd listened to him years ago.

I stare back up at Anita for god knows how long, until something flies over my shoulder and plops into my lap. A bag of M&M's sits on my legs, and I don't need to look up to know who's in front of me. I keep my eyes cast downward as Colton drops onto the far end of the bench.

"How'd you know where I was?" I ask, eyes still glued to the statue.

"I didn't," he answers, and I can feel his gaze on the side of my face. "Went to the Pantheon first, and you weren't there, so I figured I'd try here."

My lips twitch against my will. "I was going to go to the Pantheon but I knew you'd look for me there."

His breathy chuckle warms me, even as I fight to stay cold and numb. "I guess we're both predictable."

"I don't want to talk about it."

"Then we won't talk," he says.

Colton holds his tongue, the two of us listening to the noises of the park around us. Children laugh from behind the wall of a nearby school. Cars fly down the street in the middle of the park, unconcerned with pedestrians. A cannon booms, and I distantly register it has to be the daily shot the park sets off to mark noon with more reliability than the clock on my cellphone.

I continue to ignore Colton's presence, settling back into my self-loathing, when something small and hard hits my cheek.

"What the hell, Colton?" I spin toward him. He's turned his body to face me, back braced against the arm rest and another M&M poised in his hand.

"Sorry. Hard to aim without you facing me. Try two." This time, the M&M hits me square on my closed lips, and he scowls. "You're supposed to open your mouth, Quinn."

"I'm not in the mood for your ridiculous fucking game, Colton."

He narrows his eyes and tips his bag toward me. "Actually, it's *your* ridiculous fucking game."

He's right, even if I don't want to hear it right now. Colton lets the moment sit, no doubt hoping I'll cave like I have so many times in our past. When I don't speak, he shrugs.

"Guess I'll play with myself." A snort escapes against my will and he smirks. "Head out of the gutter, Riley."

I watch him toss an M&M high in the air, catching it easily just like he's done so many times on camera, when we'd played this game from two different continents.

"Having to read the shitty papers students didn't try on."

He holds up another piece and mimics throwing it at me. I cross my arms, and he shrugs again, tossing the candy up for himself.

"Students who don't do the work but expect you to pass them because they *really need an A*."

I feel myself softening even as I fight against it. It's such a relief to hear someone else admit that sometimes things suck, to feel like I can say it without being judged for not being grateful for the opportunity.

That's how this silly game started. We were so privileged in college—me because of my family's support and him from the full-ride scholarship that let him focus exclusively on his studies. Even knowing how lucky we were, we needed the outlet to say the things that were weighing on us. And it always worked. Releasing the bad from our bodies and out into the world freed up space for us to focus on the good.

He holds up a third candy, and this time I cave, opening my mouth wide. He tosses it, a perfect throw that lands right on my tongue. The crunch of the shell and explosion of chocolate hurtles me back in time to when we were the annoying students who didn't put in the work and *really needed an A.*

I think through all the things I hate right now—too many options, when my job sucks and my coworkers hate me. "That blank-eyed stare students give when no one wants to speak."

I'm loving the work, but that doesn't mean it's all perfect.

"Yes," he yells, pointing a finger at me. "That's the worst!"

I smile slightly, still unwilling to give myself over entirely. I pull open my bag of M&M's and toss one to him. My aim isn't as good, and he dives, barely catching it.

"All the extra things I have to do to qualify for tenure. I just want to do my research and teach in peace."

Another tossed to me. "The politics of it all. I hate having to watch what I say to try to keep them happy." He opens his mouth, but I cut him off. "No trying to make me feel better. This is the Bitching Game, and only bitching is allowed."

He lifts his hand in surrender and opens his mouth for

another piece. "The insecurity of this field. If I don't get tenure, I'm fucked."

I have no doubt he'll get tenure if he keeps things up the way he has for the past year. His research is brilliant, his students love him, and the whole university is up his ass. He's their new darling. Even his association with me hasn't dimmed his shine, if the way the other faculty on the program flock to him is any indication.

He tosses another one to me. The next answer comes out of my mouth without my consent. "That there's nothing I can do to be accepted by them." It comes out as a whisper, and I hate the weakness in my voice.

It isn't until the words leave my mouth that I realize I don't just mean the Rome professors. I mean all of it, the professors here and the ones on campus constantly belittling and embarrassing me. I mean my brothers, who didn't care enough to keep in touch. My mother, who was fine throwing away a relationship with me. And my father, who still thinks of me as a petulant child.

I study my hands, unwilling to see the pity in his eyes, until Colton's knees come into view at the periphery. He's as close as possible without being in my lap, serious eyes trained on my face.

"They don't deserve you, Chaos." He speaks with such conviction. I don't know who exactly he means, but I can't help but believe him. "Inez told me what happened."

A shudder racks my body. "Their minds are made up. I've tried to engage between classes or at group dinners—tried to make a positive impression—but I'm met with silence. And I don't know what to do or how to fix it. And I know it all sounds ridiculous, but the staff are hurting and I love them and I love Billings and I want to make it better, but I can't if they won't meet me halfway."

I don't realize I'm crying until he wipes the tears away.

"They're assholes," he says.

I sniff. "Stop saying the right things."

He chuckles and flicks away a tear that had made it to my chin. "I'm never going to sit by while you cry."

Sincerity is etched on the lines of his face: his tight jaw, the worry lines around his eyes, the softness of his gaze.

Those eyes ensnare me. They're like the canopies of the oak trees that never change colors where I grew up in Florida. A deep, dark green with flecks of brown, like the trunk peeking through the branches. But when the light hits just right—like it is now—they light up. Light greens and yellows dancing through the darker shades, shifting like leaves on a cool lake breeze.

Home.

I suck in a deep breath. "You can't protect me from every-thing, you know."

"I can sure as fuck try." He smiles widely, and I'm powerless to resist the urge to kiss his dimple. I savor the feel of him under-neath my lips, his light stubble that tickles me. I breathe in his comforting woodsy scent. His answering inhale echoes in my ears and goose bumps run up my arms.

I sit back quickly, nearly breaking my back on the stiff metal armrest. These moments have to stop, because when I think the word *home*, I mean it. He is my home. And I won't survive losing another family's love.

Colton clears his throat. "Now about the professors."

I sigh, dropping my head back. "I appreciate you wanting to help, even though you can't do anything."

His brow furrows again. "Hold that thought."

He digs into his messenger bag and pulls out an enormous sheet of paper and what looks like a handful of chess figurines. He dumps them all onto the bench between us.

"And that's for...?" I ask.

"Our first strategy meeting," he says, looking over the junk with a serious expression, like the pile holds the mysteries of the universe. "We have four people we need to sell. It won't happen by eating bitching M&M's."

He flattens out the paper, which I realize is a comically large tourist map of Rome, complete with cartoon images of the top sights. He places the figurines in the middle of the map.

"Welcome to your war room," he says with a giant, almost boyish smile. "Hold that thought."

He stands from the bench, running off into the park until he grabs something off the ground, coming back with a large stick.

I bite back my smile. "And that's…" I gesture to the stick.

He looks offended. "It's our plotting rod. To push the figurines around."

"It's a stick."

He scowls. "Don't judge my plotting rod. This was a last-minute plan."

"I think you watch too many medieval TV shows, Colton."

He ignores me and starts organizing the figurines around the map. "We've been going about this the wrong way. We can't rely on them seeing and appreciating your work. First, we need them to like you so they want to help you."

"Is that why you're helping me? You like me?" I ask with a teasing voice, like we're middle schoolers talking about the upcoming dance. I flutter my eyelashes at him.

He grabs another M&M, this time intentionally hitting me right between the eyes.

I rub my forehead. "Ow! When did your aim get so good?"

He smirks and turns back to his map. I swipe the black queen and knights off the table and hold them up in question.

"Where did this all come from?"

"I have a chess set back at the apartment." He snatches them back. "You're the queen, obviously. Inez and I are your knights."

"And the professors are all pawns? Oh, they'd love that." He chuckles. "How does this work?"

"We woo them. Take them to places around the city that you

have special access to." He pushes a figurine to the Borghese Gardens. "I say we start with Sydney Larsen. She's tenured, so switching sides won't be a risk for her. And you have some killer connections for museums to warm her cold, art-loving heart."

I stick my thumbnail between my teeth, chewing on it while I think through Colton's situation. "This is a risk for you, Colt. You're actively plotting with the staff."

His brow furrows, and he stares off for a few seconds before shaking his head. "I'm not worried about that. Have you met me? No way I'm not getting tenure."

But I can see the cracks in his confidence. He laid out his fears so many times over the years. I know how stressed he is about making the payments for his mom's house, how he wakes up in a cold sweat from nightmares about his pre-tenure reviews going poorly. He literally *just* mentioned he was scared of the insecurity of the field, and now he's putting on a brave face. Risking his greatest fear for me.

"Colton—"

"It's not a risk," he says, cutting me off.

"Yes, it is," I say fiercely.

A soft smile takes over his face. "Fine, it's a calculated risk. We succeed or fail together. I believe in you, and it won't be risky for me after you win over all the professors. What do you say?"

A wave of peace settles over me. For the first time in a long time, I'm not fighting this fight alone.

A slow smile creeps over my face. "I say it's time to woo some stuffy professors."

10

COLTON

JUNE — NINE WEEKS TO WIN OVER THE FACULTY

Maybe Quinn's right and the professors are determined not to get along with her, but there's no way that an art history professor is going to turn down access to the Galleria Borghese after hours, even if it means spending time with Quinn.

The scent of flowers from the villa's garden wraps around me as I wait for Quinn and Sydney to arrive. A few days ago, I watched over the top of my book as Quinn approached Sydney in the lounge. Quinn stood over her, although *over* may be generous when Quinn barely topped her while she was sitting. Sydney looked up at her in confusion, astounded that Quinn was talking to her.

"Dr. Larsen, I wanted to invite you to a site visit I have for one of our art history interns."

Sydney's mouth pinched. "I'm grateful for the invitation, but unfortunately, I can't join you. My schedule's too tight to fit something like that in."

Quinn feigned disappointment, even though we both knew she was expecting the rejection. "I understand, but it's such a shame. I always love spending time in the Galleria when the crowds aren't clogging up the space around Bernini's masterpieces."

Quinn shook her head, keeping her face peaceful. I snorted into my coffee, but turned it into a cough, waving off the concerned looks from the surrounding students who were unaware of the way Quinn masterfully pulled her puppet strings.

"The Galleria?" Sydney called out to Quinn's retreating back.

My beautiful and shockingly devious best friend met my eyes, her own lit with excitement and satisfaction, and I'd nearly gone to my knees before her.

Now, I spot them from afar, Quinn's infectious smile beaming across the park like the sun. Sydney walks next to her with a much more subdued smile, but at least a pleasant expression on her face.

Sydney's black hair is back in a messy braid, and she fidgets with her rumpled outfit as she stares at the museum's facade. She was granted tenure almost two decades ago, so she can't lose her job for voicing her support, but she can still make enemies. We need to give her a reason to rock the boat.

The first step: help her fall in love with Quinn. Should be easy.

"Good morning, ladies," I say as they reach me.

"It's good to see you, Colton," Sydney says as we settle into step together.

"Thank you for letting me join you."

"I didn't know you had an appreciation for Bernini," she says with an approving nod.

"I didn't at first. If it wasn't from antiquity, I didn't care. Quinn was the one who showed me... let's call it the error of my ways."

She turns to Quinn with a questioning look. "You two knew each other before this?"

I smile at Quinn. "We've been friends since undergrad."

"That explains it," Sydney says with a little laugh. "We've all been wondering what would compel you to attach yourself to her little ultimatum."

Quinn goes rigid, that brilliant smile falling for a half second before she plasters something much less compelling across her face.

"I attached myself to the *proposal*," I say with lethal calm, "because I think it has value. *My* priority is the well-being of the Billings students."

Sydney rears back slightly, her cheeks going pink.

Quinn quickly cuts the awkwardness. "I was a classics major, like Colton, but I spent my summers in Rome with my father, and no artist can compete with Bernini. One of my close friends from those summers became an assistant curator here." Her lips curve up at the memory of her friend, and I fight the urge to trace that smile with my fingertips.

Tomasso became a close friend of mine, too. He has the same quiet, focused energy I brought to my own studies, and we spent plenty of nights commiserating over the heavy load of our post-graduate work.

I turn my attention to Sydney. "I've reviewed the students' journals with Quinn, and I've been impressed with your student's work here. Catherine, right?"

A small smile graces Sydney's face. "Yes, she's a superstar in our department."

"I can see why. You should take a look at how Quinn's coached her through this experience. I think you'll be equally impressed."

She eyes Quinn speculatively, but we're interrupted before she can speak.

"Quinn! Da quanto tempo!"

Tomasso rushes over, nearly tripping over himself in his excitement to see Quinn. He's short and stocky, with rich brown skin he inherited from his Nigerian mother and round glasses that give him a studious air. He plants a kiss on each of Quinn's cheeks, and her smile's so large I think the little balls of her cheeks may pop off.

"Tommaso, come stai?"

The two of them launch into a fast-paced conversation in Italian, one so smooth and natural that I can hardly follow, even with my fluency. Sydney watches with wide eyes pinging back and forth.

Quinn introduces him to Sydney, whose face turns a satisfying shade of pink when her own Italian comes out much more stilted than Quinn's.

"It is no problem," Tomasso says with a smile. "I speak English very well, so we use that instead. Si?" Sydney smiles tightly in response. "Bene. I am excited to talk about Catherine's work. I am very pleased that Quinn approached me about hosting her."

We gave Tomasso the basics of the situation ahead of time, and I have to fight hard to keep the shit-eating grin off my face while he goes on to rave for the next half hour about Quinn's brilliance. At one point, Quinn subtly pinches his arm and gives the tiniest shake of her head.

Too much, Tomasso.

"Quinn and Colton, you take some time to walk around and enjoy while I talk with Dr. Larsen about her research."

"Oh, please, call me Sydney," she says with a brilliant smile. "That goes for you, too, Quinn."

Quinn nods gracefully, but I can tell her body is vibrating with energy, like a dog commanded to stay when they want to rush over and lick the shit out of their owner's face.

I dutifully follow her out of Tomasso's office—maybe I'm the dog—and wait for the explosion I know is coming. Three gallery rooms over, Quinn turns and launches herself at me. I wrap my arms tightly around her, fear of knocking over priceless art reigning in my desire to swing her around in a circle.

My face turns into the crook of her neck, savoring that

citrusy scent. She pulls back like she's been shocked, and I mentally kick myself. Physical touches had been second nature between us when we were younger, but since I came home, she's started getting weird after, even when she's the one who initiates it.

She walks a few feet away and then back to me, like she has to move her body or risk exploding.

"It worked," she whispers, paranoid that the sound would echo through the large, seventeenth-century palace.

I smile, and Quinn's eyes flick down to my dimple before she pokes it with her pointer finger.

"Step one, complete," I say.

"Now for the fun part." She links her arm through mine like she has a hundred times over the course of our friendship, and I question whether I'm imagining the tension between us.

I wasn't lying when I said I love Bernini, but I see nothing except her today. She raves about how his statue of David is a brilliant study in movement while I mentally rave about the way her features shift and her hands gesture wildly. I fixate on the gasp that escapes that perfect mouth when we come to her favorite, Apollo and Daphne. Even though she's seen it a thousand times, she looks at it like it's new, like she's spent years yearning for it and the real thing's blowing her dreams out of the water.

I recognize it from the way I look at her.

"What's so brilliant about it is how we get to experience her transformation. It's one piece, a single giant block of marble, yet as we walk around it we see Daphne change as though it is happening in front of us. By the time you reach the other side," she says as we complete our first of what will inevitably be many loops, "she's gone. No sign of the poor nymph trying to outrun a demanding god."

I chuckle. "I'm plenty familiar with the sculpture, Chaos. You've made sure of that."

She looks up at me, eyes trapped somewhere between her admiration for the sculpture and annoyance with me. "I can't help it. I could talk about it all day. It's the most incredible thing I've ever seen."

"I can understand that urge." My voice is quiet—maybe too quiet for her to hear—but her soft gasp tells me she did. Her eyes are uncertain, like she's trying to put together a puzzle, and I keep flipping the pieces back over. I can't have her sorting out the whole picture, not when there's an edge of terror in those deep brown eyes that twists my stomach in knots, so I paste on a self-deprecating smile. "I've been known to go on about Rome."

She smiles back, but there's still something questioning in her gaze that terrifies me.

"Bella, I knew I'd find you here."

We both jump, the moment gone in an instant as we turn to find Tomasso striding into the room, Sydney trailing a few feet behind, looking closely at another sculpture. I like Tomasso on any given day, but today I love him, swear my allegiance to him, owe him a life debt for saving me from myself. Because if Quinn had pressed me, I don't know that I'd have been able to stop myself from confessing everything.

After saying our goodbyes, Sydney stops us outside of the palace.

"Thank you for inviting me. This is an incredible opportunity for Catherine, and I recognize she wouldn't have gotten it without you."

"I appreciate that, Sydney." Quinn pauses to see if she reacts poorly to her using her first name, even after getting permission in front of Tomasso. Her shoulders straighten, a smile playing on her lips when Sydney doesn't object. "My connections got her resume in front of them, but it was the education she's received from you that got her the internship."

Sydney beams at her then, a genuine smile of mutual respect. I hold in my sigh of relief while Sydney's within hearing range.

Quinn takes a step closer. "Partnerships like this between faculty and staff can change the students' lives. I know it's against Billings culture, and that's intimidating for a lot of people. When I say I love Billings, I mean it, but we can make it better if we're willing to work together."

Sydney looks out over the garden, leaving the two of us in suspense for a moment that feels like an eternity. But finally, she turns to Quinn, stretching a hand out to her.

Looks like we can flip the color of one of our pawns.

As we walk through the Borghese Gardens, I peek at her over Sydney's shoulder and mouth, *One down.*

Three to go, she mouths back.

11

QUINN

JUNE — EIGHT WEEKS TO WIN OVER THE FACULTY

Damn, I'm good.

I may still have a shit ton of work to do to win over the faculty, but I am the uncontested queen of choosing AirBnBs. I can't be topped.

The greens and yellows of the rolling hills stretch out before me, peaking and dipping between each other like waves on the ocean. The scent of jasmine floats up the hill to where I'm perched on our terrace, fighting for dominance over the espresso wafting up from my hands. I close my eyes, savoring the cool breeze and the escape from the heat of Rome.

This last-minute mini-vacation is worth every cent.

A few days ago, I dropped down on the lawn of the Borghese Gardens next to Inez. "Can we go on vacation?"

She laughed, and rolled onto her stomach, propping her chin on her hands. "Is Rome not enough for you?"

I nudged her with my foot. "Of course it is, but the past month has been stressful for both of us. We deserve to get away for a couple days. Dr. Guarino and Dr. Aguilar are taking the students to Venice and Verona this weekend. Let's go somewhere, too."

She chewed on her lip. "I was actually planning on taking the train to Florence for the day on Saturday."

"Tuscany's perfect! We can find a villa, drink good wine, and not think about work for two whole days."

Inez started picking at her nails, something she always did when she was nervous. "Well, I was actually going to visit someone."

I widened my eyes at her. "Inez García, are you going to see a boy?"

She rolled her eyes at me and pinched her lips against a smile. "No, nothing like that. I can't seem to find any luck in that area. Just an old friend I'm meeting up with. But maybe we could do the whole villa thing. Bring Colton, and you two can hang out on Saturday while I'm gone."

I nodded. "Okay. I'll find something perfect for us."

And, at the risk of sounding full of myself, I delivered. The house itself is small, more bungalow than villa with three tiny bedrooms and a living room we can barely fit in, but it's cheap and comfortable, and the interior isn't the pull, anyway. Every bit of the indoor squeeze is worth it for the incredible outdoor space, set at the top of a hill with views in every direction. There's a terrace with a stunning pergola and creeping vines, the perfect spot for a morning coffee. The other side of the house faces a wide lawn with a pool, the deck lined with lounge chairs. The edge of the property is dotted with Italian cypress trees, like tall, skinny sentinels set up to defend us from the stress of the outside world.

We rented a car and headed up Friday, spending the entire afternoon and evening lounging outside and swimming in the pool. That night, the three of us piled into the small kitchen to make aglio and olio pasta, which took all of four ingredients but still felt like a massive accomplishment when none of us are cooks. As I looked around at my best friends—my family—I thought life couldn't get more perfect.

And it won't end here. This will be our life forever. We'll head back to Boston and get together for home-cooked meals and laughter over wine. The three of us will lounge on the quad on those warm summer days when students flee campus, and in the evenings, Inez and I will force Colt to watch the latest Netflix rom-com with us, as entertained by his sarcastic commentary as we are by the movie itself.

I'm feeling hopeful. The type of hope I haven't felt in years. A professor is on board. Truly, fully on board. Yes, I still have three more to go, but after getting Sydney's buy-in, it feels possible for the first time. I'll come back from this weekend refreshed and ready to dive in.

A splash comes from around the corner of the house, and I round it to find Colton swimming laps in the pool. I've just made my coffee, and this boy's already getting a workout in. The energy levels are honestly absurd.

He stops after another lap when he spots me, throwing me that smile with the dimple that makes my whole body heat like I've thrown myself into a giant pizza oven. Colton pushes himself up and out of the pool, the water sluicing down his toned chest and stomach, and my mouth goes completely dry. He grabs a towel off the lounge chair, and even from twenty feet away, I can see the way his muscles bunch as he runs the towel over his hair.

I want him. Want him so badly that I don't think I'm going to be able to stop myself from doing something stupid, and that thought is terrifying enough to make me want to beg Inez to take us with her.

What if I let myself indulge in him the same way I'm going to indulge in Tuscan wine this weekend? Just once. I think of the look in his eyes while we were at the Borghese, indulgent as always, but with an undercut of hunger that seems to have been there consistently since we got to Italy. It doesn't feel one-sided.

"Enjoying the view?" Inez says from behind me, and I jump, my tiny cup of espresso flying into the air before tipping and pouring the hot liquid down the front of my pajamas.

I glare at her while she laughs. "Look what you did!"

"Just pointing out what *you* were doing," she says, her eyebrows wiggling a bit.

"I have no idea what you're talking about," I say haughtily, and she laughs again.

Colton comes up behind us, whipping out the towel in his hands. It catches me lightly on the hip, the slight sting sending a rush of heat to every corner of my body. Inez raises a knowing brow at the way my skin flushes. When I turn to face him, he spots the coffee all over my shirt and bursts out laughing.

"Shut up," I say, crossing my arms over the offending stain.

He covers his laughter with a cough, wrangling his broad smile back into a serious line. "Excited for today?"

"God, yes," I say "Give me an overly excited Italian person explaining the science behind wine that I'll avidly listen to in the moment and forget by the time the liquid hits my tongue."

He chuckles and drapes the small towel over his shoulders, leaving his defined chest on display. "Or, I could go to the store and buy a dozen different bottles of Tuscan wine and we could stay at the pool."

Tempting, him in low-slung swim trunks pouring me another glass of wine while I lie on a pool float.

"That's what we did yesterday. I want to go out and see the world."

"I wish I could go with you," Inez says, playing with the soft silk of her shirt.

Something's off. She's meeting up with a friend, but doesn't seem happy about it. "Are you sure you don't want me to come with you?" I ask.

Inez smiles tightly. "No, you guys go. Have fun, and you can tell me all about it over dinner tonight."

I nod, unable to shake the feeling that she's hiding something from me, but I head inside to get ready.

An hour later, Colton and I are ready to be picked up by the driver we hired so we could both indulge, leaving Inez to use our rental car. We make our way out to the car before I realize I left my phone behind. I run back into the little house to find Inez pulling on a blazer.

Her lucky blazer.

"What is that?" I ask, pointing at the offending piece of clothing.

She bought it our first year of graduate school before we started our internship interviews. After receiving offers from every single university she interviewed with, she dubbed it her lucky blazer. She's worn it for every interview and important meeting since. The abstract teal and white design has faded over the years to something softer, but it's no less beautiful than the day we found it on the sale rack at Saks.

Inez looks like a deer caught in the headlights. "I thought you left."

"Forgot my phone. Why are you wearing your lucky blazer to 'get together with a friend'?"

She starts chewing on her lip. "Okay, don't freak out. But I'm meeting with Dr. Lascano."

My brows pull together. "From graduate school?"

She'd been a professor in our program, teaching class virtually from Florence where she worked for Scuola Leonardo da Vinci, a massive Italian language school and study abroad program. I'd completely forgotten about her existence, but I'd only taken one class with her while Inez had worked closely with her for several classes, including an independent study.

"And you need your lucky blazer to meet with Dr. Lascano?" I ask, even though I know the answer in my bones.

"I'm not taking a job," she says quickly, reaching her hands out to me, but stopping before she touches me as she thinks about her next words. "I'm just… thinking… about a job."

I sputter. "But… but we *love* Billings."

She winces again, and I feel guilty, like I'm jabbing her with a needle over and over again. "I *do* love Billings. It's a great school, and it would break my heart to leave Boston and you. But it has a lot of problems, too."

Obviously, I know Billings has problems. I'm literally working my ass off to try to fix them. We've spent eight years bitching about the professors, but neither of us has ever seriously considered leaving.

Until now.

"We always said we were going to fight to fix the problems. If everyone runs away from the problems, they'll just get worse. Remember? That's what we've always said."

Billings has been our home for the past eight years. We're a family—a better family than the one I got at birth. Inez and I love how small the campus is. The way we run into students while walking from meeting to meeting, and how they're always happy to see us even though they know we're going to bug them about following through on whatever we're working on.

Our supervisors are solid and believe in us. They pay us well—for higher ed, at least—and support our growth and professional development. The campus is beautiful and right in the middle of the city. It's perfect, or will be if we can work things out with the professors. And I'm on my way to improving that, one faculty member at a time.

Most importantly, we agreed we would fight this thing together. That we'd stand by each other's sides. And now she's leaving? Without talking to me, or even mentioning that she's considering it? I feel completely blindsided. Abandoned.

"I know," she says placatingly. "And I really do believe that. But if this initiative passes, my job won't be the job I love anymore. And I'm tired. I don't want to fight anymore."

"So you've decided?"

She shakes her head. "No, I just want to explore the option."

I turn my head away, blinking my tears away. They blur the painting of the Tuscan countryside hanging on the wall, the greens and yellows and reds swirling together like a Van Gogh painting. "Why didn't you tell me about this?"

We've been each other's sounding boards for every step in our careers. She helped me decide I didn't want the job at the large public university I interned with, and I helped her prepare for the presentation that was required as part of the Billings interview process. How didn't I know she is considering leaving?

She shrugs, a sad smile on her face. "I don't like conflict."

I'm flooded with guilt as I realize she didn't tell me because she didn't think she *could* tell me, and my reaction to the news is proving her right. She's a grown woman, capable of making her own choices without consulting her friend. I'm not being abandoned, even if the buzzing in my veins says otherwise.

A broken little sob escapes me. "Of course I'll support you. I want you to be happy."

She steps forward, taking one of my hands between both of hers. "I know. But I knew you'd be disappointed, too, and I don't want to disappoint you. You're my best friend."

"You've never once disappointed me." I sniff, pasting on a smile and infusing as much excitement as I can into my tone. "What's the job?"

"Director of Health, Safety, and Security," she says, rolling her lips together as her eyes shine.

"Well, fuck, Inez," I say, tears springing back up in my eyes, both because I'm happy for her and because I know I'm losing her. How can Billings compete with a job that's literally all about crisis management?

Inez nods, her own eyes filling with tears, and I pull her in for a hug. We stand in the middle of the tiny living room, clutching each other and crying.

"You're going to be so fucking good at that job."

"I haven't gotten the offer yet. Dr. Lascano set up a special Saturday interview because she knew I couldn't get away, but I still have to get it."

"There's no way they'll meet you and not pick you."

"But I haven't decided, even if they do," she says. "I don't want to leave Billings, but I don't know if I can keep going."

There's still a chance. I saw a ray of hope at the Galleria Borghese with Sydney, a little hint of what our campus *could* be like if we find a way to work together. It would be supportive and collaborative, all the things Inez and I always wanted. She won't leave if we can finally make that a reality.

I kiss her cheek as I pull away. "They definitely won't offer if you don't fix your makeup."

She wipes under her eyes, laughing. "Oh gosh, is it bad?"

I run my thumb under her eye to swipe off some of the mascara that flaked off. "Nothing a little touch-up won't fix."

She nods, a little hiccup escaping her. "I love you, Quinn."

I swallow thickly, fighting down another round of tears. "Love you, too."

We fix our makeup side by side in the little bungalow bathroom, giving each other one more hug before running to our respective cars. I watch her pull away, turning in the opposite direction from where we're heading. Already pulling away from me.

Colton's in the back seat when I slip in.

"You okay?" he asks quietly.

"Fine," I say, pasting on a smile.

He lifts an eyebrow that clearly says I'm full of shit. I shoot my eyes over to our driver and back. As happy as I am for Inez, losing her after being together for a decade makes me feel raw, and I don't want to lay my heart out right now. He nods and turns his attention back to his phone. But every five minutes of the forty-five minute drive, I feel his eyes back on me.

All I can think about is how things will change if she leaves. She's been my only close friend in Boston for a decade. My go-to person for weekend plans and after-work drinks. If she leaves, it'll just be me and Colton. And if I let myself explore something physical with Colton and it backfires on me, who else would I have? It'd be like the beginning of grad school all over again, with a best friend across the ocean and no one else, and that had been the loneliest, darkest time of my life.

If Colton doesn't feel the same tension, I could mess up our whole dynamic by making a move he isn't interested in. And if he *is* interested, we could still fuck it up if one of us decides we want more.

I need to keep my focus on winning over the faculty, on keeping my dream of the three of us in Boston together. The last thing I need is another complication.

COLTON

SOMETHING'S WRONG. I don't know what it is, but Quinn's barely said two words all day. My chatterbox is gone, leaving blank smiles and faraway looks in her place. I want her back. I need her addictive laughter and the conspiratorial glances that come right before she makes an inappropriate comment.

A very passionate man stands in front of the table, which sits six other guests who are fully engrossed in his speech. The Chianti mountains rise in the distance behind him, each peak lowering in elevation the closer they move toward us, like kids lined up on risers for a class photograph. Picturesque villas dot the slopes, and the weather's perfect—warm but with a breeze to keep us all comfortable outside. A setting for an incredible day, if Quinn were actually here.

"There are other regions where you can get fine wine," the man says, "but the Chianti region will always be a league above. Our deep, complex flavor profiles have made our wines famous around the world."

The audience murmurs their agreement, everyone but Quinn grabbing the glass he indicated to take a sip before pairing it with the slice of cheese he suggested.

"Now, there are many classifications for Chianti wine, and I will not bore you with the details, but if you take one thing from this lunch pairing, remember to look for the black rooster on the bottle. If you see a rooster, you can confidently pick up the bottle knowing it has come from this region and meets certain quality standards. Plus, you have the convenience of not having to read the label as your vision becomes more impaired!"

He grabs one of the bottles off the table, bringing it close to his face and squinting at the rooster like he's too drunk to read, then nods and mimes drinking it straight from the lip. Everyone laughs, and he waves us off to finish our wine and enjoy our lunch. I look over, but Quinn still has that same distant look in her eyes.

"What's wrong?" I finally ask, popping another piece of cheese in my mouth.

"What?" she replies, blinking up at me like she forgot I'm here.

"You've barely spoken since we got in the car. What's going on?"

"Nothing," she says with an exasperated laugh. "Can I not just be quiet?"

I turn to face her fully. "Yes, you can be quiet, but I know your quiets, and this isn't a comfortable one. Your brain is running so fast I swear I can hear a whirling like your computer fan is trying to cool it down."

Quinn chews on her bottom lip. "I'm fine."

I point to the man from the presentation, who's now leaning against the far wall talking to another employee. "He made a joke about being too drunk to read the wine label and mimed drinking Chianti Classico from the bottle, and you didn't even crack a smile."

"Wait, really?" She blinks at the man like she's finally waking up to the world around her. "Okay, I guess I have been a bit distracted."

My lip twitches. "I noticed."

She tugs her lip between her thumb and pointer finger as she looks at the food in front of her. "I don't want to talk about it."

"You're going to talk to me eventually," I say.

"I know, but not right now." She smiles, even though it doesn't reach her eyes.

She shakes out her arms like she's warming up for a sprint, then grabs her glass of Chianti and downs it in one gulp. Someone gasps in horror of her treatment of wine said to have been made from the blood of the gods.

"Okay," she says. "I'm here. I'm present. Let's do this."

I raise a wry eyebrow. "Are you? Because if you're going to zone out all day, we could've gone to the Etruscan museum like I wanted to."

There's a small museum in the area with one of the best collections of Etruscan artifacts. Quinn argued this was a work-free weekend, and I argued I was a *Roman* historian, not an Etruscan historian. Apparently, learning about Rome's cultural predecessor is too close for consideration.

"I'll take you to the museum if you really want," Quinn says with an indulgent shake of her head. Her brow pinches a little, then she turns back to me with a determined expression. "Didn't Alessandra study the Etruscan civilization?"

I jolt. "Alessandra as in my ex?"

The two of us dated during my first year in Rome. She was a senior at the American University of Rome with every intention of going back to the States after she finished her degree, so it was casual. When she decided she was going to stay in Rome for graduate school, I had to tell her I didn't want something serious. We'd stayed friends over the years, but I don't get why Quinn was bringing her up now.

"Yeah," Quinn says. "You mentioned she's interviewing at a museum in Boston, right?"

"Yes," I say slowly, dragging out the single word. "Why?"

She shrugs. "Thought you two might reconnect when we get back. She seemed like a great fit for you."

"A great fit," I repeat, trying to wrap my head around where this was coming from. "She's a good friend, but we weren't right together."

She hums, popping a green olive into her mouth and chewing thoughtfully. "What about Bex who works in health and wellness? I think you two would get along."

"Get along? What the hell are you talking about, Quinn?"

"Oh, or Alyssa in the alumni office?"

I grab her arm as she reaches across the table for another olive and turn her body fully to face me. "What the hell's going on here?"

She swallows, her throat bobbing with the action. "Just, you haven't dated anyone in a while and I thought it might be nice for you to explore your options."

I scoff and reach for a piece of prosciutto. "I'm good. Thanks."

"But why?" she asks, almost desperate. "Why haven't you dated anyone?"

I freeze, the food halfway to my mouth. In over a decade of friendship, she's never pushed me on this, and I've always been grateful not to have to lie. Obviously, I can't tell her the truth. *I don't date because I've been madly in love with you since we met and it wouldn't be fair to the other women.*

I give her a partial truth instead. "This industry's intense. For the past decade, I haven't known where I was going to end up. I got lucky with my offers, but if the only tenure-track offer I received was at the University of Alaska Fairbanks, I'd have bought a parka and been on the next flight."

"But you're on the tenure track now," she says. "You'll be in Boston for the rest of your working life."

"I hope so, but there's always a chance I get denied tenure."

On paper, I *should* get it, but there's no guarantee until it's official. The thought of losing my job and having to fight with the other people in my field for the ever-decreasing tenure-track positions is nauseating. Universities would look at my CV and wonder exactly what's wrong with me that made Billings throw me away.

I suck in a deep breath. "But if Billings decides to part ways with me at any of my pre-tenure reviews, or shit, at my final tenure review, I'll have to go where the next job is. I have too many responsibilities not to be selfish with my choices."

Quinn's smile is sad. "Only you would think choosing your job security so you can financially support your mom is the selfish choice."

I shrug. "Maybe selfish isn't the right word, but my mom's security is my number one priority. Being in a relationship means factoring another person into your plans."

"And you've never met anyone you wanted to do that for?" she asks.

Her eyes are so earnest as she asks this, and I realize that she really has no idea. No idea that I've spent the past fourteen years factoring her into my plans, even when she doesn't ask me to. She is and always will be the biggest pro on any list about Boston.

But she isn't asking about her. She's asking about romantic partners.

"No," I say. "I've never met anyone I was willing to change my plans for."

She nods, a little divot forming between her brows like she's sad for me, and I fight down the urge to smooth it out with my thumb.

"But you're one to talk," I say, the corner of my mouth kicking up. "Why aren't we talking about finding you a significant other?"

The thought twists something in my stomach, even though I want her to find happiness.

She chuckles. "Don't think that's in the cards for me, Colt."

That twisting in my gut turns a cold, heavy feeling. "What do you mean?"

Quinn waves her hand. "Forget about it."

"No, tell me."

She laughs, but the sound is brittle. "Come on, you know me better than anyone. I have more trust issues than Rome has ruins. Relationships just end up being stressful and annoying."

"So… what?" I ask. "You're going to stay alone for the rest of your life?"

"Not alone. It sounds like you're committing to the bachelor life. How do his and her rooms at the old folks home sound?"

She laughs, but I can't force one out myself. I don't want that life for her. She shows more love in a single day than most people show in a lifetime, and she deserves every bit of happiness this life offers. "You deserve more than my grumpy ass next door."

"True. If you're this grumpy at thirty-two, imagine what you're going to be like at eighty." I nudge her shoulder, and she giggles. "Kidding! Your friendship is plenty. I don't need the flowers and candles and romance to feel fulfilled. And there are ways to scratch that itch without having to deal with the inevitable drama of dating."

An unexpected fire lights my veins at the thought of her *scratching the itch*. I hate the idea of her picking up some random person who won't care enough about her to make sure it's everything she deserves. She should be with someone who'll worship her, who'll stop at nothing to have her writhing and screaming their name to the exposed beams of our apartment. Someone like me.

The devil on my shoulder is back, whispering filthy things about the way she watched me when I got out of the pool. The spark of heat in her eyes and the way her sweet, pink tongue peeked out to swipe across her full bottom lip. She isn't completely unaffected. If me being the one to touch her is an option, I don't want to give her space for anyone else.

My hand closes around a leg of her stool and I tug it an inch closer to mine. I lean forward, catching her gaze. Her eyes flick down to my lips, and I go molten.

"And who exactly," I say, my voice dropping to an octave I didn't know I could produce, "do you plan to scratch the itch with this summer?"

Quinn's eyes go wide, then she twirls to the table, grabbing the second glass in her tasting row and throwing it back like the first. She coughs a couple times like some of the liquid went down the wrong pipe. "I'll figure it out. Maybe Tomasso can introduce me to someone."

My stomach drops. What the fuck am I doing? If she was interested in me, even physically, she wouldn't be trying to set me up with half of Boston.

"Good idea," I say, clearing my throat as I shift my stool away. "He introduced me to someone a few years ago."

"Oh, yeah?" she squeaks out.

"Yeah, it was a perfect setup. Exactly what I wanted."

A breath gusts out of her. "Great."

"Great," I parrot back.

Fuck. I'm being an asshole. I have no right to be upset about who she does or doesn't scratch her itch with.

The man from before claps his hands, drawing everyone's attention again as the next course of our lunch comes out, along with another set of wines to taste. Quinn chugs the last of our first round drinks before the waiter can sweep it away, giving me an awkward smile.

When he finishes his next round of explanations about these wines and why they're paired with these dishes, Quinn turns back to me. "I'm sorry. I made it weird with all the dating stuff."

"I'm sorry, too," I say. "Your concern is sweet, but I don't want a relationship."

Her eyes are serious and maybe a bit sad. "I hope you reconsider that, because you have so much to offer someone."

I hear the message underneath. She wants me to find

someone to be happy with, but it won't be her. If I want to keep the most important relationship in my life, I need to accept that. So instead of moping, I turn my attention to having as much fun with my best friend as I can.

THREE WINERIES LATER, we stumble back to our AirBnB. Quinn's singing an old Giusy Ferreri song that was on the radio constantly when we studied here. It had poured out of every restaurant and shop for months. I haven't thought about it in years, but hearing her sing it hurtles me back to those precious days with Quinn.

She tries to pull off a spin on the dramatic chorus, but gets tripped up at the last second. I grab her biceps, yanking her back against my front as I stumble myself, my body losing all sense of control after the influence of so much wine. Quinn drops her head against my chest before tilting it to look up at me.

"My savior," she says.

So fucking beautiful.

"Thank you," she giggles, and I realize I said those words out loud.

Her cheeks are flushed from the wine and her eyes are back to their full brilliance, and holy shit, I love this woman more than anything in this world. I sway toward her on instinct. Or maybe that's the wine, because we both stumble forward, my arms wrapped around her waist as we devolve into laughter again.

When we reach the door, Quinn has to bend down and put her face inches from the keypad to type in the code, just like the winery tour guide joked we'd need to.

"This is ridiculous," I say through my laughter.

The keypad finally flashes green, and Quinn yells, "Vittoria!"

Inez is reading a book in the living room when we come in, and Quinn's laughter abruptly cuts off.

"How was your visit with your friend?" Quinn asks, something tight in her voice.

Inez smiles, but it looks more like a wince. "It was amazing."

Quinn lets out an almost manic laugh. "That's awesome! So exciting! Hey, why don't we break into one of these bottles, yeah?"

She twirls toward the kitchen before either of us can respond. I raise a brow at Inez, but she shrugs and follows after Quinn, talking to her in a low voice.

The rest of the night's a blur of more wine and probably not enough charcuterie for our dinner. After a whole day of drinking, Quinn and I are both ready to pass out by ten, but when I finally settle into bed, I can't shut off my brain.

Things have shifted between us, and I don't know if it's a good thing or not. We've both grown and changed since college, but I still love her as much as I did when she dropped me off at the airport ten years ago. More, even. And the idea of losing her presence in my life still guts me. Of course I want her, but I'd take a lifetime of her friendship over a few hours of something physical.

I'm staring at the ceiling when there is a light knock on my door.

"Yeah?" I call, pushing myself to lean back against the wooden headboard. The door cracks open, revealing Quinn.

"Can I come in?" she asks with a quiver in her voice.

"Of course," I say, and she scrambles onto the other side of the full bed, laying her head on the pillow facing me. I mirror her position. "Finally ready to talk to me?"

Her lips quirk up, but her eyes stay sad. "I was kind of a buzzkill today, wasn't I?"

"You're never a buzzkill."

"It's sweet when you lie to me," she says, her smile growing.

"Fine, you were a bit of a buzzkill." I laugh, and she reaches out to poke my dimple. "But only because I was worried about you. What happened?"

Quinn chews on her lip. "Inez wasn't visiting a friend today. She was meeting with Leonardo da Vinci."

I suck in a breath through my teeth. "Is it safe to assume you mean the school and not that one of the greatest minds of all time has been reanimated?"

Quinn laughs and flops onto her back, the first full smile I've seen all day stretching her mouth wide. "You're the worst."

"Thank you," I say, and she turns back to me, the smile fading to something softer. "Was she meeting about a job?"

Quinn nods. "She's tired of all the tension on campus and is considering other options."

I watch Quinn closely, the way she constantly rolls her lips together like she's actively fighting whatever words are trying to escape and how her gaze looks past me to the little window like she can't handle sustained eye contact or risk breaking.

"And you're scared about what happens if she takes it?"

She blinks quickly. "Of course I am. We've been together for a decade. First in graduate school, and then both starting at Billings right after graduation."

"The nice thing about living in the twenty-first century is we've got great technology."

"I know, but what if we lose touch with her across an ocean?"

"You didn't lose touch with me," I say.

Her eyes snap back to mine. "Yeah, but you're you."

A warmth unfurls in my chest. I've always been happy that Quinn found Inez, but there's a little part of me that will always feel a bit jealous that she has someone else who fills a similar role to me. Hearing that I'm different is a confirmation that she feels all the same big emotions that have always swirled around our friendship.

"Why am I any different?" I ask, partially to challenge the belief that she'd lose Inez and partially because I want to hear it.

She shrugs and starts tracing the pattern of the quilt between us. "I don't know. You just are. You're my person."

I reach out to capture her hand, twining our fingers together, fighting off the urge to pull her closer and wrap my arms around her.

"Do you know why I kept in touch with you all those years? Why I planned dinners and travel and dates around our call schedule?" I ask, and she shakes her head, her beautiful brown eyes wide. "Because you're more than my best friend. You're light and joy, mixed up with just enough sarcasm to keep it interesting. You believe in your people and fight for them, and you love with everything you are. Inez knows this just as much as I do, and if she *does* leave Boston, she'll fight for your friendship just like I did. Once someone's been on the receiving end of your love, it's impossible to walk away."

"More people I've loved have left than stayed," she whispers. She's crying softly, and I reached out to wipe a tear away.

I hate her family. Hate that they made her question the people who do love her. "I think we can both agree that Inez has more quality in her pinky finger then the whole Riley clan combined."

Quinn laughs through the tears, and I move close enough to press a hard kiss to her forehead before settling back on my own pillow.

She turns her face slightly into the pillow. "I love you."

Quinn has told me she loves me hundreds of times over our friendship. It doesn't matter that it isn't new, my heart still shoots around my chest. "I love you, too."

"I'm just going to close my eyes for a minute," she says, her body relaxing into the mattress.

I chuckle. "Sure, Chaos."

When I open my eyes in the morning, she's still there, my hand clutched in hers like she couldn't bring herself to let go even in sleep.

13

COLTON

FOURTEEN YEARS AGO

"You're failing."

I blink up at my academic advisor, an accounting professor I've only met once when I started at Chadoin a few months ago. He's set up behind his massive wood desk in his massive leather chair, while I'm in a chair barely big enough to fit me. Did he consciously set up his office to be an overbearing prick, or was it a subconscious decision to compensate for something?

"I'm sorry, what?" I ask.

"I don't know how much clearer I can be. You're failing. I received your midterm grades, and you're failing every class except your general education class." He flicks his eyes to a paper on his desk with a sigh. The guy doesn't even know what I'm taking. "Roman history."

Dr. Christensen's eyes burn into me from across the desk, challenging and judgmental. They say *you're not worth the time it takes to explain this,* and the part of me that has always believed people's comments about not being good enough to get out of my small town shrinks in on itself. My eyes drop closed, but my mom's face floats behind my lids. Her belief in me and my duty to succeed.

"Okay. What do I do?" I ask, letting that determination to provide for her swallow up every self conscious fear.

He has no idea what that question costs me. My whole life, I've been the one who doesn't need help. My grades were the best. I read—and enjoyed—the assigned books. My teachers held up my work as examples of what to do.

I knew I wasn't doing as well this semester as I did in high school. My classes are boring and I can't seem to keep up with the constant stream of assignments shouted at me like stock floor traders. But saying those words out loud, admitting I need some guidance, feels like giving up my identity. The only thing that makes me special.

"Don't fail," Dr. Christensen says blandly.

"You don't say. The thought never occurred to me."

He doesn't take kindly to my sarcasm, face going all pinched. It doesn't make me less worried, but I feel a certain satisfaction at his anger. He's sitting there acting like he hung the moon, and I'm nothing but shit on his boot.

Then I remember this man controls my future, and I need to check myself before I get kicked out of school.

"Forgive me, sir. What happens now?"

"With grades like these, I don't see you bringing them up, so your scholarship will be forfeited. You can stay another semester to see if you can get off academic probation on your own dime, but we won't be wasting ours. Not everybody is cut out for college, and I'd suggest you think about that long and hard before you make your decision about next semester."

His words wash over me like a bucket of cold water. He isn't telling me what to do to improve. I'm a lost cause. Maybe there's a reason no other Miller has made it out of Grand Creek in five generations.

"Thank you for informing me, sir." I nod to him, gather my backpack, and leave without a backward glance.

The rest of the morning passes in a daze. I sit in class, but don't hear a word that's said. Something about metrics and data and sales. In Roman History, Quinn sits beside me, blabbing on like usual. Dr. Cassia says something that includes the words *forum* and *column*, but I can't tell you more than that with a gun to my head.

I shuffle out of the classroom with Quinn in tow, the words still pouring from her mouth. My mind isn't here, but I nod along.

Silence, which has been lacking in my life since I met this girl, finally makes me stop and look up. Quinn's studying me with a worried face.

"What's wrong?" she asks.

I shrug. "Nothin'."

"Liar. What's wrong?"

"I told you, nothing's wrong."

"I know me talking and you grunting is kinda our thing, but you haven't even been doing that today. So I'll ask again: What's wrong?"

"Leave it, Chaos."

"No. What's wrong?"

"Leave it the fuck alone, Quinn!"

She pauses, her eyes wide. I've never yelled at her, but the questions are too much. I can't tell this perfect girl with her perfect grades and perfect life plan that my own has gone to shit in the span of one meeting.

"Well, now I'm definitely not *leavin' it*." Her pathetic imitation of my drawl comes out in some exaggerated *Forrest Gump*-type accent. She looks up at me stubbornly, refusing to let me push her away. "Stop being a closed-off dick and talk to me."

"Why?" I ask, exhausted and overwhelmed.

She steps closer, craning her neck to keep eye contact, and I let my eyes follow the curve to the place where her pulse beats. I want to gather her up in my arms and kiss her there. Want to fall into her and feel something besides this raging disappointment in myself.

"Because I'm your best friend. And if you can't talk to your best friend about these things, they'll eat you up inside. I won't let that happen to you."

Her eyes are pure steel, spine straight, hands clenched. She's 100 percent certain about her role in my life. I've been over here analyzing every conversation, staring at her longingly, waiting for any sign that she wants me like I want her. And she's been over there thinking about what a good friend I am. Hurts like a bitch.

But I also realize she's right. I may spend most of my days dreaming of her, but she *is* my best friend.

I sigh and drop onto the curb. She lowers herself down next to me and takes my hand between her small ones, leaning her head on my shoulder with her face tilted toward me.

"Please talk to me."

I look down into her wide brown eyes. Her blond bangs fall in front of them, and I push them back.

She huffs. "I hate these bangs."

"Yeah, I know." She's spent the better part of the past month bitching about them. Her eyes go serious again, settling in to wait me out.

"I'm going home. To West Virginia."

"For Thanksgiving? I thought it was too expensive. I was going to surprise you and stay."

My heart tightens in my chest. She really is the best person I know.

I steel myself before looking at her again. Time to rip off the Band-Aid. "No, Chaos. For good."

She laughs nervously. "That's not funny."

"Good, cause it's not a joke."

Her eyes bounce between mine, like if she stares hard enough the joke will make sense. When I give her nothing, she jumps up. Her expression goes from confused to pissed in half a heartbeat.

"What the fuck, Colt? Why would you do that? You worked your ass off to be here."

I take a breath, drumming my hands on my knees to work up the courage. Once I say it, it's real.

"I'm flunking out. My advisor called me in this morning to tell me."

She starts pacing. Other students split around her, grumbling as they go, but I don't think she even notices them.

"Okay, it's not going great right now, but you haven't failed yet. The game's not over until your grades are locked in. What did your advisor suggest?"

I laugh, a sound devoid of humor. "That I should consider if I'm meant to be here."

The fire in her eyes could burn anyone in their path. I've seen her blush a couple times when someone annoys her, but now she was turning bright red in pure, unbridled fury.

She anchors her hands on her hips. "Tell me *exactly* what your advisor said."

I walk through the meeting. How he said I'm gonna lose my scholarship. How I can pay my own way and try to bring up my grades, but I should consider if it was worth it.

It isn't. Affording this school is so far out of my reach it may as well be on Saturn. I'd be stuck paying off those loans for the rest of my life, and my mom needs money sooner rather than later. I'll have to get a job and hope one day I'll get to try again.

"And he gave you no suggestions or action items to bring up your grades?"

"Nothin'."

"Bullshit. I'll come up with the plan myself. First, we're going to schedule a meeting with the department chair. Your advisor was out of line and needs to be held accountable."

I grab her hands, forcing her to stop her pacing.

"It's done, Quinn. He said I wouldn't be able to bring up my grades, and without my scholarship, you know I can't stay here."

Her eyes fill with tears. It's breaking my heart that I'm causing her pain. That I'm hurting everyone who matters in my life. Momma's going to be so disappointed in me. She'll still want me to go to school and take out loans to help. It'll take even longer for me to support her. God, she'll be working until she has one foot in the grave.

Quinn grabs the sides of my head, forcing my eyes back to hers and stopping my spiral.

"Don't do that. Don't give up on yourself because one douchebag doesn't believe in you. I know how colleges work. I've lived on them my whole life. I'll come up with a plan if you promise to fight like hell to stay here. You deserve to be here. Plus, life would suck without you."

I don't know what I did to be graced with this perfect little spitfire. I doubt she can change my situation, but if it gives me a few extra smiles before I have to leave her, I'll do whatever she wants.

"Okay, Chaos. Lead the way."

14

QUINN

JUNE — EIGHT WEEKS TO WIN OVER THE FACULTY

WHEN I LEFT for Tuscany last Friday, I thought I'd come back relaxed and ready to jump into the work of winning over the last three professors. Instead, there's a restlessness underneath my skin that makes me feel like my entire body's buzzing. Inez spent the drive back to Rome telling us all about her interview, how kind everyone was and how her old mentor took her to get the best panini of her life after the meeting. Knowing how much she loved the team at Leonardo da Vinci doubles the pressure of the summer. If I have any hope of keeping her in Boston with us, I need to show her I can get the professors to play just as nicely.

I'm in one of the shared offices grading journals when a rap sounds on the doorframe, and I look up to find Sydney and Dr. Aguilar.

"Are you busy, Quinn?" Sydney asks, and I'm sure the way my eyes widen in surprise looks ridiculous.

I scramble to cover my shock at her seeking me out. "Just getting some grading done, but I could use a break. How can I help you two?"

The women come into the office, Sydney flipping the second chair away from the other desk to face mine as they settle across from me. "I was telling Andrea about our visit to the Borghese."

Dr. Aguilar smiles at me, a genuine smile that shocks me even more than them asking to speak with me. "Impressive work."

I struggle to find my words, but finally settle on, "Thank you, Dr. Aguilar."

She chuckles. "I think you can call me Andrea. We're all practically living together this summer."

"Tell that to Dr. Guarino," I mumble.

Andrea continues. "Sydney told me you were the one who coached her student through what field she wanted to intern in this summer?"

I shrug. "That's what I do. There's a lot more you can do with an art history degree than people think, so we talked through some options to figure out which aligned more with what she likes about her major."

Andrea's brows raise. "I'll be honest. I thought your office mostly maintained a list of internship opportunities for students." I physically bite my tongue to keep from making a snippy comment about how my job is a lot more involved than that. "But after hearing what you did for Catherine, I was thinking we could talk about how to collaborate on internships for the English department."

"Oh," I say. "Of course. I don't know if this class will run in Rome next year since… well, you know. But I can start compiling ideas."

"I meant for back in Boston. Our students are so bright, but they struggle to figure out what they want to do after graduation. I'd like to change that. Maybe some workshops in our junior seminar on different jobs that you can use an English degree for?"

My mouth opens and closes like a fish. I've been trying to get partnerships like this set up for eight years.

"Yes!" I say, too enthusiastic, and both women shift back slightly in their seats. "Sorry, yes, I have a lot of ideas. You can do so much with an English degree. What field are most of your students interested in?"

"Publishing is the most common one, but that may be because it's the most visible option related to English."

"It can't hurt to start there. We could also sit down with the alumni office to identify some alums in the field who can share about their experience and maybe help students get a leg up. We've done something similar with the architecture department, and it's been a huge success."

Andrea hums. "I never thought about working with the alumni office. I always thought of them as the people who bug old students for money."

My smile is tight. I get why that's what she thinks—it's what the faculty see—but we're so much more than their limited knowledge. "Well, they're that, too, but there are so many ways the other departments on campus can support the academics if given the chance."

My voice is bordering on desperate and both Andrea and Sydney know it, but there's a spark of interest in their eyes.

Andrea nods. "Great, if you wouldn't mind setting up a meeting when we get home?"

"Of course not. I'd love to," I say, and Andrea chuckles at my overly enthusiastic response.

"I look forward to it," she says, going to stand.

"But Andrea," I say quickly, and she settles back into her seat. "If the initiative separating faculty and staff on campus passes, this project—and a lot of others that would benefit the students— will be a lot harder to figure out. You do recognize that, right?"

She shares a quick look with Sydney before facing me. "You have my tentative support. My tenure review is in two years, and I can't risk losing it after working toward it for so long. If you get all the Rome professors on board, I'm more than happy to support this, but I'll be honest. Sticking my neck out alone makes me nervous."

I nod, slipping my hands underneath the desk so she can't see the nervous way my fingers twist around each other. "Then let's get everyone on board."

Getting Sydney's respect at the Borghese was a great step, but this is like an Olympic long jump in comparison. It's what I always hoped for our campus, taking all these incredible offices and unique skills to best support our students. I had given up hope that this type of large-scale collaboration was possible.

I log off the computer, too hyped to sit and read student journals. This is my shot, and I need to celebrate. I pull my phone out of my bag, ready to text the group chat that Colton labeled *Quinn's Knights* in a fit of unexpected whimsy, but when I open my phone, I have a dozen missed calls and a half dozen texts from Inez. I read them as I started walking toward the door.

INEZ

Hey! Can you give me a call?

Did you see my text? Call me

Where are you? I need to talk to you

Quinn, please call me back as soon as you
see this

Are you at the school? I'm on my way to
you now

I hear voices from around the corner in the living-room-turned-lounge, one so distinctly recognizable I can't block it out no matter how many years I've spent trying. My legs are moving of their own accord as I walk right into my worst nightmare. I numbly glance down at the last text.

I'm so so so sorry. I didn't want to text you this but I don't want you blindsided. Your dad's university is the other one who rented the space. I swear I had no idea. Call me.

I raise my eyes from the phone to find my father in the middle of the room, the professors from my program and his gathered around while he enthralls them with some story or another. Colton's there in the middle, Dad's hand clapped on his shoulder.

"Riley," Andrea says as she sidles up to the group. "You aren't related to Quinn by any chance, are you?"

Dad chuckles, but it has a hard edge to it. "Ah, yes, the prodigal daughter."

The prodigal son returns to his father. Dad needs to work on his analogies. The whole room turns to face me when I step through the doorway, everyone riveted to see what will happen after Dad's dramatic description of me.

He watches me, his eyes calculating. "Quinn."

"Dr. Riley," I say back with equal coldness.

"How's your *class* going?" He asks with enough of an emphasis on the word to tell everyone around us he meant the word ironically. He chuckles and sends an amused look around the rest of the professors.

"It's amazing," I say with a hard smirk. "And Andrea and I were just talking about ways to collaborate when we get back to campus."

Dr. Guarino scowls at Andrea and she gives him a little, half-apologetic shrug.

Dad smiles that viper's smile. He walks over and slips his arm around my shoulders, the first physical contact we've had in a decade, and my skin crawls. "My daughter here was the most brilliant mind in her year for my field, and she gave it all up."

"I was *not* the most brilliant mind. That was Colton, and you know it. He's the one who won the Harrow Fellowship."

"Yes, the fellowship. One road block, and she gives up everything. You know how this generation is with a bit of adversity." He says that last part to Dr. Guarino, who chuckles and nods along, and my blood boils.

My father continues as if he's a Roman senator addressing us all from the floor. "We were so disappointed when she decided not to go the professor route like the rest of the family. My three boys followed in our footsteps, but Quinn here had to be different."

"I'm literally teaching," I say through gritted teeth. "Those comments don't even make sense anymore."

"Ah, yes, I heard about the real faculty member backing out and them needing you to step in."

"How did you hear that?" I ask. I sound like a petulant child and I hate it. "Are you checking up on me?"

He rolls his eyes at Dr. Guarino, who gives him a sympathetic shake of his head, before turning back to me. "I'm your father. Of course I check up on you."

It takes everything in me not to pop off about how I don't have a father anymore because he decided the letters after my name were more important than a relationship with me.

"It's unfortunate," Dr. Guarino says, "that we couldn't find an actual professor, but the students seem happy enough and at least we didn't have to cancel the class."

"I *am* an actual professor," I say, vitriol in my tone. "I designed this course myself based on years of study. *I* lead the in-class discussions. *I* grade their papers and host office hours and field their questions. You want experience? I'll show you eight years working closely with students and employers to make sure internships are valuable learning experiences. You need research to consider me worthy? I'll email you my graduate thesis. Which, by the way, was published in an academic journal. What I won't do is let you stand there and diminish the work I've done so you can justify passing a rule on campus that hurts everyone but you."

The whole room goes quiet. Even Colton's stunned into silence. Dad's colleagues watch with wide eyes, enjoying the college drama that doesn't affect them. Next time, I'll bring them popcorn.

"This seems like a peaceful work environment," my father says with a chuckle, like he isn't the one who riled all of this up to begin with.

"The joys of staff/faculty interactions," Dr. Guarino replies, giving my father a long-suffering look. "It shouldn't be such a problem after this summer."

Colton steps forward, but I stop him with a shake of my head. I'm done hiding behind him and pretending like I'm less than.

I lift my chin. "Dr. Guarino, if you'd like to review my CV or have a genuine discussion about the future of Billings, I'd be happy to address any concerns you have. But only if the conversation is approached from a place of learning and openness." I turn my back on him and my father, facing Sydney and Andrea. "Thank you for seeking me out earlier. We're going to do great things for our students together."

Not could do. Going to do.

Their stares burn into my back as I turn without another word. I won't let Dr. Guarino's negativity or my father's disdain steal the victory of my conversation with Andrea.

And I won't lose this fight.

HOURS LATER, Colton leans in my room's doorway, rapping lightly on the frame. I meet his eyes in the mirror where I'm removing my makeup.

"Scale of one to ten, how shitty was today?" he asks.

"A solid seven," I say, running the make-up remover under one eye.

He shrugs in the mirror. "A seven's pretty damn good."

"Wait, what's a shit show? A one or a ten?"

His lip quirks. "One is the worst, ten is the best."

"Then my day was as shitty as the way you phrased your question. Solid three."

"I'm proud of you," he says, and I can't help but scoff.

"Proud of what? That I torpedoed my career because I can't hold my tongue? That I'm going to bring you down with me?"

"Proud that you stood up for yourself. Nothing you said was untrue, even if it takes a while for it to seep into Giancarlo's brain."

Giancarlo. Because I'm the only professor he demands use his title. Because in his mind, I'm nowhere near his equal.

Colton pushes off the frame and walks over until he's directly behind me in the full-length mirror. He's a head taller than me, leaving me with a view of his sharp features above me. "Put your makeup back on."

I raise my eyebrows and cross my arms over my chest. "Excuse me?"

He sighs and rubs his hand over his face, like what he's about to say is physically painful to him, and a second later I understand why.

"We're going dancing."

15

QUINN

IT TAKES us fifteen minutes to walk from our apartment to the club across the river in the Testaccio quarter, and I miraculously make it the entire way in heels without tripping on the cobblestones. Music floats down from the surrounding rooftops, pounding in my veins. This is exactly what I need. To give myself over to the music and think about nothing else. Not the blowup in front of the professors or the very tempting job Inez is considering or what this change on campus would mean for my own work.

I spot Tomasso pacing in front of the club, and he waves enthusiastically when he catches sight of us. Then his eyes land on Inez, and he trips over his feet, landing on his knees. She rushes forward and grabs his arm to help him up.

"Grazie. Scusa," he says as he gets to his feet, pushing his glasses back up his nose. "You must be Inez."

"I am," she says, a pretty blush painting her cheeks. "It's nice to meet you."

Colton nudges me with his elbow, widening his eyes when I look up at him.

"May I escort you in?" Tomasso asks, offering her his arm.

She giggles, slipping her arm through his. "I'd love that."

Colton snorts next to me, and I elbow him hard in the side. He lets out a little oof, and then whispers, "Come on, it's like we've stepped into one of your period movies."

"It's adorable," I whisper back. "This summer's been stressful for Inez. She deserves a little fun."

"The band tonight is great. You will love them, Quinn," Tomasso says as he guides us inside and up to the roof, his eyes never leaving Inez's face.

The lights are low everywhere except along the bar, and the dance floor is already packed. Inez squeals and pulls me out, and I glance over my shoulder at Colton, who settles at the bar with Tomasso at his side, whispering frantically and sending Inez longing glances. Colton says something back, clapping him on the shoulder and pushing him in our direction. His eyes sparkle when he catches me watching him, and he gestures that he'll order me a drink, the move so reminiscent of our college years that the world shifts in front of me, Colton's hair growing out and his face taking back on the softer features of his early twenties.

Tomasso was right. The band's fantastic, playing a mix of covers and originals. The three of us dance together, though it slowly transitions from us all dancing together to me dancing next to them. I'm starting to feel solidly like a third wheel, and my eyes automatically seek out Colton. He's still at the bar, though now there's some woman cozying up to him, and I ignore the swirling in my stomach. If he wants to hook up with a gorgeous Italian woman, it's none of my business.

I fight to lose myself to the music, but my eyes keep wandering to him. He leans against the bar, all relaxed and casual and confident. I see a glimpse of his smirk, but I'm relieved to see no dimple. That woman may flirt with him, kiss him—hell, even fuck him—but that dimple's mine.

I catch her hand landing on his forearm—exposed by those

damned rolled sleeves again—her head thrown back in laughter. Why the hell is she laughing so hard? Colton isn't that funny. She leans forward to whisper something in his ear, and a weird, growly sound escapes my throat.

I push my way off the dance floor to join Colton like it's a compulsion. As I approach, she excuses herself with one last flirty glance in Colt's direction. He hands me a rum and coke without a word, and I take a couple long gulps to calm myself.

"When are you getting out there?" I ask with a little shimmy.

"Never, and you know it."

I face him fully, studying him over the lip of my glass as I take another sip. "I figured someone would have taught you to love dancing by now."

"If you couldn't get me on the dance floor, there's no one in the world who could." He holds my gaze and my heart jumps in my chest. Is he saying… "I mean, the badgering. It was constant."

He laughs at his own joke, and I force one myself as I push him. Of course, that's what he means. And what I *want* him to mean. God, I'm acting like a lunatic tonight.

"Not even the bombshell?" I ask, wagging my eyebrows to cover my scowl. "She's been looking at you like you're a nice plate of *tartufo*."

"Who?"

I clench my jaw. "You're full of shit. The tall, skinny brunette with the great boobs who's been hanging all over you since we walked in."

He shrugs, and my blood boils. "Not my type."

I don't believe him for a second. She's everyone's type. "Great boobs aren't your type?"

His eyes flick down to my cleavage and the heat in my veins shifts to something else. I remind my overeager libido that he isn't expressing interest. He's a heterosexual male. I say boobs; he looks at boobs. That's it.

He chuckles. "Never said that. I said *she* wasn't my type."

I shift uncomfortably. "So, you're going to stand by the bar all night?"

"That's the plan," He salutes with his drink.

"You're the one who suggested we go dancing!"

He tilts his head to the side. "I suggested we go out so *you* could go dancing to cheer you up, so go. Dance. Cheer up."

"Fine. Be boring. If you need me, I'll be out there having a good time."

I stomp off, simultaneously frustrated as hell and confused by that frustration. Colt refusing to join the dance floor is nothing new. He hates dancing. It was a constant all four years at school. I'd pester him to come out on the floor. He'd say no. I'd tell him he was no fun and happily head off. But now his rejection twists around my ribs, constricting like a snake.

What the hell is happening to me?

I just keep thinking about Colton *scratching the itch* with the beautiful woman hanging all over him. Or the *perfect* woman Tomasso introduced him to and all the other women who touched him when I was across an ocean, only getting glimpses of him through the phone. And I hate that no matter how much thinking about those things pissed me off, I can't act on it.

Less than a song later, warm hands slip around my waist. I tense for a heartbeat, and then the scent hits me—cedar and old parchment—and my heart leaps into my throat. Colton pulls me back against him, and now my heart is beating so hard I can hardly hear the music. He starts swaying, not even close to being on beat. But he's out on the dance floor with me for the first time.

Colton's breath gusts against my ear. "Why are you mad at me, Chaos?"

"I'm not mad," I call back over the music.

With the way our bodies are plastered together, I can feel him shake his head. "Liar."

But he doesn't push, doesn't question it or demand an answer. He sucks in a breath when I run my hands down his corded forearms, linking our fingers together and tugging his arms so they're wrapped fully around me.

When the song ends, he starts to pull away, and my grip tightens on his arm. "Please?"

His shuddering breath blows against my neck, and I have to fight to hold in a moan. "One more."

His hands slide across my stomach, stopping to grip my hips as we settle into a rhythm. My eyes drop close as I let myself fall back into him, the bass pounding in my ears and pressure at my back sending me into full sensory overload. His fingers stretch over the fabric of my tight dress, sliding and flexing like he can't keep them still.

I've danced with better dancers—people with perfect rhythm and years of experience under their belts—but I've never wanted a dance to go on forever like this one, and I think I may go into full-blown mourning when it ends.

When the next song starts, I try to twist in his arms to face him, but he lets go of me, quickly taking a step back. "You got your dance, Chaos. Two of them. I'll be at the bar."

He doesn't look back, and the loss of his body heat leaves me cold, even in the warm Roman night. I try to refocus on my friends, but I can't stop looking back at him, posted at the bar with his eyes glued to the whiskey in his hands.

I don't want to look at him this way. Don't want to be so focused on him and desperate for his attention. But it seems unavoidable tonight, and I think I need to go home, go to sleep, and reset my head tomorrow.

"I'm done for the night. Want to head home?" I ask Inez.

"Noooo," she whines. "Aren't you having fun?"

"Yeah, but I'm exhausted."

She looks over at Tomasso, who smiles and nods. Oh god, these two are already communicating without speaking. They're going to be one of *those* couples this summer, aren't they? "You go. I'm going to stay with Tomasso for a bit longer."

I point at Tomasso. "You keep her safe. If she doesn't make it home perfectly happy and healthy, I know where your whole family lives."

He laughs, pulling me in to kiss each cheek. "I'll guard her with my life."

I look over at Inez, still hesitant to leave her. She grabs my face between her hands. "Quinn, the past month's been exhausting. I need this. I'm a grown woman, and I'll only have one more drink. Go home. I'll be fine."

I smile and kiss her cheek. "Make good decisions."

"Too late," she hollers and twirls to the music, and Tomasso's delighted laughter cuts through the air.

I walk over to Colton at the bar. "I'm heading home. You staying for a bit?"

"Hell no," he says.

My heart jumps, and I remind myself that he's choosing to get out of the club, not stay with me. I loop my arm through his like I did the first day we met, determined to be *us* again, without all this weird swirling in my gut, and the two of us walk home.

The streets are still alive, even late at night. The restaurant terraces are full of groups sipping limoncello while they chat. Waiters congregate on the edges, unconcerned with pushing out patrons to turn over their tables. An accordion plays from one of the nearby piazzas, and as touristy as it may be, the music gives the city a romantic air. I could spend the entire night walking in silence with Colton, breathing in the life of the city.

But since I'm wearing torture devices other women like to call fashion, I force him back to the apartment and kick my heels off the second we walk through the door, moaning in relief. But as I head to my room to crash, I remember a whole other problem.

"What's wrong?" Colton asks when I groan.

"Inez did the zipper of my dress, and I can't get it down. I'm gonna have to sleep in the damn thing."

"I'll get it." He stands from where he had dropped onto the couch and gestures for me to join him. I stare at him with wide eyes. This seems like a line we shouldn't cross. "What? It's not like I haven't helped you out of a dress before."

My brain is conjuring images of Colton helping me out of this dress. Of him kissing along the low neckline and ripping it down the center because he's too desperate to use the zipper. Of him dropping to his knees in front of me...

God fucking dammit.

"Yeah, but..."

He scoffs. "But what?"

"It's not really appropriate now," is what comes out, and his brow furrows, clearly confused. He doesn't know I'm secretly going into a jealous rage when sexy Italian women hit on him and having explicit visions like a super horny oracle.

"How the hell is that not appropriate?" he asks.

Shit shit shit. I have to get him off this topic. He can't know where my head went when that woman touched his arm, the urge to rip it away from his body and replace every woman's touch with my own.

But that's the perfect solution. Turn my weird comment around to the person who made me lose my mind in the first place.

"I don't know if your girl would appreciate you undressing another woman," I say with a wiggle of my eyebrows.

He steps toward me. "Yes, Anonymous Woman's heart would break."

I pinch my lips between my teeth to keep from laughing again, taking a step back before his hand can land on my arm. "I'd never disrespect Anonymous like that."

His eyebrows shoot up, and he takes another step forward with an infuriatingly sexy smirk on his face. "Of course not. And me seeing your bare back would be the ultimate disrespect."

I start backing away from him, my heart galloping in my chest as he continues to advance. "I'm a girl's girl."

He lets out a sharp laugh, stalking me around the living room with a predatory gleam in his eyes. "Very funny, Quinn. Give it up."

"You'll never catch me!"

When he lunges, I squeal, twirling away and bolting across the room. He's a step behind, his laughter echoing through the room. I'm sure I have him beat, but as I round the dining room table, I find the bench pulled out, blocking my exit. I stop short to avoid hitting it, Colton's arms encircling my waist as he collides with me, barely keeping us from toppling over.

Laughter racks my body until I look up at him, and all traces of amusement disappear in an instant. He's watching me with the same greedy expression from that day in my apartment with the lingerie clutched between us. He takes one small step away, letting his hands slide across my stomach before settling on my hips.

"You're a menace," he says, voice low, his breath coasting over my cheek and shooting electricity down my spine. "Now, shut up so I can get you out of this dress."

I don't trust my voice, so I settle for a whispered, "Okay."

I shiver when his fingertips brush the nape of my neck. He grabs the metal pull, working it down. The rest of the room disappears, the noise of the city fading away until all I can hear is the sound of Colton exposing my back.

A quarter of the way down, it catches. Colton tugs, trying to free it.

"Goddamnit," he says as he tries pulling from different angles. A laugh bubbles up in my throat as the tension in the room fades. This feels like us, me laughing and him scowling.

Finally, the zipper breaks free and Colton continues its trek down. He lets out a victorious whoop.

"So proud of yourself," I say with a glance over my shoulder, not realizing he'd shifted closer. Our eyes lock in on each other, and my stomach swoops.

"It's the small victories," he says, maintaining eye contact as he starts unzipping the dress again, more slowly this time, like he's savoring each click of the teeth. My spine curves slightly as his thumb follows the line down to the top of my ass, and a little sigh escapes my throat.

We still haven't looked away, and every cell in my body feels like it's vibrating. His thumbs hook on either side of the material, running up my naked back. The straps fall from my shoulders, the dress held up by my arm across my chest.

His fingertips skim over my shoulders, his eyes tracking the progress as they flit over the draped fabric.

"Wasn't too disrespectful, right?" he asks, his voice teasing, but he's breathing as heavily as I am. "Modesty intact. Strategic hand placement, like an ancient statue of Aphrodite."

I swallow thickly, trying to gather back my scattered brain cells so I can think with something besides the heavy ache between my legs.

"I'm disappointed in you," I say, forcing levity into my voice. Colton's gaze flies to mine. "This is Rome. I'm not Aphrodite. I'm Venus."

His eyes flare.

"Fuck it," he whispers.

A second later, his mouth descends on mine.

It's... fuck. It's perfect, with the exact right pressure before he nips at my lip, begging me to join him in the madness. I whimper into his mouth, my own opening for him as he deepens the kiss. He kisses me like we've been doing it for weeks, months, years, and he's spent every second studying exactly what I liked. This doesn't feel like our first.

"Delicious," Colton murmurs into my mouth. "Just like I knew you'd be."

I turn to face him fully, releasing my hold on the dress so it pools around my waist, and he wastes no time pushing it over my hips. It falls to the floor in a heap, leaving me in nothing but my lace underwear. Colton steps back to take me in, a low, desperate groan tearing from his throat.

"Quinn," he murmurs, his fingertips making a trek from my hip bone up to my breast. His hand trembles slightly, the only outward sign that he's as affected by this moment as I am. We both moan as his hand closes over me.

He brings his mouth to my neck, his tongue stroking the wildly beating pulse point. My hands can't stop moving, exploring his chest and shoulders the way I wanted to when I ran into him after his shower, slipping underneath the hem of his shirt to savor the hard panes of his body. Colton moves down to my breast, taking my nipple between his teeth, and a shudder rolls through me.

"Shit, Colton. Yes."

He groans against my sensitive flesh, growling, "Say it again," into the hollow between my breasts before taking the second nipple between his lips.

I can't focus beyond the overwhelming pleasure of his mouth. "What?"

He stands to his full height then, towering over me as he wraps my hair around his hand to tilt my head back. His eyes are blown black, feral and sexy as hell. "Say my name, Quinn."

"Colt—"

He smashes his mouth back into mine before I can get the final syllable out, like he can consume his name on my lips, like he can claim me with a kiss. And I want that, want this man who seems to know my body on pure instinct to lay a claim to me in a way that will ruin me for all other people.

Colton's other hand comes around to the small of my back, pulling me against him so I can feel how hard he is. He walks me back toward his bedroom, never breaking contact, until he has me pinned to his bedroom door. I rip my mouth away from him, sucking in heaving breaths as his lips move across my jaw and back down my throat. His tongue against my skin is all-consuming.

He whispers words against my neck, nothing more than sounds pressed into my skin until a few float up. "Perfect. So goddamn perfect for me."

"Please, Colton. Please touch me. I need it."

He slowly slides his hands over my soft stomach until they dip under the lace, pulling back to watch my face with a fascinated gleam in his deep green eyes. "Is this where you need me, Chaos?"

I nod quickly, and his lips quirk up, just enough to give me that adorable dimple. The compulsion to reach up and run my thumb over the indent is strong, but it's washed away when his fingers slip down another inch to find how soaked I am.

He drops his head into the crook of my neck. "Quinn. You're so fucking wet. So sweet and ready for me, aren't you?"

"Yes," I say, more breath than word as he circles my clit. "More."

The curve of his smile against my skin is almost as erotic as his fingers, slipping inside of me and creating the perfect feeling of fullness as his thumb takes over on my clit. "Whatever you need, Chaos. Anything you need, I'll give it to you."

I need him, around me and in me, as overwhelmed by this insanity as I am. But I'm too close to use my words anymore. All I can do is clutch to his waist and force myself to breathe.

"Yes, Quinn," he says, pulling back to look at me. "Come for me. Fuck, I need to see it. You have no fucking idea how badly I need to see it."

And then it crashes into me, and I'm crying out, close to sobbing at the relief as the most powerful orgasm of my life wracks my body.

I tremble as I slowly come down from the highest of highs. When I open my eyes, Colt's watching me, heat and promise and reverence in his gaze. He holds eye contact as he slips his fingers out of my underwear and between his own lips, his eyes closing on a groan as he samples me.

"Fuck, Chaos. I always knew you'd be my favorite flavor."

I want to stay in the moment, to push this man onto his back and ride him until we both forget our names. But one word in that sentence hooks its claws in my chest and won't let go, no matter how hard I try to shake free.

Always.

"What?" I ask, slipping out from between him and the door. Colton collapses forward, arms braced like his body can't catch up to the sudden loss of contact. He lets his head fall forward, banging lightly against the wood.

He's gorgeous like this, half undone, hair mussed from my hands and lips swollen from my own. My body screams to keep going, begging to see just how beautiful he'll be when he's undone completely.

But that word repeats in my head. *Always, always, always.* This attraction isn't new for him.

"What do you mean, *always*?" I ask.

He pulls himself straight, running a hand down his face. "We don't need to talk about this."

"I think we do," I say frantically.

Colt rubs the back of his neck. "Come on, Quinn, who isn't attracted to you?"

I've received plenty of romantic attention, even though society tells me I'm not desirable as a plus-size woman. But Colton never gave me any sign that he was interested in me until things started getting complicated this summer. Or had he, and I'd been completely oblivious?

"Why didn't you tell me?" I ask.

He shrugs. "Didn't seem relevant."

"Didn't seem relevant?" I shout, and he shrugs again.

I start pacing our living room, my mind whirling. He's been attracted to me from the start. How did I not see it? And what does it mean now? Does he want something more with me, or is he just physically attracted to me? If he wants something, can I give it to him? Am I even capable of being in a stable relationship, or will I self-sabotage like I have so many other times until eventually our relationship implodes and takes our friendship with it?

"I'm freaking the fuck out, Colton."

He takes me by the shoulders, leaning down to bring our faces level. "Will I probably always be attracted to you? Yes. Look in a mirror. But I love our friendship. I'm not asking you for more, so please stop spiraling about what this means. We're us, and in the choice between your friendship for life or a hookup, I'd choose you every time. No contest."

A hookup.

I know that's what this is. He just talked to me last weekend about not wanting a relationship—not being able or willing to put someone's needs before his own—but the way my heart clenches, I don't know if I can do my usual friends-with-benefits thing this time. He's too precious, and it's too complicated.

"You're right," I say, stepping back. "We're best friends, and we shouldn't mess with that. Starting now, no more funny business."

He scoffs. "Funny business?"

"Yes," I say, planting my hands on my hips. "No more kissing and touching. Just friends, right?"

He nods, turning away slightly. I just catch sight of him adjusting himself with a wince.

"You're still hard?" I ask, a laugh escaping me.

His brow lifts. "You're still naked?"

I look down at my still mostly exposed body. "Oh, shit!" I push past him and shimmy my dress back on, leaving the zipper down but myself protected. My very own gladiatorial armor.

"Are we good?" he asks.

I force a smile. "Of course."

One side of his lips hitch up. "Good." He clears his throat. "I'm gonna take a quick shower."

I snort. "Sure. Makes sense." I press my lips together to keep in my laugh.

He shakes his head, his eyes sparkling. "Don't be a dick."

I lift a hand. "I wouldn't dream of it. Go take care of yours."

He runs a hand over his mouth, ineffectively hiding his smile. "You're gonna think about it, aren't you?"

I swallow thickly. "Of course not."

One eyebrow lifts, and it's infuriatingly sexy. "Not even a little curious?"

I squirm under his gaze. Of course I'm curious. I want to know what he looks like when he's lost to his pleasure. Do his shoulders slump forward when he finishes? Or do his muscles go taut, his head thrown back in pleasure and exposing the line of his neck? Will he think of me?

His smirk grows. "Only seems fair, don't you think? I saw you. Seems a bit imbalanced."

"Colton," I say, a reprimand in my tone.

He lifts his hands, backing toward the bathroom. "Your choice. You know where I'll be."

He slips into the bathroom, giving me one last heated look before letting the door swing closed between us.

16

COLTON

I'M WELL and truly fucked.

I'll spend the rest of my life thinking about Quinn's mouth. Nothing else will compare. Not now that I know she tastes like summer—fresh and light with a touch of lemon, even through the bite of the alcohol. It's like the citrusy smell that's haunted me since we met is so much a part of her that I could taste it on her tongue. Not when I've heard the sounds that leave her lips—the little whimpers that give way to low moans when she loses herself to pleasure. When *I* make her lose herself.

I fist my dick before the shower door's fully closed, my other palm slamming against the tile wall of our tiny shower as the hot water pours over my body. My mind has conjured all sorts of images of Quinn over the years, but this is different. The sounds in my head aren't manufactured. The image behind my eyes of Quinn's face—her brows pulled together and her mouth dropped open—isn't a guess of what she looks like. Her sweet taste is still on my tongue.

And I've never been so hard in my life.

I grip the base of my cock, trying to slow down the release that's headed my way with the speed of a train. This should be drawn out. Savored. The memory of us together will never be as fresh as it is right now, and I want to soak in every second possible.

I slowly stroke up, letting my hand drift over the sensitive head as I remember the way her hands slipped under my shirt and her nails dragged over my abs. In my head, it's Quinn touching me, letting her exploration go lower. It's her hand wrapped around me.

"Fuck," I groan. "Quinn."

The wooden bathroom door creaks, like someone's leaning against the other side, and I pause. As much as I teased Quinn about joining me, I didn't think she would. She was so freaked, and I figured she'd pretend like it never happened. But she's there, too curious to walk away, and I can't help the way my lips curve up.

"Chaos?" I call out.

I hear a little squeak, then nothing for a few seconds. But I'm patient. She's worth the wait.

"Yes?" she finally answers, and her voice is higher than usual.

I sigh in relief. "Get your ass in here."

There's another pause, and then the door slowly opens, her body slipping through the crack before she leans against it. I turn to face her, the warm water running over my shoulders and down my chest.

The glass walls of the shower leave all of me exposed to her eyes, and my balls tighten when her gaze slides down my body, pausing for a long moment on my cock before they fly back up to my eyes. Pink stains her cheeks, and she's so beautiful like this that I can't hold in my groan as I give myself a rough tug.

"Are you coming in?" I ask. "It'll be a tight fit, but we can make it work."

Quinn shivers at the innuendo, her eyes flicking back to my cock. I love my usual talkative Quinn, but there's something so sexy about her being shocked into silence by my body.

"Quinn?" I prompt when she doesn't answer me.

Her eyes fly back to mine, and she shakes her head. "Can I... I want to watch."

I give myself another rough tug. If it were my choice, I'd have her in here with me. I want another chance to feel her, to have her wet, thick curves pushed against the hard lines of my body, but fuck, there's something so hot about her wanting to watch me.

"Whatever you want, Chaos, but talk to me. I want to hear your voice while I make myself come."

She whimpers, and my eyes drop to where her thighs squeeze together, seeking some relief. I want to ask her to drop her dress again, to let me watch her while I touch myself, but I don't want to push her too far.

"What were you thinking about?" she asks.

"You," I say, my eyes roving over her body. "About how if you hadn't stopped me, I'd have gone down to my knees and gotten a taste straight from the source."

She whines, and the sound is like a caress. Her soft noises and the warm water and my tight grip almost send me over the edge, but I slow down, pulling myself back from the edge at the last second.

"The sounds you make," I say, my breath coming faster. "They're gonna be the fucking death of me."

"Colt." My name is a moan on her lips, and I groan in response.

"Keep. Talking," I say through gritted teeth, my hand speeding up. "And keep those eyes on me."

She bites her lip. "I wish I was in there with you. I wish I could touch you."

Holy fucking shit. Her saying she wants to touch me is the hottest thing that's ever happened in my thirty-two years of life. "Fuck, I'm gonna come, Chaos."

"Please," she says, more whimper than word. "Let me see it."

That's all I need, every muscle going taut as my body jerks, my release painting the glass that separates us as I chant her name. I'm tempted to close my eyes as the sensations flood my body, but I don't want to miss a second of Quinn, so I keep my gaze pinned to her through it all as I continue to rock my hips, wringing out every ounce of pleasure possible.

Once I finish, Quinn lets her body collapse against the door, her eyes falling closed.

I'm breathing heavily, and my head finally drops forward, breaking my view of Quinn. "Fuck, Chaos. That was hot."

Hot doesn't begin to cover it. That was an out-of-body experience. The most erotic sexual interaction of my life, and she never even touched me.

"Yeah. But we can't do it again," she says, and my head pops back up. "We're even now."

I catch her eye through the glass, holding her gaze for a long second—one where I consider yanking the glass door open and tugging her in here with me, kissing her until she forgets about the lines she's drawn. But in the end, I nod, and she slips out the door, leaving me with nothing but her scent hanging in the air.

I slump against the side of the shower as the adrenaline leaves my body. The contrast between the cold tile and hot water helps clear my head.

She's right to call it off.

If she thinks sleeping together would ruin our relationship, I don't want to take the risk. Her friendship's the only thing I want more than a night with her.

So I'll leave it be and let the memory of her taste on my lips sustain me for the next fifty to sixty years.

Fuck.

THE NEXT MORNING, I pace the living room, glancing at the clock every ten seconds. The minutes are ticking down, and Quinn's door still hasn't opened.

She doesn't have to come with us this morning. None of the other faculty members chose to, but I thought she would. I'm hosting a tour of the Colosseum and Roman Forum for the students, open to the whole program, but elective for anyone who isn't in my class.

Quinn sleeping in shouldn't surprise me. She's done this tour a dozen times between her dad and our study abroad. Why would she choose to stand out in the blistering heat for a couple of hours just because I'm the one leading it?

Inez pops her head around the corner. "We need to leave if we want to beat the students there."

I send one last pathetic, longing glance at Quinn's closed door before following Inez out.

The line for the Colosseum is already a mile long by the time we get there. Thank fuck for educational passes that let us hop the line. I try not to smirk at the glaring tourists as I lead about seventy-five students past them.

The words flow from me without a thought. I've done this tour enough that it's a mindless task. My mouth talks about tunnels and pulley systems and gladiators fighting lions, but my mind's on Quinn.

Is she hiding? Did she avoid coming this morning because she regrets last night? Did we already ruin our friendship?

By the time we finish the Colosseum, the students are already dragging. We still have the whole forum to tour, and it'll be even hotter without any shade to give us a break from the brutal summer sun.

I let Inez take the lead, gathering, counting, and leading the students across the Piazza del Colosseo to the center of Roman life. The piazza's packed, as usual. Massive tour groups, pop-up stalls selling kitschy souvenirs, Italian men in plastic gladiator armor charging ten euros for a picture, and I take up the rear to make sure we don't lose anyone on the walk.

The Italian stone pines shoot up on either side of the path once we escape the main piazza, their high, wide canopies casting shade over the sidewalk. I close my eyes for a moment, enjoying the way this bit of cover keeps the cement from heating like an oven. When I open my eyes again, the group's a dozen feet away, and I heave out a sigh. We have another hour of this before I can escape into the air conditioning.

"I'm here. I'm here!" Quinn calls out, and I turn to find her rushing toward me. "Sorry! I fell back asleep after my alarm went off."

I glance over at the students, who keep following Inez like good baby ducks. "If you were one of my students, I'd tell you to get lost if you can't make it on time."

She drops her voice, even though the students are far away. "If I were one of your students, you'd be fired for last night."

I pull in a deep breath, fighting the urge to reach for her. "So we aren't pretending it never happened, then?"

I watch her out of the corner of my eye as her teeth worry her bottom lip. "Is that what you want?"

"I don't fucking know. What do you want?"

She takes a deep breath, her hands clenched in resolve. "I'm not good at filtering myself, and I don't want to start now. We've always been able to talk about everything. It happened. It was weird. One day, it'll be a funny joke between us."

I can't swallow around the lump in my throat. "Weird?"

"I don't mean weird like bad! I mean it was weird because we're us, you know? But it was great. Like, really great. But weird. Right?"

A pessimistic scoff tears from my throat. "Don't hurt yourself, Chaos. It's fine."

She sighs. "I'm just worried."

I know where it comes from. She's been taught that when

things get difficult, the people who love her walk away. I'll show her, however long it takes, that I'll never leave her.

I pull her to a stop, positioning her with her back to the students disappearing into the forum, oblivious to what their professors are getting up to behind them. I take her face between both of my hands and plant a fast kiss on her forehead before forcing her to meet my eyes.

"You won't lose me. Ever. Stop stressing about something that isn't going to happen. You're stuck with me forever, for better or for worse."

Her laugh, low and smooth, lights me up. "Did you just say vows to me, Colton Miller?"

I drop my hands and roll my eyes, walking around her to catch up with the group. "It's a turn of phrase, Quinn. And I'll be much more creative when I say vows to my future wife."

There'll be no future wife. I'll have casual relationships and fun hookups, but I won't subject a woman to a life with a man who can't give her his full heart.

We make it to the Arch of Titus, the epic entrance to the Forum, and I'm all business again. Inez drops to the back of the group with Quinn while I take on the role of Dr. Miller, who has to be engaging enough to keep seventy-five kids in their early twenties interested in rocks and ruins in ninety degree heat.

It's not working. I'm losing them. I'm losing myself, and I live for this shit. It's too hot. We should have split this up over a couple of days instead of tackling it all at once.

"The ruin behind me was one of the most important spots in Rome: the temple of Vesta, the goddess of the hearth. The Romans believed if the fire that burned here went out, Rome itself would fall."

"Can't be that strong of an empire if a burned out fire would bring it down," one student says, gaining laughs from her friends.

I chuckle along with them. "The power of superstition. Or faith. Depends on who you're speaking with."

"The temple is famous for its vestal virgins. Romans considered the role to be the greatest honor for both the women and their families. They protected the fire, among other responsibilities, including the obvious one their name would imply—*maintaining their virtue.* The punishment for not doing so was extreme: the government would bury them alive."

I look out at the wide eyes of the students. That fact never fails to shock. The idea of lifelong celibacy on the threat of death is inconceivable for these twenty-somethings.

One frat bro laughs. "Good thing Rome doesn't do that anymore, because all the chicks in our program would be six feet under."

I walk over to him. "I figure most of our program would be buried. But at least we'd have you around to tell our story."

I clap him on the shoulder while the other students holler at his expense. Quinn snorts—that ridiculous yet somehow perfect sound—and I can't hold back the smile that splits my face.

When I turn to the students, they're staring. Mouths agape and eyes wide. A few shoot excited glances at each other, then back at me and Quinn. I school my face and clap my hands together to get everyone on track as I walk to the front of the group. "That's the last inappropriate comment we'll hear in this class. And yes, even those of you who aren't in my class are in class if you decide to join one of these excursions. Got it?"

The students nod.

"We're done for today, so explore for as long as you'd like. I'd suggest climbing to the top of the Palatine Hill to see the view before leaving. You're free. Get the hell out of here."

The students scurry off like ants. Some of them head straight for the slope to Augustus's palace at the top of the hill, and I hang back to give them some space.

Quinn comes to lean with me on the boulder, Inez on her other side. Who knows what this one boulder has seen in the millennia since Rome's height, and we're using it as a bench. "Calling out a student's virginal status in class?"

"He's a dick and needed to be put in his place. I'm not dealing with that bullshit all summer because he thinks putting down women for having sex makes him cool."

She laughs next to me, a soft sound that burrows under my skin.

"I'm going to head up the hill," Inez says from her other side. "Anyone joining me?"

"Let's climb," I say, as much to burn off this energy as to see the view.

We reach the top, walking through Augustus's gardens before finding a spot at the railing overlooking the city. This is one of Rome's historical hills, a peak that sits over the bustling ancient city. I close my eyes, breathing in the scent of the flowers and letting myself imagine the great emperors of Rome in the same location, looking down at the houses and politics and commerce that all depended on their choices.

I think—for the thousandth time—about how I almost missed this. How I almost let my fear, my belief that I wasn't good enough to make it, keep me away. Now that I have it, I'm not letting it go.

"It's gorgeous up here," Inez says, and I open my eyes to find both women staring out at the ancient metropolis.

"It's always been my favorite spot," I say.

Quinn sighs. "That was my problem. I've always loved Rome, but I love the modern city. Honestly, besides the palace, I kind of hate walking through the ruins. It's hot and miserable. I was never like you or my dad, who felt a connection to these dead people."

The memory of Quinn and Richard's exchange at Giolitti makes me sick. I know the issues go deeper than her losing the fellowship, but it seems like the catalyst. I can't shake the guilt.

"Why did you come today?" I ask Quinn.

Her eyebrows pull together, and a teasing smile pulls on the corner of her mouth. "To hear you, of course."

My heart explodes.

A strand of blond hair floats across her face from the wind. I tuck it behind her ear and let my finger run down the line of her jaw for a second before pulling my hand back. Her eyes go a bit frantic, then she abruptly turns back to the view, clearing her throat.

"I'm going to head out," she says.

"We'll come with you," Inez says, walking over to the bench where she set her bag.

"No need," Quinn says quickly, shooting a nervous glance in my direction. "I think I'm going to go take a nap. Tired from the late night out."

Quinn's never been a napper, especially after sleeping in, and the way she steadily keeps her eyes away from me makes it perfectly clear this is more about avoiding me than anything.

I shove my hand in my pocket to keep from reaching out. I owe it to her to keep this strange urge under control. Quinn's the reason I'm here, the one who kept me afloat when my life almost fell apart around me, and losing her would be like a ship losing its anchor. I can't let that happen.

I've wrangled these impulses into submission for fourteen years, I can find the way to do it again.

COLTON

FOURTEEN YEARS AGO

QUINN KEEPS her back straight as she stares down the administrative assistant at the desk across from her. She has on a professional outfit, a pencil skirt and blouse that's bringing up sexy librarian fantasies I didn't realize I had until now.

I'm less confident, but no less professional looking in my slacks and button down.

"I still don't see why I had to wear my damn church clothes," I murmur.

"Because we want him to take us seriously," Quinn hisses. "We don't want him thinking we're some ignorant freshmen he can push around."

"We *are* ignorant freshmen he can push around," I grumble.

The door of the department chair's office opens, and a stern-looking man steps out.

"Mr. Miller and Miss Riley?"

Quinn stands and smooths down her skirt. She marches over with her hand outstretched, like we're meeting him for a multi-million dollar merger. He smiles at us like the kids we are as he shakes it.

How the hell did she talk me into this?

I have no idea what we're doing. I didn't even know what a damn department chair *was* until she explained it. But this is her world. She said her mom's the chair of her psychology department. Her dad's the only name bigger than Dr. Cassia's in their field. Her two oldest brothers already finished their PhDs, and her youngest brother is well on his way to his, too. If she says this is the right call, then that's what we'll do.

"Thank you, Dr. Murphy, for agreeing to hear our concerns," she says.

He laughs, like we're an amusing distraction from his important duties, and I shrink further into myself. Maybe I can disappear now and save Chadoin the work of kicking me out. Dr. Murphy gestures toward his office and we follow him inside.

Once we're seated, Dr. Murphy turns to me.

"Mr. Miller, can you explain to me why we're meeting today?"

I wipe my hands on my slacks, sweat breaking out on my brow. Quinn gives my foot a reassuring nudge.

"Well, you see, sir, I've been havin' a bit of trouble with my classes this semester. My advisor and I met last week, and the meeting didn't go too well. Quinn thought it would be..." She puts pressure on my toes with her foot. "*We* thought it would be a good idea to discuss the situation with you."

"How did the meeting not *go too well?*"

"He told me I was going to flunk out and that perhaps I'm not cut out for Chadoin, or college in general."

Dr. Murphy nods thoughtfully. "I can imagine that would be difficult to hear. But it's the responsibility of our professors to give students feedback on their performance."

"With all due respect, Dr. Murphy, you're wrong. That's not what this professor was doing, and I think you know it." Quinn cuts in.

He rears back.

"Now, excuse me, young lady." He puffs himself up, ready to

light into her, but she isn't having it. She jumps to her feet, standing at the edge of his desk.

"No, sir, I don't excuse you. I've spent my whole life on campuses. I've seen deans and department chairs and professors with all different approaches to how they work with students. But there is one trait that's always consistent with the good ones, the ones worthy of the title of professor. They don't give up on students who are willing to put in the work to improve, especially not a few months into college.

"This young man is extraordinary. He came here with no family or friends to guide him. He's done *everything* himself. Chadoin gave him a full-ride scholarship because they saw that work ethic. They saw his potential. There are resources here on campus that Colton didn't even know about because his *advisor*, if we can call him that, couldn't be bothered to tell him."

Quinn clenches her jaw and holds her chin high. I can't pull my eyes away from her. She's ferocious and confident and eloquent. And all to support me.

I've never had someone willing to fight on my behalf.

And I've never loved anyone like I love Quinn.

She turns to me. "Did your advisor ask why you're struggling?" I shake my head. "Did he tell you about tutoring services?" Another shake. "The Writing Center? Office hours where you could talk to your professors?" Another shake. She turns her attention back to Dr. Murphy. "What's the point of having these resources if you don't tell students about them?"

Dr. Murphy waves his hand. "I'm sure Dr. Christensen is planning to send those resources."

She leans over his desk, hands planted, eyes boring down on him. "He told him the university wouldn't waste any more money on him. Does that sound like the words of someone who plans to provide resources?"

Dr. Murphy has the sense to look ashamed. "You're right.

That's an inappropriate comment for a faculty member, and I'll speak with him."

"I also expect your support when he approaches his professors about his grades." *Goddamn, she's ballsy.* She lays a sheet on the desk in front of him. "Here's the plan we've written out."

Dr. Murphy's eyes scan the page, his eyebrows raising. "This is impressive, Ms. Riley. More thorough than most of our advisors."

"That says more about your advisors than it says about me, sir," she says, but the small flush that covers her cheeks betrays how pleased she is. She worked hard on it and deserves all the praise she can get.

Dr. Murphy passes the sheet back to Quinn. "I'll tell his professors he's coming, but he has to do the work himself."

"We're not asking you to hand him better grades. We're asking for a chance for him to improve without being treated like dirt. Chadoin University is an exceptional institution. Much better than it's shown itself to be toward Colton."

With that mic drop, she pulls me toward the door before Dr. Murphy can come to his senses and realize we had no right to demand anything of him.

Before we can escape, he calls out, "What are you studying, Miss Riley?"

She turns back to look at him. "Classical civilizations. Why?"

"A shame. You'd be a shark in the boardroom. We could use that in our program."

"I'm only a shark when someone I care about isn't being treated right. I'm sorry to say your sales metrics could never rile me up like that. But thank you for your support."

"You're welcome. And Mr. Miller?"

I stiffen, waiting for whatever new insult will be hurled my way.

"Sometimes a student's grades are low because the transition to college is hard, but sometimes it's because they're in the wrong field. Your grade is nearly perfect in your history class. Ask yourself why you're studying business. That might be the first step to getting where you need to be."

Quinn and I walk in silence through the outer offices, through the hallways and courtyards as we make our way across campus. Dr. Murphy's question plays on repeat in my mind. Why am I studying business? Because it feels safe? Because it's what Momma and I talked about all those years, me getting a business degree and making something of myself for both our sakes?

Quinn vibrates with energy beside me. She's waiting for me to say something, but I can't think past the arguments swirling around in my head. Plus, I'm worried if I open my mouth, I'll declare my undying love like a total ass.

Quinn eventually breaks. "Okay, are you mad at me? I should have let you take the lead, and I came in and bulldozed everything. Please tell me how you're feeling because I'm losing my mind."

I pull her in for a hug, pressing a hard kiss to her forehead. It's too far, but I can't stop myself. It isn't even a romantic kiss. The kiss is because of everything she is. Kind, supportive, tough. And mine. Maybe not my girlfriend, but she's still mine.

"I'm not mad. You're a fucking superhero."

She blinks away tears. "Really?"

"Yes, Quinn. No one's ever had my back like that. It was incredible. Thank you."

"You're welcome." She tucks herself under my arm as we walk over to the dining hall for lunch.

"I was thinking about Dr. Murphy's comment," I say.

"Oh, yeah? What about it?"

"I majored in business because it seemed like a smart move, but I hate my classes. And it can't be a smart move if I'm gonna flunk out because I'm miserable."

"So what *do* you like, then?"

"I love our Rome class. But what the hell would I do with a degree in that?"

She raises a brow. "You realize you're talking to someone getting a degree in that, right?"

"Yeah, but you're gonna be a fancy professor, and that's amazing, but so few people get to do that. My mom's counting on me to get a good job after graduation. I can't just study what's fun."

"Why not? You can get a good job studying anything if you put in the work to figure it out. Would you rather take the easy route now and be miserable for the next fifty years, or research your options and be happier in the long run?"

It's a fair—if fucking terrifying—point. "Can I really throw away all my plans?"

Quinn shrugs. "What we want out of life can change with new experiences, and I think the best thing we can do is follow that instinct wherever it leads."

I run a hand through my hair. "And what if I'm not good enough to make it?"

"You'll never know unless you try." Quinn's smile is soft. "Maybe you won't become a professor, but you're smart and passionate. And you have a very, *very* pushy best friend who wants to see you succeed. You'll be fine. And if you *do* decide to go the professor route, I happen to know a pretty well-respected member in that field."

She wiggles her eyebrows at me and I laugh.

"Dr. Colton Miller has a nice ring to it, doesn't it?" she asks.

Who knows? Crazier things have happened.

QUINN

JUNE — SEVEN WEEKS TO WIN OVER THE FACULTY

I'M FINE.

Completely and totally fine.

I'm not hiding in my room. My books just need organizing.

I'm not avoiding Colton. It just so happens that our schedules have been opposite since *that* night.

That epic night.

Get yourself under control, you horny bitch.

I thought we were fine, but when Colton touched me at the forum, I felt the electricity of it through every inch of my body. I wanted to climb him like a tree, and at the same time, I was terrified by the reaction. What if I can't get this under control? I'll lose him.

My bedroom door creaks open and Inez peeks her head in.

"She's dressed," she says, over her shoulder. A second later, she and Colton push into my room.

"What are you doing?" I sputter as she throws herself next to me on the bed and Colton walks to my closet, sliding the hangers one by one along the metal pole.

"You've been weird," Colton says without looking away from his search.

"No, I haven't! I've just been busy."

"Nope, you've been weird," Inez says, lowering her voice. "Is this because of me? The job stuff?"

I squeeze her hand. "No, not at all."

I'm still worried about her leaving, obviously, but I feel more positive after my conversation with Andrea. I'm being weird because a week ago I had my other best friend's hand down my underwear and then talked him through his own orgasm, which is totally fine and I'm super chill and not at all freaking out.

My eyes shoot to Colton's, who has finally looked back at me, and I give my head the smallest of shakes so he understands I haven't looped Inez in on the latest… developments. She's perfect and lovely and supportive, but she's also a surprisingly pushy hopeless romantic who already thinks Colt and I should be together, and I don't need her getting ideas.

"It's just been a lot all at once," I say, my eyes still locked on Colton's, and he nods slightly.

Inez grabs my hand. "Well, we're here to break you out of it."

"So because I've been weird, not saying I agree"—I've definitely been weird—"you're messing around in my closet?"

"We're going out tonight," Colton says, eyes back on the shirts and dresses.

"How do you know I'm not busy?" I ask indignantly.

He turns and points back and forth between me and Inez. "Because you two are codependent and she'd know if you had plans."

"We're not codependent." I turn to Inez for back up.

She scrunches up her nose. "You come into the office to have me check your breath before each class."

"The room is tiny! I don't want to subject my students to onion breath!"

Colton raises an eyebrow. "Codependent."

I raise a brow and lean toward him. "Jealous?"

His lip quirks in that not-quite smile. "I plead the fifth."

I huff a laugh. "Fine. Where are we going?"

As I ask, he pulls something from the closet and tosses it on the bed—a red floor-length gown with stunning embroidery. I raise an eyebrow.

"We're going to *Turandot*." He holds up his hand to stop me when I open my mouth. "And, yes, I know you're going to say it's flawed, but it's the only thing playing right now, so you're shit out of luck."

I've loved the opera my entire life. The magnitude and drama of it all. Everything's big. The costumes and the sets and the voices. Their extreme emotions are revered, and for someone who was constantly told her enthusiasm and joy—everything about her, really—needed to be tamped down, it's a relief to sit with something even bigger.

I dragged Colton to plenty of shows during our college years, and he didn't care for it nearly as much as I did. In other words, it put him to sleep. Literally—every time. It got so ridiculous that we started making bets on how long he'd last, and whoever won got to choose the next movie night. I ended up spending half of those shows watching him instead of the stage.

I raise an eyebrow. "You hate the opera."

He smirks. "Yes, but you love the opera. They're at the Baths of Caracalla, so there's a little something for me, too."

The Baths were one of the largest structures of Roman life; brick, concrete, and marble mixed together to create a towering complex. Like almost everything from ancient Rome, it fell to ruins over a millennium ago.

The ruins are beautiful in their own right, but a few times a month, the Rome Opera House sets up a stage within the structure. It breathes new life into the crumbling construction and gives audience members a one-of-a-kind experience.

Inez gathers the pile of fabric onto her lap. "Quinn, this is an actual gown. Why did you pack a gown?"

My brow furrows. "I said I packed for every potential activity."

Her eyes bug out. "Some people will be in jeans and t-shirts, and you can't wear a sundress?"

"Just because *they're* going to be underdressed doesn't mean I have to be. There are—"

"Few opportunities to get dressed up, and the opera deserves our respect," Colton finishes in a ridiculous impression of me. I toss my pillow at him, and he stretches one arm straight in front of him, snatching it out of the air before it comes close to making contact. It's hot, and I hate him for it.

Inez stands, shaking out the dress so she can lay it flat on my bed before heading to the door. "I personally didn't pack something fit for the Oscars."

"Boo," I call at her back, and she laughs, her long dark curls shaking behind her. "I'm gonna look silly dressed up all by myself."

Colton walks over to the bed, tossing my pillow back and forth between his hands. "Don't worry. I have a suit."

I'm too busy picturing Colton in a suit to notice the pillow flying at my face.

FUCK ME, that's a suit.

This isn't my first time seeing Colton in one, but that was back when we were in school, when what he wore was practically an ill-fitting bag, a hand-me-down from some guy in his hometown. He used to yank the sides of the gray jacket over his chest, like tugging the fabric would make it magically alter to his slim body. It'd been almost compulsive when we sat at the banquet for the Harrow Fellowship, a bunch of kids dolled up just in case we were the one out of five to have their lives changed overnight.

This is *not* that suit. The black fabric's perfectly fitted to the lines of his body, his sleek tie the perfect, tempting tool to grab and yank him forward. He still fiddles with his clothes, but now when he tugs on the sleeve of his shirt, it's like watching one of those ridiculous but somehow still hot as hell cologne commercials play out in real life.

Colton's eyes land on me, and I can feel his gaze as it follows the path of my formfitting dress, clocking the slit that comes to my upper thigh. I shiver under his watch, and all my concerns from earlier come flying back. How are we supposed to move forward with all of... whatever this is between us?

His eyes settle on the curve of my hip, and I heat up to the point of near combustion. I have to tell him this is too much, that I need time and space to reset and get rid of this sexual tension so we can be us again. I'll never move past it when he looks at me like that.

"You may want to pull the dress out of your underwear before we leave," he says with that little lip quirk, and all those warm, confusing feelings fly out the window.

He isn't checking me out. My ass is hanging out. Anyone would notice that, and thankfully he's kind enough to point it out instead of awkwardly ignoring my little show.

I tug the material and smooth it out. "You're a fashionista now?"

He chuckles, and I love that rumbling sound. "Don't need to be a fashion designer to know dresses aren't supposed to break public decency laws."

"Tell that to Rihanna."

He keeps fiddling with his sleeves and jacket. At first, I think it's because he feels as awkward as I do with all of this, but then he starts bouncing on his toes like he's physically incapable of staying still.

I eye him speculatively. "What's going on with you?"

"What do you mean?" he asks, the words coming out in a rush as he glances at his watch. "Do you think Inez will be ready soon? We should probably get going. It may get crowded."

"It's less than fifteen minutes away. We'll be fine."

"Yeah, you're right. I'll take care of a few things since we have the time," he says, gathering the books I left on our dining table and dropping them in my room before rushing back to fold the throw blanket on the couch. When he moves on to straightening the decorative bowls on the shelves, I know something's up.

"Are you on something?" I ask him, only half joking.

"What? No, of course not," he answers, still moving.

"In all the years I've known you, you've never talked like that. Or *moved* like that. What drugs did you take?"

He stops walking suddenly, his body swaying forward like it hadn't expected to stop. Colton brings his hand to his heart. "I swear to you, no drugs are in my system right now." He starts moving again, then abruptly stops. "I lied to you."

"I knew it!" I yell, pointing at him.

He lifts his hands. "Not what you think, but caffeine is technically a drug."

"Caffeine?" I ask, he nods happily, bouncing on his toes again. "How much have you had?"

"Solamente tre."

"Three? You had three espressos?"

"No, doubles."

"Colton! Three double espressos? Your heart's gonna explode."

He shakes his finger at me, eyes narrowed like he's letting me in on a secret. "But I won't fall asleep."

"Because you'll be dead!"

"Colton's dying?" Inez asks as she comes bounding out of her room in a sundress completely at odds with my gown. She's glowing and adorable and perfect, and yet I still shake my head.

"You look stunning, and yet you disappoint me," I say.

She smiles and twirls, the light blue fabric making her brown skin pop as it flows around her. "Some of us have to make do without our entire wardrobe to choose from."

I sigh, loud and overly dramatic, which is perfectly on brand for a night at the opera. "You have so much to learn from me."

Colt looks at his watch again, moving to the door as he speaks. "We need to get going."

Inez sends me a questioning look, and I just shake my head as we follow him down the stairs, a good flight behind his fast, long stride.

We take a taxi instead of relying on public transportation, and Colton's knee bounces for thirteen of the fifteen minutes spent in the car. A week ago, I would have placed my hand on his leg to help calm him. I'd have leaned into him, laughing into his shoulder about the ridiculousness of the situation. But now I resist the urge, trapped inside my head, the anxious buzz of his body matching the anxious buzz in my mind.

I spot Tomasso as soon as we pull up, and my skin goes uncomfortably tight. Inez is out of the taxi and halfway to him before I can open my mouth.

I turn to Colton on my other side. "Is this a double date?"

"What?" The pitch of Colton's voice goes up several octaves and his whole body tenses.

"Sorry," I jump in, shifting the fabric of my dress so I can climb out of the cab without tripping. Colton's hot on my heels. "Obviously it's not a date. It's just I saw Tomasso and he and Inez have been so... attached this past week. I freaked myself out."

Colton smiles, but the severe lack of a dimple tells me how forced it is. "I don't want it to be like this between us."

I sigh and drop my head forward. "Me neither."

"I know last week was... intense. But we've survived worse, right? Like that time we holed up in your apartment for a week with the flu? You were so fucking gross, and I still kept you around."

"Oh yes, you cleaning up my vomit is totally the same as me watching you come all over our shower," I say, completely deadpan.

He rubs a hand over his mouth to hide his smile, but after a second, his eyes go somber. "I swear, I reached out to Tomasso because he had connections to get us last-minute tickets, and I wasn't about to tell him he couldn't come when he was helping us out."

"No, of course not."

"You have nothing to worry about. I'm just trying to enjoy this summer. This is a fun friend outing. Nothing more."

"No, I know."

"I'm serious. I'm not trying to date you. Or anyone."

I get it. I don't want to date him—or anyone—either, so I don't understand why the words feel like a grip around my lungs, making it hard to breathe.

"Now that this is sufficiently awkward," I say with a little laugh, "let's head inside."

Colton rubs his hand across his brow and gestures for me to go ahead. Inez and Tomasso, who haven't stopped talking since they met on the sidewalk, have almost reached the entry gate, and the two of us fall in step behind them on our very platonic, not at all uncomfortable friend outing.

COLTON and I both gasp when we enter the ruins, for very different reasons.

I'm blown away by the magnificence of it. When you see an opera in a theater, the stage design is elaborate. Intricate backdrops and gigantic moving set pieces to complement how massive the story is.

But not here. Why design an elaborate backdrop when it'll never be able to outdo the grandeur of the Baths of Caracalla? Instead, there's a simple, flat stage with a few props to set the scene, and it's the most glorious set I've ever seen.

Colton, on the other hand, is not amused.

He runs both hands up into his hair. "The stage is *on* the ruins! What are they doing? They're going to damage the integrity of the site!"

"Calm down," I say with a laugh. "The stage is temporary and sits above the ruins so they don't get damaged."

"I'm looking right at it! It's *on* the Baths!"

"The magic of the theater," I say with a flourish. "I promise you, proper precautions have been taken."

"I don't see how it's worth the risk," he mumbles.

"Poor Colt," I say teasingly, and his scowl fades to a soft smile. "Let's find our seats."

Inez and Tomasso have already made their way there and are talking with their heads bent together. I don't think they even look at the stage. What a waste.

Colton's still vibrating with caffeinated energy when the sun fully sets and the show begins. I can't stop myself from glancing his way every few minutes, but he sticks to his word, staying awake and ripping his paper program to pieces.

We settle back into our seats for the third act, and my whole body tightens in anticipation of *Nessum Dorma*, arguably the most epic tenor aria ever written. Prince Calaf stands in the middle of the stage, singing of his love for Princess Turandot and how he'll win her hand and her love. It's visceral, the type of all-consuming music that made me fall for the opera in the first place.

As the last *vincerò* echoes off the ruins, I look toward Colton with tears in my eyes, only to find his head tipped forward, completely passed out. I laugh, the sound swallowed up by the thundering applause that he blissfully sleeps through.

He's going to feel like crap if he sleeps like that, so I lightly tip his head to the side so it settles on my shoulder and ignore the squeeze in my chest that feels eerily similar to the way the tenor's performance made me feel. Colton stays like that for the rest of the show, sleeping peacefully through pithy recitatives and the resounding chorus and a death so heart-wrenching it has me crying again.

As the opera ends and everyone gets to their feet for the well-deserved standing ovation, I nudge Colton.

"Colt," I say quietly. "The show's over."

He tilts his head, looking up at me with a sleepy smile, then snuggles back into my shoulder.

I chuckle, and shake him more forcefully. "Time to go."

He sits up suddenly, blinking around at the other attendees, still clapping enthusiastically around us. "Son of a bitch!"

Now free from the weight of Colton's head, I stand and join in the applause. "Now we know six espressos aren't enough."

"I tried," Colton says, standing up, too.

I peek over at him. He looks genuinely upset, like this was a test he failed when really it helped something settle into place for me. We're more than an—admittedly incredible—night. Colton and I are fourteen years of history, love, and support. A couple awkward conversations can't strip away all of that. I won't let it.

"You did better than usual," I say with a smile. "But you know what this means?"

He rolls his eyes, but his dimple pops. "What are you going to make me watch this time?"

"The modern-day classic *Get Over It*. Tomorrow night. No complaining allowed," I say with mock sternness.

Colton's dimple pops. "I wouldn't miss it."

QUINN

JUNE — SIX WEEKS TO WIN OVER THE FACULTY

"Aperol Spritzes and bikinis!" I cheer as I burst into Inez's room. "Three days of hot springs and calm Mediterranean waters."

I pull up short when I realize my best friend's no more than a lump under her bedspread. "Baby girl, what's wrong?"

The blanket starts inching down. First, her fingers appear, then her tired eyes, and then her red nose. She sniffs and turns her face into the pillow. "I'm dying."

"No! But Ischia!"

She huffs out a laugh. "There's no way I'm taking a train down to Naples, walking around Pompeii in this heat, and then sitting on a ferry for an hour and a half."

We fought for this assignment. Our program has weekend trips for the students, and each requires two university representatives for liability purposes. Dr. Guarino and Andrea took the students to Venice and Verona the weekend we went to Tuscany. Dr. Keck and Sydney are taking the students to Florence in a few weeks. But we have an odd number, so when the time came to discuss the southern Italy trip—a stop at Pompeii for Colton to lecture before heading on to Ischia off the coast of Naples—Inez and I argued that we should both join.

Ischia's a small island next to Capri, less touristy but no less beautiful. It's famous for its festivals—one for each patron saint, which may outnumber the actual residents. While it's less academic than some of the other trips, we argued attending one of those festivals is a vital cultural experience.

Plus, beaches.

But now Inez can't pull herself out of bed and all that hard work's gone down the drain.

"God, this sucks," I say as I drop on the bed next to her.

"You'll be fine. We only need two representatives, so it'll still work with you and Colton."

My heart jumps. Things between me and Colt have been back to normal this week, just as long as I ignore the way my stomach dips whenever he gets close. But a weekend away? It feels risky when we're still on shaky ground.

"We need to find someone to replace me. It can't be too hard to convince one of the other professors to go to a gorgeous island for a few days, right?"

"No!" she says with too much force. "I'd feel so guilty keeping you here. You're going."

"Like hell I am. If you're dying, then I'll be here feeding you soup until the end."

She scooches up to the headboard and lays her head on my shoulder. "I love you. You know that?"

"Good, 'cause it would be awkward as fuck if you didn't when I'm obsessed with you."

She laughs. "I'm not letting you miss Ischia. I feel like death, but I'm not *actually* dying. It's just a crappy cold. You'd spend the whole weekend watching me sleep."

"I'm committing to the Edward Cullen-level of creepy, and you can't stop me."

"Please go. I'll feel horrible if you stay."

I sit up, turning to get a better look at her face. She's sweet and wonderful and, as an extension of that, has a terrible poker face. "You swear you're okay?"

She smiles. "I swear I'm okay."

I chew on my lip. "So, just me and Colton?" My voice is oddly high, and I see her eyes narrow.

"Yes." She draws out the word like it's a question. "Is that a problem?"

"Nope." I pop the *p* at the end, and she raises an eyebrow.

"You're lying! Why is it a problem?"

I groan and look up at the ceiling, unable to meet her eyes. There's a very good chance she'll make this into a capital T thing, but I've tried to keep it to myself for the past two weeks, and I'm losing my mind. "We may have kissed after we went dancing."

Her squeal echoes through the apartment, and I'm beyond thankful that Colton's out.

"What does this mean?"

"Nothing," I say. "We're attracted to each other, but we both agree we're just friends and hooking up again isn't an option."

"Hooking up? You said you *kissed*!"

"And that wasn't a lie. Then we touched a bit. Or, at least, he touched."

And god, did he touch. His hands and mouth lit me up in a way I didn't realize was possible. If that's what he could do with a few kisses, what could he do if I got him between my legs? I can't stop thinking about it, even though I need to.

I'm *not* going to mention my foray into voyeurism, or that all I can seem to hear is the way he chanted my name when he came.

She throws her body flat on the bed, thrashing and screaming like she's undergoing an exorcism. "I knew you two would get together!"

"That's not what's happening here."

"Why not? You two have so much potential. And I want you to be as happy as I am."

She and Tomasso have been spending time together for literally two weeks, but I'm not going to point out that it isn't some epic love story like she's written in her head.

She squeezes my hand. "Why not give him a chance? You haven't really dated anyone in the ten years I've known you."

I cross my arms. "I've dated at least that many people in the same number of years."

"You've gone out with people, but those connections have been about as deep as the frog pond in the Boston Common." She raises her brows in challenge.

I cross my arms. "I dated Jas for almost a year."

Inez grew up with Jas, and when Inez introduced me to her group of lifelong friends during our first year of grad school, I slid in seamlessly. It was years before things started shifting between Jas and I. Inez said she was cool with us dating, even though I could tell it made her nervous. It hadn't been a clean breakup, and I'd lost all of them except Inez, who now awkwardly schedules her social life around us.

She makes a skeptical *mm-hmm* sound. "Can we call that dating? More like exclusively hooking up. Jas only made it that long because she never makes a fuss about anything. The second you two started arguing, which is a normal part of a healthy relationship, you dumped her."

I flinch at the description, even though it's accurate. It always goes the same way. I meet someone and developed feelings while everything is fun and interesting. Then, we start arguing, or they cancel plans last minute or forget to call me back one day. I start slowly spiraling and imagining all the ways they're going to leave and disappoint me, and I cut it off before we can get there. I recognize the pattern, *know* I'm doing it, but can't stop myself. Over the years, I decided that the frustration—and self-loathing, when I was unable to control my reaction—wasn't worth it, which is why it makes more sense to focus on the fun.

Inez continues with her sales pitch. "Everyone deserves a great love! And with your best friend? How could you beat that?"

I groan and drop back on the bed next to her. "Why do you only hear what you want? I said we stopped!"

Inez purses her lips. "If you say so. But we'll see what tune you're singing after a romantic weekend in Ischia."

I scoff. "A weekend with a hundred students. Who could resist that sort of romance?"

She sighs happily. "I love love."

I throw a pillow at her face as I stand up. "You need sleep. One more word, and I'm staying home to smother you with my love and affection."

She mimes locking her lips, but she starts humming as I walk away. It isn't until I make it back to my room that I realize she was humming ABBA's "When I Kissed the Teacher."

THE FEW HOURS it takes to travel south are uneventful. A short train ride to Naples, where I mostly switch between reading and counting heads to make sure no students wander from our train car, followed by a bus ride to Pompeii.

The sprawling archeological city stretches before us with Mount Vesuvius's ominous presence looming in the background. We'll spend a few hours here with Colton lecturing about the insight provided into ancient Roman culture by this city, frozen in time by a devastating volcanic eruption.

Like the rest of Italy in late June, Pompeii's blistering. The ancient concrete sucks in all the sunlight until we're baking like Naples's famous pizzas. But the students stay engaged, equal parts stunned and horrified by the plaster casts of the victims, eternally trapped in their final moments. I'm happily surprised by the level of respect they show—

Until we get to the brothel.

At the sight of the well-preserved frescoes over each door along the long hallway, their raging newly-not-teenage hormones go wild. Each one displays a different sex act—boy, were the Romans creative—and the students can't keep it together. Eyes go wide. Giggles bounce off the ancient walls. Frat boys mime the corresponding act for what they consider the funniest photo of all time.

I lean against the wall, watching them with Colton. "College students are disgusting. We were never this bad."

He raises his eyebrows. "I'm positive I have a picture of you groping the ass of an ancient statue at Hadrian's Villa. But please, tell me more about how they're worse now."

I nudge him with my shoulder and try not to think about how the contact sparks against my exposed skin. I also studiously avoid looking at the frescoes when I'm this close to my friend who I should definitely not be thinking about doing those activities with.

It's a relief in more ways than one to make it back onto the bus. I stand in front of the breeze pouring out of the AC vent until we reach the pier, determined to get one particular fresco out of my head. The man on his knees for his lover, head buried between her thighs just like Colton said he'd have done if given the chance.

No. Bad Quinn.

An hour on the ferry, and we're pulling up to one of my favorite places in the world. Ischia looms ahead of us, the volcanic island rising out of the Bay of Naples like a gift from Neptune himself. It's the largest of the islands, dotted with small towns of colorful buildings, pristine beaches, and locals who are excited to meet the tourists who chose their island over the more popular Capri.

Colton looks over and beams, and right before my eyes, he's twenty-one again, nervous about taking a weekend away from his research, but capitulating to his annoying best friend. It was a weekend of complete freedom amid the stress of our upcoming finals.

Once at the hotel, Colton gathers the students while I handle check in.

"We're giving you freedom to explore this weekend," he says. "The San Giovanni Festival is a wonderful cultural experience. Do *not* overindulge in the Nocillo liquor. Professor Riley and I aren't here to babysit you, so keep it together."

I bite my lip at *Professor Miller's* attitude. Domineering and sexy as fuck. I bet that's how he is in bed, too. Pinning my hands over my head while he moves inside me. Flipping me over and yanking me up by the hips up to get the perfect angle.

Fuck.

This is going to be a long weekend.

I call the students' rooms as the front desk manager passes the keys to me. Once I confirm everyone has a room, I turn back for our own keys.

"Bene. Here I have your room key," the manager says as he pushes one large metal key across the counter.

"And the key for the second room?" I ask, even as my heart starts shooting around my chest like it snorted a line of cocaine.

His eyebrows pull together, and he shifts between shuffling papers and glancing at his computer screen. "No, signora. One room."

I glance over at Colton in time to see him visibly swallow. I pull out my phone. "Excuse me one minute."

The phone rings until it goes to voicemail. I hang up and call again. On the third call, Inez picks up. "Hi bestie!" She sounds bright, happy, and very noticeably not sick.

"One room, Inez?"

She bursts out laughing. "Oops!"

"What the hell?" I glance back to make sure no one's paying attention.

"I must have messed up the reservation," she says with an innocence that rings fake even through the phone. "How lucky that I got sick or someone would be sleeping on the street!"

"You're a meddling little shit."

She just laughs. "Have a great weekend with your boyfriend."

"He's not my boyfriend," I frantically whisper, but she's already hung up.

I drag my feet back over to the desk. "You don't, by any chance, have another room available, do you?"

He shakes his head. "I apologize, signora. We are booked for the festival. Most of the island has been for months."

I grind my teeth together.

Colton places a soft hand on my shoulder. "It'll be fine. We've shared hotel rooms before."

He's right. We traveled together while we were studying and it was never a problem. It had also never been a problem when he helped me with zippers before, and we saw how that turned out.

But Italian hotel rooms typically have multiple twin beds. We'll each have our space, get through the weekend, and head back to Rome.

Colt grabs both of our suitcases as I lead the way up the stairs, pausing at our door with one last desperate look down the hall before sliding the key into the hole.

I take a few steps into the room and stop short. Colton runs into me, steading himself with a hand on my hip, which only makes my already racing heart gallop faster.

Because right there, in the middle of this old Italian hotel room, is one. Tiny. Full. Bed.

"You've gotta be fucking kidding me," Colton mutters.

I turn to get a 360 view of the room, praying for another bed.

All I find is a love seat against the wall, too small for even my short body.

We're fucked.

I face Colton, hoping to read his thoughts on his face. We stare at each other for what feels like days without speaking until he finally opens his mouth. Every muscle in my body tightens in anticipation, but no words come out.

Instead, Colton lets out a giant, booming laugh. He bends at the waist, hands on his knees as he struggles to get control of himself.

I walk over and smack him on the back with my purse. "This. Is. Not. Funny."

He straightens but is still trying to force in breaths between his laughter. "It kind of is. You're horrified, and that's the smallest bed I've ever seen."

I tilt my chin imperiously. "The heroes in my romance novels would offer to sleep on the floor."

"Then the heroes in your romance novels are dumbasses."

"Can't be that dumb. They get laid because they're gentlemen."

Colton stops laughing then, though the devious glint doesn't leave his eyes. "Chaos, are you trying to act out one of your romance novels?"

I sputter. "No! Obviously not."

He crosses his arms over his chest and his biceps bulge. I hate them. I want to bite them. "Because it kind of sounded like you were propositioning me."

I groan. "You're so evil! You know that's not what I meant, but you like watching me squirm." I look at the bed again and feel a spike of adrenaline. I start pacing the too-small hotel room. "It's just a really small bed and you're not a really small guy and I take up plenty of room too and then there's the whole... you know, and now we're going to be stuffed into this bed and we have this new history, which I know is oxymoronic, and—"

"Quinn. Stop." He grabs both of my shoulders. "We'll be fine.

We've shared a bed before and it wasn't a big deal. Yes, we hooked up, but we agreed to stop. You know I'm not going to try anything when you said no."

He thinks I'm worried he's going to push for something to happen? Of course, he wouldn't do that. I'm worried about what *I'll* do.

It all feels too charged. Every glance at his strong profile or every smile I earn. The mouthwatering way he rolls up his sleeves while lecturing. Those. Damn. Biceps. And worst of all, it's totally one sided. Yes, he admitted his attraction from college. And yes, he's still attracted to me by his own admission. But there's been nothing since. No heated stares or glances at my lips or longing looks when he thinks I'm not watching. And I'm always watching. Why is it so easy for him to pretend like nothing happened?

It's unfair to be annoyed with him for respecting my boundaries. If he were the type of guy who would push for something not offered to him, he'd never have become my best friend in the first place. I just wish it were as easy for me as it is for him.

I force a smile. "Of course I trust you. It's not that. It's just a weird situation."

He drops a chaste kiss to my forehead, the same quick, friendly kiss he's given me our entire friendship, and my whole body heats in response. Why am I like this?

I try not to think about that bed while leading the students to our group dinner.

I focus on anything but that small space while students chat me up about their internship experiences.

I ignore the fact that Colt is on the other side of the door while I get ready for bed, shimmying into my too-short sleep shorts and tank top.

Colton's already on his side of the bed when I come out, and I slip under the blanket.

We both lie on our backs, legs perfectly straight and arms at our sides, like two corpses laid out for burial preparation.

Colt clears his throat. "Well, good night."

"Yep. Good night."

Like I'm actually going to sleep.

COLTON

THE SMELL of citrus and sunshine fills my nose as I come out of the fog of sleep. I shift, moving to stretch my stiff muscles, when I realize I'm not alone. A warm, lush body is wrapped around me.

Quinn and I are facing each other. My arms encircle her, and she's buried her face in my chest with our legs twined together. I sigh and shift closer, brushing a soft kiss to her shoulder, savoring the feel of her body against mine.

Everything about it is perfect.

Except a few seconds later, my brain wakes up enough to process that it *isn't* right. She was worried about exactly this. She made it perfectly clear that she doesn't want anything with me, even if she is attracted to me. I know my best friend, and I know she's struggling to readjust after what we did together. I need to extricate myself from this situation before she wakes up and starts spiraling.

I inch my leg out from between hers, but she buries her face more deeply in my chest, pulling in a deep breath while I hold my own.

She moans, grinding her pussy against my leg, and I bite back my groan. She's dreaming, letting out little whimpers and sighs that take me from hard to a fucking rock.

I try to pull back again, and her fingers wrap in my shirt.

"Colton."

I freeze. The way she says my name, breathy and desperate, short-circuits my brain. Maybe she isn't asleep. Maybe she woke up in my arms and wants this as badly as me. "Quinn, are you awake?"

She blinks her eyes open, recognition slowly filling her gaze.

A heartbeat later, she pushes herself away, scurrying to the other side of the bed like a crab. In her rush to get away, she forgets the bed is barely wide enough to fit our bodies, and she falls off, landing flat on her ass.

I sit up and look over the edge, losing the fight against the laugh bubbling in my throat.

"Okay there, Chaos?"

"Oh, yeah," she stammers, rubbing her sore rear end as she stands. "Of course. Obviously. I'm totally fine. This is no big deal."

My heart plummets when she doesn't laugh. I've never seen her this flustered. Her nervous eyes shoot around the room, landing on everything except me. She's uncomfortable. *I* made her uncomfortable.

Logically, I know I haven't done anything wrong. I was asleep, and she snuggled up to me as much as I did to her. But she wouldn't be this uncomfortable if she didn't know the way I'd felt about her. This was why I kept my feelings to myself for so long. She's too kind, too concerned with my discomfort. And there's definite discomfort.

"I'm sorry."

Her frantic eyes shoot over to me. "You're sorry?"

I clear my throat. "Yeah. For the cuddling and the arms and, you know."

Her eyes flick down to where I've positioned the blanket to

hide my very obvious erection. She can't see anything, but knowing she's looking makes my dick strain harder against my shorts.

She turns on her heel and rushes off to the bathroom, slamming the door shut without a word.

Maybe I *should* have offered to sleep on the floor.

CLEARLY I'M A MASOCHIST, because I spend the day at the beach with Quinn. She gave the students some suggestions on where to explore, but beyond that, we don't have to see them until the festival starts this evening. Our day is completely our own.

All my plans to spend a nice, platonic day proving to Quinn that she doesn't need to be uncomfortable around me disappear in a burst of adrenaline when she whips that cover-up over her head. Her breathtaking curves are wrapped in red nylon, and my wildly unhelpful brain supplies endless images of me burying my face between her round thighs, licking over the slick suit. I spend hours trying to distract myself with baseball and my grandfather, determined not to look at her. I've been fighting like hell to keep my eyes off her for weeks, ever since she rewired my brain chemistry in our bathroom, and I can't break now. Not when she's already feeling weird.

"You coming in the water?" she asks as she pushes off her blanket, brushing some sand from the back of her thighs and drawing my eyes back to her ass.

I yank my gaze back to her face, terrified she caught me checking her out, but she's looking out over the water with a giant smile on her face. I pull my knees up, leaning my elbows on them to hide anything that might make this day even more awkward.

"No way. It's the festival of San Giovanni. There are swords and knives out there."

She drops her head back and laughs. "You're going to let a children's story keep you out of the Mediterranean?"

No, but I'm going to let my very obvious hard-on keep me out of the Mediterranean.

"Those stories come from somewhere, right?" I say instead. "I'm happy on this towel with my book."

Hurt flashes across her face, covered quickly by a smile. "Okay. Have fun!"

My heart pinches, and I almost follow her. But I can't stand up without making things worse. This morning was a fucking mess, and the last thing our friendship needs is another awkward moment.

What it *does* need is for her to think everything's fine. For her to brush off this morning as a natural, albeit uncomfortable, reaction to us being pushed up against each other in our sleep. We have to stay in the same hotel as the students, and with no other rooms available, this is our only option. I refuse to make the next two nights uncomfortable for her.

I watch her walk into the water, hands playing over the waves as the sun glints off her bright blond hair. She giggles as a local boy splashes her. The sound skips across the sand until it surrounds me, and I groan, wondering how I'm supposed to get through this weekend, much less off this beach.

I've been able to manage my reaction to her for fourteen years. But our hookup was like a hole punched in the hull of a boat, and now the water's pouring in and I'm drowning.

I somehow gain enough control to walk to the water's edge. Quinn's wet, drops of water clinging to her eyelashes.

"You're coming in?"

"I'm actually heading back to the hotel to shower."

Her face drops. "Oh. Okay. I'll head back in a bit."

Her new friends pull her attention away from me with a splash as she sputters through her next laugh, sea water sliding down her beautiful features. I'm left to watch her, wishing things were different—that I was stronger—before dragging myself off the beach.

Back at the hotel, I end up in the shower again. This proximity to Quinn is turning me into a pathetic schoolboy who needs to jerk off multiple times a day. She's everywhere, and I can't resist popping the top of her shampoo to get a whiff of her scent, one hand clutching the bottle while the other wraps firmly around myself.

And when I feel the sweet relief of release, I pray it's enough to get my head on straight before the festival tonight.

HOURS LATER, as the students file into the tiny lobby, my head is decidedly *not* on straight.

"Listen up, everyone," Quinn calls out, and they obediently—and shockingly—turn their attention her way. "We're heading to the main square. There'll be food for sale, so make sure you have some money on you.

"In the square, you can see the *La 'Ndrezzata* dance. Joey, I could hear you groaning before I even finished the sentence." She points at a student and everyone around him chuckles. "But I promise it's cool and you should check it out.

"You're all adults and of legal drinking age here. I won't tell you not to partake, but the Nocillo is strong. Dr. Miller and I are here to help if you need us, but please don't make us spend our pseudo-vacation taking care of drunk undergrads."

The students all laugh.

"Definitely try it, if you drink alcohol, because it's a special liquor you can only get for this festival. It's made with walnuts collected a couple of days before the festival at night by a woman. Why a woman? I don't know. Get out there and ask a local!"

I bite my lip to keep from smiling at Quinn. She flourishes in this setting, toeing the line between advisor and friend.

Approachable in a way I've never been. I envy the way she easily moves between her roles. Everything in her demeanor, even her language, shifts as she settles into each position.

She waves a hand, and everyone falls in line as she leads them into town. The streets are packed with tourists and locals alike pouring into the square to enjoy the festivities. A large stage is set at the back of the piazza up against the plaster buildings, somehow more charming for their chipped paint.

Quinn hoists herself onto the side of a lamp post and calls out. "Okay, everyone. Here we are! Areas to check out." She gestures to different parts of the square. "Stage where the folk dance is happening. Harbor, where you can watch the boat parade." She points straight up to the sky. "And finally, where you can see the fireworks. In case you couldn't figure that one out for yourselves."

Some students chuckle and some roll their eyes, but they all hold a level of affection in their gazes.

I call out from the back of the group. "Get out there and have fun. But not so much fun that you ruin our night."

The students scurry off, leaving me with Quinn. She rushes over to me, bouncing on her toes. "Boat parade?"

My stomach growls. "Let's grab something to eat first. There's plenty of time."

She pouts. "If I don't get a spot soon, I won't be able to see anything."

"Then I'll put you on my shoulders. I'll make sure you see it."

She snorts. "Yeah, that's not gonna happen. Come with me. We'll grab something later. We won't watch the whole parade, just a few boats."

I send one last longing glance towards the food stalls and let her drag me onto the Ponte Aragonese. Quinn's fingers slot through mine, and my heart skips a beat. It feels so right, our hands wrapped together, a small point of connection even in a sea of other people. But it only lasts for a few seconds before she realizes what she's done and yanks hers away like she's been burned.

"Sorry," she mutters.

We shouldn't be this awkward. She's held my hand walking through crowds dozens of times, and it was never weird. That night was the best of my life, but if this is how it's going to be between us now, I'd take it all back.

The sun's setting over the harbor, nearly gone now and casting a pink and orange glow over the calm, lapping water. Slowly, the space around us fills, bodies pushing us more tightly to the edge as everyone tries to work their way to the front.

Quinn sends me a victorious smile. "See! I told you my plan was better."

My stomach disagrees, but it's worth it for the way her dark eyes sparkle, like there are stars hidden in their depths only I can see.

The crowd continues to surge forward, shuffling us around until Quinn's pushed into me, her back to my front. All I can think about is how easy it would be to slip my arms around her waist and inch her back farther, to drop my lips to the curve of her neck, the spot that's tempted me from the first time I saw her. I bite my tongue hard enough to draw blood, desperate to distract myself.

She turns to face me, every curve of her body dragging across mine. I don't know if this is heaven or hell.

She tilts her head back to look at me. "I'm sorry. It's packed. I swear, a few boats and we'll get out of this crowd."

Someone pushes me forward. My hands come down on the top of the stone wall behind her, trapping her body between my arms. She fists the material of my shirt as she steadies herself, and I barely keep our lower halves from touching. Thank god, because one brush would make my issue obvious.

I'm not sure if it's a conscious decision or not, but Quinn's fingers flex in my shirt, tugging my face closer. Her other hand settles on my stomach, trailing down to the top of my jeans, and I close my eyes to hide the way they roll back in my head. When I open them, our gazes clash, her brown eyes going even darker. Her hypnotic lips part on a gasp. It'd be so easy. Two, maybe three, inches, and my mouth would be on hers again.

Someone shifts behind us again, breaking our staring contest and bringing me back to myself. I clear my throat. "I think I'm going to grab food now. You enjoy the parade and I'll meet you in the square."

She chews on her bottom lip. "Are you sure?"

"Yeah, I'll see you soon."

"Okay." She forces a smile and turns back toward the water. I watch her for a minute, unable to move. It's subtle, but her hand comes up to touch the corner of her eye in a quick movement that has my heart clenching.

I don't know what the fuck is wrong with me. All I know is I can't turn it off after waking up next to her, wrapped up in her scent, her touch, her voice when she said my name. A persistent part of my brain argues she wants me, but one word muttered in her sleep doesn't overrule the dozens of words she's said consciously.

I grab pizza from one of the local shops, then find a rickety table, unhappily munching down while keeping an eye on her from a distance.

My phone vibrates on the table, and my heart stutters at the 304 area code. West Virginia. Unknown numbers never call me from West Virginia, and my mind fills in all the possibilities. My mom's sick. There's been an accident or a fire or a burglary.

Breaking out of the trance, my hand shoots forward, answering on what's likely the last ring. "This is Colton Miller."

"Hey, man," says a voice I don't recognize. "How you been? It's Bobby."

I wrack my brain for a Bobby and come up empty.

When the silence stretches uncomfortably, he elaborates.

"Bobby Campell. From high school? We sat next to each other in American history."

A blurry image takes shape, a short, skinny white guy who would pop into the seat next to me every third class and promptly fall asleep. I wonder how he got my number, then remember it's Grand Creek. Everybody's in everybody's business.

"Hey, Bobby," I say absently, eyes pinned back on Quinn. "What can I do for you?"

"I sent over a contract for the new countertops for your mom's house. Not to rush you, but I need that deposit before I can order anything."

He rattles off a number that has me choking on my own spit.

"That's not what my mother and I agreed to," I say when I recover.

"She decided to upgrade from the laminate to the marble."

"I didn't approve that," I shout.

I'm lightheaded and my leg starts bouncing, the movement rattling the iron table. We talked about a budget. We got it all in place. I can cover it—just about—but not if she starts adding more things without talking to me.

There's a long, awkward pause on the other end of the line. "Okay, well, you two need to talk this out. If this job isn't going to happen, I need to take on another one."

I dig the heel of my palm into my eye. "I'm sorry, man. I'll sort it out."

Within seconds of hanging up with Bobby, I call my mom.

She answers on the first ring. "Didn't expect to hear from you while on your big trip."

"Momma, did you change things for the kitchen renovation?"

She huffs. "What a way to greet your mother."

"I'm serious. I got a call from your contractor about a new contract?"

"It's just a small change," she says.

"Thousands of dollars is a 'small change'?"

I can hear papers shuffling around in the background. "The marble is so much nicer. Let me take a picture of these pages and I'll send them to you so you can see."

"We set a budget for a reason."

"Oh, come on! You're off on a fancy island in Italy, but some marble countertops for your mother are too much?"

She laughs, but there's a bit of hurt underneath. When she looks at me now, she sees this hotshot professor, one who's flying all around the world. There's no doubt in her mind that I can handle these changes to the budget.

And the hard part is, if I had stayed on my original career path, figured out a way to do better in my business classes and got a job in investment banking or private equity, it really wouldn't be a big deal to cover the few thousand dollars to give her the kitchen of her dreams. But I made the selfish choice, and now we're here.

"This is our home, Colton. If this isn't worth investing in, what is?"

That's all she's ever wanted, a home that she can make her own. One that doesn't have the threat of increased rent hanging over her head. I think about the string of apartments we bounced through my entire childhood, the ones with things constantly breaking and landlords who refused to help. Or even worse, the dingy one-bedroom apartment she moved us into before my senior year to save enough money to visit colleges, the two of us trading off between the bedroom and the blow-up mattress in the living room because she said that big brain of mine needed good rest at least a few days a week. Momma gave up the little comfort she'd carved out in this world to give me what I needed.

I sigh, already knowing I'm going to capitulate. It won't be *too* hard to move things around. I may need to look at moving to a cheaper part of the city after my lease is up, but extra time on the T is worth her feeling happy in her home.

"Fine, but no more changes to the budget," I finally say.

"Who knew I was raising such a cheapskate?" she jokes.

"I'm serious, Momma. No more. Please."

She agrees, but I can tell from her teasing tone that she doesn't get it, that she'll keep making assumptions about what I can handle and keep pushing until I break. We hang up as Quinn squeezes her way through the crowd to where I sit.

"Who was that?" she asks.

"My mom."

She stands up straighter. "Is everything okay?"

"I don't know." At her concerned expression, I quickly add, "She's fine. Just… money stuff."

She sinks into the chair next to me, taking my hand between hers and massaging the muscles in my palm. "Want to talk about it?"

I run my free hand over my brow. "I… I want to support her after everything. But I don't know how to tell her she's asking for too much, that I don't have enough to support her."

My voice breaks on the words as guilt floods me.

"I obviously can't talk about healthy family relationships," Quinn says, keeping her eyes on my hand, her fingers still moving like having a job makes this conversation easier. "But I can speak to love, and you and your mom have that. And can't anything be worked out if you're starting from a place of love?"

"Yeah," I whisper, and when she looks up and smiles, her dark eyes crinkling into crescents, my pulse races.

I squeeze her hands before extracting mine and using it to nudge the pizza box and the glass of Nocillo toward her. Her smile grows even wider, and I want to throw myself at her feet.

"You got me food?"

I shrug. "I figured I was standing in line, anyway."

We sit in companionable silence while she eats. The crowd in the square's getting rowdier, the Nocillo doing its job and loosening everyone up. I watch her watch the festival, so beautiful and carefree in a way she hasn't been all summer. Bright and addictive, just like she was when we came here at twenty-one.

Over the past decade and a half, I've become an expert at keeping the wall up between my feelings for her and our friendship. I've been respectful and welcoming to her significant others without letting my jealousy take over. We'd fall asleep together on my futon after a long day of studying without it turning into anything more. We've gone to the movies or dinner or the goddamn opera without me wondering if it was a date. But I can't seem to think straight today, and I'm so fucking mad at myself. How many magical moments like this will I miss out on with my favorite person because I can't wrangle my dick under control?

I clear my throat. "I think I'm going to head back to the hotel. It's been a long couple of days and I want to get some sleep."

"Are you sure?" Her voice cracks on the last word, and the hurt reflected in her eyes feels like a blunt sword thrust straight into my stomach. "The fireworks haven't gone off yet."

"Yeah, go have fun. See you at the hotel." I turn before I can see more of the pain reflected at me. I make it a few steps before turning around. "Call if you need me, okay?"

"Yeah. Will do. See you later." She won't meet my eyes, turning her attention back to the pizza box, and another rush of shame shoots through me.

Back in our room, the bed taunts me. It haunted me all day, a specter settling over us. I get ready for bed, changing into plain black running shorts and a t-shirt. But despite what I said to Quinn, sleep isn't an option. I sit down on the large love seat and pull out a book to try to relax. No luck. I pull out student essays to grade—nothing like undergrad writing to put you to sleep—but even that doesn't work.

The door creaks open an hour later. Her head peeks in, and when she sees me on the love seat, she doesn't smile. "Glad I'm not waking you up."

"Yeah," I say awkwardly. I settle the book I picked back up on my lap. "How was the rest of the festival?"

"Good. Great." She shifts from foot to foot, and I wonder if it's a nervous tick or if she partook in some more Nocillo. Finally, she settles her hands on her hips and faces me head on, determination brightening her eyes. "But we need to talk."

I run a hand through my hair. "I'm sorry. I shouldn't have left, but I was tired."

She narrows her eyes and points at me. "Liar." I try to stand up, and she shoves me back onto the love seat. "You've been weird all day."

"No, I haven't," I say, even though I definitely have.

"Yes, you have. We both have. I hate being like this," she says, a pleading note in her voice, "and ignoring it isn't going to make it go away."

"Quinn, we're fine."

"No, we're not, and we need to talk."

"There's nothing to talk about." *I just need to figure out how to stop wanting you so badly and we'll be golden.*

"You're either a liar or in total denial," she says, crossing her arms.

She's so beautiful this way, strong and passionate and not willing to take any bullshit. I start to harden—fuck, I'm a mess— and I know it'll only get worse the longer we speak. Avoidance is the only logical way to handle this.

I stand from the love seat, but Quinn abruptly steps in front of me, determined to finish this conversation. Our bodies collide, and Quinn gasps at the feel of me pressed against her stomach. Her mouth opens in a perfect *oh* shape that has me imagining all the things I could do with it.

We hold each other's gaze, neither speaking as the moment stretches between us. I brace for what will follow—her shuffling away and avoiding me for the rest of the trip, or her letting me down easily. We promised not to go there again, and I'm the one breaking that rule.

But instead, Quinn's hand comes to my hip, so close to where I desperately want it that I have to stifle a groan.

"Sit down, Colton," she says, softly pressing my body back onto the love seat. "Please."

I go willingly, hypnotized by her wide eyes. She slowly places a knee on either side of my lap, like she's giving me time to stop her. When I don't—how could I?—she lowers down, then intentionally rocks herself over me, never taking her gaze away from mine.

"What are you doing?" I barely get the words out of my mouth.

"Just for a minute," she murmurs.

A minute, a second, the rest of our goddamned lives. She can do whatever she wants to me for as long as she wants.

She whimpers. "Doesn't it feel good?"

Fuck yes, it feels good. Hearing those words on her lips makes me groan and drop my head on the back of the love seat. "We—fuck— we said we wouldn't, Chaos."

"I know." She runs a hand through my hair, and I open my eyes to find hers, desperate and mesmerizing. "I've tried so hard to be good, but I can't anymore."

She's tried to be good? I've been fucking dying all day. Was I so focused on keeping her from realizing I was completely lost to her that I didn't see that she was right there with me?

"All day?" I ask, the words choked.

"All day, all week, all year."

"Fuck, Chaos, you're killing me," I say, my breath coming faster with each shift of her hips. "Me, too. All year."

Longer.

"And that's why…" She trails off when she finds a particularly pleasing angle, her words fading into a moan. But I know what she's trying to ask.

"You want to talk about why I've been weird? You need to hear me say it?"

She lets out a sigh. "God, yes. Please."

I wrap a hand around the back of her neck, dragging her ear to my mouth. "Because you made me hard all day. After waking up with you wrapped around me and your scent in my nose and your perfect fucking body rocking against my cock, I've fought like hell to keep from giving the people on this island a show they didn't pay for."

"Fuck. Colton," she moans my name, and I want to swallow the sound.

Her hand snakes inside my running shorts and whips out my rock-hard dick. I look down between us as I help her shift my shorts down my legs, my hips bucking into her hand. I've dreamed of that hand wrapped around me more times that I can count, and that sight alone is almost enough to undo me.

I instantly miss her touch when she lets go, but she doesn't make me wait. She replaces her hand with her lace-covered pussy, her heat branding me through the fabric as we both work her over me.

"It's not enough, Colton."

She inches my shirt up, and I rip it over my head. Her hands trace the lines of my chest and stomach before pushing her panties to the side. I finally—*finally*—get to feel the pussy I've spent half of my life fantasizing about, pressed against my cock. Fuck, she's already so wet. Her hips tilt so I can put pressure right where she needs, both of us getting worked up past the point of insanity.

She whines with every swivel of her hips, and I'm so fucking close already.

"You know you're my best friend, right?" she asks.

"Yeah," I groan back, my hands squeezing so tight on her hips that I know there'll be marks in the morning. "Mine, too."

Her head drops to the crook of my neck. "But I can't stop. I don't know how to stop."

"Then don't," I pant. "Please, Chaos. Please don't fucking stop."

"I want you so much. Please, Colt," she whimpers against the shell of my ear. "All I'd have to do is lift my hips." She does just that, brushing her entrance over the tip of my cock. "You could be inside me in a heartbeat."

I moan into her neck, a deep, guttural sound of regret. "I don't have a condom."

"If you've been tested since the last person, I don't care. I have an IUD and am clear."

My head yanks back in surprise, tilting hers so our eyes meet. "You'd trust me with that?"

She watches me, her fingertips following the same lines as her eyes, like she's mapping me. Weighing me. She smiles softly when her eyes find mine again.

"You're my Colt. I'd trust you with anything."

At her words—the trust and care of them—my heart squeezes in my chest. I bring her lips to mine for the first time tonight, pouring every ounce of my love for her over the past fourteen years into a single kiss. This moment, her wanting me and choosing me, is a dream I never thought would come true.

"Please, Colt," she pants against my mouth. "Let's take the edge off and everything will be fine. Back to normal."

A stone settles in my gut.

I'm a fucking idiot.

Here I am, thinking she has feelings for me, too, when she's just drunk and horny. I might as well be a sex toy, the vibrator she pulls out when she's desperate. I was about to pour my guts out to her, offer her every part of me, when the only part she wants is my dick.

"That's what you want? One time?"

She nods before the words are even out of my mouth. "I can't stop thinking about what it would be like. Can you?"

Of course not, but that's not a new problem for me.

She pushes on, determined to convince me. "We can get it out of our system and then we'll be fine. All this awkward tension will disappear. We'll be us again."

There's no getting this woman out of my system. I've tried for a decade and a half, and it's impossible. She's as much a part of me as my own soul at this point.

The idea of having her is so fucking tempting, I almost say yes. But she didn't want this a couple weeks ago. She's been drinking tonight. How can I trust that she truly wants it and that it isn't just an effect of the alcohol?

"We're not having sex."

"Why not?" she whines, and it makes me want to flip her over my lap and spank her.

"You're drunk and we need to stop." My hand tightens on her hip, stilling her movements.

"I'm not drunk."

"I saw you drink at least one glass of Nocillo, and I know you well enough to know there was at least one more. You can't say you haven't been drinking."

"Drinking, yes. Drunk, no. Tipsy at worst."

"Still too drunk for this." I close my eyes, knowing I'll break if I look at the fire in hers. "You're not wasted. But I'm still not fucking you when you aren't 100 percent sober."

She whimpers, dropping her lips to my ear. "Would you fuck me when I *am* 100 percent sober?"

"Quinn," I say, forcing out the stern voice that makes my undergrads cower.

She groans. "You're no fun."

"You said that once freshman year, and it took all my self-control not to pin you to that twin bed and prove how fun I can be." She whimpers, and I bury my face back in her neck, breathing in her intoxicating scent and running my lips along the enticing curve. "And here you are, testing that self-control all over again."

Quinn takes my hand, sliding it along her thigh and under the hem of her dress. When I stop at the junction of her hips, she brings it between her legs, guiding two fingers inside, and her pussy clenches around them.

Hot and tight. Perfect. She's everything I've spent years fantasizing about. Everything I've tried and failed to find with a dozen other women.

She's just everything.

So what if she isn't offering more than one time? If that's all she wants, I'll take it. I'll take anything this woman wants to give me. My heart will feel like it's gone through a wood chipper by the end, but I don't care.

I pump two fingers inside of her, grinding my palm against her clit. She moans loudly.

"See how fun I can be?"

"Says the guy who won't fuck me," she says, shooting for indignation, but it's undermined by the breathiness of her voice.

"Tomorrow," I pant against her lips, knowing there's a very serious chance when the sun comes up she'll remember this is a terrible idea and never let me touch her again. "The second the alcohol's out of your system, I'll give you what you want. *Anything* you want."

I pull my fingers from her, and she cries out in protest. She'll have to wait, because before giving her what she wants and letting her walk away, I'm going to explore her the way I should have the first time. I devour her delicious mouth. My hands run over every inch of her. Across her chest that heaves under my touch. Down her thighs that settle over me, the weight of her body reassuring me that she's here, that this isn't a dream.

She moans, sliding her hand down her curves to replace my fingers between her legs. I grab her wrist before she can put pressure where she needs it. I want to give this to her. To be the one responsible for her pleasure. To burn the feeling of what I can give her into our memories. Something to keep me warm when she leaves my bed.

"Please, Colton," she says desperately.

Her words go right to my dick, and I grab her by the hip and start working her on me again. I lean forward, using my other hand to yank the front of her dress down.

I dive on her, sucking and biting at her nipples. Her breath comes faster, and I know I almost have her there. My hands move around to her ass, gripping her tight, and she moans loudly at the bite of pain.

"That's it. Take what you need. Think about how good you'll feel when I'm finally inside you."

God, please let her still want that tomorrow.

She whimpers, moving herself along my shaft, and I go back to playing with her tits, imagining her heat wrapped around me.

"Fuck, Quinn. So beautiful. So fucking good. Always so fucking good for me, aren't you?"

"Oh god, Colt. I'm gonna come."

One last drag against me and she lets out that moan, the one that's been on repeat in my mind for the past weeks. It's like a strike of lightning through my body, pushing me over the edge as I come between us. I can't even be embarrassed that I came so quickly when I have her, sated and smiling on my lap.

She leans back to look at me, her fingertips tracing the line of my lower lip, and I shiver. "There's that smile I love so much."

I know what she means. She loves me, but not like I want her to. But it's hard to remember that after what just happened.

Once in bed, Quinn tucks herself against me. I run my hand lightly over her hip as her breathing evens out.

I know I'm setting myself up for heartbreak. But for tonight, I'm going to let myself enjoy her body next to mine and the way my heart feels complete for the first time in my life. I place a kiss on her forehead, a light brush of my lips this time.

"I love you, Quinn Riley."

QUINN

Is it possible to be hungover and horny at the same time?

My eyes are still closed, but the bright morning sun is already pushing knives into my brain. Colt's arms band around me, holding me against his firm—and in certain places, fully hard—body, and the contact sets me on fire. I push back against him, and he moans sleepily in my ear.

One hand slides from where it's grasping my breast, skimming over my stomach to my hip. He pulls me back as he pushes forward, grinding himself on my ass. We both moan.

"Fuck, Quinn," he whispers, kissing the spot where my neck and shoulder met. "You're gonna be the death of me."

"Worth it?"

He runs his hand back up to my chest, massaging my breast before tugging my nipple through my tank top. "Without a doubt."

I pinch my eyes shut more tightly to block out the headache and focus on his brilliant hands, but Colt reads the stiffness in my body. He slides away from me and pushes up on his elbow, looking down at me with a cocked eyebrow.

"Hungover, Chaos?"

"Of course not. Perfectly fine. Keep touching me."

He scrutinizes me for five seconds, and I fight to keep my face serene. Suddenly, he bursts out into a loud—and off-key—rendition of "O Sole Mio."

I squeeze my eyes shut again and blindly reach to cover his mouth. "Fine. I have a slight headache."

His grin falters before he drops beside me, noticeably keeping his hands to himself.

"We shouldn't have done anything last night." He's upset, more at himself than me.

I roll to face him. He's staring up at the ceiling with his brows pulled together.

My fingers grip his chin and turn him toward me. "I was tipsy, not drunk. I'm just in my thirties. Looking at alcohol gives me a hangover. You have nothing to feel guilty about, I promise."

His Adam's apple bobs and I fight the urge to lick up his throat.

"And don't think I forgot your promise. I'm fully sober now."

His pupils dilate, the green slipping away like a shadow taking over a forest. There's danger there, and my veins are injected with another hit of desire.

"You still want that?" he asks, his eyes boring into me.

"Absolutely," I say. "Don't you?"

His jaw tightens, and I worry for a second that he's going to say no, that it's too much of a risk for our friendship, and he'll leave me here burning.

"And you're happy with this just being physical?" he asks.

Physical is good. Hot. I don't want to ruin our friendship with romantic feelings, and Colton already made it clear that he isn't willing to factor anyone else into his plans. We're on the same page.

"Don't worry, Colton, I'm not asking you to be my boyfriend or anything," I say, and his body sags in relief. My heart pinches, which doesn't make sense. Why should I care that he doesn't want to be my boyfriend when I don't want to be his girlfriend? I wiggle my eyebrows to cover up the little sting of rejection. "I read somewhere that orgasms cure headaches."

He chuckles, and I marvel at how my body can have simultaneous yet opposite reactions. Goosebumps fly over my skin while my head jackhammers.

"While I'd love to fuck the headache out of you, the aspirin on the bedside table may be more effective."

He stands and heads for the bathroom, and panic floods me. He's walking away, giving my brain space it definitely doesn't need. Space that will fill with the questions and worries that had been pushed out by pure need.

I take a deep breath. I've done friends with benefits plenty of times. Why would anyone pass up good sex with someone they can trust completely with their body? The complications come when you mix feelings with orgasms, and that's a line we both agreed not to cross.

This doesn't have to be complicated. I want him. *He* wants *me*. Sex has never been a big deal to me. It's a way to feel good. Is it better with someone I care about? Of course. But so is everything else. Talking and cleaning the house and going to the grocery store. I've always been able to separate the feeling from the act, even when hooking up with a friend.

I grab the pills and toss them back. "What about your promise?"

"One time. That's what you want, right?"

There's a challenge in his eyes, and I feel like I'm being tested on a subject I've never studied.

"Yeah, don't you?" I ask.

He rolls his lips together. "Of course. Let's save it for when you're feeling better."

"But I want it now." I sound like the brat from Willy Wonka, imagining myself trashing the factory because I didn't get my golden goose.

He walks back to my side of the bed, taking my head between his hands and pulling me in for a deep kiss, completely unconcerned with my morning breath.

Pulling back so our lips are a hairsbreadth apart, he whispers, "I have too many dirty things I plan to say in your ear to have you wincing every time I talk. Patience, Chaos."

He gives me one lingering kiss and heads to the bathroom without another glance.

Meanwhile, I'm a puddle.

COLTON NUDGES me towards the entrance of the thermal park. The stunning resort is designed around the natural healing properties of the volcanic island's water. Properties that my still-pounding head seriously need.

The manicured pools and waterfalls are set into the cliffside, creating the illusion of cascading waters. It's exactly what I need right now. To sit in the pools, close my eyes, and let everything go but the feel of the water on my skin. I rub at my temples again.

"The pools will help," Colton says from behind me. I can hear the smile in his voice, and I want to elbow him in the stomach. Then, his hands land on my shoulders and expertly press into the knots on either side of my neck, and all's forgiven.

"I'm not going in the freezing ones," I say. "You can't make me."

He chuckles and continues steering me towards the pool. "Noted. We'll start in the natural cave. From what I remember, that pool's warm and the cave will keep the sun out of your poor, hungover eyes."

"You're the best."

He throws his arm around my shoulder, and we walk in companionable silence towards the cave at the back of the resort.

If we did this day properly, we'd move through the pools in

the order the resort suggested, each change in temperature and length of time designed for optimal relaxation and healing. But right now, I need to stay submerged.

We toss our clothes and towels onto a nearby chair. The air in the cave is cool, tucked away from the heat of the Mediterranean sun. The warmth of the water and the chilly bite of the air ease the tension in my body, and I drift over to the back corner of the cave. I lean against the natural wall, the edges of the cliffside digging into my back like the island itself is giving me a massage.

I open my eyes and breathe a sigh as the pain in my head fades. Colton makes his way to me, his eyes dark in the dim light. No one else has made it to this pool yet. We're closed off from the rest of the guests, and I shiver at the predatory glint in his eye.

I wet my lips as he closes in, and his eyes track the movement.

"Remember the last time we were here?" I ask.

He lets out a cross between a scoff and a laugh. "Yeah."

"What's that scoff mean?" I ask, narrowing my eyes.

"It means I definitely remember you running around in a tiny bikini," he says, his voice as dry as the Sahara. "Not the easiest day of my life."

"Would you say it was… *hard*?" I roll my lips together in an attempt to bite back a smile at my truly horrendous joke.

His arms land on either side of my body. "That was terrible, and you should be ashamed of yourself. But yes. It was very, very hard."

The press of his lower half to mine makes me gasp. He runs his nose along my jaw. The way he inhales, like my scent is sustenance and he's starving, makes my heart tighten. I grasp his shoulders, wrapping my legs around him.

"Do you want to head back to the hotel?" I whisper.

He leans back and quirks an eyebrow. "No need to rush this. I want to spend the day with you."

I bite my lip against the smile. How does he know the perfect thing to say?

The idea of spending the day together without the awkwardness of us pretending we aren't attracted to each other is exactly what I need. His willingness—no, his request—to put off sex to get more time with me is everything. It's a relief to know that in a few hours, when our one time is up and sex is back off the table, this connection will still be there.

I lean forward and give him a light kiss. "That sounds perfect," I whisper against his lips.

He groans and deepens the kiss. We may not be running back to the hotel, but we're only human.

I hear the voices before he does, unwrapping my legs and using them to push him across the pool. His eyes are still dazed as the new swimmers come around the corner to join our oasis.

"Quinn!" Markus calls out, and I realize the poorly timed interruption is a group of our students. Thank god we stopped when we did. The last thing we need is the students gossiping about how they found two professors grinding against a cave wall on a school-sanctioned trip.

"She's Professor Riley while here," Colton barks from the other side of the pool. I send him a chastising look. His frustration isn't an excuse to snap at poor students. He rolls his eyes and moves back next to me.

Markus looks chagrined, and I almost elbow Colton. The kid's a goofball, but it's clear to anyone watching that he idolizes Colton. "I'm sorry, Dr. Miller. Habit from back home."

"Don't worry about it, Markus," I say with a smile. "It's not a big deal. Right, Dr. Miller?"

Colt holds my gaze for a second before turning back to Markus. "Honest mistake."

Markus visibly relaxes and swims closer while the rest of the students start horsing around. "Have you two been here long?"

Colton shoots me a look that says *this is why I'm not friendly with the students*, and I smother a laugh.

"We've been here for a bit," I say. "I didn't know you all were coming to the thermal park."

"Yeah! It was on the list you gave us of places to visit around Ischia, remember?"

Colton sends me a flat stare, continuing his new practice of communicating solely with his eyes.

"I'm digging this new mute you," I whisper.

He pokes me in the side, and I let out a little yelp.

"We'll leave this pool to you," Colton says, tilting his head toward the stairs. "It's time for us to move on to the next one."

"Have fun, guys. We'll probably see you around," I say as I swim over to the exit. This day's going to be a lot less interesting with our students swarming the place.

Colton stands with our clothes, which he holds in a strategically placed bundle.

"I'm going to the cold pool," he grumbles, and the loud laugh that explodes out of me draws curious stares from the students.

"See you in the hot tub when you're done," I call after him.

The hot water soothes me, washing away the lingering effects of last night. Colton slides in across from me a few minutes later, looking less grumpy but still not thrilled. "I can't believe you told them about this place."

I hold my hands up. "Inez and I made that list a month ago. I completely forgot!"

He grabs my foot under the water, kneading the muscles even as he continues shaking his head. "How's the mission to get Dr. Keck on board?"

I lean my head back on the tile and let the scene above draw me in—the blue sky, dotted by green palms and white birds. A moment of peace before Colt starts giving me a hard time.

"I haven't made much progress in the past couple weeks."

He pinches my toe, and I yelp and glare at him. "Because

you've been avoiding me or because you've been avoiding your dad?"

"Why not both?" I spread my arms wide, a manic smile on my face.

He shakes his head, a scowl on his handsome face. "You're not as cute as you think you are."

I lean forward, lifting an eyebrow. "Liar."

He chuckles and pushes his thumb more firmly into the arch of my foot. "Fair. But you can't keep hiding."

"I know," I say softly, then sigh. "I have a plan. Or a plan to make a plan. My friend—the one who comes up from Orlando every year for that internship program—is in Italy with her fiancé and their kids. We're getting together next week to catch up and brainstorm. We'll figure something out. We have to."

"Would it be the end of the world if the initiative passes in August?" he asks, no judgment in his tone. It's one of the things I love best about him. If something I say doesn't make sense to him, he doesn't placate me and move on to the next topic. He asks questions—thoughtful, sometimes difficult questions—because he wants to get me.

"When I started at Billings, they sold me on a small, collaborative campus. Passionate, respectful people from all departments working together to help the students. I don't think they were *lying*, per se. More like they were hopeful that the culture was shifting when it wasn't."

He nods, his hands switching to my other foot. "But can you still do the work without working with the professors?"

I nod, trying to work out the best way to describe it to him. "Remember the situation your freshman year?"

He levels me with a flat stare. "Yeah, I remember when I almost flunked out of school. Thanks, Chaos."

I wince, but push on. "You were lucky that I grew up in this world and could coach you through that. I knew what resources were available. But what would have happened to you if someone else had taken that seat before me? Someone who didn't know higher ed like I do?"

"I'd have been fucked. Trust me, I think about that all the time."

"There are students—thousands of students—who have no idea I'm on campus. Students who need my help and guidance. This initiative will make it harder for me to reach them for no reason other than stupid workplace drama. It's unfair. And unacceptable."

He runs his tongue over his teeth, nodding thoughtfully. "Fair enough."

"And then there's the Inez of it all. I can't let her be scared off. She loves Billings."

His brow furrows. "Didn't you say two days ago that you wanted whatever was best for her?"

"Yeah, to her face! But I'm not *really* okay with her leaving. Do you not understand how friendships work at all?"

"I guess not." Colton's lips quirk as his hands keep moving, working their magic. The tension slips away with each stroke of his fingers. "But someone did tell me that what we want out of life can change with new experiences, and the best thing we can do is follow that instinct wherever it leads. Don't you want that for Inez?"

I scowl at him and tug my foot out of his grasp. "Don't use my own words against me. It makes you look like an asshole."

He laughs then, loud and invigorating, and I'm relieved the sound doesn't hammer in my head anymore. My favorite smile of his—the big, broad one he saves only for me—stretches across his face. I lean forward, keeping distance between us for any prying eyes, and run my thumb quickly over his dimple. His eyes soften, and it takes all my self-control not to kiss him. We hold each other's gaze, the warmth in his eyes making it hard to breathe, like I sunk under the water's surface for too long.

I push out of the hot tub. "Let's move on. I'm getting overheated."

We spent the rest of the morning and early afternoon swimming in the different pools, chatting about everything and nothing, before heading back to town for one of those beautiful Italian lunches with as many hours as there are courses.

There's a shift when we head back to the hotel, like we both know we're walking toward a moment that will change everything. I'm not hungover anymore. There's nothing stopping us from exploring this tension between us.

After all of our rushing and our inability to keep our hands to ourselves, I expect us to fall into bed as soon as we walk through the door. Instead, we stand in the middle of the room, looking around like the answer on how to move forward will be written across the wall in bold letters.

Colton clears his throat. "So, um, we should probably shower after the pools."

I nod. "Yeah. Of course. That makes sense."

The shower's even smaller than the one in our apartment, barely big enough for one person to squeeze into, and I'm grateful for that fact right now.

"You first?" we both say and then awkwardly laugh. This is painful.

"Please, go ahead, Colt." I need a minute to put myself together.

He pops back out a few minutes later with a towel slung low on his hips while he rubs another one over his wet hair.

"Sorry, I should have brought my clothes." He winces, and I know it isn't a ploy to stand in front of me practically naked.

I let my eyes run down the panes of his chest before grabbing my own clothes and sprinting into the bathroom.

Why is this so awkward?

We both want this and know the other wants it, too. We're

comfortable with where the relationship's going and know what it means. It should be a no-brainer.

But now, faced with the possibility—and without the liquid courage of last night—I'm freaking out.

After my own quick shower, I comb my hair out as I gaze at the tiny bathroom mirror with unseeing eyes. He's on the other side of the door, skin probably still damp. And I'm here in nothing but the thin hotel towel that barely fits around my curves.

My clothes are right there. I can put them on, walk out of this room dressed and put together, like I wasn't in here imagining all the filthy things I want to do to that man. They could be a line of defense, like my dress had been the other night. A layer of protection as I fumble through this awkward moment.

Or, I can walk out in this towel like he did—okay, slightly less innocently—and get what I've spent the past month—okay, the past year—craving.

Before I can second guess myself, I fling the door open, my clothes forgotten on the bathroom counter.

22

QUINN

I HEAD STRAIGHT for the full-length mirror, positioning myself in front of it as I comb the hair I already combed in the bathroom. But he doesn't need to know that.

I keep my eyes away from him, but my stomach jumps when I hear his fingers stop clacking against his keyboard.

"Chaos?"

"Hm?"

"Where are your clothes?"

I look at him sprawled out on the love seat, clothed in nothing but athletic shorts. I let my eyes wander over his body, across those wide shoulders and along the strong biceps and down the line of brown hair that travels his abdomen until it disappears deliciously beneath his shorts.

"Look who's talking," I say, gesturing to everything he has going on.

He chuckles and pushes himself to stand. "I'm dressed."

"Barely." I try to infuse my tone with as much derision as possible, but it comes out breathy.

He smirks and walks closer. "I'm not the one without pants."

I look down at the towel that reaches halfway down my thighs but just meets in the middle. The tiniest shift and you'd see everything. "I'm covered more than you, assuming nothing slips."

His eyes run down my towel, taking in how easy it would be to get me out of it. I let it slide a bit, but catch it at the last second and tuck it back in.

I smile innocently at him. "Oops."

He growls. Literally growls. His eyes are turning more feral by the second, and he's starting to look more predator than man. "Teasing ain't nice, Chaos."

"That mountain boy's coming out, huh? I must be getting to you." I step closer and whisper, "Who says I'm teasing?"

He pauses, one heartbeat of hesitation, and then he's on me. His long legs close the distance between us in two steps. His hand grabs the back of my neck, hauling my lips to his. He wraps my wet hair around his fist, tugging to angle me where he wants. My stomach swoops, then tightens along with the rest of my body.

He grabs my towel with one hand, ripping it from my body and flinging it across the room in one fluid motion. He steps back, seeing me completely naked for the first time.

"Fuck. You're so hot."

He pulls me back into a kiss and walks me back until I'm pinned to the wall. The abrasion of his shorts reminds me I'm the only one exposed. There's something addictive about being on display, Colton's groans and wandering hands broadcasting how much he likes what he sees.

"Always so fucking wet for me," Colton whispers as he slides a finger inside me.

"It's been a constant struggle since you came home."

My moan mixes with his as he uses the heel of his hand to apply pressure to my clit, and I grind against him. My hands dive into his hair, desperate for something to cling to, something to ground me in the flood of sensation. When I tug at the soft, short strands, he grunts, and I yank my hands away.

"I'm sorry," I pant.

"No," Colton says, his voice low and harsh. He grabs both my hands and slides them back into his hair. "No, don't fucking stop."

I grip his hair tighter as his head lowers to my breast, and my whole body jolts against the wall. He brings his hands around to my ass, kneading each cheek before he starts to lift me. My stomach swoops and I push him back. I try to move past him, but he cages me in with his arms. He isn't letting me off so easily.

"What's wrong?" he asks.

"Nothing, I just figured walking over to the bed is better."

"Why?"

This isn't how I expected my naked strut from the bathroom to go. I gesture to my body as I roll my eyes. "Not the type of girl people pick up."

I love my body and have no interest in changing it to fit the ideal society pushed on us before we were old enough to understand what fat actually is. At the same time, I'm a plus-size woman, and that rarely translates well to being carried.

Colton pushes his hands into my hair and angles my head so our eyes meet.

"You're not too much for me," he says, pinning me with his intense gaze. "What I want right now is to feel your legs wrapped around me, and then I'm going to fuck you on every surface in this hotel room, including the walls. Understood?"

I can't speak. His tone leaves no room for argument—not that I want to argue when he speaks that way. I struggle to focus on anything beyond the intense ache between my legs, but all I can see is him and the picture he's painted.

I'm able to pull myself together enough to nod. The corner of his mouth kicks up, and then I'm in the air, his arms wrapped securely around my ass. My legs wrap around his waist and the glorious pressure of his hard dick between my legs has my eyes rolling in the back of my head. He pushes me against the wall and grinds into me, wrenching a moan from my throat.

Colt supports my weight with one hand, and I almost come at the show of strength alone. His other arm comes around to push his basketball shorts to the ground, leaving us naked together for the first time.

"Are you sure about the condom?" he asks, his voice hoarse. "I picked some up earlier, so we have the option."

"Yes. I trust you. Please fuck me."

No more encouragement needed, he lines himself up and lowers me onto him. Colton's mouth is at my throat, choked moans and whispered pleas pressed to my skin as I slide farther and farther onto him. I reel at the perfect feeling of fullness when he's seated.

But after a few seconds, when he doesn't start moving, I worry lifting me up is too much.

"Colt? You okay?"

He breathes heavily. "I spent nearly half my life dreaming about this pussy. I need a minute, or this one-time thing is gonna turn into a one-minute thing."

My heart pinches at his reference to our agreement. One time. That's all I get with him, and immediately it feels wrong. We fit together perfectly and the thought of never feeling him again makes my body clench, and not in the way you want with a hard dick inside of you. I shift to shake it off.

His fingers dig into my ass. "Stop moving, Quinn."

"Yes, sir," I say, and he groans into my neck.

After a few more seconds, he finally starts moving, slowly and deliciously deep, the friction making my head drop back against the wall with a small thunk. He moves faster, thrusting his hips while bouncing me in his arms like it's nothing. My orgasm creeps closer, made more intense by the feeling of weightlessness and of his strength around me. I feel completely secure with this man—I instinctually know that he has me. That he'd never let anything hurt me.

He leans down to take a nipple between his teeth, and that

steady climb turns into a full-blown rocket. It shoots me off, and I scream his name toward the ceiling.

With my legs still wrapped around his torso, he walks us over to the bed. He lets my body run the length of his as he sets me down, lightning sparking at each point of contact. I run my hands down his forearms, the blue veins standing out from the effort of keeping me pinned against the wall.

"I'm nowhere near done with you. Get on the bed," he says, and I whimper as I scramble back onto our tiny mattress. He grips himself, giving one long, slow tug. "Good girl. Now touch yourself."

My head tips back as I moan, one hand running down between my legs while the other clasps my breast. Within seconds, though, my eyes seek out Colton again. The distance lets me see him—really see him—for the first time. I want to trace the lines of his body with my fingertips, feel the strength of those thick thighs. But mostly, I want his incredible cock inside me again.

When my perusal makes its way back to his face, I realize he's doing the same to me. "Venus in the flesh," he whispers, like he's talking to himself, not to me.

I reach for him. "I need you back inside me."

He tuts as he crawls over my body, stopping to lavish kisses on my stomach.

"We need to work on your patience. I'm living out all of my fantasies." He drags his tongue up my core, stopping to suck my clit into his mouth, and I groan and arch my back. "And you coming on my tongue is definitely on the list."

Good. Fucking. Lord.

I don't make him wait long. I can't, not with the way he savors me. There's no teasing. His tongue traces the lines of my lips before pushing inside me. He licks me like he wants to explore every part of me, like it's more for his enjoyment than mine, and that thought pushes me over the edge again.

He shifts back up my body and kisses me deeply, letting me taste myself on his lips. He rolls his hips against mine, and I wrap my legs back around him to angle myself perfectly.

His eyes met mine, and half a second later, he fills me with one hard thrust.

"God, yes," I scream.

He buries his face in my neck, licking and kissing his way to my ear. "I propose we change our deal from a one-time thing to a one-night thing."

I huff out a laugh. "Seconded."

"Thank fuck, cause I'm not gonna last much longer and there are so many more things I want to do to you." One hand comes down to my hip, squeezing tight and pinning my body where he wants me.

"Yes, please," I pant.

"I'm close, Quinn. What do you want?"

"Don't stop."

He takes my earlobe between his teeth, giving it a soft tug that sends a shockwave straight to my center. "I'm gonna need you to use those words you're so fond of. When we're together, you say what you want. In explicit detail."

His accent has come back in full force, and his twang is doing things to me. He's my Colt, but a new, sexy version who likes dirty talk and fucking me into the mattress.

I grab his ass, pulling him as deep as possible. "Come inside me."

He groans. "You're so fucking sexy."

He thrusts a few more times before he swells and explodes, the sensation sending me over the edge as I join him in oblivion.

Neither of us move, both trying to recover. He shifts away, but I tighten my legs around him.

"Not yet. Please."

He nods into the crook of my neck and grinds his pelvis

against mine. The pressure on my clit sends aftershocks through me, and I sigh in his ear.

After an eternity, he rolls off me and flops on the bed. His dimple's on full display, and I lean over to kiss it, slipping my tongue out to flick over the small indent. He laughs, so light-hearted it's almost a giggle, and pushes me away.

"I've never done that before," he says.

I raise my brows. "Had someone lick your dimple?" He rolls his eyes and I faux-gasp. "Or sex? Colton Miller, were you a virgin?"

He scoffs. "I think it was pretty clearly not my first time."

"Conceited dick." I laugh and smack his chest.

"Want to see conceited? Wait until you see my recovery time."

Goosebumps spread over my body when he drags me across the small bed. We lie there, legs twined together and my hand tracing patterns over his chest.

Even with the rest of the night still to go, I don't know how I'm supposed to have my fill of him. And that thought scares the shit out of me.

23

QUINN

JULY — FIVE WEEKS TO WIN OVER THE FACULTY

INEZ BARRELS into me the moment I open the door. "You're home!"

I laugh and wrap my arms around her. "You're feeling better."

"Yeah, weirdest thing, right? I felt perfectly fine the next day."

"So strange." I roll my eyes at her and fight to keep my mind off what her trickery led to. She knows me too well and will read every memory of his hands and lips and tongue if I give an inch.

She waves her hand. "We could have found a room at another hotel for Colton." She peeks at him over my shoulder, committing to her lie. "I'm sure you'd have appreciated a weekend away from the students."

"I can hardly think of anything more appealing than that." His tone's neutral, but his amusement—and the breath-stealing memories of the previous night—burrow under my skin.

Inez turns back to me. "Okay, can we talk about how tan you are?"

I look up at Colton. "She's much nicer than you."

He sighs as he slips past me with our suitcases in hand. "If it's red, it's not a tan. It's a burn."

Inez throws her arm over my shoulder, and we follow him into our living room. "I got a bottle of wine. Let's go sit on the Tiberina and you can tell me how it went. You too, Colton."

"Thanks for the offer," he says, "but I need to prepare for this week's classes. I'll let you two catch up."

Inez protests weakly while I protest more vigorously. I want some time with Inez, but the second we're away from Colt, she'll start badgering me for details.

She goes off to the kitchen to pop the cork and grab some cups. As soon as she's out of view, Colton steps close, his already low voice dropping another octave. "This weekend was incredible."

"Yeah," I say, so eloquent in my breathlessness.

My hand lands on his chest, testing the muscles underneath, and his chest rises faster in response. His own hand comes to the side of my neck, his thumb tracing my bottom lip. He brings our foreheads together, our noses grazing in the softest, most electrifying way.

"Come to my room when you get home," he whispers, the breath of his words fanning over my lips.

I pull back a few inches so I can see his eyes. They hold a trace of vulnerability, but no uncertainty. I can't lie to him—or myself—and say I don't want that, too.

A clang of plastic cups flying across the floor interrupts us. We turn around to see Inez staring. Her eyes are wide and a bit manic, like she can't decide whether to cheer or yell or faint. Instead, she lifts an arm and points back and forth between us.

I chew on my lip and look up at Colton. "I guess that's one secret out."

"If it's supposed to be a secret, maybe you shouldn't make out in our living room," Inez says, but her eyes are smiling and her body vibrates with barely restrained excitement. "I'm so happy for you two! I knew it would work!"

"What would wor—"

"Oh, we aren't—"

Colton and I both start talking, cutting each other off.

"You know what? I'll let Quinn explain. I'll see you later tonight." He sends one last long look my way before heading off to the safety of his room.

"I knew you two were gonna fall in love! Tomasso said my meddling was going to get me in trouble, and I can't wait to tell him he was wrong."

I shush her, glancing at his closed door and praying the wood's thick enough to block Inez's booming voice. "That's not what this is, and this conversation requires a glass of wine. Get me to the Tiberina, and I'll give you the details."

I distract her from what she really wants to know along the way with stories about the trip until we're comfortably settled on the hill. This is one of my favorite spots in Rome, a small island in the middle of the Tiber river between Trastevere and the Jewish Quarter. It's a popular place to hang out in the summer, when the *Lungo Il Tevere* summer festival takes over the banks of the river. Pop-up restaurants and bars draw people from across the city. Others, like us, bring their own drinks and sit on the grassy knoll, enjoying the views. I take a sip of my wine, closing my eyes while savoring the fruity flavors and the rush of the river around the island.

I take a fortifying breath and asked her the question I'd been avoiding for the past couple weeks. "Have you heard anything from Leonardo da Vinci?"

"You must be really desperate to put off this conversation if you're willing to talk about the other job," she says with a smirk.

"I'm not stalling," I say, mostly telling the truth. Yes, I want to avoid the Colton-sized elephant in the room, but she hasn't talked about the other job at all. I want her to know I'm here for her, even though the idea of her leaving crushes me. "Any news?"

A small smile crosses her lips and she takes a sip of her own wine. "They asked me to come back to meet the rest of the team. No offer yet, but Dr. Lascano says it's a really good sign."

My stomach bottoms out. She's one step closer to leaving me, and I've set myself back a few dozen steps by snapping at Dr. Guarino and then hiding out. But I don't want her to think she can't talk to me, so I paste on the most realistic smile I can manage.

"Inez," I say, throwing my arms around her and just barely keeping my cup of wine from splashing down her back. "That's incredible! When are you going back?"

"The same weekend Dr. Keck and Dr. Larson take the students to Florence, so I'll have to be very, very sneaky."

That's three weeks away, which means I have three weeks to show her we can keep the initiative from passing before she has to make any sort of decision.

"No more stalling," Inez says. "We aren't leaving until I get details about this weekend. I'll burn the damn bridges down if I have to."

"Those bridges date back to antiquity, you heathen."

"Don't care. Spill. Now."

I sigh and face her. "We slept together."

She whoops. "Finally! It's so romantic! I'm going to be maid of honor, obviously."

I laugh and grab her hands. "Slow down. We aren't together."

She blinks her large brown eyes. I can practically hear the cartoon tinking sound. "But... you slept together."

"Contrary to what some people believe, sex doesn't always lead to a romantic relationship. It was a one-time thing."

"But... you were kissing. I saw it."

"We *weren't* kissing. Our faces were just... really, really close."

Her confusion is adorable. My little romantic can't understand why we haven't rushed to the altar already.

I launch into the story, leaving out some of my more... confusing reactions.

When I'm done, her eyes are sad. "Quinn, you have to tell him how you feel."

"I didn't say I had feelings for him. I said I enjoyed sleeping with him."

She levels me with a flat stare. "I've seen you with dozens of people—"

"Dozens seems a bit much, doesn't it," I mutter.

She rolls her eyes. "You know what I mean. I've seen you in relationships—even if I'd hardly call them that—hookups, and one-night stands, but I've never seen you like this."

"Like what?"

"Scared."

The word clangs through me. I'm not scared. I'm fucking terrified. The sex was incredible, but what if everything's different now? What if we get awkward around each other and slowly drift apart? No more sarcastic comments and dimpled smiles. No more baking pumpkin pie with Gerry on Thanksgiving and no waking him up on Christmas morning.

I've cared about the other friends I've hooked up with, but I've never loved one of them before, not like I love Colton. Platonically, of course. *That's* the deeper emotion Inez is reading.

But his words, *come to my room,* repeat in my mind the entire walk home, and I'm helpless against the urge to knock on his door. This is probably a terrible idea, but I'm just self-destructive enough to want to see how it will play out.

A half second later, it swings open. Colton's on the other side, his face surprised but hopeful.

"One more time," I say.

"Yes," he breathes out, relief and hunger on his face. His hand closes around my arm, tugging me inside and pushing me against the door before it fully closes. He devours me, and I fall head first into the kiss. This is what I need. Hot and hard. None of the emotional bullshit Inez was spouting.

I move down his neck, nipping at the skin, and Colton's low groan feels like a caress between my thighs.

"Y'all were gone for a while. Did you eat?" he forces out. "We could go get dinner first if you're hungry. Or gelato, maybe?"

I don't need anything approaching a date right now. I need to focus on what this is. Two people with an overwhelming attraction having fun on sort-of-vacation.

I push him back a step and kneel before him. "I can think of something I'd like to lick more than gelato."

His eyes roll into the back of his head as I free him from his pants, running my tongue along the underside of his shaft. I take him in my mouth, twirling my tongue around the tip as Colton softly brushes my hair back from my face and murmurs praise.

My chest tightens. If our friendship's going to survive crossing this line again, I need to make sure I don't mistake consideration for affection, so I take his hand and weave it into my hair, tugging on the strands to show him what I want. What I need.

"Fuck, Quinn."

He releases my hair for a second to rip his shirt over his head, then gathers it back, using his tight grip to keep it out of the way, and I take him deeper until his cock hits the back of my throat. His other hand sweeps over my cheek and down my neck, tightening around the back in a greedy, possessive grip.

"You're so pretty like this. I fucking love you on your knees for me."

I relax, taking him another inch, and a surge of satisfaction bursts through me when his palm comes down hard on the door like he needs the extra support.

My hands grip his ass while my head bobs, and I let my nails bite into the flesh. His hips jerk at the sting, pushing him deeper. I moan, and Colton's gaze blazes into mine.

"Is that what you want, Chaos? You want me to fuck your sweet mouth?"

I nod, and his grip on my hair turns more demanding, his hand and hips working in tandem. He takes complete control, and I accept everything he gives me, running my hands over his defined stomach and letting my nails scrape over his strong thighs. He's stunning. Savage and desperate and possessed, and I don't know how I'll ever look away from him.

"I swear to god, if we keep going, I'm gonna come down your throat."

I hum my consent, my whole body tight and overheated from seeing him lose control. He lets out another string of curses and my name before pulsing in my mouth, my body pushed back against the door as he jolts.

There. Hot, but nothing romantic about him fucking my mouth. This can stay just sex.

Colton looks down at where I'm kneeling and runs a finger down my cheek. He places it under my chin, tilting my face up to his, watching in fascination as I swallow. He's a handsome man on any day, but when he's rumpled and undone like this, I've never seen anyone so beautiful. I want him beyond all reason, and just like last time, I know tonight won't be enough.

"Venus," he murmurs, his eyes falling closed as his breathing evens out, and my heart skips a beat.

I run my fingers through my hair as I stand up. Colton's looking at me with a combination of lust and orgasm-fueled reverence that could be easily confused for something else. And shit, I think I want the *something else*, and that isn't acceptable. He told me he doesn't want a significant other, and I told him the same.

He's been the most stable relationship in my life for fourteen years. Part of me thinks if there's anyone in the world who could handle me, it's him. But a bigger part is afraid that in truth, I'm just not worth sticking around for when it isn't easy. And if I lost him, I wouldn't survive it.

This is all Inez's fault. She put this complication in my mind, made me see things that aren't there, and I need to get my head on straight. I start pacing the room like I can outrun these feelings, but the tiny bedroom is like a chariot track, and no matter how quickly I run, it always circles back to him.

Finally, I stop and turn him, asking a question that's both electrifying and terrifying.

"This is just sex, right?"

COLTON

I'M STILL TRYING to piece my mind back together. This woman just sucked my soul out, and she wants to talk about this now?

I drop down into the armchair in the corner of my room, my head falling back so I'm looking up at the ceiling. My chest is still heaving and if I answer now, I'll probably declare my love and blow up our entire friendship.

"Give a man a second to recover, Chaos."

When she doesn't laugh, I look up to find she's started pacing the room again. The lush bottom lip that gave me more pleasure than I imagined possible is tucked between her teeth, and she's tapping her fingers on the side of her leg like she always does when trying to keep herself from talking. She looks terrified, and it's all my fault. I could feel the love shining from my eyes as I looked down at her, so perfect on her knees for me, and now I've scared her off.

Quinn stops in front of me. "Colton, answer my question."

My eyebrows draw together. "Isn't that what you want? Just sex?"

Her eyes go wide, like a sweet baby deer. "Yeah, obviously that's what I want."

I nod, even though I feel like I've been thrown into an MMA ring with no training and am getting the shit beat out of me.

"I'm freaking out, Colt," she says.

"Why are you freaking out?"

"Because," she says at an octave I've never heard from her. "This is the sort of thing people freak out over. We've hooked up twice now."

"Technically four times." My lip quirks up at the memories of the night before, and Quinn smacks my shoulder.

"Stop being cute," she says, like it's the most painful thing she's ever experienced.

I grab Quinn by the waist and pull her to a stop between my legs. "You're scared about our friendship? We felt like us on the trip home, and that was after we slept together. I don't feel like it's ruined. Do you?"

She chews on her lip again and shakes her head.

"Right. Because there's no universe where you aren't my best friend. No choice that could be made to drive me away."

She rolls her lips together to try to hide her smile. "Promise?"

I groan. "Yes, I promise. Damn, you're needy."

She laughs and pushes my shoulder, the light back in her eyes.

I pause, doubting if I should ask this question but desperate to know the answer. "If you're so scared, why did you come to my room tonight?"

"I don't know," she says quietly, and I lift a brow. "Because... because I wanted to."

My heart does a flip in my chest. I'll never get tired of hearing her say she wants me. I give her a little tug, and she falls onto my lap, legs going to either side of mine. Her mouth is an inch away from mine when I whisper, "Good. I wanted it, too."

Our lips touch, and I combust all over again. Will she ever not wreck me completely? I can't imagine a day when even the smallest touch from her won't electrify every cell in my body.

An idea comes to me, one that will probably leave me

destroyed at the end. I never should have kissed her, never should have let myself see what I'll spend the rest of my life missing, but it's too late for that now. The damage is done. Shouldn't I take as much happiness as I can while it's available to me? If she wants me for now, I'll gather as many of those memories as possible, like a squirrel hiding away food for the winter.

I pull back so I can see every microscopic reaction to what I'm about to suggest.

"I have an idea," I say.

She blinks away the haze in her eyes. "An idea…"

"We have another five weeks here. We're too busy to meet other people. And even if we did, it's not like it could go anywhere since we're leaving. What if we… don't stop?"

"Don't stop having sex?" she asks, her eyes wide.

"I don't think I'll be able to continuously fuck you for the next five weeks, but I appreciate the vote of confidence," I say drily, and she punches my arm.

"You think we should keep hooking up for the rest of the summer?"

"Why not?" Besides the inevitable heartbreak coming for me in five weeks' time. "Neither one of us wants to stop. We know and trust each other, and we're together all the time anyway, so it'll be convenient."

"You sure know how to make a girl feel wanted," Quinn deadpans. "Convenient may be the sexiest thing I've ever been called."

"Do you want pretty words, Quinn? For me to wax poetic about your dark eyes and soft skin?" I ask, and her eyes go wide as she frantically shakes her head.

She looks away, and for the first time in our friendship, *I'm* the one fighting to keep my mouth closed. I want to give her the space to think about this, not steamroll her into a physical relationship.

"If we're going to do this, I think we should set some ground rules," she says.

My heart soars. She's in—or at least seriously considering it—which means I'll have five more weeks of this. Of the connection and heat that comes with being with Quinn, so much deeper than anything I've experienced with any other woman.

"Rules?" I brush her hair back from her shoulder, letting my fingers play over the sensitive skin where her neck and shoulder met. She shivers on top of me.

"To avoid confusion about what this is. So that neither of us forgets that it's casual."

I freeze and look up at her. She's worried that I'll get too attached, and it's a fair concern. What she doesn't understand is that I'm already too attached, so attached that I'll cling on after she leaves me because a life without her is inconceivable. I'd rather watch her live her life with someone else than not have her in mine.

I run my tongue over my teeth. "What do you need?"

She blinks rapidly for a couple seconds, then seems to steel herself. "Nothing physical except sex. No snuggling up for movies or sweet goodbye kisses. No holding hands while we walk through the market. All heart-to-hearts need to stay clothed. Our friendship and our physical relationship stay separate. This is just sex."

I ignore the way my ribs constrict my internal organs at her words. She can't offer more than this, and I won't try to force more from her than she's willing to give.

"Got it. Just sex."

I remind myself of that while we go another round, Quinn pushing us back to a fast, punishing pace any time we veered toward something sweeter.

Just sex.

I chant it as we lay next to each other, sweaty, exhausted, and more satisfied than I've been in my life.

Just sex.

And when she drapes herself over my body, I remind myself

that she's staying because she's worn out and doesn't want to walk the dozen steps to her own bed, not because she craves the physical connection like I do. I fall asleep to the constant refrain.

Just sex. Just sex. Just sex.

At least, for her.

~

I JUGGLE the cellphone in my hand, too much nervous energy in my system for my hands to stay still.

The past four days have been an emotional roller coaster. Quinn and I came to an agreement last night—three times, to be exact—but the emotional bomb of the weekend is still hanging over my head.

"You're asking for a broken screen," a voice says, and I jump, fumbling the phone and barely catching it before it hits the cobblestones.

Richard is standing in front of our school's door, shifting his messenger bag higher on his shoulder as he exits.

I smile sheepishly. "Not my best habit."

He lets out a long sigh. "There's another habit of yours I wanted to talk to you about."

My brow furrows. I can't think of anything I've done that would bother him. "Yes, sir?"

"I was talking to Giancarlo Guarino in the common room a couple days ago. He mentioned you've been making a stir on campus."

"I wouldn't call it a stir," I say with a little laugh that Richard doesn't return. "All I did was offer to be a resource for Quinn's class."

"We talked about this, son." He claps me on the shoulder. "No making waves until you're established on campus. Follow the path I set out for you, and everything will be fine."

"I wasn't going to leave her up there alone," I say, some of my frustration edging into my voice.

"She's made her own decisions," he says in the tone of a placating parent. "Don't throw away your future over some misguided feeling of obligation."

My stomach plummets. "I believe in what she's doing, and she's getting the professors on board. It's not a risk."

Richard sighs again and pats my shoulder. "Think about what I said. It'd be a shame to lose another promising mind to my daughter's whims."

He turns and heads down the street before I can respond. I want to yell after him that this isn't a whim. This is the result of years of hard work on Quinn's part. But by the time I rediscover my voice, he's been swallowed by the crowd.

I lean back against the stone wall, thinking through everything Richard said. The churning in my gut makes me sick, but I remind myself that it's just Giancarlo causing trouble. We still have five weeks to win him over.

I close my eyes and release a heavy breath, finally biting the bullet on why I'm pacing to begin with and pulling up my mother's contact. Might as well tackle all the turmoil at once. It's early, but she'll be up. She's always been a morning person, like me.

It rings three times before she picks up. "If this isn't the perfect way to start a day, I don't know what is."

"Hey, Momma," I say, unable to keep the smile off my face, even as adrenaline flows through my veins.

"How're you doing, sweet boy?"

I chuckle. It used to drive me crazy when she called me that, especially in front of the other kids in high school. But now it feels special, a recognition of all the effort she put into me when I was little to make sure I could be who I am today.

I struggle with what to say next. We need to talk about her spending—for her to understand where I stand financially—but I don't want to disappoint her.

I decide to start with a softball. "How's the renovation coming along?"

Her tinkling laugh comes down the line. "Colton Ford Miller, actually interested in my decorating schemes?"

"I show interest in your life," I say with a scowl she can't see.

"Sure, sure," she says. "Don't get your panties in a twist. I know you care about me. But you've never been good at faking interest for things you don't enjoy."

I clear my throat. "Well, I'm asking now."

"It's already so beautiful, Colton. I just know it's going to be perfect. The way it opens up to the living room? So much natural light and such a great flow for the space. Della and Lettie are gonna be so jealous."

Momma and her never-ending competition with the neighbors.

"That's great to hear," I say. "Look—"

"I haven't thanked you yet, have I?" she asks. "Pretty sure I've been too busy busting your chops, but you know how proud I am of you, right?"

"Of course I do," I say thickly.

"I'll admit now I was a bit nervous when you called to say you were switching from your business major to Roman history. Seemed so impractical at the time. But look at you now. Stable and happy and making a name for yourself, with enough left over to help your crazy old mom. I don't know why I ever doubted you when you're clearly the smartest of us all."

"You've always been smarter than me," I say, and I mean it. She's brilliant, but with her circumstances, leaving Grand Creek was never an option.

"You're a sweet little liar. Hey, I was thinking about cutting back my hours at the factory," she says, and I'm glad that we aren't on a video call so she doesn't see my wince. "Since you're done with your PhD and at a stable job now."

It's what we always talked about. My whole childhood, I told her she worked too hard, was too exhausted and overwhelmed. I begged her to cut back, telling her that I didn't need the latest SAT study guide or a private tutor if it meant she was going to drive herself into the ground to get it for me. And every time, she'd say it was her turn to work hard, and that I'd have my turn after I finished school.

Here's where I should speak up. It's my chance to set the record straight about my finances. To tell her the reason I didn't come home for so many years is because I couldn't afford to, not because I was busy working. To mention how I've been living on beans and rice for the majority of the year so I can cover my rent and her mortgage. To explain that the reason I say yes to each new project is because I'm desperate to give her what she deserves, not because I can afford it.

But instead, I say, "That's so great to hear, Momma." I tug at the collar of my shirt that suddenly feels too tight.

"Really?" she says, her excitement palpable. "It'll be so nice to have some free time! I was thinking about starting up a book club. Not one where we read books, obviously, but one of those book clubs where I buy a ton of cheap wine and everyone gets drunk and gossips about what's going on in town."

She's so happy. This is the future I promised her, back when I was going to be a bigshot finance guy with enough money to charter a plane between New York and Grand Creek. It's the future she expected when she worked herself to the bone to support me, an unspoken agreement. One I threw away when I decided to change my career path for my own enjoyment.

She loves me, but her dreams for me—and, by extension, for herself—have always spoken the loudest.

You're going to be the one who makes it out, sweet boy.

Our lives will be better. You'll see. With that giant brain of yours, everything's gonna work out.

You just watch. Get that fancy degree of yours and things will turn around right quick.

The image—and paycheck—she conjures when she hears the word "professor" doesn't line up with reality. I can't tell her that the job I chose doesn't come with the money she always expected for me to make. I was her hope for a better future, and I can't bring myself to break that mirage.

"I should prep for class," I say.

"Of course. You get outta here, fancy professor man," she says. "I love you."

"Yeah, I love you, too," I say, hanging up before she can take note of the tremor in my voice.

I'll find ways to make it work, skimp where I need to, and I'll keep working toward my own success in the name of providing for the both of us. No matter what.

And as much as I hate myself for it, Richard's voice echoes in my head.

No making waves until you're established on campus.

QUINN

TWELVE YEARS AGO

"WE'RE GOING to Orvieto this weekend!" I say, bouncing next to the table where Colt's studiously ignoring me in favor of a book as thick as his biceps. "I was telling Roxanne the other students wanted to see a smaller town, and she told me to run with the idea. She let me organize it all!"

"Cool," he says without looking up.

"Are you listening to me?"

We're finally in Rome together. The hundreds of hours I spent researching scholarships paired with the thousands of hours Colton spent waiting tables paid off, and I've been so happy to spend months introducing my best friend to the city that captured his imagination. But he's spent the entire semester with his nose buried in these books.

He sighs and sets down his pen, looking up at me. "I'm listening. What's up?"

I know he's excited about his research, but he's been so focused we've barely seen each other. I miss my best friend.

I spent a lot of time recently with our study abroad coordinator, Roxanne, helping with the organizational stuff for our trip.

It's so much fun, and this is the first big thing she let me take over.

I explain that to Colton and try not to get frustrated when his eyes flick back to his notebook.

His eyebrows pull together. "How does that relate to ancient Rome?"

My whole body shakes with my frustration as I let out a loud groan. "Not everything has to be about work. We're allowed to do other things."

"That's great, Quinn. Have fun." He turns back to his work, dismissing me.

"'Have fun' as in, you aren't coming?"

"No, we have a couple weeks until the end of term, I need to finish this paper, and you already roped me into Ischia next weekend. I don't have time for this, too."

"One day trip won't kill you. Your work is amazing."

"It's not where I want it."

Heat blisters under my skin. I get that he's passionate about his work, but this is important to me, and he's dismissing it like it's nothing. "Oh. I'm sorry. I forgot how much more important all these dead people are than your actual friends."

He lets out a pessimistic laugh and turns back to me. "You want me to blow off my work to run around Italy with you? I need to get this right if I'm going to have a future in this field."

I roll my eyes. He's so dramatic. I've read his work, and Dr. Cassia's going to fall all over herself to praise him when the time comes. "And one day's going to be the difference?"

He stands and starts pacing the room. "I don't know, but I'm not taking that risk for anything. Even you. Maybe you should spend a little more time on your work, too."

"I'm not worried about my work. I *know* I'm going to be successful."

He explodes, his anger wafting off him in waves. "Of course

you do. You have the money and the connections and everyone believes in you. Some of us have to work for our place in life."

I feel his words across my face like a slap. "You think I don't deserve my success?"

"I didn't say that. But I *do* think you're so used to being told this'll be your life that you don't stress about it."

"Or maybe," I say, fighting between tears and fury, "you're taking it out on me because you're afraid you don't have what it takes."

I pushed it too far, not to mention the fact that it's a complete and total lie. He's so much better at this than me. His words hit too close to home, and instead of reflecting on his fair assessment, I lashed out.

He breathes deeply through his nose. "Fuck off, Quinn."

He turns back to his books without another glance. My stomach clenches as tears flooded my eyes. "I'm sorry."

"I don't have time for this." He flips another page without looking up. It's a dismissal, the proverbial door slamming in my face.

"Talk to me," I say.

"No."

I walk over and slam his book closed, and I see him flinch at my treatment of his beloved text. "Yes. I'm not leaving here until we deal with this."

"Why?" He sounds exhausted, and I suddenly wondered if I've missed the signs of his stress and fear while I was running around Italy like this is an extended vacation. He'd been terrified about changing his major, that he wouldn't be able to get a good job and support his family. I'd figured those fears had gone away when he aced class after class, but I was letting my own background and resources affect the way I look at the situation. He's scared, and I was too distracted by my own fun to support him.

"Because we love each other." He raises his brows, and I roll my eyes in answer. "Shut up. You know I love you. You're my best friend."

He drops his head back, staring blankly at the ceiling.

I try again. "Please. I was wrong, and I don't want to leave it like this. I miss you, and I was an asshole because I want to spend time with you and felt like you didn't care. But I get it. It's a lot of pressure, and I'm a dick. Please forgive me."

He stands, pressing a kiss to my forehead as he pulls me into his arms. "I miss you, too, Chaos."

"I didn't mean what I said. Your work is incredible."

His sigh vibrates through my body, and my muscles relax. "I'm sorry, too. You're not riding on your dad's coattails. You're brilliant all on your own."

"But I kind of am, aren't I? Riding on Dad's coattails?" I whisper the words, like I'm afraid if I say them too loud my father will hear them all the way across the Atlantic.

He tenses, then lets go of me. He leans back on his desk and watches me in that thoughtful way of his, weighing each word before letting them out. "You want my honest opinion?"

"Always." The answer flies from my mouth, even though I'm terrified of what he'll say. Colton never minces his words with me, and I don't want him to start now.

He pauses for another few seconds, leaving me in terrible suspense. "I think you're great at this stuff. I also think you hate it."

"That's not true," I blurt out indignantly. Colton crosses his arms and stares. "Fine. I'll keep my mouth shut until you finish."

One side of his lips curves up. "Thank you. You aren't stressed about any of this—grad school, fellowships, and doctoral programs—but I don't think it's because your dad will bail you out. I think it's because this isn't what you want."

"Of course I want it. It's the only thing I've ever wanted."

He raises his hands. "I know. But you don't seem happy."

"I'm not unhappy. It's just... how can I sit in a musty library when *life* is right outside my door? We get a few more weeks here and I want to explore it all."

He takes my hand in his. "I'm not judging you. If you say this is what you want, great. But you're the one who said what we want can change."

I think about the conversation I had with Roxanne a few weeks ago where I laughed it off when she said I'd be great at this type of work, even as a spark of something lit up behind my ribs.

But there are plenty of cool jobs I'll never actually pursue. I'd also like to run tours around Southeast Asia, or work as a food critic who gets paid to eat at the best restaurants in the world, or become Channing Tatum's personal assistant.

Dad and I spent years working out my future. I'm going to teach, like the rest of my family. I'm going to work with Dad on research and continue the Riley legacy. I can't imagine how he'd react if I told him I wanted to do something else.

So when Roxanne offered to mentor me through the application process for the higher education program she went to, I brushed her off. I can't give up my whole identity on a whim. And I can't imagine what my parents would say.

But as Colton watches me patiently over the books that seem to draw him in while repelling me, I wonder if he's on to something. And if Roxanne's on to something.

I'm not deviating from my plan.

But one conversation, for curiosity's sake, can't hurt.

QUINN

JULY — FIVE WEEKS TO WIN OVER THE FACULTY

COLTON WAS right about me hiding. I was acting like a coward, and that's not who I am. So I decided, for this week at the very least, I'm going to put myself out there.

I start by meeting up with my friend Juliana and her family. We met when she and her now-fiancé came up to Boston to recruit students for their internship program. They work closely with the faculty in the architecture department and have somehow charmed all of them. If there's anyone who can help me win Dr. Keck over, it's these two.

Jules and I are sitting against a tree enjoying the shade while Ben and their girls are out in a canoe on the small, artificial lake. Her youngest, Sophie, stands up in the boat, throwing her arms wide and calling out that she's queen of the world. Ben intentionally rocks the boat, and Juliana jumps to her feet when Sophie almost topples over the side.

"Ben Thomas, don't you dare," Jules calls out to Ben, and he shoots her a wink over his shoulder, sputtering when the ten-year-old splashes water in his face, her sisters cackling on the other side of the boat.

Juliana settles back on the grass next to me. "Those two are going to be the death of me."

She can grumble all she wants, but it's so clear how much she loves the bond Ben's developed with her kids.

"Are you sure you're good to watch the girls tonight?" Juliana asks, chewing on her lip. "They're… a lot."

"Of course. You and Ben deserve a date night while on vacation. Inez and I already got all the snacks and have movies queued up. We're gonna pump them full of sugar and borderline inappropriate content before we send them back to you two to manage. I told Colton it was a girls' night and to find something to do."

"Oh, yes," Juliana says, her eyes sparkling. "The famous Colton."

"Jules…"

"The elusive *best friend*"—the emphasis on the words show how little she believes them—"I've heard so much about."

"Yes, my best frie—"

"Whose name you say all breathily now. That's not how you said it a couple years ago." She takes a dramatic breath. "*Oh, Colton.*"

"It's a hundred degrees today. I'm panting from the heat."

"Yeah, I believe you're in heat."

"Juliana Ryan," I say, all mock outrage. "Your children are ten feet away."

"Don't try to be all moralistic now," she says, nudging me with her elbow. "You asked me if I was sleeping with Ben when they were only *five* feet away, so that leg you're standing on looks a bit wobbly."

"Yeah, but I'm the irresponsible auntie type. You're a mother."

"Mothers like to hear about their friends getting their brains banged out as much as the next woman."

I laugh, covering my face as I lean back against the hard bark. "I'm not gossiping about my sex life."

"So there *is* sex."

I glance at her out of the corner of my eye. "Again, I'm not talking about my phenomenal, mind-altering sex life."

Juliana hollers and claps, earning a questioning look from Ben.

"Such a perv," I say.

"Hey, it's been a tough summer for you, and there's nothing better for stress relief than a steady stream of orgasms."

I have no doubt she gets plenty of those if the way she eyes Ben's back—muscles shifting under his shirt as he rows their boat back to shore—is any indication. He gracefully hops out of the boat, helping each of the girls onto the dock, and Juliana sighs.

Ben drops onto the blanket next to Juliana, pulling her onto his lap while the girls run off into the open field. "What are we talking about?"

I open my mouth to change the subject, but Juliana gives me a devious smile and says, "Quinn's sex life."

Ben groans, dropping his face into the crook of Juliana's neck. "Are you going off about Colton again?"

I gesture toward Ben, glaring daggers at Juliana. "How does he even know Colton exists?"

Juliana narrows her eyes. "What's the big deal if he's just a friend, Quinn?"

I narrow my eyes right back, but can't come up with a response.

Ben places a soft kiss on Juliana's cheek. "Lay off, baby. For all you know, Colton's ugly."

"He's really not," I say, sighing wistfully, to which both Juliana and Ben laugh. "But it's nothing serious. Just sex."

Ben scoffs, and Juliana reaches over to pinch his side.

"Do you have something to say, Mr. Thomas?" I ask, crossing my arms.

"Just that I've heard that before," he says, turning to Juliana. "How'd that work out for you?"

She lifts her left hand, twisting it this way and that so her engagement ring catches the light. "Worked out great, I'd say."

His smile softens, and he pulls her in for a kiss, whispering *I love you* on her lips.

I groan, dropping back on the blanket and tossing my arm over my eyes. "I get it. You're in love and adorable and you can fuck right off. Will you guys just tell me how to win over this professor so I can go enjoy my spinsterhood in peace?"

"Which professor is it?" Ben asks as Juliana slides off his lap.

"Lynn Keck."

He nods, running a hand through his thick, dark hair. "I went into her class when we were up there in April. She's into classic designs and wasn't excited about a program in Orlando because she thinks the buildings are too austere. Anything classic or unique might soften her up."

I light up. "I could take her class out to the Villa d'Este!"

He clutches his chest. "Oh damn, I fucking *love* the Villa d'Este. That's perfect."

Juliana glances between us. "What is it?"

Ben's eyes light up, going full architectural fanboy. "It's a Renaissance palace with these incredible gardens. A literal architectural masterpiece. You have a connection there, Quinn?"

I shrug. "No, but I'm sure my friend Tomasso does. The museum world is small. And there's no school-sanctioned trip this weekend, so if I could set it up…"

Ben nudges Juliana. "You should go with them."

She guffaws. "What?"

"Seriously," he says. "You'd love it. And you can help soften up Lynn."

My eyes go wide. "Oh my god, yes please."

Her mouth opens and closes, looking between us. "What about the kids?"

"What's an afternoon away in the scope of a two-week family vacation? I can handle the kids for a few hours," he says with an eye roll. On cue, Clara starts screaming about something Sophie did, and he grimaces. "It'll be fine. I'll take them to that gladiator school thing you were looking at and go get an espresso."

"Sophie with a sword? Lord save us," Juliana says, rubbing a hand over her forehead. "But okay, let's do this."

"Thank you thank you thank you," I say, throwing my body into hers and tackling her onto the blanket.

She laughs. "We'll see if you still want to thank me after Sophie conquers the city."

MY FRIENDS ARE THE BEST. Tomasso was able to get us a last-minute private tour for the Villa d'Este and Juliana's sacrificing her vacation to help me, even if she insists being away from the kids for a full afternoon is a vacation in and of itself.

We have about an hour until I'm supposed to meet Juliana, Dr. Keck, and the two dozen students who decided to join us. Just enough time for me to pop over to the school to print off an attendance list, but when I enter the office, I stop in my tracks.

My father's set up behind the desk to the left, a pair of reading glasses perched on his nose. He didn't need reading glasses the last time we spoke—fights not included—and the reminder of how much he's aged during our estrangement makes my heart tighten. No matter how much he's hurt me, he's still my father.

He glances up and startles when he spots me. I'm clearly unexpected, and the rare break in his exposure shows a flash of pain. "Good morning, Quinn."

"I just need to print something off really quickly. I can use the other printer," I say, turning to leave.

"How's the class going?" he calls at my back. His words sound sincere, and when I look back, I don't see any sarcasm or disdain.

I pause, wondering how much I should say. We'd been so close when I was younger, and the child inside me still believes he loves and cares.

"It's going well," I say, smiling slightly.

He huffs. "I knew you had it in you."

I bite my lip to distract from the moisture filling my eyes. This is by far the most praise I've received from him since the day I told him I wasn't going into the PhD program he picked out for me. "Thanks, Dad."

He smiles, always a small thing, but meaningful nonetheless. "Would you like to come to dinner with me tonight?"

My stomach swoops, and I let myself imagine what reconciling with my family would look like. I'd never be able to trust them fully or pick holidays with them over spending them with Colton and Gerry—my true family—but the truth is, I miss them. I miss my dad's gruff commentary on life and the way Christian and Joshua would roughhouse. I miss hiding underneath Dad's giant desk after I pulled a prank on one of them while Bradley pointed them in the wrong direction. I even miss Mom, the cold shake of her head when we were out of control.

I loved them all so much, and maybe reconnecting could heal something in me, the part of me that broke when I realized how easily I was thrown away.

"Sure," I say. "That sounds great."

His smile grows. "Perfect. You remember Dr. Livingston?"

My own smile falls in response. Of course I remember Dr. Livingston. He's one of the half-dozen friends of my dad's who offered me a spot in their graduate program after Colton won the fellowship. A part of the same group Dad used to trot me out in front of when I was in elementary school to list all the Roman emperors in order. A fun little party trick to entertain his friends.

When I was young, I thought it was him celebrating our connection. I believed we were bound on a deeper level because of our shared love, that him pushing me toward his field was a sign of how special I was to him. It wasn't until I was grown that I realized I was a pawn to show off, one that was easily sacrificed when I was no longer protecting the king.

Dad continues, completely unaware of the spiral inside me. "Dr. Livingston is in town for the week, and I thought you two could connect and discuss you joining his program next year."

"Why would I join his program, Dad?" I say, pure exhaustion seeping into my tone.

"You've done well in the classroom this summer. It shows I was right all along about the correct path for you."

"Dad, that's not—"

"You'll be older than most of your peers, but it's all about the quality of the work you produce."

"I have no—"

"There'll be some people, like Colton, you'll never be able to catch up to, but you can still make a substantial—"

"Dad," I shout, and he finally stops talking. "I'm not switching my career. I have no desire to go back to school."

His gaze softens. "I know losing the Harrow Fellowship to Colton was a heavy blow, but you're giving up all your talent because of one bad moment."

I want to scream, to sit him down and unload every thought and feeling I've had about how he's tried to manipulate and control me. To dissect everything with the fellowship until he understands that I'll never choose to get back on his path. But he won't listen, and it would bring up drama long since buried that would put Colton in the crosshairs.

He sighs when I don't speak, like I'm a disappointing child. In his eyes, I guess I am. "Why are you being so stubborn about this, Quinn? Don't you miss your family?"

I blink back tears. Of course he'd make the estrangement my fault. "That's your fault, not mine."

"Your brothers miss you. And your mother. Do you know

how much it hurt her that you barely even said hello at Bradley's engagement party?"

I doubt Mom thinks much of me at all, just like I rarely think of her. The two of us were never close. Gerry's who I go to for motherly love. As for my brothers, my guess is they've gotten comfortable with this estrangement and don't care enough to resolve it. I was never important enough to them to begin with.

Either way, I'm not reorganizing my life for a handful of people who don't love me enough to respect my wishes. And I'm not going to stand here feeling guilty about the consequences of my dad's actions.

"This was a great chat, Dad," I say. "We'll have to take a rain check on that dinner."

I leave the office and head to the second one farther down the hallway, determined to squash that split second of hope. Leaving Rome at the end of summer will be hard, but having a thousand miles between me and my father again? That's definitely something to look forward to.

LOOKING up at the palace looming over us, this was absolutely the right choice. Dr. Keck loves the unique architecture, and I love that this trip includes at least three hours of forced interaction with me.

Dr. Keck's been the hardest to pin down on this trip. I'm pretty sure she's been actively avoiding me, but she's softened up a bit in Juliana's presence, chatting about the students in the architecture major that Dr. Keck thinks may be the right fit for Juliana and Ben's internship program next year.

Now that our tour of the palace is over, we have some time to wander the extensive gardens, some of the most elaborate in the world. Miles of unique grottos and architectural features that accentuate the natural beauty of the landscape.

Each section of the garden is more impressive than the last, a marvelous combination of flora, stone, and water that weaves together to create a fairy land. Everything from giant, towering features that dwarf the viewer to intimate, bubbling brooks tucked in private alcoves, nothing but the sound of pounding water and chirping birds to keep you company. A peaceful paradise.

And then the rowdy college kids show up. I stumble upon a group of my students standing below a fertility statue fountain. The female bust has about thirty breasts, water shooting out of each nipple. The students are all laughing and taking inappropriate pictures, tongues hanging out like they're catching the water.

I snap a quick photo and shoot it off to Colton.

ME

College students are gross: Exhibit C.

COLTON

That's one we don't have in our collection.

ME

This generation is more creative than us.

I slip my phone back in my purse and dive into my pitch to Dr. Keck. She listens, engaged and respectful, and I feel a surge of hope.

"Look, I'm not going to be much help to you," she says when I finish, and my heart sinks. "I'm an instructor. I'm not on the tenure track, so my voice will carry less weight on something like this."

"You're still a professor in the program. Your support would make a difference."

She shrugs. "But it's dicey. My contract is year-to-year. It's a lot easier to boot an instructor, and I love my job. And, at the risk of sounding dismissive, our program already has a great professional development component. We don't need extra help from the staff."

"Is it conceited for me to assume you're talking about the KMG internship program?" Juliana jumps in, and Dr. Keck chuckles. "Did you know Quinn helped design that internship?"

Dr. Keck eyes me speculatively. "If you designed it, why haven't you been at any of the meetings?"

I straighten my spine. "Because I haven't been invited by the faculty. Juliana reached out to me on her own."

Juliana nudges me with her elbow. "Quinn's being uncharacteristically modest right now. She's the reason the program is so successful. I'd have been completely lost that first year without her."

She hums thoughtfully. "If you're involved with the curriculum, you should be in the meetings next year."

My heart races. That's way more than I expected from her. "I'd like that."

She nods once. Definitive. "If all the other professors are in, then I'll support you, too. Otherwise, I'm sorry."

"I have everyone on board except for Dr. Guarino. And I have a month left to sway him. Maybe with all of your help?" I give her a cheeky smile, and she laughs.

"Good luck. He's old school."

"Well, I'll have to change that, then. Won't I?"

She gusts out a sigh. "Fine. I'm in."

I barely hold back a squeal and the desire to throw my arms around her. Dr. Keck laughs and continues down the walkway.

I sidle up to Juliana. "You're the fucking best!"

"That was all you, babe!" she whispers back, hip checking me.

One person left to go. Yes, he's the hardest, like fighting the final boss in a video game, but I believe in us. And it's something Inez can keep in mind when she goes back to Florence for her second interview.

When we get home, I rush right into Colton's room. I ignore

him asking how it went and fly right to his desk where we set up our war room. I smack one of the white pawns off the map, grab a black pawn from the set on his bookshelf, and plop it down with a gratifying thunk.

Colton runs over to me, lifting me up and swinging me in the air as he kisses me.

And again, I spend the night in his bed.

COLTON

JULY — THREE WEEKS TO WIN OVER THE FACULTY

I GLARE at the half dozen tomes laid across the desk. This article is due by the end of the summer, and with only a few weeks left, I can't get past the hump. I'm supposed to get on a call with Richard soon to discuss it, hoping that will jog an idea.

My phone buzzes, breaking my standoff with my computer.

QUINN

I finished my meeting with the employers early.
You around?

I smile at the screen. One text from her, and everything's better. Not fixed, but better.

The past few weeks have been the best of my life. Lunch together at the local sandwich shop between classes. Dinner around our giant wooden table. And every night, she's in my bed. If it weren't for the threat of the summer's end hanging over us, I'd think I'd died and gone to heaven.

We'll still have our friendship when we get home, but this slice of paradise—the one where I spend every day devouring her stream of consciousness and she spends every night coming apart around me—has an expiry date that's quickly approaching. How will I pretend her walking away doesn't gut me?

I shoot back a response.

ME

Have a call with your dad to work out some issues in the article. Give me an hour?

QUINN

Lucky you.

Her sarcasm is laced with hurt, and it makes me ball my fists. She deserves so much better than she gets from him.

Less than ten minutes later, the FaceTime app on my computer lights up with an incoming call from Richard Riley.

"Colton. How are you doing, son?"

Great! Fucking your daughter every night and loving every second.

Probably not the best opener, so I go with something more neutral. "Could be worse. You heading to Venice soon?"

He grumbles something unintelligible. "I don't see why we have to take these students to different parts of Italy. They're adults."

I personally had a great time—life-changing, really—on my university-led weekend trip. But, again, I'm not sharing that with her father.

"I'm sure they appreciate it," I say instead.

"What a waste of the last two weeks in Rome," he harrumphs.

The reminder that we are coming up on the end of the summer shoots through me. Our program goes a week past Richard's, but that final day is looming, like the Grim Reaper waiting to drain the life out of me.

Richard sighs, snapping me out of my doom spiral. "Let's hear this challenge you have for me."

I run through the premise of the article and the limitations of my research. There's a reason he's so respected, even if he is a terrible father, and by the end of our call, relief washes over me. We sorted it out. I'll get this published and add to the growing list of reasons I'll eventually be granted tenure.

As we prepare to hang up, Richard clears his throat. "How's Quinn?"

It's like a shock from an electric fence hearing him say her name. Ten years, hundreds of calls, and dozens of dinners, and he's never asked about her.

"She's great," I say, unsure how much she'd want me to share with him.

The papers on his desk rustle as he moves them around, creating a static sound that muffles his words. I barely make out, "A shame she chose not to come to dinner."

I grit my teeth. She told me about dinner, how he was planning to ambush her. He should have been begging for the chance to spend time with her, not diminishing her accomplishments from this summer and trying to force her back into the box he created.

"You should ask her about her work," I say. "You'd be proud."

He grunts. "Her internship class."

I bite the inside of my cheek to slow my response. "It's impressive what she's accomplished."

"Well, she was never lacking in ability. Drive and follow-through, on the other hand…"

I need to take a breath, a step back, anything to keep me from biting off his head. "With all due respect, she's plenty driven. She convinced the faculty—who were dead set on their plan—to give her a chance to prove them wrong. And she hasn't coasted her way through the course. She created something incredible with little guidance or support."

He rolls his eyes, an undignified look on a man of his age. "I'm glad she's getting her act together. Now if we can help her see that the mistakes of the past few years can be reversed, she'll go back to school."

"I'm not planning on convincing her of anything. Her job makes her happy. She doesn't need to change."

"She broke down when she didn't get the Harrow Fellowship and threw away everything she spent her life working toward. Excuse me if I don't praise the fact that she's doing an okay job."

"Who do you think you are?" The words are out of my mouth before I can stop them.

Richard's eyebrows disappear into his hairline. "I think I'm her father. Who the fuck are you?"

"Someone who actually knows her." *Someone who loves her.*

"Think long and hard before you keep talking. You have shown incredible promise, and I'd like to continue our working relationship, but I value respect more than talent."

It's a clear threat. A powerful, insufferable man waving his dick around to reinforce that he can treat people however he wants because no one will stop him.

Recommendations from people in the field are vital for tenure review. Dr. Cassia will always support me, but if I have the top scholar in the field bad-mouthing me, moving forward will be a lot more difficult. But stopping the next words out of my mouth is impossible, like trying to catch a wave on the beach.

"And I value loyalty over respect," I say. "So here's the truth. Quinn isn't good at her job. She's phenomenal. She has every student and almost every faculty member eating out of her hand.

"Your daughter's brilliant. If she wanted a PhD in Roman history, she'd have one. She chose to do something else with her life. You're choosing to miss out on a relationship with the most incredible person I've ever met because you think you know better for her than she does. So no, I'm not going to think before I tell you that you're royally fucking up every day you choose not to be a part of her life."

His face goes bright red, a trait I've never had cause to learn Quinn inherited from him, and I can make out beads of sweat pooling on his lip even through the grainy image of the video call. Now that I've finished my tirade, a ball of anxiety settles in my gut. The fire in his eyes scares the living shit out of me.

What was I thinking?

"Thank you, Dr. Miller, for your unsolicited feedback," he says. "Good luck on your academic journey. You'll need it."

He ends the call before I can respond, and I stare at the blank screen. Adrenaline courses through my limbs. I need to move, to do something to make me forget that I may have fucked up my career when both my mom and I are dependent on my salary.

I turn toward the end of my desk, swiping the books off with a yell. My body turns with the movement, and I stop short when I see Quinn standing in the doorway. My breath rushes out of my body.

She's wearing that damn white lingerie.

I scan her body, my own responding even amid the fear and anger running through my veins. When I reach her face again, she has tears in her eyes.

"You defended me," she says.

"Yes."

"But you were counting on his recommendation for tenure."

I pull in a deep breath and nod. "That was the plan."

Her gulp is audible, and she blinks quickly. "He can be really vindictive, Colton."

"I know."

She closes the distance between us, going up to her toes and pressing a featherlight kiss to my lips. A shudder racks my body. The vulnerability and gratitude in that kiss wipes out any regret I have. I'd do anything—sacrifice anything—for her to know she's loved.

She deepens the kiss, and I wrap one hand around the back of her head. I let her maneuver us to the plush chair in the corner. I drop back when my legs hit the seat, expecting her to come down with me. Instead, she stands between my legs and runs her hands through my hair. My eyes drift closed, and I plant a soft kiss on her wrist.

"You brought the lingerie," I say, my voice coming out husky.

"You told me to."

I did, but if I told the Colton of two months ago that Quinn would both listen to the suggestion and allow me to see her this way, he'd have assumed I'm on drugs.

She runs her hand down my neck and over my chest, continuing down my torso in a slow, addictive slide. She kneels between my legs, looking at me from under her lashes as she unbuttons my pants.

I place my hand over hers. "You don't have to do that."

It's not like it's the first time, but I don't like the idea of her doing it as a reward. She deserves to be supported because she's her—gorgeous, dazzling her—with no expectations.

"Please." That word on her lips wrecks me. "I want to."

She shifts my pants down my legs, removing them completely before sitting up on her knees, undoing the buttons of my shirt with steady hands. She undresses me slowly, almost reverently, until I'm completely naked before her.

She grips me, and my head drops back when she twirls her tongue around the tip. I let out a deep groan, my breath turning ragged. She hums in response, and my gaze is immediately drawn back to her. I can never keep my eyes away from her for long. Her gaze stays on me with every leisurely bob of her head, and my heart clenches at the trust in her eyes even as I feel the familiar tinge at the base of my spine.

"Stop." I barely force out the word. "I want to be inside you when I finish."

Her smile is so sweet, almost shy, when she pulls away. She stands between my knees and slips one strap off, followed by the other, before she lets the lingerie drop to the floor in a pool of white lace. The look on her face, open and unguarded—is it too hopeful to say loving?—freezes me in place. Her underwear slips over her hips, dropping to join its pair on the ground.

She climbs into my lap and kisses me. I want to wrap myself up in her, to feel and taste every inch like it's the first time, but she pulls away from me. Her fingers map my face, my jaw, my neck; her eyes shine with so much affection I can hardly breathe.

Quinn notches me at her entrance and lowers herself torturously slow. Our eyes never leave each other. I can't think beyond her perfect heat wrapped around me, squeezing me tight.

There's none of the frenzied energy that normally drives us. No hard, punishing movements. My cock swells, but it's the sensation in my chest that's driving me to the brink. It's like my soul is swelling, too. Like it's trying to escape my body, reaching out for hers as if they were always meant to be one. Like it recognized something from the beginning and finally sees the hope that its pair will recognize it, too.

Quinn's eyes fill with tears, and I bring my hand up to wipe away the couple that escape.

"Quinn, what's wrong?" I want to take away her pain, to stand in front of her and defend her from anything that threatens to hurt her.

"Nothing's wrong," she insists, running her hand through my hair.

"If that were true, you wouldn't be crying."

"I'm not sad. It's just… I feel…" And when I look in her eyes, I see it. There's no heartbreak, no fear or insecurity. I can see what she can't say yet. I'm not a convenient fuck or a living vibrator. I'm more to her. *We* are more.

And I know she's not ready to deal with what that means, so instead I pull her forward for a soft kiss and place my forehead against hers.

"Me, too," I whisper. The closest I can come to saying what I mean without scaring the living shit out of her.

Because what I want to say is that I'm hers, so utterly and

completely that I could never belong to anyone else, even when she doesn't want me anymore. She's my best friend, my Venus, the love of my goddamn life, regardless of whether or not I'm hers. And all I can do is hope what I see on her face isn't a desperate figment of my imagination.

We don't say anything else as she kisses me and begins to move. The only sounds are our soft breaths and sighs. When we come together, my face buried in her neck, I fight to swallow down the words again.

If she needs time, I'll give it to her.

I've waited this long already. And she's worth every second.

QUINN

THE NIGHTMARE STARTLES ME AWAKE, shaking the entire bed as my body shoots up. The dream's already hazy, fading into a jumble of distorted images and disjointed storylines. But the feelings are still there. The shame and fear. The hurt. And the knowledge that it was about Colton and the life that had been stripped away from him for defending me.

I'm still shaking, trying to reconcile my brain's response to yesterday's events.

The movement must have woken Colt, because he sits up next to me, placing a soft kiss on my shoulder. "Quinn? You okay?"

I force a jerky nod. "Yeah. Weird dream."

He yawns, a ridiculous, over-the-top sound that chases away some of the darkness inside me. "Wanna talk about it?"

"No. I'm good."

He nods against my shoulder, wrapping his arm around my waist and pulling me down with him. The casual intimacy makes my heart squeeze.

"Let's go back to sleep," he says.

No way I'll sleep with the jittery feeling under my skin, but I place my head on the pillow next to Colton's, his arm thrown over my middle as I attempt to force the issue. After a few minutes of my squirming, Colton chuckles, his laugh vibrating from deep in his chest and through my body.

He throws his feet over the side of the bed. "I guess we're up, then."

I watch in confusion as he grabs a pair of jeans and slides them on.

"I'll go back to my room," I say.

He rubs a hand over his sleep rumpled hair. The gap in his curtains offers just enough light to see the way his muscles flex. "Nope. We've got plans."

I laugh and grab my phone from the bedside table, shooting a quick glance at the time. "Plans? At two o'clock in the morning?"

"Yes, ma'am," he answers, sounding more awake with each word. "I've been meaning to set an alarm anyway, so this dream you refuse to talk to me about"—he pauses and sends me a chastising look—"knocked something off my to-do list."

He keeps moving around the room, grabbing clothes and shoes like it's completely normal to go from a dead sleep to leaving the house in the middle of the night.

"Where are we supposedly going?" I ask.

"We haven't done the Trevi yet."

"The Trevi?"

He flicks on the lamp and I wince at the influx of light. "Yes, Quinn. It's this famous fountain where people throw coins to guarantee they'll come back to Rome one day. Surprised you haven't heard—"

His sarcastic response is cut off by a pillow to the face, while I laugh so loudly I worry about waking up Inez. "Fuck off. I know what the Trevi is. My question is why we'd get up now instead of stopping by while we're already out in the city."

His brows pull together. "You hate the Trevi during the day."

He's right, of course. The Trevi Fountain is one of the most epic sights in the city, a massive fountain the size of half a football field with elaborate travertine sculptures butting up to the building behind it.

Unfortunately, it's also one of the most popular sights in Rome, and during the day it's flooded with tourists, so packed that you can hardly make it to the edge of the fountain, much less enjoy the magnificence of the art. When the sun's up, visiting the Trevi's transactional. Get to the front. Throw your coin. Move over for the next person.

But at night, with the sculptures illuminated by dramatic lighting and no tourists to overpower the rush of the millions of gallons of water, it's perfect. I dragged Colton and our other friends there more than once after a drunken night out.

"Colt, were you actually going to set an alarm?" I ask.

He scoffs. "We certainly aren't partying until two in the morning anymore."

I chew on my bottom lip. "You're kind of the sweetest." He busies himself with getting ready to hide his pleased smile. "But we don't have to do this."

He throws one of his shirts at my face. "Get your ass out of bed, Chaos, or I'm leaving without you."

I laugh and slip his shirt over my head to make the dash back to my room for my own clothes.

Ten minutes later, and I'm following Colton down the cobble-stone street to his Vespa. The restaurants and bars around us are closed, but the city's never silent, laughter and music streaming to the street from house parties continuing into the early morning.

The drive isn't far, less than fifteen minutes with the roads clear, and I nestle into Colton's back, using the excuse to snug-gle up.

Colton parks his Vespa a few blocks away, knowing I'll want to savor the joy of walking up to it. The tight streets of Rome make for the most epic reveals, narrow, almost claustrophobic walkways giving way to large piazzas hosting heart-stopping sights with no warning. My skin tingles when I hear the rush of the water from around the corner, so close, but still out of sight. A siren's song drawing us in.

And then it's there. Oceanus lit up above the pool, shining like the god he is. Two horses sit at his feet, one bucking and one docile, a vivid representation of the unpredictability of the sea. It's massive and wild, a bit gaudy, but so essentially Roman.

The fountain doesn't belong solely to us tonight. There's a group of drunk kids—maybe study abroad students, though thankfully not ours. Colt and I watch as they toss at least five Euros each into the fountain while trying to get the perfect picture. I'm sure the Roman charities that receive all the money thrown in are more than grateful for drunk people.

Besides the very generous college students, there's a couple nestled back on the stadium-style cement benches facing the fountain, the woman straddling the man as they push the boundaries of Italy's public decency laws. Colton snorts, placing a hand on the small of my back to lead me to the far side, away from the mayhem and potential sex show.

He slips a coin into my hand with a small smile before turning his back to the fountain, using his right hand to toss the coin over his left shoulder in a practiced move.

I twist to face away from the fountain, following the same precise movements. There are specific rules for this ritual. It doesn't matter that my logical brain knows it isn't real when Rome's on the line, so I relish the plunk as my coin sinks below the surface.

I sit on the curved edge of the fountain and let my fingers play through the pool. "This is the most Roman thing ever, isn't it?"

He tilts his head as he takes a seat beside me. "I can see that. It's a bit ostentatious, but Rome's always been about big displays. Wealth, art, power. It's carved in the lines of its sights."

"True, but I didn't mean the fountain. I meant the legend. There are wishing fountains all over the world." My hand creates ripples across the surface. "People stop and toss in coins, praying for their deepest wish to come true. To find love. To get that promotion. To get pregnant. All their dreams, poured out into these tiny scraps of metal. But not here. Here, you throw in a coin to guarantee you come back one day. Because if you're in Rome, what else could you wish for other than the joy of seeing it again?"

"No other wish could compete," he says.

I glance over to find him watching me, that same soft smile on his lips and a gleam in his eye that makes me wonder if there *is* something else he'd wish for. Heat rushes through my veins, and I have to look away. I glance over his shoulder, my eyes catching on the most awkward conversation piece possible.

The Fountain of Love.

The drinking fountain has two spouts with the same fresh drinking water that's available all over the city. Those streams cross before landing in a large basin. Legend says any couple who drinks from the fountain at the same time will have a life full of love and faithfulness.

"Have you ever drunk from it?" Colton asks quietly, almost reverently.

Both of us keep our eyes glued to the fountain. "Nuh-uh. You?"

He clears his throat. "Never had someone I wanted to drink with."

I think I hear an unspoken *until you* at the end of that sentence, and I can't say if the rush I feel is joy or terror.

Things feel different after the confrontation with my dad. I've never had someone stand up for me like that. No one in my family has been willing to cross him. No one *ever* chooses me.

Until him.

"Colt, do you—"

A splash keeps me from finishing the sentence. I twirl around to find one of the college students resurfacing, sputtering while his friends howl. A sharp whistle sounds from the roof of one of the buildings on the piazza where a police officer is stationed to watch the fountain. Another officer rushes down the steps to the water's edge.

I try to rein in my laughter at the sight of the large man trying to catch the student, who flops around like a slippery fish near the fountain's edge as he tries to avoid being caught.

"Let's get out of here," I say.

Colton places a hand on my arm to stop me. "Were you going to say something?"

His deep green eyes are so earnest, so hopeful, that it's suddenly blindingly obvious. This means something to him beyond our friendship and a really great sex life. The answer to the question I was going to ask—if he thought we could be more than a summer hookup—is a resounding yes. It's equal parts tempting and terrifying.

I gulp and send another glance back at the students. Was that a sign? Maybe I'm not ready for something real with him and would destroy our friendship by asking for more. Maybe I'm too broken—too insecure underneath all the noise and bluster—to maintain a healthy relationship. Colton doesn't deserve someone half in.

Or maybe I'm just a coward.

Either way, the moment passed.

"It wasn't important. Let's go home and get some sleep."

His jaw tightens, but he doesn't push me on it, and I'm grateful for how well he knows me.

When we get home, I tell him I'm going to my own room since it's too late for us to hook up, kicking myself when that furrow appears between his brows. And instead of spending the night next to the person who's quickly becoming everything, I spend the night alone, staring into the dark and telling myself I need to figure this out before we both get hurt.

I AVOID Inez's wide eyes as I pick my way through the stalls of the Campo dei Fiori market, a large piazza packed full with tents. While the market has seen a drastic uptick in stalls selling kitschy souvenirs since I was last here, the fresh fruit and vegetables are still some of the best in the city.

"So you're telling me that this man, the one you've been having incredible, wild sex with"—Inez's voice drops low on the word *sex*, like she's worried the old lady selling fruit will judge us —"stood up to your father, a man who could make or break his career."

I gulp, but hide it with a quick word to the vendor, requesting a bundle of fresh cherries. She slips out a produce bag with a sly smile and a wink before gathering the fruit.

"Yes, that's what I'm telling you," I finally say to Inez after paying and moving away from the stall.

"And then he made sweet, tender love to you?" she asks with stars in her eyes, and I snort. "And *then*, he took you to one of your favorite places in the middle of the night just because he knew it would make you smile?"

I sigh heavily. "Yes."

She squeals loudly enough to draw stares. "Oh my god, he loves you so much! Tomasso and I are going to need a double date ASAP."

My stomach clenches, but I force an eye roll. "No double dates. And of course Colton loves me. I'm one of his best friends."

"You know what I mean. He's *in* love with you."

My heart joins in with my stomach's roiling, my throat going dry. After last night, her words don't sound wrong. They sound the opposite of wrong, but I don't know if I can trust it. What I *do* know is if I give Inez an inch on this, she'll take a mile.

"It's just sex," I say, and the words taste like ash in my mouth.

She pulls on my arm to stop me from walking up to another vendor. "*Mija*," she starts with a bite to her tone.

I groan and stomp my feet like a toddler who didn't get her way. "Can't you let me have this?"

"I could, but willful ignorance isn't a good look on you. Don't you want to be happy?"

Of course I want to be happy. Who would say, *no, I actually want to be miserable. Thanks.* But what happiness actually looks like is a completely different question.

I don't know what would happen if I told him I wanted to try for real. Right now, it's easy. We're friends and fuck like bunnies on the side. The best of both worlds.

I've never been more comfortable in a friendship than I am with Colton. He accepts me fully and completely, and there's never been a moment I've questioned that. But that's as friends. It's easy not to get scared or antsy or insecure in a friendship.

But if we tried to be more? I could struggle with the same issues that had plagued every other relationship until we explode and take out our friendship in the blast. I don't know how I'd handle it if he ended up like Jas, who can't even make eye contact with me.

But if we end this thing when we leave as planned, we can guarantee our friendship. I can keep him.

And isn't that the most important thing?

Inez watches me curiously, and I realize I'd stared off into space for god knows how long. I force a smile. "I'll think about it."

She squeals and flails her arms. "The double date?"

"Absolutely not. But everything else you said."

She throws her arms around me, the tomatoes in one of her bags swinging around to hit me in the gut. "That's so much better than I expected from you!"

"Don't get ahead of yourself," I say, linking my arm through hers.

She sighs, looking around us like she needs to savor every

door, every alley, every stone. "Only three more weeks. It's gone by so fast."

"You may be back here before you know it," I say with forced levity. She had her second and final interview with Leonardo da Vinci a few days ago and is expecting an offer or rejection any day now.

She slips her arm around my shoulder. "I don't want to talk about that right now. I just want to enjoy what we've created here."

I lay my head on her shoulder as we continue walking. "You've done an amazing job."

She lays her head on top of mine, the two of us continuing to walk like conjoined twins. "I've been so nervous I was going to ruin the entire program."

I pull back to look at her as we make our way toward the river, the sound of the water rushing around us. "It's been perfect. Absolutely perfect. I'm so proud of you."

She sniffs and pops a quick kiss to the top of my head. "I'm so grateful you're here."

"Always." We clutch each other tighter, making our way back into our neighborhood and the life we've built here. A life that's made me happier than I've been in a long time.

But it's temporary. In a few weeks, we'll be gone. Some other college will move into our school and another person will take over my bedroom.

And, if everything else in my Roman life is temporary, how can I be sure what Colton and I are feeling isn't temporary, too?

QUINN

JULY — TWO WEEKS TO WIN OVER THE FACULTY

THE ENTIRE SUMMER has been leading to this moment. After three months of new and exciting challenges that have changed their lives forever, my students ready to present.

It's also my last-ditch effort to get Dr. Guarino on board.

He's resisted every attempt to connect with him. Enticing him with things around the city? *I'm from Rome. There's nothing new you can offer me.* Asking for his advice? *I don't have time to hold your hand.* Using the other professors to sway him? *I'm shocked you all have bought into this absurdity.*

But I have one last, shameless card in my hands. For all his asshole tendencies, he does care about his students. He couldn't say no when Anthony, a business and Italian double major, begged him to watch his presentation.

He's now sitting at the back, flipping through composition papers and ignoring the other students, until Anthony takes the stage.

It's perfect.

He talks about the industry-specific words he learned that

aren't taught in his Italian classes, explaining how this experience took his language skills from excellent to professionally fluent. And he does it all in perfectly accented Italian, much to the confusion of the students in English-speaking internships who don't know much beyond hello, thank you, and where's the closest gelateria?

My eyes ping-pong between Anthony and Dr. Guarino through the presentation. He nods along, and I even detect a small smile when Anthony spouts off what I believe are the Italian words for capital expenditures and dividends.

I breathe a sigh of relief when he opens the floor to questions. Dr. Guarino throws out three in rapid succession, using specific business terminology like he's hoping to trip Anthony up and give himself an excuse to continue his Quinn hating in peace. Anthony—bless him—never fumbles. Dr. Guarino's left with one last question. "How has the work in this classroom—not at your internship site—benefitted you?"

Anthony's quick to answer. "It's been life-changing. Professor Riley made all of us reflect on our experience and how it connects to what we're studying. The internship would have been a good experience on its own, but this class and Professor Riley's expertise on professional development took it to another level. It was the best experience of my college career."

I meet Dr. Guarino's eyes across the room, and I fight hard to keep the smirk off my face. I didn't even prep Anthony with that answer. It was all him, and I feel vindicated in ways I never imagined.

After a pause, Dr. Guarino nods. "Very good, Anthony."

I lift my eyes from him, and they snag on the open classroom door. My father stands there with his brows drawn together, eyes pinned to the student who just praised me. He meets my gaze for a second before walking away.

A small part of me wants to chase after him, like when I was a little girl, running through the Forum to keep up with him, leaping off ancient stones like my very own jungle gym. His program officially ends today, which means he's leaving and I can walk through the school without looking over my shoulder, but it also means that glimmer of potential has run its course. I shake off the moment, refocusing on my students.

When the last presentation wraps up and I release everyone, Dr. Guarino stays behind.

"Impressive work, Professor Riley."

I bite back my smile. It's the first time he's used the term professor when addressing me. It has to be a good sign.

"Thank you, Dr. Guarino. It was a challenging and rewarding summer for us all."

He clears his throat and squares his shoulders like he's preparing for battle. "I can admit when I'm wrong. I didn't expect you to succeed, and I'm pleasantly surprised."

"So I can tell the other faculty members that you're on board?"

"Non posso crederci," he mutters. "I have some thinking to do."

"Is that a yes?" I ask as he turns away from me.

"That's not a no."

I smile at his back as he leaves the classroom. I'll take what I can get. "I appreciate your support, Giancarlo."

He stops in his tracks. "You may still call me Dr. Guarino."

Small wins, then.

I vibrate while waiting for the last of Colton's students to leave his room. I bounce by the door, desperate to release some of this energy until I can talk to him.

That wasn't an official yes from Dr. Guarino, but it might as well have been. In a couple weeks, all five professors will stand up in Boston and say this program was a success. That the initiative will harm students more than help them. This won't just be a step toward healing the Billings culture. It'll be a fucking leap.

While I'm waiting, Inez wanders up, staring at her phone in a daze.

"Inez," I call, the excitement nearly bursting out of me, and she jumps like a cat trying to escape water. She looks terrified, and my enthusiasm drains out of me. "What happened? Is everything okay?"

She blinks down at her phone again and then back at me. "I got it."

In the excitement for my own victory, it takes my brain a few seconds to catch up.

"The job?" I ask, and she nods. "Congratulations!"

I wrap my arms around her before she can see the way my lip quivers.

"What am I supposed to do, Quinn?" she asks.

I pull back. My knee-jerk reaction is to tell her to stay in Boston, to beg her not to leave. But she doesn't need my trauma dumped on her when she's making one of the biggest decisions of her life.

"When do you have to give them an answer?"

"Three weeks. They said they recognize it would be a huge move and want me to have time to think about it. Which is a good sign for the work environment, don't you think?"

A breath whooshes out of me. Three weeks means we'll be back in Boston, and we'll have proof that the faculty and staff can pleasantly work together. That may be the difference between her staying or going.

"It's totally a good sign," I say. "I can't tell you what to do, but I can tell you that I just had a really great conversation with Dr. Guarino."

Her eyes go wide. "He agreed to back off the initiative?"

I tilt my head back and forth. "Not *officially* yet, but he's going to. And he said he was *wrong*, Inez. Wrong! I doubt the man's ever said that word before. So, you know. In case that changes anything."

She smiles, but it's wobbly. "He held out for so long."

I take her face between my hands. "Whatever you decide, that school is going to be so lucky to have you."

She dips her head. "You're right. And we have so much to celebrate. Dinner tonight? You and Colton, plus me and Tomasso?"

"Stop trying to get us to double date," I say with a laugh. "But yes, I'd love to go to dinner with my three closest *friends*."

She gives me a disbelieving laugh before heading down the hallway as the students started pouring out of Colton's classroom. The excited jitters over getting Dr. Guarino's approval mix with the nervous jitters over Inez, and I'm going to explode if I don't get to talk to him within the next fifteen seconds.

When the last student leaves, I slip in and lock the door before running to Colton. At the sight of him, the nerves settle. Whatever happens with Inez, all five professors have admitted the value I bring to campus—and, by extension, the staff in general. I did what no one besides the two of us thought was possible. I jump and wrap my legs around him, something I've never felt comfortable doing in my entire life, but he's already proven he can—and will—catch me. I brace my arms on his shoulders and devour his mouth.

He laughs against my lips. "Not that I'm complaining, because I think this is how you should always greet me, but what's with the attack?"

I wiggle so he'll set me down, loving the way our bodies slid together. "The students finished their presentations."

He smiles, and I pop onto my toes to peck his dimple.

"So you're pretty much done," he says. "The last class is just a discussion to fill time, right?"

"Yes, but that's not why I'm freaking out." I do a weird wiggle dance. "Dr. Guarino came to the presentation. He said, and I quote, 'I can admit when I'm wrong.' It's done. I got them all."

I start humming the *Pokémon* theme song as I continue my

dance. He sputters a bit, then breaks out in the biggest smile, leaning down to pull me into a deep kiss.

"I'm so fucking proud of you," he whispers against my lips, and tears prick my eyes.

"It's not all sunshine and rainbows," I say, pulling back. "Inez heard back. She got the job."

"Quinn," he says softly, like I'm breakable and he has to handle me with care.

I wave my hand in front of my eyes in an attempt to dry the tears before they fall. "God, I'm a mess. Why am I crying? Today's a good day! I got Dr. Guarino on board and my best friend got a job offer."

"You can be happy for her and sad for yourself, Quinn. It doesn't make you a bad person. Has she decided?"

I shake my head. "No, she has a few weeks to think about it."

He kisses my forehead, and I lean into the pressure that grounds me, just like it always has.

"Either way, she'll be there with you when you present in Boston. And so will all the professors."

And so will Colton. By my side—cheering me on—just like we've always been for each other.

3 0

COLTON

TEN YEARS AGO

I DON'T WANT to be in this cold ballroom, even if Quinn's brilliant smile almost makes the trip worth it. This is the moment Dr. Cassia has been pushing us toward for the past three years. The Harrow Fellowship, the most prestigious award in the world for undergraduates studying ancient history.

It gives you access to the top research facilities, faculty advisors, and funding through the completion of your PhD. They take one student a year in each area of study, which means Quinn and I are competing against each other. I didn't even plan on coming to New York since Quinn's going to win. I'll be happy for her, of course, but I'll also have to watch my dreams go down the drain. I don't think I'm strong enough for that.

Quinn begged me to come, batting those giant brown eyes. She swears I have a shot, that my work is as good as hers. I don't disagree with her, but she's also a legacy to the program. Her father won it forty years ago, and it'll take something huge to steal the spot from her. When I said as much, she pouted and said I should come to support her. Four years, and I still haven't sorted out how to say no to her.

So here I am, getting ready to watch as the girl of my dreams walks away with the program of my dreams to the city of my dreams, leaving me behind with nothing.

We're at a round table with Quinn's family and Dr. Cassia. I wish I had my mom's steady presence, but she couldn't get off work. I've barely eaten the fancy five-course meal they serve us, my leg bouncing incessantly as the announcer moves through the winners—China, Egypt, Greece, Mesopotamia—inching our way down the program to Rome.

The emcee stands at the podium as the screen behind him displays the five finalists for Rome. I tug at my oversized suit jacket, like that can somehow make me fit in with the rest of the people on display at the front of the room. My scowling head-shot's situated right next to Quinn's, which shines like a beacon.

"And here to announce the winner is the student's faculty advisor, Dr. Gianna Cassia."

Dr. Cassia wiggles her eyebrows at the two of us as she stands and heads toward the stage. Quinn squeezes my hand and chews on her bottom lip. I want to pull her into my arms and assure her she has nothing to worry about, even while I'm fighting to keep the moisture out of my eyes.

"Thank you for joining us tonight," Dr. Cassia says. Her confident, slightly accented voice booms through the room. "This is the first time in over a decade that I haven't been involved in this decision, which means it's the first time in over a decade that I've had the honor of working with a student of this caliber.

"It's a rare moment in a professor's life when they interact with a student they know will dominate their field. It's a shocking experience when the person is only eighteen years old."

She pauses, and I grin down at Quinn. She came blustering into Chadoin like a hurricane and blew everyone away, even the woman she spent her life idolizing.

Dr. Cassia continues. "Now, that doesn't mean those early essays were great. They were still the work of an eighteen-year-old with no substantial training. But I saw the potential, even then. The ideas were insightful and unique. Once given the proper guidance, their work became even more impressive. Their research will greatly impact the field, and I'm honored to have had the chance to mentor them.

"Everyone, please join me in congratulating this year's recipient of the Harrow Fellowship for Ancient Roman History..." She pauses for dramatic effect. Quinn and I turn towards each other. "Colton Miller."

The fuck?

I continue to stare at Quinn as her face breaks out in a giant smile. She stands and throws her arms around my neck, but I'm frozen.

This doesn't make sense. My research is good, great even, but not better than Quinn's. She pulls me to stand and pushes me toward the stage in a daze.

When I reach Dr. Cassia, she pulls me in for a hug. "Congratulations, Colton. I've never seen a student more deserving."

She guides me to the podium. Fuck me. I didn't prepare anything because it seemed like an exercise in masochism. And now I have to speak in front of a giant room with no preparation. Sweat beads on my forehead and I think I might pass out. I look into the audience and see Quinn nodding encouragingly.

I keep my eyes on her the entire time, knowing I won't make it if my gaze wanders. "Thank you for this incredible opportunity. I'm honored to have been selected and I look forward to working with the foundation in Rome next year."

I lift the award and nod out toward the crowd. Short and sweet.

I make it back to the table on unsteady legs. Dr. Riley leans over to shake my hand. "Congratulations, son. Welcome to the Harrow family."

"Thank you, sir." I turn to Quinn. "I'm so sorry. I don't know how this happened."

Her eyes shine, and I know she's holding back for my sake. "You have nothing to be sorry for. You deserve this. I'm so happy for you, Colt."

"What are you going to do?" I ask.

She shrugs. "Figure it out. Go to grad school. Find a job. Live my life."

Dr. Riley puts his arm around her shoulders. "There are plenty of other opportunities, Quinn. We'll write up a plan, and I'll cover the costs so you can pursue what you're meant to."

She smiles tightly at him. "Thanks, Dad."

Quinn begs for us to explore New York after the program wraps up. If it'll make her smile after losing, I'll do anything she wants. I drag my tired and emotionally exhausted body down the sidewalk as she points out interesting buildings and cool bars.

She pulls me into one and plops me down on a bench along the bar.

"I can't believe you get to be in Rome all next year," she says as she sips her drink.

"Yeah. Me neither. I didn't think I stood a chance."

She grabs my chin and forces my eyes to hers. "Stop. Right now. You don't see yourself the way everyone around you does. You're *brilliant*. Brilliant and creative and so fucking talented. They'd have been idiots not to pick you."

"You realize you were my competition, right?"

She laughs, an airy, genuine sound I wouldn't have expected to hear right after losing the fellowship she always expected to win. "I knew they were going to choose you. Why do you think I was so adamant you come tonight? I had no doubt because I've seen your work."

She's right. I *am* fucking brilliant. I received the most prestigious fellowship in my field. Why am I still second guessing whether I have something to contribute? And to top it all off, I beat out someone incredibly talented, not to mention incredibly connected. That wouldn't happen unless I deserved it. Unless what I brought to the table was unique and worthwhile.

That thought settles into my bones. I'm going back to Rome. Without her. I'm torn between the overwhelming relief that my future is still on track and the desire to throw it all away to stay close to her. This beautiful, strong, overwhelming girl who pushes me toward my dreams, even when it means me stealing hers.

My eyes fill with tears. When I try to blink them away, she shakes her head. "You can cry, you know. You don't have to be all strong, manly man and all that."

I laugh as a tear slides down my cheek. "I'm gonna miss you."

She shifts on the bench and wraps her arms around me, laying her head on my chest. "You're going to forget all about me once you're off living the big life in Rome."

"There's nothing in this world that could make me forget you, Chaos."

She tilts her head but keeps it on my chest. "Promise?"

I kiss her forehead, taking a minute to breathe her in. Even with the distance, her request is an easy promise to keep. This girl's in my bones, and nothing will get her out.

"I promise. You're unforgettable."

QUINN

AUGUST — ONE WEEK TO WIN OVER THE FACULTY

My last class.

For an opportunity I barely wanted, this summer has been a game changer.

As always, we're sitting in our little, cramped room for our Wednesday morning class. But unlike the other Wednesday mornings, no one's mind is fully here today. The internships are done, there's nothing else to discuss, and it feels like a waste of time. I'm sure the students are just as anxious to get out of this room and soak in their last few days in Rome.

We have one last group dinner tomorrow night, and then the program's officially over. Students will head off, some to the airport to go home and others to travel for a couple weeks before the fall semester kicks off back in Boston.

And I'm going to get one week in Rome with Colton. One more week to figure out if I have the guts to accept more from him.

One of the students half-heartedly answers my latest discussion question. I'm starting to wonder if I should call it for all of our sakes when Colton comes barreling through the door.

"I'm sorry for the interruption." He turns serious eyes on me. "There's an emergency and we need to cancel the rest of class. Professor Riley, I need you to come with me right away."

"What's going on?" I ask, nausea settling in my gut.

The students chime in alongside me.

"Is everything okay?"

"What's going on?"

"Did something happen at home?"

Colton lifts his hands, mustering all the professorial intimidation he has. The students cut off immediately, and I'd have laughed at the power he holds over them if I didn't feel like I'm going to puke.

"I assure you, there's nothing to worry about. It's a personal matter Professor Riley needs to attend to, so please gather your things and enjoy your last days in Rome. Professor Riley, come with me quickly."

My heart's in my throat, my stomach churning as I hurry after him.

We rush up behind a crowd standing at the door—Colton's students, who he already dismissed.

"Let us through, guys," Colton calls out.

"Dr. Miller, you don't want to go out there right now. It's pouring."

Colton glances over his shoulder at me. His stern mask never breaks, but I see the glint in his eyes. The expression eases my nerves, and he sees the question in my eyes. *What are you up to, Colt?* He shakes his head, glancing sideways at the students.

"Thanks for the heads up, but we need to get through. It's an emergency."

The class parts like the Red Sea, and Colton subtly grabs my hand to pull me behind him.

"What the hell is going on, Colton?"

"Everything's fine. Trust me. You'll be happy if you do."

He tugs me after him as we run through the rain, not bothering with umbrellas. The chilly water is refreshing in the Roman heat, soaking us through in seconds. He tosses me a helmet as we reach his Vespa.

"Move faster, woman, or all of this'll have been a waste."

I laugh, but do as he said. "I'm going as fast as I can, asshole."

He speeds off as soon as my hands wrap around his torso. I can feel the definition of his abs through the wet button-down shirt and fight the temptation to follow those lines lower. Not the safest option while driving in the rain. He flies through the streets with the confidence of a local, swerving around tourists milling about and turning corners at top speed despite the rain-slicked streets.

The world passes us in a blur as I try to get my bearings. I know the city well, but I'm lost between the rain pelting my visor and the speed of the Vespa.

I finally catch sight of something I recognize. Largo di Torre Argentina shoots up out of the busy intersection, the ancient pillars helping me get my bearings. I spent a lot of time at the cat sanctuary there when I went through my preteen kitten-obsessed phase, and it holds a special place in my heart. Only in the absurdity of Rome would they turn the site of Julius Caesar's assassination into a feral cat sanctuary.

Colton takes a hard right as it flies by us, shooting down a glorified alley. My heart stills as I realize where we're going. How did I not realize as soon as I saw the rain?

He comes to a hard stop next to the mammoth of brick and concrete. Even the rough rear facade of the building, worn down from millennia of exposure to the elements, speaks to me like no other building ever has. Colton pulls as close as we can get before the barrier blocks off traffic.

"You didn't," I say as I pull the helmet off as quickly as I can.

"Didn't what?" he answers with a brilliant smile. He pushes

the kickstand down with his foot as I throw my helmet onto the seat. "Fake an emergency to get us both out of class when I saw it was raining outside?"

"You're unbelievable."

"I know, but if we stand around talking about how wonderful I am, we'll miss it."

He grabs my hand, both of us sprinting down along the side of the building. Summer rain in Rome never lasts long, and this is probably our last chance. We skid to a halt, both of us slipping on the wet pavers as we reach the front of the Pantheon.

As always, the building takes my breath away. The size and majesty. The history this building has seen over the last two thousand years. Cement pillars the size of a redwood tree dwarf the tourists crowding under the awning to escape the rain, using one of the oldest buildings in the world as an umbrella.

This structure has seen the rise and fall of empires. And here I am. A part of it, if only in the most inconsequential of ways.

Colton's smile grows as our eyes lock before we take off again, dodging around tourists to get into the building.

I marvel at the circular interior. At the elaborate marble floors and altar. The intricate tombs of famous artists and leaders encircling the church like the gods who once held their place, reminding us of the grandeur of Rome and the littleness of our own lives.

But none of that majesty compares to the center of the building, my favorite site in the world. Rain pours through the oculus in the roof, a gaping hole the width of two cars. It pounds the floor, driving most tourists to the edges of the building to avoid the splash zone.

The effect is magical. A 150-foot waterfall pouring into an ancient temple-turned-church. It's a breathtaking combination of the power of nature and what humans can achieve when motivated. It makes me feel small in the most beautiful way. My heart swells, awed that I'm lucky enough to experience this.

"Are we doing this?" Colton whispers from next to me.

Unable to speak, I nod.

He grabs my hand again. The two of us hop the velvet rope, and he pulls me with him under the stream of water. The tourists watch us like we've lost our minds as he spins me around in the rain, our laughs echoing through the massive chamber. He dips me, bringing our lips together before lifting me upright.

"I can't believe you did this," I say again.

"I know you don't have windows in your classroom." He shrugs, turning almost sheepish under my praise. "We only have a week left. I didn't want you to miss it. But for appearances' sake, let's make sure the students don't know we blew off class to dance in the rain in an ancient temple."

Our eyes meet, and feelings rush through me faster than the rain through the oculus, washing away the doubts that have plagued me.

This is my best friend. Someone who has seen me at my worst and still wants me. The man who seems to know me in a way no one else does. My person, who makes me laugh and stands up for me when he doesn't have to. Who canceled his class at the first sign of rain to give me the thing I love most. Or, at least, the thing I *had* loved most.

"I love you," I say, my mouth speaking before my mind can even finish processing that *that's* what I'm feeling.

But I'm suddenly so certain of what this is, and certain that we're strong enough to take on whatever challenges in life may come our way. Colton and I are partners. We always have been. And I don't want to spend another day forcing my feelings down out of fear.

His eyes widen. It isn't even close to the first time I've said those words to him, but we both know this is different. I wait for what's probably a second but feels like days. My heart hammers in my chest and I will him with my eyes to tell me what he's thinking.

"Signor e signora," a sharp voice comes from behind me, breaking the moment. A priest makes his way to us with a deep frown on his face. "I must ask you to leave. This is a church. Your behavior is unacceptable."

"Mi dispiace," we say in unison, fighting to appear apologetic as we join hands again and speed walk out of the church. Our laughter breaks free again the minute we exit the building.

Colton tugs me through the crowd under the awning, leading me around to the side of the building. He backs me up against the rough concrete, rain still pouring over our bodies as he places a hand on either side of my neck.

"Did you mean it?" he asks, his voice low and husky.

I nod, unable to force a single word past my lips until I hear what he has to say.

Tears fill his eyes, then his dimple appears, followed by the widest smile I've ever seen grace his perfect face. He pulls me up to kiss me, and I feel it in every corner of my body.

He pulls back, his eyes sweeping over my face like I'm more mesmerizing to him than all the ruins in Rome. "I love you, Quinn. So fucking much."

He kisses me again, and just like that, I'm complete.

3 2

COLTON

AUGUST — ONE WEEK TO WIN OVER THE FACULTY

QUINN SNUGGLES UP on my lap in the large armchair we pulled over to the window so we can look out at the view. I run my mouth down the curve of her neck, settling her more firmly on my lap.

It has been thirty-one hours since Quinn told me she loved me—not that I'm counting—and my mind can't quite comprehend it. We've spent every one of those thirty-one hours in bed. But now we have to split up for different dinners, and I hate the idea of not being by her side. The second I get back, I'm dragging her to bed where she belongs.

"This view is incredible," she says.

"Is that why you've been sleeping with me all summer? You're pissed I got to the room before you, so you're employing other strategies to access it?"

She chuckles, and the way her body vibrates from the noise goes straight to my dick. "It isn't the worst thing I'd do for this view."

I nip at the spot where her shoulder and neck meet before

sliding out from underneath her, and I love the way she reaches after me.

"Don't leave," she whines, and it takes every ounce of self-control I have not to lift her perfect ass up and slide back in place.

"I can't keep Dr. Cassia waiting," I say, even though I want to.

It's more important than ever that I maintain my relationship with Dr. Cassia now that Richard has it out for me, so when she planned a last-minute visit to her family and asked me to grab dinner, I made it work, even though it means I'll have to miss the goodbye dinner. And worse, I'll have to be away from Quinn.

"Want to join?" I ask, even knowing she won't say yes.

She rolls her eyes, a teasing smile playing on those full lips. "I think one professor skipping the final dinner is enough, don't you?"

"Oh, come on. The students are much more interested in talking to each other than us. They won't care. She'd love to see you."

She runs her thumb across her bottom lip. "Things ended kind of strangely when I decided not to go into the field. She didn't agree with my choices, and our last conversation was... tense."

My brow furrows. "You didn't tell me that."

"It wasn't *bad* bad, like with my parents. She just said I was making a mistake. I didn't want to cause issues between you."

I lean down, arms braced on either side of the chair. "Anyone else I need to hate?"

She nudges my shoulder. "Stop, I don't hate her, and neither should you. It's just a bit awkward, and I've had my fill of awkwardness this summer."

"Okay. I'll be back later tonight." I lean down and kiss her goodbye, savoring the fact that I can.

She chuckles against my lips. "This is a thing we do now?"

"Damn straight it is." Technically, we still haven't discussed what we are to each other. Silly, when we've both said I love you, but still a necessary step. "We should have a conversation, shouldn't we?"

"You mean we can't just be friends who are in love with each other and fuck on the side?" she asks, a teasing glint in her eye.

"The uncertainty may get tiring after fifty or so years."

She bites her lip, her deep eyes twinkling. "You think you'll still like me in fifty years?"

"I was always going to like you in fifty years. You letting me see you naked is just an extra incentive," I say as I walk over to the door. "But if I don't leave now, I'll be late. Talk when I get home?"

She smirks. "Don't spend the whole dinner with your mentor thinking about how I'll suck your dick tonight."

I groan and grip the door handle so hard the edges cut into my skin. "You're evil."

She laughs. "See you soon, Colton."

I rush out of the apartment before I blow off Dr. Cassia to drag Quinn back into bed. I need this meeting. She wants an update on my research, and I need her opinion on how to move forward after the shit show with Richard.

She's already seated at our favorite restaurant when I arrive. She kisses each cheek and couples it with a tight squeeze. "You look well."

"Thank you, Dr. Cassia. You too."

She rolls her eyes. "Colton, I've told you many times to call me Gianna. We're colleagues."

I chuckle as I tuck my napkin onto my lap. "Still feels weird."

"Well, practice, dear. Now, tell me all about this summer."

I fill her in on my classes and involvement with the Rome program, plus the research I'm hoping to publish. We brainstorm on how that will impact my standing at Billings and the pre-tenure review I have coming up next year.

"I did run into one issue," I say as the waiter clears my entrée and sets down dessert. I wanted to leave this for the end of the meal. I know it will lead to a lecture, and I didn't want it to spoil my steak.

Dr. Cassia—Gianna—lifts an eyebrow. "What?"

I clear my throat. "An argument with Richard Riley."

"What sort of argument?"

"It was about Quinn."

She shakes her head. "I always knew that would end up being an issue with Richard. Is she here this summer?"

"She's teaching a class in the program with me."

She beams. "That's fantastic. She always had a way in front of people. I'm sure she's doing a superb job."

I glance down, moving things around the table to distract from the dopey smile I get whenever I talk about her. "She is. But while talking to Richard, she came up. He said some... unflattering things about her."

"And you defended her honor." She smiles indulgently at me. "You always were sweet on her."

I don't touch that. She's been my mentor for twelve years, and our relationship has always been more personal than the one with Richard, but talking about my love life is a step too far for me.

She settles further into her seat, crossing her arms. "So, how bad was it?"

I rub my hand over the back of my neck, keeping my focus on the plates in front of us so I don't have to see her reaction. "Bad. He gave the impression he's going to tank my career."

She sucks in a breath. "Call him as soon as we're done here and apologize."

I look up then. "Absolutely not. He was wrong."

"Of course he was wrong. But sometimes you have to eat your words to keep your career moving forward."

"That's bullshit. And weak."

Her eyebrows raise to her hairline. "Weak? It's real. You have lived in a bubble of support since you entered this field. I'm not saying you're not immensely talented, because you are, but you are also very, very lucky. Richard and I have pushed for you, your opportunities and positions. You may not find the field so welcoming when one of its leaders is against you."

I rub both hands down my face. "So I throw away my morals and beliefs for a job?"

"Do you know how many microaggressions I've smiled through? How many subtle sexist comments I ignored as a woman pursuing a PhD in the eighties? I fumed and swore and screamed to my family and friends, but I kept my head down until I got tenure. Then, and only then, was I able to make real changes. You need to do the same."

I grumble, "I'll think about it."

She watches me for a beat of silence, then nods. "Now, besides derailing your career, tell me how Quinn's been."

A smile spreads across my face and Dr. Cassia—Gianna— chuckles. "She's great. I'm supervising the first class she's teaching, and she's doing an amazing job."

"I'm glad she changed her mind about her career path. I always thought she should have stuck with our field. Granted, I could have voiced my opposition in a kinder way. I've always regretted that."

"She's not teaching history. We have an internship program and she's teaching a class for those students."

Gianna hums as she chewed a bit of her dessert. "So, she stuck with it."

I nod. "It's part of what Richard and I fought about. He thinks she had a mental breakdown after losing the Harrow Fellowship, and that's why she didn't pursue her PhD."

She laughs. "Seems like that plan of hers backfired."

My eyebrows draw together. "What plan?"

"She thought when she gave up the fellowship, her father would let go of his plans for her."

I feel like someone's punched me in the gut.

Gave up the fellowship.

"But she didn't give up the fellowship. She didn't get it." *Please tell me she didn't get it.*

"She asked me to keep it quiet. Richard would have been furious if she publicly pulled out of the running, so she asked to keep her name up, but pulled out of consideration."

My throat goes tight. When did swallowing become so difficult? "Did she get it, then? Or she pulled out before the choice was made?"

"She got it. I called her into my office to celebrate before it was formally announced, but she went off about how she didn't deserve it and didn't want it. You two never talked about this? I thought you told each other everything."

Apparently not.

Every interaction about the fellowship comes slamming back into me.

You have nothing to be sorry for.

You deserve this.

I was happy for you then, and I'm happy for you now.

They'd have been idiots not to pick you.

She was never upset about losing the fellowship because she never lost it. And I didn't win it. My best friend handed it to me.

Dr. Cassia keeps talking, unaware that she's taken my world apart in one sentence. A single thread pulled from a tapestry, and the whole thing unraveled. I've been so confident in my career, and it's all been built on that one day in April when they called my name instead of Quinn's.

It isn't about beating Quinn specifically. But I read her work. It was good. And I know how much pull her father has. He's one of the past recipients, for Christ's sake. The community witnessed her grow up and watched the progression of her career. They were rooting for her.

And in my mind, beating her meant I had to be better than good. Better than great.

Now I'm questioning everything. The impostor syndrome Quinn talked me out of years ago slams back into me in full force. Am I really good? Or am I the best mediocre option after the real winner said no?

And, more terrifying, is my success mine, or is it actually the result of Richard and Dr. Cassia pushing me forward? Do I have a completely false sense of my worth?

And, most terrifying of all, if my success is based on the support of people in the field, have I screwed my chances of tenure by pissing off Richard Riley?

I *have* to get tenure. If I don't, I can't cover my expenses. My mom would lose the house she loves so much, the first true home she's ever had.

I'm not only down a recommendation, but now I have someone who's actively working against my success. Even if I were willing to walk it back—which I'm not, Quinn doesn't deserve that—I don't think Richard is the type to forgive and forget. A few subtle comments here, a rejected conference presentation proposal there, and he'll make it clear where he stands on my work.

I move through the rest of the dinner on autopilot, numb to the world around me. But that numbness mutates into fury as I walk home. How could Quinn do that? How could she hide this from me, let me believe that I won it on my own merit?

But all other thoughts fly out of the window when I walk through the door to our apartment to find something so much worse than the fight I'd already started in my head.

33

QUINN

T HE DIFFERENCE between where this summer started and where it's ending is astounding.

I'm at the final dinner for the program, sandwiched between Sydney and Lynn. The students laugh and joke at their own tables, trading stories about the summer and swiping away sneaky tears that escape now and then. I remember that feeling, the heartbreaking realization that life will never be this perfect, this magical, again. That even though these people and this moment will live vividly in my mind, the beauty of this moment will never be recaptured.

To my utter shock, the faculty and staff table is just as comfortable. We share our own stories, and when I speak, the professors give me their undivided attention. I even earn a few chuckles from Dr. Guarino. I catch Inez's eyes, widening mine in shock.

I was shooting for mutual—if begrudging—respect this summer, but this is so much more. It's fun and honest and comfortable, and I can see the future of Billings. The seven of us coming home and setting the new standard, the others following behind and reaching for the bar we've lifted.

"Oh, Quinn," Andrea says from down the table. "I spoke with the English department chair yesterday, and she loves the workshop idea."

I flick my eyes over to Inez, letting her see the flash of excitement I smother in the name of being professional. "That's great to hear! We can get it on the calendar as soon as we're home. If everyone's on board, I can probably get the first one set up within the first month of the semester."

"I knew you'd jump right on it," Andrea says, clapping her hands together.

"She is shockingly efficient, isn't she?" Dr. Guarino says, his tone dry, but there's a sparkle in his eye I've only seen directed at his students.

I smirk back at him. "I'm endlessly disappointing to you, aren't I?"

He laughs, his whole body shaking like a little Italian Santa Claus. My heart soars at being a part of this little family. Of them seeing my value and welcoming me. *Celebrating* me.

The dinner passes without anything of note, us eventually ushering the students out of the tables so the restaurant can clean up. There are tears and hugs and a million pictures as the students desperately try to capture everything.

Once the students wander off, I turn to Inez. "We headed home?"

She chews on her lip. "I… I'm going to meet Tomasso for a drink. There are some things we need to talk about. I'm going to tell him about the job offer." She drops her voice to a whisper on the last words, shooting a nervous glance to where the professors stand a few feet away.

"Oh, wow," I say. "That's big."

She hums, towing me further away. "We've been casual since I've always planned on leaving, but if I'm staying? An hour-and-a-half train ride is way different than a nine-hour plane trip. I don't know…"

Tomasso's a great guy. He would treat her the way she's always deserved to be treated, but can she really know him well enough after only two months to make that call?

"Are you sure?" I ask, unable to stop myself. "That's a big move for a man."

Inez meets my eyes, her own steely in their determination. "He's not why I'm taking it."

And like a wave crashing over me, I finally realize that all my resolve to show her Billings is still the place for her was completely misplaced. This job is what she wants. Not to get away from the toxicity of our school or to be close to Tomasso, but for herself. I spent the summer obsessed with winning and keeping her, but I never stopped to consider if she wanted to be won over to begin with.

A breath whooshes out of me, and when I smile, it's genuine. She'll be incredible in this role, all crisis management, and what more can I ask for my best friend than for her to be happy and fulfilled? Her smile back's massive and tinged with the smallest bit of relief.

I raise an eyebrow. "Okay, but Tomasso's a pretty big pro, isn't he?"

Inez giggles, chewing on her bottom lip. "I think I love him, Quinn."

She's always been a hopeless romantic, but she isn't one to throw the word *love* around. I can see her future with him. Starting long distance, then she'll transfer to the Roman branch of Leonardo da Vinci. Them having a half-dozen kids running around when Colton and I visit over the summer. The idea of her leaving Boston still breaks my heart, but I'd never want her to sacrifice her own happiness for mine.

I wrap her in my arms, resting my chin on her shoulder. "I could not have parted with you, my Nezzie, to anyone less worthy."

She laughs, but I can hear the tears within it. "How can I leave you? Who will drive me crazy during my *Pride and Prejudice* rewatches by saying all the lines five seconds before the actors?"

I pull back, squeezing her upper arms. "I'm a pro at this. Monthly video calls where we press play at the same time so we're perfectly synced. Weekly calls so we can hear each other's voices and know everything's okay. Daily texts so we still know every detail of each other's lives."

"And summers?" she asks.

"And summers." With the professors from the program speaking out against the initiative—especially Dr. Guarino, who was its staunchest supporter—the rift won't happen on campus, and maybe that means I'll get to run this class again, too.

And if not, I'll just have to rearrange my finances—a lot—to prioritize visiting her.

I give her one last kiss on the check and rush her off to meet her man, holding back the tears in my eyes until she's safely around the corner.

I jump when Dr. Guarino speaks behind me. "May I have a moment?"

I swipe away the tears before turning to face him. "Of course, Dr. Guarino. What can I do for you?"

"I have some exciting news for you," he says. "I spoke with President Munchen a few days ago."

Here it is. The moment I've been working and fighting for all summer. He called our president to say he no longer supports the separation initiative, that he sees the value of faculty and staff collaboration and will stand before the faculty senate and back my argument against it.

"I know I was hard on you this summer." *Yes, you were.* "I was very stuck in my ways, and I'll admit I didn't think you could successfully lead this class." *Just say it.* "I was wrong." *Fuck me, I love those words.* "I know it's not my place since I'm not in the business school, but I wanted you to hear it from me. Billings would like to offer you a faculty position."

There's a record scratch in my head.

"I'm sorry, what?" I ask.

"You know President Munchen has been working on professionalizing our curriculum. We've already approved an on-campus internship course based on the curriculum from this summer. The business department planned on splitting the half-dozen sections between the existing faculty, but when I told her how well you did this summer, we both agreed you should take them on instead."

"That's a full-time position," I say, and he smiles like I meant that as a positive thing. "How am I supposed to do two full-time jobs on campus?"

His smile falters. "Well, you'd have to leave the staff position, obviously. I mean, you won't be able to do both after..."

My stomach bottoms out as I realize what he's saying. When he told me he was wrong—that he was impressed with my work—he didn't mean he was switching sides. He was talking only about my work, not about what it means for Billings.

"You're still supporting the initiative," I say, my voice hollow.

He shakes his head like following the path of this conversation is too much for him. "Why wouldn't I?"

"Because," I say, the pitch of my voice rising, "I proved this summer that staff have something to contribute to the academic side of our campus."

"*You* have something to contribute. *You* taught the class beautifully, and Billings would be lucky to have you teaching this course full time."

"You were never going to give this a real chance, were you?" I ask.

He rolls his lips together, almost apologetic, which is infuriating when he's destroying my job in a few sentences. "The experiment is flawed by nature. With such a limited sample size, we can't reach any valuable conclusion. I know you don't understand how research works—"

"I *do* understand research. I've done my own—hell, I've even published my own—but this wasn't an official study—"

"You're right. It wasn't. This was the faculty appeasing President Munchen. That's it. We know what this campus needs and have decided on its future."

"But you admitted you were wrong!"

"About you," he says calmly, and I want to poke him until he gets as pissed off as I am. "And I hold true to that belief. You have so much to give, and this faculty position will allow you to keep contributing."

Will. Not would. It's a foregone conclusion in his mind that I'll take the position because he thinks I have no other options. He thinks he can bully me into it, just like my father thought he could bully me into living the life he wanted for me.

"I'll be honest," Dr. Guarino says like he hasn't been brutally honest all summer. "You have potential, but we're not willing to continue dealing with all the other issues on campus, the incessant requests and interruptions, just to see what may happen with that potential. If you want to see your new plans through, this is the way to do it."

My hands are shaking, and I clutch them together to hide it. "Please don't do this, Dr. Guarino. We could make things better if we worked together."

His smile is so condescending I want to vomit. "Let's be realistic about this, Professor Riley. Even if I did stand against the initiative—which I won't—do you really think that would make a difference? I'm not *that* powerful on campus. These are deep-seated issues, and believing a few professors saying you did your job well this summer will change anything is simply naive. There's nothing that can be done to stop this train. All you can do is step out of the way or let it hit you."

I want to rage and scream and break something, but I'm shocked into silence. Why had I let myself believe I succeeded? I should have known that even though he admitted he was wrong,

Dr. Guarino would find a way to justify maintaining the status quo.

He pats me gently on the shoulder. "Think about it."

He doesn't wait for a response before walking away, making it a dozen feet before I can find my voice again.

"I'm going to fight this," I say, somehow infusing strength I don't feel into my tone.

He turns back to me, nodding his head. "That's your choice. You will be the one responsible for any fallout, for you or anyone else who supports you."

But if Dr. Guarino's out, who even will consider supporting me? Not Andrea, who's jumpy about doing anything dramatic this close to her tenure review or Lynn, who just wants her contract renewed next year. Maybe Sydney, since she doesn't have much to lose. But what does she have to gain?

The only person I know will stand with me is the most vulnerable of the group. He's done everything in his power to support and protect me since the moment we met, even to his own detriment. Colton has sacrificed so much for the people he loves.

But I can't let him sacrifice his dreams for me.

I CRY the entire way back to the apartment.

I cry for the lost hope, the belief that I could find a way to make this work.

I cry for the pain this is going to cause Colton, the way he's going to react when he finds out.

I cry for the future I'd imagined earlier today, me and Colton back in Boston, loving our jobs and loving each other.

It's so tempting, the idea of staying. Of asking Colton to figure this out with me, because I know he'd say yes. Selfishly, I don't want to be alone. I want to be the priority, the one worth sticking around for.

But I know what will happen. He'll become public enemy number one of Dr. Guarino and the other professors. And if he loses tenure—if he isn't able to keep Gerry in the house she loves so much—he'll resent me eventually. Love only stretches so far before it breaks, and seeing his love for me dissolve would destroy me.

It takes way less time than it should to pack my bags. A process that took days back in Boston is done in less than half an hour, like the universe is telling me this is the right decision and ushering me out of this beautiful bubble we've built. I'm hollowed out—broken and exhausted—by the time it's done.

I glance around our apartment, this perfect haven of joy and love, and snap a few pictures. The perfect tool to torture myself with back in Boston, like an empty stage I can use to set the scene for my masochistic daydreams.

My phone says I still have fifteen minutes until my taxi will be here, but there's nothing else for me to do. I'm tempted to sit on the couch, to let myself dissolve into a puddle of tears, but I can't. If I let myself fall apart, even for a minute, I don't think I'll be able to put myself back together.

So, I keep going. I'm like a shark. I can't stop moving or I'll die.

I look for something productive to do while I wait. Colton's notebook is sitting on the dining room table, his favorite pen laying across the top, and I realize that even if what I'm doing is terrible, this is something I can do right. At least I won't leave him with nothing.

I tear a page out, sitting at the table with the pen clutched in my hand as I desperately try to figure out what to say. That it's all for him? That he deserves to achieve his dreams? That I love him? I start writing, hoping it will magically come to me.

Colton,

I'm sorry

I can't figure out what to say beyond that, staring blankly at the page. He deserves more than a note, but I know if I wait to see him, he'll try to talk me out of it, and I'm terrified that I'm not strong enough not to let him.

Before I can figure what to say, a key is fitted into the lock. I pray it's Inez, home early from her drink with Tomasso. But from the way the air's sucked out of the room when the door opens, I know it's him.

Heavy footsteps follow, then silence. I can feel him right behind me, close enough to see over my shoulder to where the incriminating paper rests on the table. Maybe he'll be mad enough that he lets me leave without even talking about it. I'll slip away like a dream so vivid you wonder if it actually happened.

But that's not Colton's style. He's never let me get away with anything, and I know he's not about to start now when he says, "Quinn, what the fuck is this?"

COLTON

I'M PISSED. More pissed than I think I've ever been at Quinn. I was already mad when I arrived, but finding her here in our home, suitcases around her and a piece of paper that just says, "Colton, I'm sorry," in front of her makes me feel like there's a fire under my skin.

"Quinn, what the fuck is this?"

She turns slowly to face me, complete and utter panic on her face. "Colton…"

The silence that follows my name speaks so much louder than anything she could have said. She's leaving me. Leaving me with nothing but a half-hearted note, and she doesn't even have the decency to say it.

"I asked a fucking question, Quinn. What is this?"

She looks away, blinking rapidly. "I'm leaving."

"Yeah, I fucking got that from all the bags," I say, my voice rising. "What I don't get is why, when three hours ago we were talking about the next fifty years together."

She covers her face with both hands, a shudder moving through her body, followed by a deep breath, like she's steeling herself for this conversation. When she removes her hands, it's not my Quinn looking back. It's something fake. Artificial.

"The professors aren't backing me," she says with perfect calm. "Dr. Guarino's still supporting the initiative."

That halts the rampage I've been on. I'm still angry at her, but I see the pain underneath her facade. "But I thought—"

"Yeah, me too. You know what they say about people who assume, so I guess you can call me an ass." She lets out a pathetic laugh. I know she's trying to cut the tension with humor, but I can't even muster a quirk of my lips. "I'm going to head back to Boston. Try to set up meetings with professors who may be willing to stand against it."

"And you want to do that without me?" I ask, because that's what she's saying. She doesn't want me with her in this.

"I *need* to do this without you," she says, glancing down at the paper with her hastily scrawled apology.

"Why?" I ask desperately, stepping toward her. "Why the hell won't you let me help you?"

"Let's walk this situation through to its logical conclusion," Quinn says with absolute calm that makes me want to scream to the ceiling. "You back me, and you make an enemy of the other professors. They turn everyone against you, and with the help of my asshole father, they tank your career. You lose tenure and end up having to leave Boston for another tenure-track position or take adjunct roles and can't afford to support Gerry. You're heartbroken over it and come to resent me, and whatever we have falls apart under the weight of that, anyway."

Anyway.

Fuck fuck fuck.

I thought she was just planning on doing this on her own, but that sentence implies that she means to end *everything* with us. My stomach twists, the apartment swirling before my eyes as the panic sets in. I'm going to lose her. I just got her, and I'm going to lose her. There are things I could say—pretty words that would soothe her and help her see that my world revolves around her—but they're trapped behind something lodged in my throat, and I stand there. Mute in my desperation.

She steps closer, placing a soft hand on my forearm that's anything but comforting. "I don't want you sacrificing anything for me. You said yourself you didn't want to take anyone else into consideration so you can do what's best for your career."

"That doesn't apply to you," I say fiercely, finally finding my voice. I go to close the distance, but she backs up, maintaining the space between us.

"This summer's been intense. This whole 'us versus them' vibe, plus us adding sex to our friendship. Of course it all feels huge. But it's only been a couple months, and we're not even technically anything to each other—"

"That's bullshit," I say, but she's back to avoiding my eyes and keeps talking.

"This doesn't have to be this big, complicated thing."

"Yes, it does," I say. "There's nothing small or simple in the way I feel about you."

A small sound, like a trapped sob, escapes her throat. "I know, but I think we need space—"

"Like hell we do."

"—to let the dust settle on all the campus drama. You know you won't be able to stand by, so we can just, you know, put us on hold. Take some distance. It'll be easier for you if you don't have to watch it. The chaos will probably die down in a few months. And if you still want to see what we could be, then we can. Not, like—" Her voice breaks on the words, but she clears her throat and pushes on. "I don't expect you to wait around for me. I mean, that's a long time to go without getting laid."

She chuckles, but there's an edge of panic in her eyes, like she doesn't realize there could and never will be anyone else for me. The idea of someone else touching me—or someone else touching her, for that matter—is like a knife in my gut.

"I'm not fucking anyone else, and neither are you, Quinn. This thing right here"—I gesture between us—"this is it. For both of us, and you know it. Stop pretending like you don't."

She turns away from me, laying a hand over her eyes. This indifference is an act. She loves me as much as I love her, and I'm not letting her go without a fight.

I walk up to her. My movements are slow, leaving time for her to slip away from me if she wants to. But I don't think that's what she wants at all. I think she wants me to catch her. To hold her and reassure her and love her.

I turn her back to me, pulling her lush body against mine as I tuck my face into the crook of her neck.

"I love you," I whisper. "You're a part of me. Please don't take a piece of me away."

"I love you, too," she whispers back, and I nearly cry in relief. "But I couldn't live with myself if you gave up your dreams for me."

I pull back, placing my hands on either side of her face. "It doesn't have to be one or the other."

She has tears in her eyes, and I hate seeing her this way. "But it does. Dr. Guarino said there would be fallout for fighting against the initiative, for me and for anyone who stands with me. He *will* come after you."

For the first time since coming home, I feel a spark of fear that doesn't have to do with losing Quinn. Dr. Guarino is a good man, but he's passionate in his beliefs. He isn't championing the initiative because he hates the staff. In his mind, Billings is at a crossroads, and the only way to protect the students is through this hard-line solution. Anyone who disagrees is, in his mind, the enemy. A threat. And he'll do away with any threats.

Quinn reads the fear in my eyes, and her own mist over. "Can you look me in the eye and tell me you wouldn't regret it if you lost your job? That you wouldn't hate yourself if your mom needs to sell her house because you don't have the money to pay her mortgage anymore?"

I want to give her the same answer I've given her since I took the job at Billings—that I'm not worried. That I'm confident in myself and my abilities. That of course I'm going to get tenure. But all that confidence has been wiped away by the truth of what happened with the fellowship. I don't know if I'm good enough, not without Richard backing me or my best friend handing me life-changing awards. And I can't bring myself to ask Quinn about it while everything else is falling apart around us.

She smiles sadly and goes up on her toes to press a light kiss to my lips. It tastes like salt, and I realize I'm crying.

Her phone pings, and she pulls away. "My taxi's here."

"Quinn," I say, following behind her as she gathers her things, dragging her ridiculous suitcases to the door.

"I'll text to let you know when I'm home, but we should avoid each other on campus."

"This isn't— I mean, we can't just— Please don't leave."

She flicks away a tear, pasting on a bright smile. "A few months is nothing. It'll be fine."

And then she walks away without a single hesitation, leaving me behind with nothing but the heavy thud of the door.

I don't know how long I stare at the elaborate wooden door. The decorative swirls will be etched into my mind until the day I die. But I can't look away. To do that would be to admit defeat, to accept that this conversation—and this beautiful life with Quinn—is over.

Eventually, I move, knowing I have to do something—anything—or I'll be frozen in place forever. Quinn is the only person I want to talk to, but since she isn't an option, I call my mother.

She picks up after a few rings. "Just the man I wanted to talk to! Bobby has some interesting ideas on lighting I wanted to throw your way."

"Wh-what?" I stammer.

Momma pauses. "What's wrong?"

I clear my throat, trying to dislodge the knot that settled there the moment Quinn walked through that door. "Quinn and I broke up. Or… I don't know. I guess we weren't officially together to begin with. But she's done with me."

"Now, I don't believe that for a second."

"It's true."

She huffs. "Then what the fuck did you do?"

"Language, Momma," I say on instinct, my voice low and flat. I can feel her smile through the line, picture it like she's right in front of me, and the warmth of her love breaks me. I'm not numb anymore, not in shock or denial, and the truth of our situation hits me like a ton of bricks.

Sobs escape me before I even realize the tears are coming. I sit on my bed, clutching the phone to my ear like a lifeline, while my whole body shakes from the force of it.

Momma's shushing and murmuring encouraging words down the line. After lord knows how long, the tears slow enough for me to explain the fight and everything that happened afterwards.

"I don't get it," she says. "Why doesn't she want you supporting her?"

"Because it could cost me tenure," I say. It doesn't matter how many times I explain "tenure" versus "tenure track." She can't conceptualize a world where I don't succeed.

"And who gives a flying rat's ass if you lose tenure?"

She's so fucking flippant with this situation, like her needs and desires aren't the catalyst for all of this. "The bank who owns the mortgage on your house, for one. Oh, and the contractor who keeps convincing you to get more and more expensive shit every time he calls."

"Oh, come on! If you lose tenure, you'll just go to another university. And we can live on our savings for a bit."

"What savings, Momma? I have no fucking savings to live on!"

My phone starts ringing, and I glance at it to see she's switched us to a video call. Her face appears. The red flush of anger across her cheeks makes me think about Quinn, and I fight down another wave of tears. At this rate, I'm going to flood the apartment.

"Colton Ford Miller, what do you mean you have no savings?"

"How would I have anything saved?" I ask, years of pressure coming to a head in one second, like a pressure cooker someone forgot to lift the valve on. "I've spent all my money on you. On getting you the house you wanted right behind downtown, instead of the more practical one a ten-minute drive out of the way. And getting you the couch that was thousands of dollars more because it was a bit plushier, and giving you the goddamn marble countertops. I have nothing. I'm living paycheck to paycheck. If I lose tenure, we're *both* screwed."

Momma drops into a chair, her hand coming up to her mouth. "The missed holidays where you were working…"

I sigh. "I never said I was working."

"You let me believe you were working," she says, her voice pitching up. "I filled in the blanks and you never corrected me."

"You said it all the time when I was growing up. It was your turn to work hard to support us while I was in school, and I'd have my time later. Well, it's my time now, and I'm trying my fucking hardest to support you while doing what I love, too. If that means some missed holidays, so be it."

I slump back against the headboard. It's exhausting, arguing with the two people I love most in this world, and I don't have any more fight left in me.

"Oh, Colton," Momma says, her voice soft. "That wasn't what I meant. I meant it was my job to provide for you. When I talked about your 'turn,' I meant you would have a turn to take care of your own family one day."

"What about all the talk growing up about me being the next Gordon Gekko, minus the insider trading? How we'd be rich and buy a nice house that would be all ours?"

Her head drops forward. "I'm a terrible mother."

"No, Momma, that's not what I'm sayin—"

"I fucked up. In my head, I thought that I was building you up. I've always been happy in our little corner of Appalachia. I have the mountains and a community I love. This is my home. But it always seemed like a black hole to you. This ominous presence threatening to suck you in and keep you forever, and I thought all that talk about your potential would make you believe it was possible to get out. I didn't pause to think about how it would feel like pressure."

"Please stop. You were the best mom. I'm so lucky to—"

She lifts a hand to cut me off. "You don't need to console me. I always knew I'd fuck you up somehow. It's a mother's prerogative, after all. And looking back at all the times I've asked you for money or to up the budget you gave me, I've been a massive screw up.

"I never wanted to be dependent on you for anything, but I saw this house and was so excited about it. And you swung it, even though it was beyond what we originally discussed. I think a part of me realized I was asking too much, but it was exciting to have disposable income for the first time in my life. I took advantage of your good heart, and that's not fair."

I sniff and wipe away tears from my cheek. "You're the only reason I have a good heart. Everything I know, I learned from you. What's a bit of skimping on my end to give you what you deserve?"

She smiles. "Baby, do you think there's any world where I'd take this house over your happiness? I love it here, but it's just walls. You're my soul, living outside of my body. I'd be happier moving to a new apartment every year where you and the love of your life can visit me than in this house with you moping all over it."

The light sheen over her eyes tells me how much she means it, and I feel lighter than I have in years. Maybe ever.

Momma sighs. "Fucking hell, I'm gonna have to cancel those marble countertops."

I laugh, loud and free. "You really don't have to. Not unless I lose my job."

Her eyes go soft. "No, I need to get better about standing on my own two feet. Obviously, the support from you has helped, but I can take care of myself. Everything you've given me has been comfort, not necessity. Quinn *is* a necessity for you."

"She is," I say. She's more than a necessity. She's life itself.

"But from now on, you need to be better about telling me no. Lord knows you'll still demand to help me, but if we're gonna move forward, you need to be more honest with me."

I nod. "It's a deal."

"So what comes next?" she asks.

I rub a hand down my face. "I don't know."

"I've talked to your Quinn. A lot. Confessions over pumpkin pie and latenight chats with heavily spiked eggnog. Her trash can of a father did a number on her. She'd never admit it outright— she'd never want to give him that power—but she doesn't believe she's worth sticking around for. So I guess that's the real question. Is she worth it? If the worst case happened and you lost your job and could never find another professorship, would you regret choosing Quinn?"

It's a mirror of the question Quinn asked me. And with the pressure of supporting my mom lifted, the answer is so resoundingly clear that I feel like a complete dumbass for not seeing it to begin with.

"No." The answer comes easily. I'd miss my work, but I could never regret anything that keeps Quinn in my life.

Momma's wide, self-satisfied smile splits her face. "Then go get our girl."

COLTON

I IMMEDIATELY JUMP INTO ACTION, yanking out my suitcase and flying around the room. Choosing Quinn is so painfully obvious that I want to kick myself, or to find a way to go back in time and take it all back.

I set the phone up on the desk, Momma talking through what I should say while I throw my stuff into my luggage. I barely get it zipped around the crumpled clothes. When I come out into the living room, Inez and Tomasso are standing there, watching as I sprint around the apartment tossing the last-minute items into my messenger bag.

"Quinn talked to you?" I ask Inez, never stopping.

Inez glances nervously at Tomasso. "Yeah, she did, but what—"

"I'm going after her. I never should have let her leave."

"Oh, thank god," she says, a sweet, wide smile spreading across her face.

"What flight is she on?" I ask as I stuff my laptop into my bag.

"I don't know yet. She promised she'd text when she got it sorted out. I'll send the information as soon as I have it."

I run over and plant a kiss on the top of her head. "You're an angel."

She laughs. "I've never seen you so expressive before."

I beam at her. "I'm gonna get her back."

"Good luck," she yells as I bolt out of the same door Quinn ran through an hour ago.

I sprint towards the closest taxi stand with my luggage bouncing wildly over the cobblestones as I dodge drunk tourists. I curse the fact that I can't hail a cab like in New York. There's a line of twenty taxis when I reach the back of the stand, and I beg the closest one to take me instead of making me run up to the front cab. I again curse the damn taxi system when the other cabbies demand I honor the process and take the first one in line.

Finally reaching the front, I throw my stuff in the trunk, too impatient to accept the driver's help, and dive into the back seat. I tell him I need to get to Fiumicino as quickly as possible, and he speeds off, winding through the other cars.

We've just reached the highway, so close, yet not nearly close enough, when the traffic hits. Bumper to bumper, with no end in sight. I get a text from Inez with Quinn's flight time, which is too close for comfort, and yell in frustration.

"You need to go there faster?" my driver asks.

"Yes. I need to get on this flight to catch the woman I love," I say, playing into the dramatics of the situation.

"Do not worry," he says with a flick of his hand. "Dominico can fix this."

He pulls off the highway and slams on the gas pedal. We shoot down the shoulder at a speed that would have scared the living shit out of me on the actual road. But if it gets me there before she leaves, I'll take it.

And if I die in a fiery car crash, I hope Quinn will come to my funeral.

We reach the terminal with enough time for me to buy a ticket on her flight. I bounce impatiently as I wait in the security line, then sprint to the gate, making it just before they close the doors.

I walk down the aisle, scanning every face for the one I'm looking for. She's in a window seat, head leaning against the wall. Her eyes are closed and puffy. The seat next to her is open, but I continue a few rows back to my assigned seat. We have time, and I don't want to start this conversation only to be interrupted by the half-dozen announcements flight attendants make at the beginning of a flight.

An hour later—the longest hour of my life—the flight attendant announces over the speaker that we can move about the cabin, and I shoot out of my seat and up to Quinn's row. The person in the aisle seat looks at me funny, but makes room for me to squeeze by. Quinn's eyes are still closed, but I've seen her sleeping enough this summer to know she's faking it.

"Hi," I say. An impressive opening line.

Quinn's whole body springs up, those beautiful brown eyes rimmed in red. She looks around, confusion furrowing her brow. "How are you here, Colton?"

"I'm coming home with you, and I'm not discussing it again. We have a lot of shit to talk about on this flight, but whether or not I'm going to stand by you next week isn't one of them."

"Colt—"

"No, it's my decision, and I'm 100 percent certain of it. So stop trying to talk me out of it."

Her mouth curves up, hope shining in her eyes. "For the record, I think this is a terrible idea."

"For the record," I echo. "I don't give a fuck."

She bites her lip, turning toward the window to hide her smile for a second before facing me again. "So if we're not talking about you torpedoing your career for me, what's the 'lot of shit' you're referring to?"

I tilt my head, making sure I have her full attention. "We've both lied to each other, and we need to hash this out."

Her eyebrows shoot up. "I've never lied to you. Literally not once in our entire friendship."

"I've never lied to you, either. At least, not outright," I say, because that's the truth. "But we've both watched the other fill in the blanks with things we *know* aren't true, and neither of us spoke up."

She looks genuinely confused, and it's so cute and endearing I nearly drop the whole thing in favor of pulling her into my arms. But I almost lost her, and I need to make sure we're on the same page if we're going to jump back into this thing.

"Tell me about the Harrow Fellowship," I say.

Her face twists, panic in those deep brown eyes. This is a conversation—a secret—ten years in the making, and I know she's terrified of the fallout. She turns, facing forward in her seat instead of looking at me.

"Dr. Cassia told me at dinner. She didn't realize I didn't know, and it sent me into a tailspin. One achievement shouldn't carry so much weight, but the truth is I never believed in myself before that moment. It was the foundation all my confidence was built on, and in an instant, it turned from solid rock to a muddy marsh and everything was collapsing around me. I was too lost in my anger and fear to handle our conversation when I got home."

"I didn't want to hurt you," she says, so softly I almost don't hear her.

And I know that's the case. She was trying to protect me, just like I've spent the past year trying to protect her on campus.

"I'm sorry I didn't tell you," she says, meeting my gaze with tears in her eyes. "I didn't want you dismissing the quality of your work because of a broken system. Me getting it was pure nepotism. Your work was so much better than mine. *You* were the one who deserved it, and I didn't even want it. Please, Colton. Please forgive me."

"I know," I say softly. "I'm okay. But please don't keep secrets from me anymore, even if you think you're protecting me."

She nods, tears streaming down her face, and I lean forward to kiss them away. The temptation to turn my head a fraction of an inch, to capture her lips with mine, is nearly overwhelming. But if I've forced her to admit her own half-truth, I owe her the same.

I pull back. "I guess it's my turn."

Her eyes blink open, still slightly hazy. "What?"

I suck in a breath. It's not that I think she'll be upset by what I have to say, but it's vulnerable, laying it all out there.

"You said during our fight that this summer has been intense because of all these new feelings. And I get that's how you've experienced it, but none of this has been new for me."

She pulls her lips between her teeth, clearly confused by what I'm saying. I'm totally fucking this up.

"Fourteen years ago, I was a mess. Terrified and defensive and so fucking lonely, and then this beautiful, chaotic girl dropped down beside me and completely rewrote who I thought I was. Within an hour, you were my new favorite person. Within a week, I'd have sold my kidney for a kiss. Within a month, I knew I was going to love you for as long as I drew breath. And I've never faltered. Not for a single day. I loved you in college when I got to see you every day and while we were an ocean apart and when it was supposed to be 'just sex.' So this *big shift* you're stressing over? It's nothing for me. Just a regular Friday, honestly."

"Why didn't you tell me?" she asks, her voice cracking on the words.

I look up at the ceiling of the plane, focusing on the line of lights dotting the aisle. "Because you really are my favorite person. You never showed any signs of romantic interest in me, and the thought of losing you was debilitating. I was happy just being your friend—I'd *still* be happy just being your friend—because you're the sun. All I've wanted for the past decade and a half has been to enjoy your warmth in whatever way you'll allow me."

"Colt—"

"So you have to understand that I could never regret choosing you. I'd give up my career, never step foot in Rome again, if it meant keeping you in my life. I've chosen you every day for fourteen years, and I'll keep choosing you as long as you let me."

"What about your mom?"

I tsk. "We finally had that conversation you've been telling me to have for years. Apparently I just needed the proper motivation to get over my bullshit and tell her the truth."

Quinn points a finger at herself, the cutest smile on her face. "Me? I'm the motivation?"

I roll my eyes, and her smile widens. "The best motivation of my life."

She lets out a little watery laugh, twining our fingers together. "So I lied about your career and you just lied about loving me a lot."

I kiss her forehead. "Hey, you lied to protect me. I lied to protect myself."

I love the little smile that tilts her lips. "I can get behind that spin."

My forehead drops to hers and I let my lids fall closed, breathing in her citrusy scent. "I know you don't trust love, and I get why. But trust me. Please don't run from me again. I'll take you back every time because I'm so pathetically in love with you, but it hurts like a bitch."

She nods quickly. "No more running."

My fingers twine in the soft blond hair, and she tilts her head to bring her lips to mine. It's the softest brush of a kiss, and it's more devastating than the most passionate of kisses we exchanged this summer.

"I love you, too," she whispers against my lips. "Just in case you're wondering."

"I wasn't," I say, my mouth tilting up. "You've always been transparent as hell."

She laughs again, light and airy—so fucking addictive—and kisses me harder, nipping at my lip before she soothes it with her tongue. I groan, grabbing her hip and pulling her toward me, nearly onto my lap.

A throat clears behind me, and I turn to find the third person in our row grimacing. "Um... do you think I could maybe take your old seat?"

Quinn buries her face in my shoulder, her whole body shaking with her silent laughter.

"28E," I say. "The whole row's open, so enjoy."

"Oh, sweet," the woman says, gathering her things from out of the pocket and slipping out of her seat.

I turn back to Quinn, wrapping a hand around the back of her neck and whispering, "I thought she'd never leave."

Quinn giggles, her breath coasting over my lips before I capture them again. We kiss and we kiss and we kiss, and I hope this plane never lands. I'd live in this death tube thousands of feet above the earth forever if I could stay just like this.

Quinn eventually pulls back, and I grunt at the loss of contact, trying to pull her to me, but she leans back, tossing her legs over my lap. She intentionally rubs against where I'm so clearly hard, and I hiss, grabbing her knee.

"Unless you want to join the mile high club, you need to cut that out."

She smirks, shifting against my hard cock again. "Not opposed. But before that, I wanted to tell you an idea I had for when we get home. It'll take a lot of work over the next week before the faculty senate's supposed to meet, but if you want to help, I'd love to do it with you."

I can't help the broad smile that stretches across my face, because this is everything I've ever wanted. The two of us, together and happy and a team.

"Put me to work, Chaos."

36

QUINN

AUGUST — ONE WEEK
UNTIL THE PRESENTATION

"Absolutely not."

My chest caves in as we get yet another rejection from a faculty member, this time from a tenure-track professor in the creative arts department. We've been trying to sell our new plan for the past three days, and so far not a single person has taken the bait. We've approached professors of all different positions—tenured, tenure track, and instructors—and everyone has an excuse not to tie themselves to us.

We're meeting in Colton's office, which is about three times the size of mine. I shoot him a look from my spot across his desk and he nods slightly, giving me the reins.

I shift my chair so I'm facing Dr. Gleeson. "I know it's a big commitment, but—"

Dr. Gleeson doesn't even try to disguise his reason for saying no. "It's political suicide to go against the older faculty members, and you know that, Colton." He places his elbows on his knees, leaning toward Colt's desk in a way that seems intentionally designed to cut me off from the discussion. "We're both tenure track. Why are you taking this risk?"

Guilt settles in my bones. Hearing another faculty member so blatantly call out how dangerous this is makes my stomach roil.

Colton places his forearms on the edge of his desk, mirroring Dr. Gleeson's stance. "I have every intention of getting tenure when the time comes, which means I'll spend my entire career on this campus. Why *wouldn't* I choose what's best for the place I'm going to spend the next fifty years?"

Dr. Gleeson stares down Colton for a solid minute, weighing what Colt said against what he knows about campus. A wave of hope rises in me. He's considering it—genuinely considering it, not just humoring Colton—and if we can get him, maybe we can get enough people to make it work.

Then he shakes his head. "I'm sorry."

He gets up without so much as a goodbye, squeezing past my chair. The soft click of the door closing behind him feels like thunder ringing through the office. Colton lets out a frustrated sigh.

It isn't going to work. All this planning and stressing and hard fucking work is going to be for nothing. I'll be laughed out of the auditorium, and I'm going to take Colt down with me. He won't get tenure and will have to start over from scratch at another school. Who knows where he'll land. His new university could be across the country and I'll never get to see him.

"We need to call it," I say to Colton's ceiling.

"You're right," he says, and my stomach drops.

I've been waiting for this, the moment when he decides I'm not worth sticking his neck out for. He's been so steady, and I started to believe he'd remain that way forever.

But everybody has their limits, and it would seem I've found Colton's.

"It's been a long day," Colt says, stretching as he stands from behind his desk, a tempting sliver of skin appearing above his waistband. He walks over to the door Dr. Gleeson escaped through, flipping the lock on the door. "And you deserve a night to relax."

I blink back tears when I realize him agreeing to "call it" meant for the day, not the program.

"No," I say, the word embarrassingly wobbly. "I meant this plan. We're banging our heads against the wall."

Colton walks across the room to me, taking the seat Dr. Gleeson vacated, pulling it so our knees knock just like on the Janiculum Hill when I was ready to give up this summer. "It's not doomed."

"Colt," I say with a pathetic little laugh, "We've met with six professors and haven't gotten a single yes. All we're doing is negatively impacting the way the professors view you. There are over fifty other universities in Boston. I can find something else and still stay close."

Colton tugs my hand, pulling me from my seat and into his lap. Determination is etched on his strong face as his hands find my waist. "We're not giving up. If you need a break, that's fine. I'll handle it."

The air rushes out of my lungs. "What?"

"You've been taking these hits for eight years by yourself. You're exhausted, but I know how much you love it here. Let me fight for the both of us until you feel strong enough to fight again. If it doesn't work out, then we can talk about a plan B."

Those pesky tears are back again.

"I think I need a hug," I squeak. "Can I have one?"

Colton smiles softly, and it sets off a riot in my chest. "Always."

His hands slide from my waist around my back, anchoring me to him like he always does. The calm to my chaos. I twine my arms around his neck and lay my head on his chest, feeling the steady thump of his heart, as strong and reliable as the man before me. His chest swells against my head as he takes in a deep breath, and I turn my face into his chest in a futile attempt to hold back the tears.

"I don't want to tap out," I say into his shirt, "but if we're not giving up, we at least need to change *something*. What we're doing isn't working."

He hums, the sound vibrating through my body and down to the tips of my toes. "You need a champion."

I tilt my head so my chin was on his chest. "A champion?" I ask skeptically.

He gives me that little half smile. "Every queen needs one."

I laugh and push on his chest. "I already had two incredible knights. And as valiantly as you fought, the war still seems to be lost."

"I didn't say you need another knight. I said a champion. Someone so strong that people will think twice before issuing a challenge because they'll have to go through them."

The likelihood of finding someone who will instill fear and awe in the Billings faculty *and* who will be willing to stand beside me is infinitesimally small. It's so unrealistic it's almost laughable.

"When did you become an optimist, Colt?" I ask.

His lips quirk up an inch. "I'd guess somewhere between kissing you for the first time and you saying you love me."

I groan. "Oh my god, you're such a fucking sap now. I'm telling everyone."

"No one will believe you," he says.

I'm mid-laugh when he captures my mouth, his smile pressed to my own. As teasing as the kiss begins, it escalates quickly. Colton repositions me so I'm straddling him, and I push down, feeling the way he hardens for me. The soft grunts and hisses I elicit with the slide of my hips give me life.

His hands slip under my dress, dipping into my underwear to grip my ass as he takes control of our movements, dragging me along with the perfect pressure. I love the way he grasps me, hard and bruising, like he's worried I may slip through his fingers like water. One of his hands moves around my body until he reaches my core, already soaked for him.

"We don't have time for this," I pant against his mouth.

"Our meeting was cut short by that asshole," he says. "Pretty sure we have the rest of the day for whatever we want."

"There are plenty of other things we need to work on." The words are pathetically breathy, and they break completely when he slides two fingers inside me.

"You deserve to feel good, Chaos," he says against my neck. "Let me make you feel good."

His thumb rubs against my clit, the perfect pressure, and any other objections die on my tongue. There's no stress, no presentation in a few days that we're wholly unprepared for, no professors waiting to see us fail. There's only Colt and his hands and the safety of his body against mine.

He slides a hand into my hair, gripping tightly and angling my face toward his. "Open your eyes, Chaos. Let me see you when you come for me."

I didn't even realize they'd closed, so focused on the sensations, but I listen and force them back open. I'm instantly captured by his moss green eyes, intense and loving.

"You are spectacular," he says as he picks up the pace of his circles on my clit. "So fucking spectacular. I can't believe I get to see you like this."

"Colton—" I can't get out more, can't form coherent sentences when he's taking me apart.

"I love you, Quinn," he says, and that's enough to tilt me over the edge.

I don't have the clarity to hide my moan, but Colton's there, protecting me like always, swallowing the moan so it doesn't leave his office. His fingers keep moving, not letting up until he's certain he's wrung out every ounce of pleasure possible.

I collapse against his chest, sucking in breaths in an attempt to come down from the high.

"Feeling better?" he asks smugly.

I pinch his side, but don't have the strength to lift myself off him. "So fucking pleased with yourself."

He chuckles against my hair, dusting a soft kiss there that has my heart leaping. "Now that you're not so stressed, I have someone in mind to help us, but before I say who, you have to promise to stay quiet and let me make my whole case before you tell me no."

"That's not ominous at all," I say sleepily. "Did you get me off as a form of manipulation?"

"Are you complaining?" he asks.

"No," I say around a yawn, the exhaustion from the past few days settling into my bones. "You should use that particular form of manipulation a few times a day for the rest of our lives."

He chuckles, shifting his arms more tightly around me. "Do you agree to keep quiet while I argue my point?"

I sigh and shift backward so I can see him properly. "Fine. I'll stay quiet."

"Great," he says with a firm slap to my ass. "Here's what I'm thinking."

37

QUINN

AUGUST — LAST DAY TO WIN OVER THE FACULTY

I LOOK over the crowd of professors with a knot of anxiety in my stomach. A sea of faces stretches out in front of me. Whether they'll be friendly or not is yet to be seen. I take strength from the knowledge that Colton's behind me, all crossed arms and sexy scowls, like he's my very own praetorian guard.

We spent the past four days working non-stop and the nights wrapped up in each other's arms, with one exception. After forcing myself to leave Colton's apartment for one night of space, I took a play out of Gerry and Colton's book and called my dad. Our family needs a bit of honesty, too.

He answered the video call with a furrowed brow, which isn't terribly surprising when I haven't called him in ten years. "Is everything all right, Quinn?"

I took a steading breath. I owed this to Colton as much as I owed it to myself. "Hi, Dad. Have a minute?"

"What's going on?"

"We need to talk. And before I say anything else, I need you to listen to what I have to say before you formulate your own arguments. Can you agree to do that?"

"Quinn, I don't like the tone you're taking."

I nodded. "I'm sure you don't, but you have two choices right now. You can listen and possibly rebuild a relationship with me, which I think you might want after this summer, or you can dig your heels in for the sake of your pride and lose me altogether."

His jaw tightens. He doesn't enjoy relinquishing power, but says, "I'm listening."

"I've been letting you—letting everyone—operate under a false assumption." I take another deep breath. "They offered me the Harrow Fellowship when I was a senior—"

"What?" His face is furious, and I lift a hand. The simple movement, or maybe the harsh look on my face, cuts him off.

"You agreed not to speak." I wait for him to nod before continuing. "Like I said, they offered me the fellowship, and I turned it down. Those summers with you in Rome were everything to me, but when I went to school, I didn't enjoy it. And I didn't want to do it for the rest of my life.

"I watched Colton. He was so brilliant, and I knew I was going to beat him because of *your* name, not mine. I had new dreams, and I wasn't going to steal his because I wasn't brave enough to make my own choices. It made me sick, but I didn't have the guts to tell you that to your face. I wasn't broken by losing the fellowship like you believe. There was no spiral or depression or whatever else you've concocted in your mind that you need to 'save' me from. So if you're waiting for me to get over a heartbreak that doesn't exist, you'll be waiting for the rest of your life.

"I love what I do. And I'm fucking good at it, Dad. My students love me. The work I do with them changes their lives as much, if not more, than the work in the classroom. If you still think that makes me unworthy of your time, that's your decision, but at least I'll know you're making that decision with all the information."

His head drops forward, but I'm not done. "One more thing. About Colton, if you do anything—and I mean *anything*—to negatively impact his career growth, you will never hear from me again. I don't know if that's enough of a threat to make a difference, but I'm making it, nonetheless. You should be happy that I have someone in my life who loves me enough to support me, even at personal risk. He's my family, and I won't let you hurt him without a fight."

His eyes are hard, and I know this is going to be the most difficult part for him. It's a point of pride, and he's already proven his pride is the thing he cherishes most. All I can do is hope that I matter more underneath all that posturing.

"Well, Dad, thanks for taking my call. I have some stuff I need to focus on, so… bye."

I hang up before he can speak. Maybe I should have given him a chance to respond, but after everything he's put me and Colton through, I don't owe him a chance to argue his point. And I feel lighter than I have since I pulled out of the running for the Harrow Fellowship.

I use that new confidence in who I am to fuel me as I stand before a hundred professors who are set against me because of over a century of ingrained culture.

Colton slips something out of his pocket, dropping it into the purse I've set behind the podium. I laugh at the bag of M&M's sticking out.

The corner of his mouth tilts up. "Just in case."

"Your pessimism is showing. What happened to Optimistic Colton?"

He tries to hide his smile, but his dimple pops. "It comes in waves."

President Munchen clears her throat at the front of the room, such a small, simple action that reverberates and brings everyone to silence.

"Thank you all for making time for this meeting right before a new school year. I'm happy to see so many faces beyond the senate today. This conversation is worth our attention, even amidst the chaos. As you all know, we're voting today on the initiative to permanently separate the staff and the academics. Quinn Riley, our associate director of internships, is here to discuss an interesting alternative. I ask that you all listen to her proposal with an open mind. This would be a substantial project, but one that may be exactly what we need."

Murmurs fill the room as she steps aside, and I'm officially on. I gift myself one last look at Colton for a spark of confidence and turn back to the group.

"As some of you know, I taught an internship course this summer in the Rome study abroad program. I know, it's shocking. A staff member teaching a Billings course."

I pause as select people around the room chuckle. Others scowl. Everyone's a critic.

"The intent was to prove whether staff members can bring value to the academics before anything permanent is written into our bylaws."

Colton jumps in. "The class was a resounding success. The Rome faculty have all written up their positive experiences from this summer. They're included in the packet you received when you arrived."

I smile at him. "But, after more consideration, I didn't think this little experiment got to the root of the issue, so we're presenting another idea."

I pause, glancing around the room to catch the eyes of my allies, to draw strength from the knowledge that I'm not alone.

"Right now, the faculty and staff are on opposite sides of a cavern with a rickety bridge between us, technically able to cross over, but no one's brave enough to do it. We want to fix the bridge, give us something sturdy so that we can reach each other."

"We're not here for a poetry competition, Miss Riley," a

professor calls from the front row, and I recognize the asshole philosophy professor from the first senate meeting.

Colton steps up next to me. "Enough. If you aren't here to listen with an open mind, the door is just up the stairs." He ushers me in front of him with a hand at the small of my back.

"Thank you, Dr. Miller," I say.

His fingers twist in my dress, and I know he's going to have me say it again later while I'm on my knees for him.

"As I was saying," I continue, "none of us can figure out how to move forward. Rather than tying one hand behind our back, we propose another way forward. A new committee, chaired by one staff member and one faculty member, designed to help bridge the gap between the two vital parts of our campus. We've spent decades determined the others were helping students in the wrong way. In truth, students learn and develop through different means. We all have the best intentions, but assume the other has the worst."

The same professor speaks up again. "And, I assume, you believe you're the best person to lead this."

I dig one fingernail into my palm to distract myself from the sarcastic reply fighting to leave my tongue and smile. "As someone who has experience on both sides, yes, I do. But, if you all choose someone else, I'll happily step aside."

He won't be deterred. "And the best professor to chair it is a faculty member who has only spent a year at our institution?" He glares at Colton, and there are a few murmurs of assent around the room.

"You make a great point," Colton says. "Quinn made the same argument. Great minds, I guess. Which is why I won't be co-chairing the committee. We've identified someone more established and infinitely more qualified for that position. He has already agreed, assuming this new initiative passes."

The group looks around the room, trying to suss out who it is.

I wave my hand. "Giancarlo, will you come up to answer the remaining questions with me?"

The quiet gasps crash through the room like a wave of noise as they rise simultaneously, and Dr. Guarino walks to the stage, only scowling slightly at me using his first name, even though he agreed it would send a message about our equal partnership.

When Colton suggested him as a partner, I did exactly what Colton said I'd do. I jumped off his lap, interrupting his explanation to bitch and moan about everything he's put us through. But after I'd exhausted myself, Colton made his—unfortunately very valid—points.

I spent all summer trying to convince him that his plan was wrong and that he should throw it all out to switch to the staff's side. But his issues, the reason he spearheaded this initiative in the first place, are valid. When I presented a logical solution to both of our problems, he was shockingly enthusiastic.

"What would this committee do?" calls one professor from the back.

Giancarlo looks at me and nods, signaling to every person in the room that he's deferring to me.

"The committee would have two roles. One, we would host sessions with staff members to help them better understand expectations for in-class engagement and create a system to streamline presentation requests so individual professors didn't have to review them." Always best to start with what they'll like the best.

"Two, we'll work with faculty liaisons for each major to figure out the best ways the academics can be supported without adding more workload to individuals. We already have those liaisons identified in all but three departments. If you all could please stand?"

I watch as a few dozen professors, including Andrea, Sydney, and Lynn, rise from their seats, the physical representation of their support looming over the other faculty members. Inez sits beside them, giving me a little thumbs up as we lock eyes. She gave her notice right after she came home, and I'm going to soak up every minute of in-person support I can get before she moves in a month.

Giancarlo speaks for the first time. "This is a chance to fix the rift between the two sections of campus. I've seen firsthand the ways we can support each other if both sides are willing to humble themselves. We can continue this power struggle, or we can work to give the students the best experience possible. If helping the students isn't your top priority, it would seem you're in the wrong industry."

We field a handful of questions about logistics and expectations, and the attitude in the room shifts from apprehension to acceptance. I know, even before President Munchen calls for a vote, that it's going our way.

I turn to Colton as everyone starts filing out of the auditorium. His eyes are shining, and he slips one hand out, twining his pointer finger around my own.

"You did it, Chaos," he whispers, and I fight to keep from crying. It's done. I succeeded. All that stress, all that fear. Gone.

A throat clears behind us, and we step away from each other. Colton looks over my shoulder and his eyes grow wide for a second before he clenches his jaw. I turn to find my father, watching Colton with an unreadable look.

My stomach bottoms out. What the hell is he doing here? Did he come to berate me for giving up the fellowship? To tell me in person that I'm a disgrace to the family and more disappointing than he ever imagined?

Colton coughs. "Hello, Dr. Riley."

"Dr. Miller," my father says, and reaches out for a handshake that surprises us both. "I'd like a moment with my daughter."

Colton looks at me for confirmation before walking away. I watch him take a spot against the wall, far enough to give us privacy, but close enough to intervene if I need him.

I turn back to my dad. "What are you doing here?"

"Dr. Guarino reached out. He thought I'd like to see your work. I'll admit, it's impressive."

I sputter, in complete shock and unable to form a coherent thought. My childhood and early adulthood were spent idolizing him, desperate for his love and approval, and even though he damaged our relationship irreparably, there's still a buzz of pleasure at his words.

"I don't agree with your decision to turn down the fellowship," he says.

I shrug. "Well, that ship's sailed."

"You could have been one of the greats in our field."

"I know. But it wasn't what I wanted. Can you accept that?"

He plants his hands on his hips. "I can work on it."

It isn't much, but it's something, and a weight lifts from my shoulders.

"Dr. Riley," President Munchen says as she walks up to the two of us. "It's an honor to have you on campus. I hope you're as impressed by your daughter as we are."

"I am," he replies as they shake hands.

"I'm sorry to interrupt this reunion, but I was hoping to borrow Quinn for a few minutes."

"Of course. Quinn, I'll be in town until tomorrow night. We should have lunch tomorrow."

An acceptance almost flies from my tongue on instinct, but I pause, thinking about what I really want. "I'm in back-to-back meetings tomorrow, but why don't you call me when you get home?"

I appreciate him showing up and accepting my decision, but there are still ten years of hurt and mistrust between us. While I'm not opposed to building a new relationship—whatever that might look like—I need time to process before jumping into one.

Colt catches my eye as I follow behind President Munchen. He mouths, *What?* and I shrug my shoulders.

I follow our president to her office and sit down across the desk from her. I straighten my shoulders as she looks me over, like she can see every thought I've had and every challenge I've encountered.

"I appreciate the work you've done on this initiative. I've long thought our school would benefit from bridging the gap between the two sides, but I didn't see a way to do it until you came around."

"You're welcome. I love Billings, and I'm happy to help however I can."

Her smile turns impish. "How about helping out by taking the faculty role?"

I laugh, my head dropping back. "Nice try."

"What if I sweetened the deal?"

I shake my head. "While I'm curious what you'd come up with, I know what I want."

She shrugs, and when her eyes crinkle, and I feel a wave of warmth from her that helps me relax. "Never hurts to try."

She rises from her desk, meeting me on the other side of her desk and taking my hand between both of hers. "Thank you, Quinn. Truly. For having a vision for this campus and fighting for it. We owe you a debt. You'll let me know if there's anything I can do for you."

I smile, giving her hand a squeeze in response. "You're welcome. But there's no debt owed. Just excited to see what this all leads to."

I'm almost to the door when an idea strikes me. There really is no debt, but there is something I want. Something that would make this beautiful, incredible life I've found this summer perfect.

When I turn back to her, President Munchen raises an eyebrow.

"Actually," I say, "there is something you could do for me."

COLTON

THE UNIVERSE HATES ME. First, her dad interrupts us. Then our president. Both people she can't blow off, which I understand, but all I want right now is to take my girl somewhere private where we can celebrate.

I'm across from the door to President Munchen's office, one foot braced on the wall as I wait like the stalker I am. When Quinn steps out of that office, she looks a little shell-shocked, and I rush over to her.

"Are you okay?" I ask, resisting the temptation to cup her face. We haven't talked about where we stand on PDA on campus or when we'll disclose our relationship to HR.

She bites her lip, and my whole being fixates on that one move. I swallow my groan, but when I finally drag my eyes back to hers, I know she can see all my dirtiest thoughts.

She nods toward the exit. "Let's go to my office."

I stay a step behind her, fighting off the instinct to reach for her hand the whole way. When we get in private, the first thing we're going to do is talk about what I am and am not allowed to do in public. Scratch that, the first thing I'm going to do is figure out why she looks like she's seen a ghost, then I'll go down on my knees and worship her to celebrate her victory the way she deserves. *Then* we'll talk about PDA.

She shuts the door behind us when we reach her office, one hand on the handle and the other pressed against the door, where she pauses for two seconds like she's fortifying herself.

"Chaos," I say, stepping up behind her. "Are you okay?"

Finally, she turns toward me. "Yeah."

That's all she gives me, but she looks excited, not upset, and it soothes the monster inside screaming at me to protect her. "What did President Munchen want?"

She smiles, covering it with her hand. "She wanted to officially thank me for all the work I did."

"Okay," I say, drawing out the word. That's nice, but it doesn't explain why she's freaking out.

"Then she said Billings owes me a debt for coming up with the new committee, and I called it in." Quinn lets out a disbelieving laugh.

"What did you ask for?" I ask, stepping closer and sliding my hands over her waist.

Another laugh escapes her before she clasps both hands over her mouth. "Rome."

My brows draw together. What the fuck does she mean she asked for Rome?

"From now through the foreseeable future, you and I are guaranteed faculty spots on the Rome summer program. She's going to let me keep the internship class, and you get first dibs on the history course. We're going to Rome together, every summer, for as long as we want."

"You asked for me, too?"

Her nose scrunches up. "I may or may not have disclosed our relationship. I'm sorry! We should have talked about it first and I totally understand if you're upset with me and if you weren't ready to make it public knowledge, but there's no policy against fraternization at Billings and I was just so excited about the prospect of—"

I cut off her rambling, my lips taking hers in a hard kiss. I can't believe that I'm going to get to spend three months every year in my favorite place with my favorite person. That we'll never have to be separated while I do my research or teach.

There's no world where I'd be mad at her for telling people about us. Her claiming me publicly is the hottest thing I've ever heard—second only to her so actively including me in her plans for the future—and I want her to know it.

She squeaks, but catches on quickly. Her hands slide over my shoulders and up into my hair as she meets my passion in equal measure.

I move down her neck, my mouth leaving wet, biting kisses down her neck.

"You're not upset with me?" she asks, gasping when I nip at her collarbone.

"Fuck no," I say, my lips dragging across her skin with each word. "Tell everyone I'm yours. Stand up at the next campus-wide meeting. Send a university-wide memo. Hire a fucking skywriter, for all I care."

"I love you, Colton."

The words are barely out before I pull her mouth back to mine, crushing my lips against hers. We open in unison, like we've perfectly choreographed this dance, and I groan into her mouth.

"I love you so fucking much," I say on her lips.

She blindly reaches behind her to lock the door, and then I'm walking her backward, our mouths never leaving each other.

"You're mine," I growl, tugging her tightly against me.

"Yes," she sighs.

"And I'm yours. Today and forever."

"Forever," she moans.

I pull her flowing yellow dress, as bright as the light Quinn brings to my life, around her waist and settle her back on the desk. She fumbles with my belt and zipper, as frantic as I am to bring us together, freeing my painfully hard erection from my slacks. I pull her underwear to the side, finding her already soaked for me. Our eyes remained locked as I push inside her in one agonizingly slow push. I stop, fully seated inside of her, savoring the feeling of home.

"Fuck, I don't know how long I'm gonna last," I say through gritted teeth. "Between watching what a badass you were in that meeting and hearing you claim me, I'm right there unless we slow down."

"Please don't stop," she whimpers.

I push her back to lie flat and shift her slightly off the edge. I pull out slowly, pausing with just the tip inside of her, then slide back in, inch by agonizing inch. I keep that pace long enough to have her squirming against me before I pick it up, filling her with punishing thrusts, hands tight on her hips. She clenches around me, digging her nails into my forearms.

Our sex life this summer was amazing. Mind-blowing, even, but this is different. There's nothing hanging over our heads anymore.

"I love you," I whisper onto her skin when we finish, nothing but harsh breath and tangled limbs. I'll never get enough of saying that to her, of having the freedom to say it every time it crosses my mind.

She murmurs words I can't comprehend in my current state as she pulls me close, our bodies still joined and her legs wrapped tightly around the back of mine.

We stare at each other as the truth of our situation settles between us. I kiss her—slow and purposeful. A promise of our life to come.

"If you'd told eighteen-year-old Colton that this is where we'd end up, his heart would've given out."

She sighs, running her hand through my hair. "Fourteen years. So much wasted time."

"Not a second of that time was wasted." I lean down, giving her a soft kiss. "And you caught up eventually."

She laughs on my lips. "Thank god for this summer, and for tiny Italian beds."

I growl, the memories of our first night together flooding my senses. Back when I thought it was the only time I'd get to experience what it meant to be physically connected to the person who owns my whole heart.

We leave no room for words between our lips, wrapped up in each other and how perfectly we fit. I think back to those years of longing, of laughing with her and dying for the opportunity to touch her. I pull back slightly and lay my forehead against her, letting our noses brush as I savor the knowledge that this perfect woman I've loved my entire adult life is mine.

"Thank god for Rome."

QUINN

ONE SUMMER LATER

To MOST PEOPLE, this is probably the ugliest possible backdrop for a Roman wedding. In a city with some of the most beautiful architecture in the world, this rough brick and concrete stands out for its lack of opulence. But it's the exact spot where Colton told me he loved me for the first time, and I can't imagine swearing my life to him anywhere but this random stretch of wall on the Pantheon.

I pace a few steps back and forth, glancing back into the Piazza della Rotonda every few seconds.

"Where is she?" I ask.

"You know she'll be here," Colton says, reaching for my hand and just missing when I change directions again.

I shoot a wary look at the police officer stationed in the piazza. Technically, weddings aren't allowed to happen on the streets of Rome. Although, also technically, we aren't *actually* getting married. We took care of the legal side of things back in Boston—in a building even uglier than the side of the Pantheon—before heading here for the summer. This is more of a commitment ceremony than anything, but it still goes against the spirit of the law. I keep waiting for the officer to come over and yell at us to move along.

"We need to get started," I say, eyes still glued to the man.

Colton puts a hand on either side of my face, forcing my eyes back to him. "We're four people standing on the side of the building in a piazza where thousands of tourists congregate every day. There's nothing sketchy about it."

I look down at my flowing white dress, then back up at him with a raised eyebrow.

"Fine," he says with a laugh, "but we're not being disruptive and I guarantee that officer has much bigger things on his plate than us right now."

I let a heavy breath burst out of me. "You're right."

"You back with me?"

I shake out my head like it can send the stress flying straight out of my ears, "I'm with you."

"Good," he whispers, before placing a kiss on my lips. "Hello, wife."

I beam up. "Hello, husband."

"You two are nauseatingly adorable," Gerry says from her seat on the low wall opposite of us.

When we went for Christmas this year, we followed through with my plan for everyone to propose activities we could do together instead of giving presents. Gerry gleefully presented about why we should go to the Six Flags in New Jersey ("It's halfway between us and I'd love to see Colton's face after I force him to ride Nitro with me.").

When she was done, Colton and I stood up to present Rome. She'd huffed out that we were supposed to each present an idea, and if we were going to team up against her every year, there was no point. In the middle of her rant about how it was also outside of the budget and how Colton can't pick and choose when the budget matters, I slipped my new engagement ring out of my pocket. Colton placed her flight confirmation onto her lap, and

Gerry's complaining quickly turned to uncharacteristic blubbering.

We spent the days since we all arrived showing her around the city. She'd looked at the ruins and massive cathedrals with wide eyes, and then declared that all this concrete couldn't compete with the Appalachian Mountains. Colton whimpered and sputtered, but I just stuffed more gelato in his face. I love the way Gerry knows herself and what she wants, even if it's hard for us to conceptualize anyone not being obsessed with Rome.

She'll be here for a few more days before heading back to West Virginia, and we'll stay on for our second year teaching in the Billings Rome program.

I'm excited to take on the class without any threats hanging over our heads. My work on campus has only gotten more fulfilling as our committee—named the Faculty/Staff Collaboration Committee, because clever names in higher education are sorely lacking—has shifted the conversation on campus, and Colton's pre-tenure review a few months ago was as smooth as can be. This summer, we can enjoy the fruits of our labor.

I turn to face Tomasso, and Colton's arms wrap around my waist, pulling me flush against his body.

"Where's your girl?" I ask him, my hands settling on top of Colton's.

He shrugs. "She just told me she had an errand."

"I'm sorry, I'm sorry, I'm sorry," Inez calls from behind us, running the last few feet with a deep red rose in her hand. "You can't get married without flowers!"

I laugh so hard I buckle over, Colton's arms around me keeping me anchored to him in the most delicious way. "You didn't buy that from one of the rose scammers, did you?"

These men are stationed all over the city with gorgeous bouquets. They'll hand a flower or two to a passing woman because, in their words, *she is so beautiful.* Then they promptly demand an exorbitant amount of money from the man she's walking with.

She presents it to me with a flourish. "I absolutely did! I had to go all the way to the Piazza Navona to find one. Why are they *always* there until you want them to be?"

I raise the flower to my nose, inhaling the floral scent with a touch of something spicy, the perfect accompaniment to this moment.

"Can we get started now?" I ask, bouncing on my toes.

Our group stands in a little circle. To an outsider, it would look like we were a private tour group, listening to Tomasso lecture about the historic sight behind us. He's between me and Colton, murmuring words of love and lifelong partnership. Inez is next to me and Gerry's next to Colton, both of them wiping tears from their beaming cheeks.

When it comes time for the vows, Colton and I turn to face each other fully.

"Colton," I say, a tremor in my voice. "The day I met you, I knew you were it for me. I may not have recognized what that meant for far too many years, but I could already feel that you would be the most important person in my life. You've been my confidant, my cheerleader, my inspiration. I've spent every day of the last fifteen years in awe of you, and am so grateful that you were patient enough to wait for me to realize the awe was actually love. I love the way you murmur sarcastic comments in my ear, like my laugh is the only one you care about. I love the way you always reach for me, like being connected is the most important thing in the world. You've shown me love in all its truest forms, and I promise to continue to show you the same every day for the rest of our lives."

Colton sniffs and wipes at the corner of his eyes as Tomasso nods for him to go. "Last summer, I made a comment that I'd be creative with my wedding vows. At the time, I didn't think I'd ever have to follow through with that promise. I'd accepted that we'd just be friends, and if it wasn't you, it wouldn't be anyone. Because, since that random day in September fifteen years ago, I've only ever seen you. I've spent the past few months trying to think of something clever and unique, but all I can come up with is that I love you. That I love the way your thoughts pour out of you. I love the way your whole body shakes when you laugh, like you're letting yourself experience every ounce of joy. I love that you challenge and believe in me in equal measure. And I love that you're my best friend, that I get to see your face first thing in the morning because it's my favorite thing to look at. I swear to be your partner. To build you up through love, and to never forget how lucky I am that you've chosen to share your life with me."

Gerry slips the ring box into Colton's hand, and we both repeat the standard vows after Tomasso.

He smiles between the two of us. "So, by the power vested in me by… no one, since this isn't a real ceremony, I now pronounce you husband and wife. You may kiss the bride."

Colton takes my head between his hands. "I love you," he whispers a second before his lips land over mine.

It may not be a real wedding, but it feels like our beginning, and it's appropriate that it happened here. We pull back to find Inez awkwardly in our space snapping pictures. Her own engagement ring sparkles on her finger, one Tomasso put there not long after she moved to Italy. She told him she wouldn't leave Florence until she found a position that was as fulfilling in Rome, something she'd secretly achieved a few days ago. She pulled me aside at dinner last night to tell me she'll start the new position halfway through the summer, and that she's going to surprise him tonight after our reception.

Colton weaves our fingers together and leads me away from the Pantheon. I send one last look at the massive building, unable to stop my mind from drifting to my father. In the past year, we've made a few attempts to connect. The calls and text messages are stilted, but they're an improvement over the past, and I can at least let go of some of the hurt hanging over my head.

I texted him and my mother after Colton and I got married in Boston, and they asked if they could take us out to dinner when they come to Rome. I considered inviting them to this ceremony, but I decided I didn't owe them anything. What I wanted, more than anything, was to start our married life surrounded by the people who have always loved and supported us. As tiny as the ceremony is, it's perfect.

None of us speak as we walk through the winding streets to our final destination, a hush settled over our naturally talkative group. Within a few minutes, we reach the Trevi Fountain, thousands of tourists packed in front of it.

Colton looks down at me and says, "Sure you don't want to do this later tonight?"

I smile up at him. "No, I want to do this right now."

We walk to the far side of the fountain, waiting in a long line to reach the Fountain of Love. The two of us locked eyes before leaning down to drink from each stream for the first time. As silly as the superstition may be, I love the fact that neither of us have been here with anyone else, like we knew deep down that the fountain needed to be saved for each other.

We meet in the middle of the basin half a second before our lips touch, the sweetest, softest kiss I've ever received.

"A life full of love and faithfulness," Colton whispers.

That's the promise of the fountain, but I don't need superstition to tell me that's what we'll have. Because I see our future in his eyes. I see laughter and teasing. Challenges and fights and making up in the best possible way. I see us pushing each other to be our best selves.

I see forever with my best friend.

And it's beautiful.

ACKNOWLEDGMENTS

This is my third time writing acknowledgements, even though they'll be the second acknowledgements to make it out into the world. But that's the reality of indie publishing versus traditional publishing.

One is like off roading through the mountains. You control when you take off in the ATV. It's fast and exciting, but there's the terrifying possibility that you'll run yourself off a cliff. The other's like a roller coaster. Still overwhelming and exhilarating, but there's more of a safety net. You know someone has run their tests and checked the cars, but you also give up control, only getting on the ride when they tell you it's your turn.

I can't say yet which I enjoy more, but I can tell you I feel extremely lucky to get to experience both. And I feel so honored that you all are coming on this journey with me. All the best things in my life have come when I did something scary. Who knows if this will pan out the same way, but I'm hopeful, and I'm having fun. And shouldn't that be what life is all about?

So now to the part where I thank the people who kept me sane.

First, my agent, Jem Chambers-Black, the ultimate partner. When researching agents, people often ask whether you want an editorial or business focused agent. I never imagined I'd be lucky enough to find someone who fills both roles so perfectly. Thank you for being such a trooper and for never blinking when I throw out something insane (like deciding to self-publish another book a few months before the second book on my contract!).

Taking this plunge sounded so intimidating, and I'd never have done it without the brilliant indie authors who talked me through it (and answered a frankly absurd number of texts). Thank you ila sikorski, Chelsea Curto, Hailey Dickert, Maria Rigou, Kim Swizz, and Brittany Kelly for all your support and guidance. I hope every one of you knows just how brilliant and special you are.

To my other writing friends, thank you for standing by me, no matter how many voice notes I sent crashing out: Amanda Hopkins, Kjersten Piper, Heather McBreen, Laura Marie Meyers, Michelle Mitchell, Britt Middleton, Alexandra Vasti, Peyton Corinne, Rosie Danan, Scarlett Belford, Sarah T. Dubbs, and so many others!

To Valentina, thank you for believing in this book even when I didn't and for copyediting and proofing it with such care. I wouldn't have had the courage to take this leap without your unwavering faith in Quinn and Colton.

To Tiffani, my little ball of light! Thank you for proofreading this book and helping me fight the never-ending imposter syndrome.

To Fozi and Nela, thank you for always matching my energy, for talking through every piece of art, and for making me feel loved and important, no matter what else happens with this book.

For Jane, Ashley, Trinaty, and all the other girlies at The New Romantics. I love every one of you and feel so lucky that I'm writing at a time when your store exists. Orlando will never be the same (and thank god for that!).

To my parents, thank you for being the antithesis of Richard Riley and for encouraging every wild dream I've come up with. And thank you for sending me to Rome because I "had to study with this specific professor," even though I never did anything with my art history degree.

To my littles, Bria, Emmy, and Lucas, of everything I've done in my life, you three are by far the best. Thank you for letting me be your mom. I love you more than all the stars in the sky.

To Brandon, my partner in all things, I couldn't have done this without you. Literally. I'd have been a mess. I love you forever.

And lastly, to the readers, thank you for jumping into my world. The romance community has been a lifeline for me in these scary times, and I hope you felt some peace and joy from this book.

Thank you for reading!

ABOUT THE AUTHOR

Amy Buchanan has had a lifelong love affair with romance. After decades of devouring love stories written by others, she decided to share the ones pinging around in her own brain. She writes spicy contemporary romances with relatable heroines, swoon-worthy heroes, and loving found families.

She lives in Central Florida with her husband, pup, and three wildling children.